The Casa Martyrs

Book One of the Blazing Court Trilogy

Moti Black

Copyright © 2023 Caroline Blackler

The Casa Martyrs © 2023 Caroline Blackler, All Rights Reserved

No part of this book may be reproduced, or stored in a retrieval system, or transmitted in any form or by any means, electronic, mechanical, photocopying, recording, or otherwise, without express written permission of the publisher.

Cover design © 2023 Caroline Blackler

The characters and events portrayed in this book are fictitious. Any similarity to real persons, living or dead, is coincidental and not intended by the author.

DEDICATION

To the Autistic warriors of the world.
To those who fight for the Autistic community.
To the Autistic people fighting just to make it through the day.

And for those who didn't make it.
We will remember you.

And to Kati. Thank you.

CONTENTS

1	Kasaman	1
2	C Sharp	4
3	Black Sheep	6
4	Asana	11
5	The Devil's Hand	16
6	The Graveyard of the Forgotten	25
7	Daddy	28
8	Flight of the Fuck Up	33
9	The Tower	36
10	Redwaek	40
11	Mull'aman	45
12	Hands of Helios	55
13	The Acres	66
14	Dream Filled Cage	76
15	Timmins Cave	82
16	Kaetian Gardens	91
17	Laescenno	97
18	Into the Dark	104
19	Reverberate	110
20	Beetroot	115

21	Betrothal	122
22	The Faceless Keyboardist	127
23	Diametric Destiny	132
24	A Match Made in Kaetia	138
25	Black	145
26	The Choice	151
27	Blacker	156
28	Regrettable Day	159
29	Porcupine Fairy	165
30	The Casa Martyrs	173
31	Leap of Faith	178
32	The Fall of Constantinople	183
33	Into the Woods	189
34	Demetrius	194
35	The Misappropriation of the Blood Red Rose	200
36	Drizzle	205
37	Mathematicians Eat Babies	213
38	Insignificant	219
39	Pandora's Box	225
40	Imprints and Echoes	230
41	The Unravelling	235
42	When Gods Roll Dice	239

43	A Pain in the Coccyx	244
44	Samson and Delilah	249
45	Samson's Ribs	254
46	The Unspoken	261

| The Setting Sun: Preview | 268 |

| Glossary | 270 |

ACKNOWLEDGMENTS

I would like to say thank you to my beta readers, Coral, Erika, Kati, and Jan.

A huge special thank you goes to Kati. She's the reason this book made it out into the world. No one could ask for a better writing partner or best friend.

Thank you to my family for supporting me whilst I wrote this book. And finally, my cat, Lydia. I love you with all my heart.

1: KASAMAN

*B*elow me is the patio where my mother died, above me, the window from which she fell. These are the main attractions on a sightseeing tour and nothing more. Inside the building are the artefacts which create the meaning behind events, and I have no business left behind those walls.

As long as the front door remains closed, I am safe.

Outside, I am strong, even with the night breeze whispering ghost stories in my ear and the moon taunting me with my father's voice: "You'd be safer at home. You'd be healthier living at home. This will always be your hoooooome."

Home? All I see are bricks and mortar which speak of sanitised wealth, business success, and family failure: a pretentious erection with my father rattling around inside like a solitary bean in a gourd.

Memory echoes bounce around, drained of all meaning, benign and tinged in midnight blue. The past haunts this place, but from the garage roof, I can see all that I need to without opening the Pandora's Box of my childhood.

As long as I don't go inside, I am in control…

But I'm not in control and my past is not confined to the laws of architecture. My old bed joins me on the garage roof and then the child-size dresser appears next to it. Before long, all the furniture of my childhood bedroom surrounds me: the confines of a sanctuary that has lost its walls, but none of its bile.

The indigo curtains billow in the hot wind of the desert encroaching on my dreams. They pull and rattle on the pine curtain rail hovering in the air, as they're sucked out of the imaginary window, and thrust back into the fake room, over and over again, as if a demon were breathing life into my nightmare. Sand blows in on the wind, rattling against the pine furniture and gathering on the wicker seat of the small wooden chair. The dark blue cotton bedding with the yellow star pattern grows pale as the smaller grains cling to its surface. And the Devil is hiding underneath the bed.

Clad in my dark blue cloak, I'm ready for battle. This supernatural cloak has always protected me against the things I conjure up to fight. If it gets too much, I can pull the hood over my face and that'll keep trouble at bay. With my cloak, I can confront anything, or hide from everything.

Bending down by the bed, I reach under the valance, past those smiling yellow stars and into the more accurate representation of my childhood. Damp leaves stick to my hand. I pat the ground and sink my fingers into decomposing vegetation.

He's in here somewhere.

Insects scurry from under the bed: armoured leaves on legs, millipedes swollen to obscene proportions, swarms of hard black shells released from the nightmares you find beneath every child's bed. The undergrowth stirs against my hand, bugs crawl up my sleeves, and soon the shiny mass of the insect army covers the garage roof.

Something larger moves under my hand. It's too deliberate, too firm to be part of the under-bed ecosystem.

I seize the tuberous limb and begin to pull, entering a tug of war contest with my subconscious.

Tonight, I will wrench this beast from under my bed.

Inch, by painful inch, I drag my tormentor from his burrow. As the limb emerges from under the valance, I see that I'm grasping the scaly green hand of a demonic beast.

I try to stay calm.

I try to wake up.

I try to free my hand from the Devil's grip, so I can pull my hood over my face.

As my guard drops, the beast acts. The limb twists and writhes until our palms are pressed together, and before I can pull away, he has cordially shaken my hand and is slithering back into the darkness.

I begin to pull the hood of my cloak over my face to shut out this world, but before I manage to raise my protective shield, the Devil emerges in front of me, and I freeze.

His cloak is like mine, except much darker. Light disappears into the folds of the material, and from under the hood, darkness stares back at me.

I recognise him.

I know him.

My mouth tastes his name as I test my voice. "Kasaman…"

A name.

A name that tastes of corked red wine.

A name tied to old memories, which, as my mouth slips over the syllables, is no *longer unknown.*

Behind Kasaman, something else starts to take form. A shape. A shadow cast over my subconscious mind, recalled now to project on the canvas of a dream.

As a child, I painted this scene in many different ways: a blood red sky still dripping from a fresh slaughter and an apocalyptic plain of burning bushes and mangled bodies. From this hostile landscape rose a mountain of smooth black stone, topped with a crown of three twisted turrets.

In my mind, I see a door slowly start to open. Behind the door I will find the origins of that image.

And the black mountain waits.

2: C SHARP

Snoring erupted next to me, sending the trio of twisted turrets scattering into oblivion. Dreams recoiled, and I was left with the stale morning breath of the idiot lying next to me.

I hit him.

He rolled over to face me and smiled with the primal charm of a rotten banana. I tried to squirm away from him but was caught by a clammy hand on my shoulder and another worming its way under my waist.

He pulled me close to his sweaty, naked body, and grinned as the woodland of the dawn tried to take root. "Good morning, Kerella."

"Not really."

Pushing both hands against his chest, I launched myself out of bed, and, with a sleepy, hung-over elegance, made my escape.

I grabbed my black and red crocheted blanket from the back of the settee and wrapped it around myself before finding refuge on the piano stool. I curled up, hugging my knees to my chest, and rested my head on the keys.

Rocking gently back and forth, I let the index finger on my left hand reach out for C sharp on the keyboard.

I ran my finger up and down the dark wood.

With the power of this note, could I bring Kasaman back?

The note struck. Kasaman was called. Deep in my chest a hand stirred in the vegetation, reminding me of the pact I'd made. I hit the note again, feeling the swing of the hammer and the collision with the string: again and again, hoping to recapture the dream. The sound brought forth the comfort of the nightmare, but the battle had been more than lost, it had been misplaced.

A dark shape moved in the corner of my vision. The generic-boy-in-black-jeans, already rolling this morning's roll-up, had thought it was worth following me in here instead of going straight out of the front door.

I watched him from behind my hair, my head still resting on the keyboard, my index finger hitting C sharp sharper.

From epic battle to pathetic face-off: a defensive barrier of hair and manic note hitting versus the desire to pursue a gratuitous one-night stand past its natural life span.

Golden veins of hair passed in front of my eyes allowing me to watch the boy without seeing too much and breaking the spell. Behind my own magical cloak, I could see him, but he could not see me. He could not see what C sharp had the potential to be. I was just that mad woman he screwed last night. And I was going to win this fight, because I wanted nothing from him.

The door slammed shut with his glorious exit and I let C sharp take me back to my dream. From one note, I found the timbre of an improvisation. That idiot may have cost me a confrontation with Kasaman, but I could still turn what I had learnt from the dream into something I could hold onto. I knew I was one step closer to beating Kasaman: I knew his name, I had seen his mountain, and I was on the verge of capturing him between the keys of the piano.

3: BLACK SHEEP

A lightweight object bounced off my nose and fluttered to my knees with a reed-like cadence.

I picked the beer mat up and looked at the Black Sheep (Alc. 3.8%). Then I looked at Becca.

"Don't look at me like that. I warned you I was going to throw it. I even counted to three. It's not my fault you were ignoring me."

"I was just looking for... Sorry, I'm distracted."

"Can you at least pretend you're a normal person and give me a bit of attention whilst we share this lovely food?" She reached over, snatched three chips from my plate, and stuffed them into her mouth.

"Hey!"

"Freak tax. Bitch."

I slumped back in my seat and tried to give her my full attention.

It was hard. Being closer to Kasaman had its drawbacks. I felt him wherever I went. I was tracking him down, but by doing so, I was revealing myself to him: I could not hunt without being hunted; I could not find without being found; I could not see without being seen; I could not bite without being bitten.

Bitten. Bitten.

Realising my mind had started to wander again, I sat up and looked at Becca, who was now finishing off the rest of my dinner.

We had already discussed her new spiky red hairstyle. My eyes dropped a little; she was wearing a baggy turquoise jumper I'd better not mention in case I accidentally told her what I really thought about it. She took a sip of cider and put the glass down on the table. The dark varnish flaked in long lines, directing my attention towards my glass of white wine. Fresh drops of condensation welcomed my gaze with a globular canvas.

I drew a 'K' with my finger, parting the frosted pattern of droplets to create a window into the soul of 'K'asaman.

His dark cloak reflected in the wine glass.

I turned around as he disappeared into the packed bar, seeking camouflage amongst the goth-rock clientele. With the sumptuous parade of budget ostentation, DIY couture, pigment, piercings, and PVC, I had no chance of picking out a genuine demon from a random wannabe.

Mike was at the other side of the bar talking to a short woman with bright pink and black hair who was being affectionately mauled by her male companion. There were others in the group, but I couldn't see them through the people waiting to order drinks. No one looked like a plausible candidate to be Kasaman in disguise.

"Bit-ten." I felt the tip of my tongue on the gumline just behind my front teeth. "Bit-ten."

Another cardboard missile fluttered into my cheek and a Black Sheep fell to the floor.

"Why do I bother with you?"

"Because we share the pain of our parents shagging?" I said, throwing a beer mat back at her.

"We agreed never to mention, or even think about that." She shuddered. "I bet your dad left his socks on. No wonder mum kicked him to the kerb."

"Sounds like you have thought about it. A lot." I checked the bar to see if Kasaman had turned up.

"That's it. Ker, who the fuck are you looking for?" Her eyes widened with excitement, and she clapped her hands together. "It's a guy, isn't it? You've finally become a human being and discovered feelings that go beyond a drunken shag!" A look of nausea quickly wiped the enthusiastic overtures off her face. "Please tell me it's not the fuckwit you left with last night?"

"No, no, and no. How many times do I have to tell you I'm a strictly fuck-em-and-run gal? I'm not interested in anything else from my two-dimensional playthings."

"You really think I'm that stupid? Okay, you have your secret crush; I'll pretend I don't know."

I pursed my lips in annoyance. "I don't know why I'm even going to bother explaining this to you; I know exactly how you'll react." I paused and looked at Becca. She rolled her eyes, before pasting on a fake smile.

"Last night I had a dream. The Devil was under my bed. I grabbed his hand to pull him out, so I could confront him, but he caught me off guard and shook my hand instead. Now I can feel him watching me all the time. I'm worried I inadvertently sold my soul or something and any moment now he'll take it and I'll become evil. Since I got here, the feeling that I'm being watched has got so intense, I just know he's here."

"You shook the Devil's hand?"

"Yes." I threw back more wine to steady my nerves, shaking at the sudden naked exposure of my involvement with Kasaman.

Becca lifted her glass to her mouth to hide a smirk. After a long, drawn-out sip, she put the glass down and tapped her perfectly manicured red fingernails on the table. "Well, that was fucking nuts, even by your standards."

"I grabbed his hand to pull him out, not to shake it!"

"Strangely enough, Ker, I'm not commenting on which guys you choose to touch up in your dreams; I'm saying your attempts to change the subject are stupid, but I'll let you keep your little secret. As long as you tell me everything else you did this week."

I sighed. Here we go again. "I've been working on a new song."

"Uh huh." She said, as she pulled out her phone and started scrolling.

I went quiet to let her focus on what she was doing.

"Keep going." She instructed, waving her hand at me, but still staring at her phone.

"Oh! I got that book I was telling you about, the one about graveyards…"

Becca looked up. "You really are morbid, aren't you? What else?" Her attention returned to her phone.

I hated these interrogations of hers, they always made me feel like I was reporting to an authority figure, rather than chatting to my best friend.

"I cooked myself a risotto last night. It was a bit mushy, but edible. I finished a couple of paintings and took them to the framers. I was expecting my period to start, but it's a bit late, so I went for a nice walk up to the caves on Wednesday, then I got an Indian takeout on my way back. Oh, and on Thursday…"

"Wait! What?" She slammed her phone down on the table.

"I know I said I'd get you one, but we can have takeout next week."

"No. Your period's late?"

"Only by a few days." My stomach tensed up. How could I have been so stupid?

"Has it started yet?"

"No, but it's fine. Any day now."

"So that's who the fuck you are looking for!"

"What?"

"The father!"

"It's not even a week late, and I've been careful, pregnancy isn't an option."

"Yeah, well, we both know with you, it's possible. And it explains every-fucking-thing! The mood swings, you scanning the bar every three seconds for someone, your big secret, and that stupid dream! You're angry at this guy for getting you pregnant and feel he's forced you into a deal you had no intention of getting into, but were conned into 'shaking his hand' for want of a better part of anatomy."

As she lectured me about being a responsible adult, I returned to my hunt for Kasaman.

Pretending to be involved with what Becca was saying, I tried to catch his reflection in the rusty mirror hanging on the wall behind her head.

The two lads by the door had badly dyed black hair and unconvincing fake tattoos: definitely not Kasaman candidates. The group behind them were clearly under aged and far too clueless to be demons.

Letting my hair fall over the left-hand side of my face, I tried to see behind me without letting Kasaman know that I was looking in his direction.

"Ker?"

I snapped into attentive mode as quickly as I could.

"The father's here, isn't he? Who is he?" She pointed her finger far too close to my face and I pulled away.

"I told you, I'm looking for the demon from my dream. My period is just late; there's no 'father' to be looking for."

Becca's eyes fixed on something behind me. I spun round to be faced with absolutely nothing of interest. The woman with pink and black hair was jumping around; a generic-boy-in-black-jeans was carrying a five-pint round back to his table on his own; a more rotund girl fell out of her red lace-up corset, much to the amusement of her companions and the ridicule of the boys behind her; but there were no majestic demons in midnight blue cloaks.

"What did you see?" I asked, convinced Becca had caught a glimpse of my nemesis.

"No... I..." She ran her fingers through her hair. "I just remembered..."

She was looking far too serious and continued to stare at the space behind me.

"Becca?"

"I'm so sorry. I forgot." She leant across the table and grabbed my hands. "Look, Ker, this time, you have me."

"You know, you are definitely not the father." I said, extracting my hands and placing them under my legs.

Ignoring my levity, Becca continued. "I mean, don't run off, okay?"

All these years later, and my little lie was back to bite me in the butt.

"I'll deal with your dad, okay? But Ker, don't run away, and don't give up the chance to be part of your child's life."

"Look, I'm not pregnant. I don't feel pregnant, and I'm sure I would know if there was a little parasite growing inside of me."

"Did you know last time?"

I slugged back more wine.

"Should you be drinking?"

"That's the one thing I should be doing."

She reached over, snatched my glass from my hand, and downed the contents in one gulp.

"Right, this is what we're going to do: tomorrow morning I'll come over with a pregnancy test; no point in making plans until we know for sure. Then if it's positive we'll make a list of potential fathers and work out how to break the news to your dad once it becomes obvious."

I wanted to scream at her, "You're overreacting! I am not a child! I feel pre-menstrual, and it's not even been a bloody week, you nutter." But I couldn't. I had to keep my mouth shut and accept what she was throwing at me.

And Kasaman just loved this distraction; he could watch me as I gave Becca my soul-divided attention. He was probably right behind me, reaching out with those scaly hands, touching my hair, making his plans, learning about me.

I jumped as a hand brushed against my shoulder. I turned around, but no one was there. As I scanned the bar for the culprit, disappointment seeped in. Kasaman was not here.

"Ker!" Becca tapped the table. "Eyes on me! This is serious."

Thankfully, at that moment Mike signalled her from the other side of the bar.

"Ugh. Looks like the band's heading on."

"Can I come?"

I pictured Kasaman sweeping across a stage covered in wires, his billowing cloak swimming in darkness, a bass guitar in his hand.

Becca rummaged around in her bag. "Seriously Ker, you'd hate it. I'm only going because Mike's helping them." She threw her bag on the table. "I've forgotten my fucking purse." She sighed and rolled her eyes.

"Don't worry, I'll pay."

"That's my girl." She stood up and patted me on the head.

"I promise I won't embarrass you…"

But Becca was already walking down the steps towards Mike.

4: ASANA

The sky is thick and red; clouds of sand and blood mooch on the horizon, reaching out with cirrus fingers to caress the twisted black mountain. But it is not there to be touched; its dark imprint on the horizon is the absence of form, not a mere obstacle to light. I cannot touch it, and neither can the clouds. This illusion makes them furious.

I'm in Kasaman's world, gazing over at the black mountain through a large window. I lean on the sandstone base of the deep frame and peer down at the world below. Dark clouds float beneath me, and the ground is a long way off, shrouded in a haze.

This is a dream. My mind is creating a safe space for me to escape to, a place where I belong. A new world where people don't laugh at me from across the room, where I have friends who understand me and don't boss me around without listening to what I'm saying. I imagine there's a whole group of us: a gaggle of misfits who'll bring Kasaman to justice and peace to this land. I'll be valued as an equal amongst my peers and provide information useful to our mission gleaned from my years of reading in the library.

I turn my back on the black mountain and look around the room. It's small and sparsely furnished. There are three arched windows. They have no glass, or bars to prevent people falling out of them, but they do have sturdy wooden shutters, which are currently open to let in the evening light. The room is dominated by a four-poster bed with old cream netting draped between ornately carved wooden posts. There is a simple table with a pile of books on it, and a plain wooden chair next to the table. The only other decoration in the room is a mosaic on the wall by the bed, depicting two rows of dark figures below a red sky with twenty-two stars.

Obviously, in this world, I only sleep in this room. Through the door my friends will be waiting for me in a library, or perhaps the stables, where I have my very own horse.

If this is going to be where I escape from my life, I'm going to create the most amazing place I can, and then the real world can just fade away.

I see a dark blue cloak on the bed and feel it would be appropriate to put it on before I venture out into the unknown beyond the door. The material is rough, but the cloak is well made. A lovely brooch decorated with twenty-two stars joins the fabric at my neck, the hood is deep and hangs nicely around my face, and the bottom of the cloak floats as I swirl around.

I stride towards the door, and push the handle down, excited to see what my subconscious has in store for me behind the door.

It is locked. I bang on the dark wood and shout to be let out.

No one comes.

The light in the room is dimming. I stand by the door and look around my prison, realising how familiar everything feels.

I've been in this room before.

I run over to the largest window, unfasten the shutters from the wall, and pull the edges towards myself. I know there is a T carved on the side of one shutter, and an M carved on the other. When the shutters are closed for the night, the T and the M rest next to each other.

The letters are there, but the M has been defaced by a criss-cross scoring.

This loss hurts me more than I can explain.

I sigh, and without thinking, grab the chair, and use it to climb into the recess of the largest window. I stare out at the black mountain. Even that is falling apart, sending black shapes into the sky.

I watch as the tallest column crowning the black mountain disintegrates into a mass of black dots and disperses through the angry clouds. At first, the dots are just holes in the red sky, but all too soon, their impressive wingspan and the power of their form comes into focus.

The rotting arms, the gnashing teeth, the clawed hands.

"Redwaek!"

I jump down and close the shutters, pulling the beam of wood down to lock them with a thud. Staggering backwards, the image of the warped bodies hits me afresh, and propels me towards the smallest window.

Secured.

I stumble to the final shutter. The first of the redwaek have made it to the tower and the leader dives towards the open window. The skin on her face rips as she yowls with the excitement of attack, thick tracks of blood push down her face and drip into the air.

I release the right-hand shutter and slam it across the window, pushing my hand against the closed shutter to hold it in place as I reach for the final latch.

The redwaek has reached the window and lunges through the gap. Grabbing the hood of my cloak with one hand, she pushes her other hand underneath my protective shield. Claw-like nails dig into my scalp.

I wake up with a jolt, but can't move beyond opening and closing my eyes. The back of my head is burning in pain.

In the dim light, I see the ornately carved wooden posts and cream netting of my dream-world bed.

A hooded figure looms over me, a knife in her hand.

What part of 'safe space for me to escape to' did my brain not grasp about this dream?

"What are you doing to her?" A woman hisses from the other side of the room, moving closer with a fiery torch. "She's awake!" She exclaims.

I close and open my eyes to show her she's right.

"She's not really here; she's just dreaming." The shadow woman whispers. "I need blood from her scalp for the spell. Be quiet and keep an eye on the stairs."

Fingers rub into the wound on my head.

I feel a warm, wet stone being placed into each of my palms and a hand is pressed firmly to my forehead. I am pushed down, down, down.

My spirit slips through the bed and falls into the air. Watercolour images of cloaks, mountains, and blood surround me; as the waves crash and the tide flows over, these pictures get washed away. My head is stinging where the redwaek attacked me, or is it because that woman cut me?

Finally, I land back in the four-poster bed, my muscles twitching.

"Now she's really here."

I look up into a pale face with soft golden eyes, framed by an indigo cowl.

The woman sits down next to me on the bed and gently strokes my face.

Too drained to protest to this stranger's familiarity, I let her prop me up, so I'm resting against her bony body. She places a small wooden bowl in my hands and guides it towards my mouth. There's a foul-smelling liquid in the bowl, and I pull away as she tries to make me drink.

She's talking again, but I can't focus on her words. The Redwaek scratching at the shutters intrude on my concentration. An argument coming from the other side of the cream netting stops me from listening. The 'M', who had been scratched out, screams at me for abandoning him.

I finally tune into what she's saying. "You must be prepared, Tushenta. You are not alone in the lower realm. Others have followed you. Be careful what you say. This is the only defence I can give you."

My throat is sore, and my mouth is dry, but, scared by this warning, I manage to ask with a hoarse squeak: "I'm in danger?"

"We're all in danger." Her eyes convey the gravity of the situation as she pushes the bowl back to my mouth. "This should break down the barrier between your mortal mind and your eternal memories, but the effects will be unpredictable. You must record all that you can and be careful who you trust. You must remember the real reason you are there: the fate of Kaetia rests with you."

This time, I don't pull away from the bowl and accept the bitter drink. I feel the liquid crawl down my throat, as though the insect army is now inside of me. It infiltrates my whole body, and I lie paralysed and in pain.

The mysterious woman gently kisses my forehead before placing my head carefully back on the pillow. "Be safe, Tushenta, and think things through before you act. I love you." And with that, she slips out of my dream, leaving behind a dark blue shadow and a new name. She had called me 'Tushenta'.

Someone starts shouting from the other side of the room. She bursts through the netting, falls to her knees, and grabs my hand. She is dressed in a floating cream gown and screams at me with words I don't understand. Where my hair is blonde, hers is mahogany brown; where my pale left cheek has a scar across it, her olive-toned cheek is smooth; where my eyebrows are plucked, hers are unkempt; and where my eyes are decorated with thick lines of kohl and mascara, hers are naked. But she is me.

"They are dead because of you! There is evil in you! You only bring destruction!" She collapses in tears and disappears.

Intoxicated, berated, and confused, I lose the strength to keep myself rooted in Kasaman's (and Tushenta's) world. A deluge of memories briefly sends the neurons in my head into overload. Then darkness takes over.

When I regain consciousness, I am sat at a piano. My fingers find the keyboard and embark on a peregrination through the darker layers of my heart. A strange power is pulsing through me and into my fingers. As I play, the keys, that are usually my touchstone to reality, start to morph into strings.

I know how to play this kind of instrument: some of the strings I brush, some of them I push down. The result is a wave of Kaetian nostalgia.

I glance down at my hands; green scales have started to push through my skin. Jumping to my feet, I back away from the strange instrument. The music keeps coming even though I'm no longer touching the strings.

Someone grabs me from behind. Without looking, I know it's Kasaman. He holds me tightly, his body pressing firmly against mine, leaning over my shoulder to *gently whisper in my ear. The warmth of his breath sends electricity through my body as words pass between us for the first time:* "Question what you remember and everything you are told, because lies are the most convincing of realities. What you do with what you learn is up to you. I trust you will make the right decision. I trust you."

He pushes me back towards the piano. "First, you need to become part of the music."

5: THE DEVIL'S HAND

It was early. The sun had just started to pull itself out of the sea and its fire was still diluted. The pale semi-circle hovered on the horizon, full of water, fat and sleepy.

I stood on the balcony of my flat, looking down at the town nestled in the valley leading out to the bay. My spellbound eyes saw the view in front of me superimposed on another land: a fantastical vista created from memories returned to help me fight Kasaman, but returned without logic, understanding, or any sense of order.

The cold morning air pinched my arms and legs, and the sea breeze whipped my hair into a frenzy. The growing strawberry-gold light of the sun sank into every cell of my being and the landscape of my world started to glow. Holding my head high and alert, I concentrated on the myriad of images bombarding me. "The fate of Kaetia depends on these memories."

As the sea emptied out of the sun, sleep and dreams drained from my body. The waking state took over and real-life buildings, roads, and seascape prevailed. Pained by the loss of my fantastical world, I started scribbling and sketching, trying to catch the words, images, thoughts, and sounds that were coursing around my head.

It was a jumbled heap, craving for comprehension. I needed to reclaim this territory, this world I had found in my dreams, but with every second, I was losing vital clues. Thinking would have to wait; I needed these memories in a form I wouldn't forget.

Images fell onto the paper in front of me, long forgotten words possessed my pencils which transcribed names and phrases, and the piano called me to let it sing the songs of this strange world.

I didn't eat. I didn't want to chase away the flavour of the bitter liquid still on my lips, convinced that would break the spell. I needed to know more about this world: to remember Asana, to understand Kasaman, to learn about Tushenta, to find the 'M' who'd been scratched from the edge of the shutter.

By mid-afternoon, the spell was wearing thin, and I needed to create a microcosm to maintain the conduit between my worlds. I pulled the headphones over my ears, plugged myself into the keyboard, and let my fingers trace the notes I could feel in my alternative realm.

I channelled an epic score which swept through a dramatic and heroic rescue followed by a forbidden and secret romance based on music, art, and love. Wrapped up in the embrace of the music, I felt stronger than I'd ever done before. I felt accepted. I felt it was safe to be myself.

Memories of 'M' flowed in on the undulating melody.

Mull'aman.

Tushenta wrote this piece for Mull'aman.

Locked in an intense intermingling of music and emotion, I was transported to that world.

My world.

I was in love with Mull'aman, in awe of Asana, scared of Kasaman, and part of something larger than myself.

Something important.

I meandered through feelings, songs, and echoes. Eventually I reached the tune I'd been playing at the end of the dream. A dark rush of energy swelled up from the centre of my being; I could feel scales pushing through my skin as the music rushed by.

Then, my arm was pulled away from the keyboard and an envelope of money thrust in my hand.

Becca's abrupt appearance was not unusual; my dad had given her a key 'for emergencies', and her interpretation of 'emergency' was quite broad. Today it included standing outside in the rain.

Her face reflected a fury beyond what my lack of attention to the intercom called for; downward straggles of claret hair clung in waves to her forehead and her rosy cheeks were wet and glistened. Sandwiched between these features, her usually wide powder-blue eyes had become dark slits of anger, from which crept black fingers of mascara. This gave her a comical sad-clown appearance, with intimidating overtones.

I wasn't ready to let go of the Devil's hand and face that storm just yet. Putting the envelope on the back of the keyboard, I continued to scribble in my 'song ideas' notebook, labelling the page 'The Devil's Hand'.

Becca crossed the room. The floor was covered with visible representations of the inner workings of my mind, and she waded carelessly through the sea of images towards the French windows. A storm had arrived since I shut out the world with the headphones and I hadn't noticed the rain coming in on a strong wind, leaving splodges on the sketches thrown to the furthest edge of my floor montage.

Pulling the doors shut with exaggerated effort, Becca glared at me, as if I'd left them open deliberately to inconvenience her. I resisted the urge to object to the footprints tracked over my artwork, as I knew that would just provoke her, instead, I examined the contents of the envelope.

"Holy fuck! Where did all this money come from?"

"Mum finally sold that large canvas, and three of the little oils, and would like you to start work on replacements." With a sneer, she added: "Unless you're too busy with this crap."

She picked up a watercolour painting of Asana standing in the Courtyard of the Arcane. At the far side of the courtyard, three twisted columns of sandstone rock jutted up into the sky in front of the setting sun, causing the floor to be plunged alternately from deep red to dark shadows: twenty-two stars decorated the sky. When I looked at that painting, I felt as though I could step out into the courtyard, that I was back in my world again, that I was looking into Asana's sombre golden eyes. The power of the image vibrated through the room, and I was shocked that I'd created something so amazing without even thinking about it.

Becca looked unimpressed. "You know your dad wouldn't approve of you wasting your time like this? You should really focus on landscapes and saleable stuff. You know the rules."

A year ago, I'd grown bored of replicating the same shorelines for the same customers of the sea-front souvenir shop Becca's mother ran. Day after day, my palette was the same blend of bland of blah, so I stopped being literal with my use of colour. I got away with that, so I stopped being literal with the landscapes and their inhabitants. Before I knew it, I'd gone down the rabbit hole, along with the fairies in the clouds and the selkies on the sand. A few months later, my father marched into my flat, interrupting my disobedient exploration of the spirits of the sea. He tut-tutted for several minutes, before instructing his latest gopher to help him dispose of the incriminating canvasses, and I watched helplessly as the best work I'd ever done disappeared for good. Despite their recent breakup, my father and Becca's mother banded together to 'request' a return to 'proper' art, and Becca had been the one tasked with ensuring I obeyed the rules.

But Becca didn't give a fuck about rules or productivity.

"Okay, either my dad has brainwashed you, or there's something up. Which is it?"

"I'm not in a carey-sharey mood. Can we just keep this simple today?" She brushed the red armchair free of debris and sat down, still looking at the picture of Asana.

"Tell me what's up and then we can keep it simple."

Shifting her gaze back to the painting, she burst into tears. She continued to stare at the painting as she confessed to Asana.

"I fucked up, okay? I really fucked up. I got so off my tits last night I ended up in bed with Larry. I have no idea why. I'm such a fucking idiot."

"What? Dealer-Larry? Shit. I thought you hated that manipulative fuckhead?"

Becca managed to stop her tears, but kept her gaze fixed on Asana.

"Mike's fucking mental. He threw all my clothes into the garden. In the end, he gave me an ultimatum. Fresh start: no pills, no poppers, not even fucking weed." Her hand wiped a slate clean in the air. "Niente."

"Bloody hell, you'd better not fuck up. But there's always a spare bed here if you need one."

"Don't you fucking give me that shit, Kerella." She yelled, spinning round and pointing her finger with its long, obscenely shiny, red fingernail at me. "You're not responsible enough to have a relationship or even look the fuck after yourself. You know nothing about how normal people behave, so just leave me the eff alone. Mike's just on his 'I fucked my life up 'cause I was dumb enough to drive drugged out my brain, and now I ain't got no legs, everyone has to march to my holier-than-thou-community-centre-counsellor-bullshit."

I sighed. Now I knew the attack was coming from her self-inflicted wounds, it was easier to brush off. Still, I hated being the stop-tap to release her guilt. I snatched Asana from Becca and went into the kitchen to get caffeine, throwing the painting on top of the fridge as I passed.

When I returned with the tea, Becca was spiking up her hair and playing with her tongue stud as if nothing had happened.

I put her mug on the coffee table and threw myself back into the pile of cushions on the settee, not sure what to expect.

She rummaged in her bag, pulling out a pile of things. At the top was a pregnancy test, which she threw on the table.

"Go piss on that."

I ignored her and blew into my tea.

"Kerella!"

"I. do. not. need. to. pee. (.) It. will. have. to. wait."

She looked like she was going to launch into another attack.

Stubbornly, I kept eye contact with her as she narrowed her eyes and tried to project the blame for her shitty feelings on to me. Then, as quickly as the summer storm had passed, her mood shifted. She pushed a memory stick into the middle of the table and picked up her phone.

She sat there, stroking the blank screen, looking thoughtful and proceeding with care. It was a nice change from the bull that had arrived five minutes earlier, but equally unnerving.

"You know the band we went to see last night? The Casa Martyrs?"

I felt the blood drain from my face, and tipped my mug too far to one side, spilling hot tea onto my thigh.

"The band was called the Kasaman-as?"

"You've heard of them? I thought you didn't notice anything outside of your own little world. Colour me surprised..."

"No Becca: Kasaman!"

I paused. Becca looked confused.

"That's the name of the hooded beast thing from my dream, KASAMAN!"

"The band is called The Casa Martyrs."

I thought for a moment. "No. It's too close to be a coincidence; Kasaman must be involved somewhere."

"Not this fantasy bullshit again." Becca groaned. "Kerella, the band is called The Casa Martyrs, not The Casa Man. Whatever you think the Casa Man is responsible for, forget it. If there's any connection, you probably heard us talking about the band and then dreamt about it. Anyway, you're not letting me get to my point."

She picked up her tea, fixing me with her best 'focus on reality please, Kerella' look.

"Last night their keyboardist announced he's leaving for Australia next week, and they have this really important gig next month, some battle of the bands thing for charity, so they need a replacement ASAP. I told them you're a musical genius and could learn the stuff in a matter of days, so you'd step in until after the gig."

"You did what?" My mouth moved, trying to find something else to say in response. After trying out the start of several sentences, I formed a coherent argument. "I'm not joining a band, Becca. Especially one called The Kasa Man-tas."

"Mar-tyrs."

"Whatever. I'm not joining the band."

"Kerella, what's the point of only ever playing with yourself? It's pointless locking yourself away up here and bashing out fucking fantastic music with me as your only victim. You have your mum's gift, and you're wasting it. You may not want to join a band, but you need to."

"Leave my mother out of this. You know I don't do people and I'm crap at 'team' music." I said, making air quotes. "I'm bad band material. It will end badly. I don't do people. I don't do bands."

"Kerella, do this as a favour to me? They really need an eccentric keyboardist; you'll be just perfect. I've already promised them, and it'll earn me extra brownie points with Mike."

"No."

"You'll love their music: melodrama-rock... female vocalist..."

I gave up responding and pulled the black and red crocheted blanket over my head to escape.

"Just listen to this before you make up your mind."

She jabbed at her phone a few times, then held it above her head as it burst into song. I tried not to be interested, but the music caught me straight away. And I hated her for that.

Each note was a burr, brushing past, then refusing to let go. I was becoming lost in the terrain of the song. The composition was well thought out, layering patterns, and building to a climax. I rarely liked music I didn't write as much as I liked this song; the composer was on my wavelength. On the other hand, the keyboardist was clearly not up the task. His accompaniment copied the melody with no imagination and there were a few moments when he was slightly out of time with the other musicians.

Still, I refused to show any interest, putting all my attention into admiring my mother's crochet work from underneath my black and red veil.

"That's Mannie doing the vocals. She looks amazing. She's really short but has these huge muscles and mad pink and black hair. When she's on stage she really engages the audience."

I didn't respond to Becca's sales pitch. I was lost in the music, hoping I could get out of being in the band and somehow get hold of the sound files.

The next song came on.

It whined on about loss and death in a provocative self-absorbed manner. I loved it.

"Is that a cello?"

"Yeah, I think so. Chris plays like five or six different instruments. Weird guy. A real fucking intense wanker. But a talented wanker. You two'll get along; both of you are better with music than people."

We listened to the cello solo.

"Your dad plays the cello, doesn't he?"

"One more reason not to join the band."

Then came some male vocals: I did not like the way they made an electric charge surge through me.

If Mull'aman were to sing, he'd sound like that.

I was definitely interested.

I pulled the blanket down and pouted at Becca. "I like their music."

"So, you'll do it then?"

"No."

"Kerella, please? Just one month. You're the quickest person to hand with the ability to learn the music. They're desperate. I'm desperate."

"Becca, you know how me and people are unmeshable. I like the music, but I don't, I can't, deal with people."

"One month. And they know you're... not so good at the social thing. We've told Fus you're a bit of a head case and he's fine with that. He and Mannie are fucking counsellors for fuck's sake. It's so perfect! They might even fix you!"

"I can't." My voice was a pathetic whimper, slowly being worn away.

Becca's tone changed. "Look Kerella, do something for me for once, okay? Think of all the things I've done for you. Getting you in with the band will help me rebuild things with Mike. He'll be grateful that I found them a keyboardist, and you can tell them I'm keeping clean, and they will tell him."

I didn't respond. The keyboardist tripped clumsily through an awkward passage, before leaving the cellist to end the song.

"Here are Simon's notes on what he plays," she slapped a few grubby sheets of manuscript paper down on the table, "but they said you can try your own style as long as it fits in with the overall sound. I'll take you to the community centre on Thursday; all you have to do is go in and strut your stuff on the keyboard: good karma all round. You're into that supernatural bullshit, you have to do it, or badness will fall on your head."

Her phone launched into the next song.

Something about the music was getting to me; I knew I longed to be part of it. I just didn't want that to involve people.

I looked at Becca. She smiled and pushed the memory stick over to my side of the table, knowing she had won.

"Hmumrrrurrrurrrmmph." I moaned slipping down into the cushions and hugging my mug of tea. I pulled the blanket back over my head and sulked. In my mind, I travelled back to the dream and the music I had played. I could hear the words Kasaman had said to me, feel him pushing me towards the piano...

And then it all clicked into place.

I threw the blanket off my head. "This is fate, you know, Becca."

"Bollocks."

"No! It's all been symbolic. This Kasaman in my dream pushed me towards the piano and told me to become part of the music! All the dreams have been my subconscious getting me ready to be in the band... Kinda bland really. I think I'm a bit disappointed."

Becca burst out laughing. "You are fucking nuts! You know that?" She got up and started walking around the edge of the pool of images, now taking the effort not to tread on anything.

Her boots clonked on the wooden floor in time with the music, which had moved on to a more uplifting song about escaping the world to fly with fairies and porcupines.

It was unusual for me to leave my artwork lying around and I think the only paintings of mine Becca had ever seen was the work I did for 'Shambles', her mother's shop, as part of an arrangement set up by my father to keep me 'busy and productive'.

I felt uncomfortable that Becca was looking straight into my secret world.

She picked up a watercolour of Kasaman's mountain reaching up into red clouds.

"Interesting. What inspired this?"

"Surprisingly enough, a dream."

I reached out to take the painting off Becca.

She dutifully handed it over. "Anyway, I should head off to check in with Mike. I promised him I would cook a shit-hot dinner. You get practicing for your meeting with The Martyrs. Don't let me down. I told them you're a genius, so work your fucking arse off."

"You're a bulldozer, you know that?"

"It's all for your own good." Becca walked round the back of the settee, pulled my head back, and kissed my forehead. Then she started playing with the hair on the back of my head.

"What have you done to your head?"

I pulled away in a panic, remembering my head injuries from the night before. I felt the top of my head and pulled a small amount of dried blood from my hair.

"I... I... don't know." What could I tell Becca? That some deformed flying thing attacked me in my dreams, whilst someone else sliced into my head, and I brought the wound into real life because some deity called Asana made me drink a bitter liquid?

"Don't look so shocked, it just looks like you knocked the scab off a spot or scratched your head too hard. You make everything so melodramatic! Anyway, I'll see you later. And if you haven't done the test by then, I will give you something to be melodramatic about."

"Okay." I said, staring at the flakes of dried blood in my palm.

This blood was evidence that my dreams were real, even if they were starting to feel like a distant memory.

After Becca left, I laid out all the sketches, paintings, and notes I'd done that morning. Although they were unplanned, cascading randomly out of my mind, most half-finished, or barely started before they were discarded to make room for the next image forcing its way into my head, I could pick out a story waiting to be told in the images: a story filled with cloaked beasts and hooded figures in dramatic, dry, mountainous landscapes.

The bitter liquid Asana made me drink must have triggered something. The way I never stopped to think, just scribbled words over images over songs and tunes; the way that, when I looked away, the pictures faded just as fast as they were intense when I looked at them. There was more to this than dreams.

These memories were real.

I tried to sort the pictures into groups, then stood up to look at them.

The first group of paintings were of the Kaetian Compound's guards. I'd scrawled 'Paders' over one of the pictures; a group of four of them at sunset, perched like crows on an outcrop of rock. They wore black hooded cloaks with red streaks which started at the neck and snaked down the back. In their right hand, each of them had a thick, milky-pale sword that was nearly as long as the Paders were tall. They held short black daggers in their left hands.

One looked straight at me. Her face was covered in the traditional grainy yellow Pader face paint, with a line of blood drawn from forehead to chin, showing that she had taken a life. The area around her eyes was coloured black, marking her as a veteran of battle who had eaten the flesh of her fallen comrades.

The second group of paintings were of the people whose faces came up again and again. Mostly in red cloaks, occasionally dark green. Unlike the 'Paders', the faces of these characters were more detailed, as if I knew them well. Most of them were old, except one young man I'd drawn six times. He had a warm and familiar face, and unlike the other guests in my pictures, he wore the hood of his red cloak down. His curly, dark brown hair cascaded down his back. I could feel it between my fingers, see the colours reflect in the strong rays of an unforgiving sun, smell its woody scent.

Looking into his fertile, pondweed-green eyes now, I knew who he was. I picked up a black ink pen and knelt to write 'Mull'aman' over a painting of him playing an instrument which looked like a cross between a piano and a harp.

I stood up to take in the images swimming around my feet. I rotated slowly so I could see them all. I felt transported through them, like I was falling into another world; a world that could be more real to me than the world of Becca and my father. There I had a place, a role. Perhaps as 'Tushenta', whoever she was. In my 'real' life, I didn't have anything, except a vivid imagination and a lot of issues.

I started spinning faster and faster.

This was probably why I didn't feel like I belonged in the real world, I was too busy making up worlds where I did. I knew what I was doing was wrong. It was hardly going to fix me or make me normal. But was that a realistic option right now?

Feeling dizzy, I let myself fall on to the settee.

Hardly realistic.

Normal was out of my reach.

6: THE GRAVEYARD OF THE FORGOTTEN

This is my graveyard: overgrown, untended, and secluded. Resting in a small copse in the corner of a large wheat field, far enough away from the coastal path to avoid the annoying thoroughfare of walkers, close enough to have a spectacular view of the cliffs pouring lines of stratified rock into the sea. The church is no longer here. Their god no longer looks over this sanctuary, but the memory of death has not gone anywhere. They left the graves when they stole the stones to build a monument to their wealth and piety in a more populated and popular location.

This is my field of death, abandonment, revelation, and reality. The church had abandoned its believers, believing them dead long enough not to matter. I never would.

Since the death of my mother, I regularly 'paid my respects' to these ornate gravestones. I hated the place my father had chosen to lay my mother's corpse to rest. The digger always seemed to be bouncing out noise as it dug another hole in the death-factory-floor, and the smell of weedkiller hung around the sharp stone edges and the plastic grave décor. This overgrown graveyard in the middle of nowhere was where she would rather be, a wild and natural shrine to her passion and her life.

When I was younger, my mother brought me to this field and unveiled the history hiding underneath the grass and nettles which grew thick and possessively around the weathered slabs of slate. If it were still to be found anywhere on this plane of existence, I knew her spirit was here, not in plot 147, where the florist my father's company used, regularly delivered plastic wrapped flowers in his name.

I reached into my embroidered Prussian blue bag and scooped out a smooth white stone with a black streak running through it, which I'd rescued from North Beach, and a rough pitted ochre stone, that presented itself to me on South Beach. These gifts had been chosen with care to offer to the spirits of the abandoned. I knew they were watching over me, had helped me find my magical world, and were to thank for my period, which wasn't worrying me, until Becca had made such a fuss.

Carefully laying my offerings down by the entrance to the graveyard, I declared: "I dedicate these offerings to the Dispossessed God, the God of Outcasts, the God who knows what it is like to walk on the outside."

I ran my finger over the smooth stone one last time, and, satisfied that I'd paid tribute to whatever deity was bothering to take an interest in my issues, I pushed my way through the waist high grass to the best vantage point in the cemetery.

I lifted myself up onto the Hendersons' resting place and settled down to share the sunrise with my friend, Ergle, the angry-cherub-demon carved on the gravestone next to the Henderson's tomb. In the half-light of the pre-dawn, he scowled his welcome through menacing eyes.

I pulled out my paints and watercolour pad, and waited for the sun to make its entrance. Thin scars of white gold cut through the sky and I grabbed my brush to capture the changes in the rocks, sun, sea, and birds, encoding them into colours and shapes on the paper in front of me.

"You would love to meet a redwaek." I told Ergle as I dipped my brush into the water and ran it across the page to lighten a streak across the sky, blotting it with a rag. "They were humans once, but Kasaman stole the essence of their human spirit. Without this essence, the mind decays, yet remains trapped within the body, even after death. Because the mind contains such powerful energy, without any conscious restraint or channel to disperse, the redwaek's body physically manifests the desires that person held during their lifetime. Those who dreamt of flying may grow powerful wings, or those who talked to themselves a lot may grow another head, so their two heads can have rambling conversations that never end. But, because the mind is rotting, they have lost all power of reason and are totally insane. They are so jealous of the people still with their spiritual essence intact, their overwhelming desire becomes torturing, killing, and eating anyone who is not a redwaek."

I looked at Ergle as he grimaced through his dark slate facade, unimpressed with my discovery of these creatures.

"Oh, the sky, Ergle! You would love to fly through the Kaetian sky! The clouds look as though they are filled with blood-soaked sand, and the colours flow from dark red, to the orange of a lazy fire, to iris purple, and back again, like the sunset reflecting on water throughout the entire sky."

I could hear Ergle respond in my head. "Why would I want to fly through such a confusing sky and feel like I'm crashing about in a kaleidoscope, when I have a sky as beautiful as the one above our heads?"

I sighed and looked up at the aureate spectacle unfolding in the heavens.

Ergle was right: this real sky above my real head, in the world I really inhabited was beyond beautiful. But I was lost to my desire for a world carved into sandstone; the silhouette of a black mountain; and the courtyards, passageways, and towers I'd decided to call my home.

The morning moved on as I filled more pages with the view from the Henderson's tomb. With each painting, the view became less exciting, and I grew restless. My mind kept dragging me back to the paintings on the floor of my flat, the notebooks filled with Kaetian culture and etiquette, the maps of the Compound, and the score for Tushenta's favourite piece of music.

Eventually, the pull became too strong. I bid farewell to Ergle and headed back into town. I stopped off to buy a baguette before returning to my earthly home, only to discover it had been invaded.

7: DADDY

The conquering power took one look at me and started his annoying tut-tut-tutting.

I stood in the doorway of my flat in my black and blue dress, with the corset style bodice, and uneven shreds of lace and velvet tumbling down. A carefully designed mess of blonde hair fell loosely to the left-hand side of my face.

His eyes bored into me with compassionate disappointment, seeing only the exhibits of a useless sub-culture on a dysfunctional member of society.

His secret shame.

I addressed the man who was wearing a suit that was far too expensive for this little seaside town: "Hi Dad."

"Hello Kerella." He paused to look at his phone. "And what have you been up to?"

"Keeping busy." I said, throwing myself onto the settee.

"That's descriptive, dear."

"Well, if you must know, I walked out to the graveyard mum used to take me to."

"That's..." He took a big sigh and shook his head. "Hardly a..." He sighed again, "productive use of your time... and a little bit, well, morbid, dear. Don't you think you're taking this Goth thing a bit far?"

"It's not morbid; it's a lovely place."

"But it's hardly normal to hang around in a graveyard."

"Well, 'normal people'," I made air quotes, "don't know what they're missing."

He sat down next to me, so I jumped up, relocating to the piano stool. My right hand touched the keys and my mother's confrontational spirit flowed through me. "You should try it; it feeds the soul."

"I don't see how a place of death can feed the soul."

"That's because you're looking at it all wrong. Gravestones are a testimonial to how someone touched the world; they are evidence that the people who lie beneath invoked love, passion, and friendship. Gravestones are a historical monument that these 'loved ones' were part of this world, even when the world and their 'religion' have moved on without them."

He didn't have an answer to that, so looked around the room to find something he did perceive himself to be an authority on. "I see you've been engaging in fantasy again."

I imagined the gates to the Kaetian Quarters slamming shut. I was safe in my tower; my father and everything that could hurt me were on the other side of thick, impenetrable walls. But my fingers refused to be locked up. They found the piano and began dancing up and down the keyboard, silently tracing the melody to The Casa Martyr's song, 'Hands of Helios': a song that made me feel some parents didn't just see their children as problems that needed to be fixed. I drew on the strength of the piano, the comfort of Mull'aman, and the wisdom of Asana, to prepare myself for what was coming.

"You remember what Dr. Devries said? You have to try and stay grounded in the real world."

"That's just fucking bullshit from an overpaid moron who knows sod all about me. Believe me: painting a few pictures is not going to kill me. I. am. fine."

I started hitting chords to explain how I was feeling.

"Five years ago, you weren't 'fine'. I just..." He started to move towards me. "I don't want you to damage your health again, and you have to be productive and grounded in the real world to avoid that."

I paused to let a melody fill me, before responding with accompaniment:

"For too long, I let you lead this fight
against the demons that come in the night.
The evil that attacks lies in your 'reality':
maybe...
I know what is best for me?"

He hit the side of the piano and slammed the cover over the keys. I flew off the piano stool, rescuing my fingers just in time, and cowered by the wall with my hands over my ears.

He raised his hands to say sorry and signal that he was calming his approach.

"Based on your past record? No, I don't believe you know what is best for you." He looked at me with paternal consideration. "What I do not understand is why, a girl as intelligent as you are, is so determined to ruin her life: you could be so much more than this."

Then, he remembered our agreement made under Dr. Devries's supervision, and took two steps back. I stood up and returned to the piano stool.

"Okay, let's talk about 'positive ways' forward." He forgot, as always, that my input was required in creating my 'positive trajectory'. "You need to start producing more commercial artwork, enrol in some training, or come to work for me. I'm sure we can find something for you to do at the factory." He was quiet for a moment before fixing his cold grey eyes on me. "Do something, or I'll stop your allowance, young lady."

I met his threats with a blank stare aimed at the middle of his forehead.

"This is no kind of life; it's not eccentricity. I know you're trying to be like your mother, but do you think she'd really be proud of you? She was creative, yes, distracted, yes. What you don't seem to understand is, she was a highly successful professional pianist, not a weirdo in silly clothes, wasting her time scribbling rubbish with no commercial value and hanging around in graveyards trying to scare people at funerals."

I was starting to feel dizzy, so I stared at the floor. He always managed to induce nausea and make me feel like a useless child, but this was new.

"Kerella?"

"What?"

"Look at me when I'm talking to you."

I forced my focus back to his face. "What?"

"What are you going to do?"

"Produce more commercial artwork." I mimicked in a narky tone.

"Okay. For now, I will take these fantasy pictures with me. And I do not want to see any more of them. Okay?"

"No!" I jumped up. "I'll be more commercial, I promise! Just, please, don't take my pictures. I need them!"

He let out a half-grunted sigh and set about scooping up my pictures, bending them, smudging them, mixing them up.

I grabbed the pile of paintings of Mull'aman at the same time as he did. He didn't let go, so I gave them a sharp tug. The pile ripped, sending me reeling back onto the floor, my face colliding with the coffee table.

I lay there for a moment, startled, my face feeling both numb and painful. Gingerly, I felt my lip and it was bleeding, my tongue wrapped around my tooth, it moved slightly, but would survive. I glared up at the grey suit clutching an arm full of paper, card, and canvas.

"Kerella, stop overreacting, you'll only hurt yourself... Are you okay?"

I looked away and felt my lip again.

"Great. And I've got a fucking audition on Thursday as well."

"You didn't mention that before. Oh, that's a good thing. For a music group?"

"No, for the fucking circus." I pulled myself up, holding on to the settee whilst I waited for the dizziness to pass.

I glared at the buttons on my father's suit jacket. He didn't get it. He never did.

"Kerella, please. I'm sorry. Let me look at your lip."

As he moved over me, I was knocked back by whisky, claustrophobia, and violation.

"Get away from me! You aren't allowed to touch me, yet you creep in and tell lies that catch my throat with peat fumes and you think the shame will keep me silent but you're the fucking monster!" I screamed, pushing him away with all my strength, causing him to totter backwards a few steps.

As the moment of panic dissipated into the parquet flooring, the present returned with a flood, and we both stood awkwardly, not sure how to address the big black issue that plagued the Tomlinson family.

"Kerella?"

I felt sick.

"Kerella, I'm not Eddie, and I don't drink whisky, and I have not been drinking... And I would never do that to you. And it hurts me that I couldn't keep you safe. But you are safe now. Everything I do is to keep you safe."

My brain began to swell inside my skull and the voices were screaming obscenities. I clamped my hands over my ears and started stamping frantically around the room. My head filled up with nasty images. Naked, deformed people were running after me, black mountains were standing proud and erect against blood skies, hands clawed at my face, and Eddie's rancid breath replaced all the air in the room.

My breath was shallow and panicked. "Get out!"

I needed this to end. I needed Eddie out of my flat.

"Get out! Get out! Get out!"

It was only later I realised that he'd left with all my notes and paintings.

My father still lingered in my flat. Okay, his flat if you want to get technical about ownership. His smell, his tidy wake, the thought of him, the way he made me feel like a helpless child trapped in a past I wanted nothing to do with, the way he looked like Eddie.

"Ugh." I stared in dismay at the herring bone pattern of interwoven rich wooden hues, hoping if I looked long enough and hard enough, I would see my pictures again.

I couldn't accept that they were gone, and not only were they gone in the physical sense, but with their departure, I'd lost all detailed memories of my world. What did those female warriors look like? And the boy in the red cloak? Was it even red? I closed my eyes; I couldn't even remember the colour of the sky. My entire memory was made of watercolours and the tide had washed it away.

I was angry.

Scratch that.

I was livid.

I knew these images were a fleeting insight into this world and I'd worked so hard to capture them in a concrete form, only to lose them in such a way! Now they were gone, and I felt hollow, gutted, and disembowelled. I'd lost my only weapon in the fight against Kasaman, and now I was plunged into the unknown with C sharp as my only ally.

8: FLIGHT OF THE FUCK UP

Thump. Thump. Thump.

The veins in my forehead filled up with blood and tension. Dragging my fingernails over the skin brought only a moment of relief; the pain dissipated, the distraction ceased, and the pressure remained.

I had no control over anything, over this space, over my life. I was empty. I was nothing that he did not say and nothing in his eyes.

I had to escape the things he controlled: my flat, my home, my space, the things he owned, the things he gave, the things he took, and the empty space he created when he stole my paintings.

I stood in that empty space as the walls closed in and I spiralled out.

My throat hurt from screaming.

My foot hurt from kicking the settee.

My forehead hurt from the scratches.

My lip hurt from my collision with the coffee table.

I needed to escape.

Grabbing my bag, I fled as if from the Devil himself. Running through the streets towards the sea with blood and bruises on my face, smudged eyeliner around my eyes, and uneven shreds of lace and velvet tumbling down.

I took the coastal path to the south and ran until the cliffs regained their essence and gave up the pathetic charade of tamed pebbles slinking lamely into the bay.

I knew this land well; I knew the rocks better. I picked my way through the long grass and walked up to a solid rock face. I threw myself into the climb towards the hidden ledge I knew was on the other side.

The liberation of entering a space my father could never control brought an immediate wave of calm. I collapsed onto the ledge, exhausted, and drained of all the delusions that had led me to believe I could be a part of The Casa Martyrs, that I could be anything other than the local pariah.

A fucked-up piece of crap in uneven shreds of lace and velvet.

A joke.

A failure.

Dirty.

Wrong.

It didn't matter. Here on this ledge, I was free. Free from delusions and expectations; free from control and obligations. Here I only had the sea, the sky, and the rocks to answer to, and they were as feral as I was.

Here I could breathe.

As the panic and sickness provoked by the mention of Eddie subsided, the real sting started to burn. "I know you're trying to be like your mother, but do you think she'd really be proud of you?"

That was the lowest my father had ever sunk.

I sought comfort in my mother, speeding back through time until I was standing backstage listening to her play my favourite of her songs: Silver Stream. Things were so simple back then. We used to spin around, laugh, paint, collect stones, and make up songs. How could I know that it was a mask, deceiving a young child, making me believe life was full of love, magic, and adventure?

Safe.

Reality hits harder when you're so deluded.

The tide went out.

I sketched dark sketches and picked at my baguette, unwilling to return home.

The sky entered its evening ritual, leaving behind the cerulean blue and silver clouds framed with delicate yellow, and exploring the earthier hues of its palette. Memories taunted me in the clouds: each colour evoked another feeling, each shape a new association. I could hear my mother's infectious laughter, the spells she created on the piano, the sweetness of her melodies.

And then my mother found Eddie in my room that night and never forgave her husband for what his brother had done.

The music became screams, shouting, and the sound of glasses being broken in anger.

They told me she went mad. She started to drink heavily and became obsessively protective of me.

We didn't spin after that.

She didn't laugh anymore.

Everything became static and dark and broken and it was my fault.

The clouds reflected the light from the candle my mother had placed by my bed that night. In its golden aura, she told me I was a goddess. She lay on my bed, stroking my hair, whispering that I had important things to accomplish in my life, and she wouldn't let the evil in this world stop me. She told me, whatever I did, I would succeed, because I was the hero of my own story.

I knew my mother wasn't mad. My father made that up to cover his own guilt for not protecting me from his brother.

The clouds turned indigo, drizzled with dark red. The blood in the clouds became the blood on the shards of glass at the top of the stairs. In the black depths of the sea, I saw my mother's broken body lying on the patio. She was wearing a dark blue dressing gown and a long cream satin nightdress, now splattered with scarlet as her soul seeped away. Her brown eyes were open and fixed on me as I looked down from the broken window. Her blonde hair shimmered over the paving slabs, reflecting the glare of the patio light. She looked so natural and passionate, like her music. Until my father reached the body. He bent over her, pulled at her, moved her. And then she just looked dead. Something else my father had ruined.

Blood from my torn face dripped into the air.

They told me she was sleepwalking.

I never believed it.

9: THE TOWER

My spirit had been walking, but survival called it back. I fell into physical pain, remembering only the last foot of my descent, and woke to pins and needles in my arms, and a hip numb from lying on a hard surface.

I flexed my fingers, easing the blood flow back into my arms, and became aware of the cold stone under my fingertips.

It was too dark for me to see, but I guessed that I was on the floor of Tushenta's tower. Ignoring the protest from my aching body, I forced myself to move. If I were in that world, a redwaek might attack at any moment and making sure the shutters were locked could save me a painful encounter.

Flipping clumsily onto my knees, I edged forwards in the darkness. A roaring was erupting from somewhere. What monsters were there in Tushenta's world that made that noise? My mind ran through the fragments of images left in my head after my father stole my paintings.

I was not ready.

I'd lost the advantage.

(Damn my father).

Now, I needed to fight, not think.

I listened carefully. The sound was coming from outside and the shutters were all open. Not willing to get to my feet in a strange room in total darkness, I pushed my hand into the void to feel my way.

The floor wasn't there, and I lurched forwards.

Reality kicked in as I clung to the cliff face with the sea crashing onto the rocks beneath me. My fingers dug fiercely into a ridge in the rock, and I flailed around trying to find a foothold to push myself back to the safety of the ledge.

I nearly lost a nail but managed to pull myself to safety and edge away from the drop onto the crashing waves.

"I could have fucking died!" I declared to the rocks, who threw my stupidity back in my face as the echo of possibility rebounded off their cold face.

I crawled to the deepest part of the ledge and curled up in defeat, tears welling up in my eyes.

"You fucking idiot."

The sun was yet to rise, but the birds had started heckling the false dawn, weaving a painful tune, backed by the recklessness of my pulse. They were laughing, laughing at me; Darwin at his most productive, assuming birds knew about natural selection.

If I had died, they would assume suicide and it would mean nothing to anybody except my father, who would be happy because he could finally control me and put me in my place next to my mother: parallel, organised, appropriate.

I would finally fit in a box he wouldn't have a problem with. No more being dragged from one professional to another to get a second (and third) opinion. No more coaching on what to say to appear normal when I was assessed.

Not autistic.

Just dead.

I was filled with a raw nothingness that came from having all my false perceptions torn apart, the phantoms from my past rising from their grave to spit in my face, from spending the night sleeping on rocks, and from being proven delusional and phenomenally stupid.

Close the bloody shutters! Yeah, right. Maybe I really was losing sight of the line between reality and fantasy. I'd begun to hope for something, and this was my punishment. I'd believed I was worthwhile, believed I could be part of something, believed that 'The Casa Martyrs' would want a delusional freak like me in their band.

Now I was reduced to the reality of what I was.

Staring into the darkness where the sun would later tread, I tore my mental landscape down. The divine destruction had struck. I'd fallen from the tower of my false perceptions and was lying broken on the rocks. Amidst the rubble, I started to build new plans: sedated plans, realistic plans, plans based on the painful reminder that I never lived up to anyone's expectations. Plans based on the fact that my brain worked differently from most people, and I had to stay in my lane.

I let my own desire to be part of The Casa Martyrs colour my perception. I was a joke; I'd danced around in a graveyard singing their songs, thinking that would make me good enough for them.

I'd lost valuable time painting that pathetic canary sunrise when I should have been working out what I was going to show them on Thursday. I needed to perfect every last note if I were to convince them they wanted to share their music with this fuck up in dirty, uneven shreds of lace and velvet.

"Focus."

Darkness swept around me as I played their music in my head.

My father told me that my ability to recreate and listen to songs in my head was a bad thing, as it stopped me working hard to truly master my talents. To him listening to my favourite songs without hearing them, or playing a piano that wasn't there, was not a useful skill. It was just a novelty, something entertaining for a while, but of no use for business. Something that didn't fit in the real world. Something Kerella did. One of the many things about me that wasn't right.

Whatever my father may think, in the darkness, in the depths of my despair, it was useful to me. I let the sound of the birds fade into the background. My fingers traced the keys I would play, and the emotion of the music wrapped me up in silence.

The sky became less black.

I was hungry and dehydrated.

My lip was cracked from where I'd collided with the coffee table, and it had started to bleed again.

The taste of blood trespassed onto the edge of my tongue, reminding me of all the lies I'd told myself, reminding me that I was not the hero of my own story: I'd be lucky to be a stock character forgotten before the page had turned.

I should get home before it got too light, and I'd have to walk past people looking like the insane maladjust that I was.

I navigated the rocks that guarded my ledge, and as my feet hit the grass, a German Shepherd lumbered up to me and deposited a large stick by my feet.

It was rare for anyone to fight their way through the bushes and uneven terrain to explore this section of the coast. For someone to be walking their dog here, at this time of day, was inconceivable, but just in case I was awake, and a dog walker was nearby, I thought I should head back over the rocks to my ledge. The last thing I needed right now was to bump into an early morning dog walker whilst I had blood on my face, dirt on my clothes, and my hair was a frizzy, knotted mess.

"Tris!" The dog's ears pricked up and he barked at his owner who was moving steadily through the bushes towards us.

I remained motionless between two large boulders, assessing the intruder, as his dog panted enthusiastically at me. A long black cloak draped around his lithe physique and darkness stared out from under the rim of his fedora hat.

He jumped over a hidden ditch, moving as though he knew the terrain. He turned towards me, and I got a better view of Kasaman's face; the nascent light tiptoeing across the sky threw back an impression of his smudged features. My trespasser looked creepy enough to be a figment of my imagination.

This really could be Kasaman.

In the indulgence of my hybrid reality, I took too long to realise that he was now only a few metres away, and his continued presence had ruled out the possibility of him being an imagined phantom.

As his owner came around the last bush, Tris barked at the stick by my feet.

And someone, who was probably not Kasaman, stopped in front of me.

He raised his hand to his lips, to indicate he was about to ask about the blood on my face, but before he had the chance to say anything, I charged at him, knocking him into a bush.

As I ran towards the coastal path, I could feel his eyes on my back.

I would just have to cope with one more resident of this town thinking I was a freak.

10: REDWAEK

The grisly history of how Kasaman murdered my grandparents and great grandparents slips from my mind and back between the thick pages of the leather-bound tome. The book falls from my hands onto the bed.

I stare in horror at the head peeking through the tiny window. I had been listening out for the beating of redwaek wings; or the squawking, squealing, and howling redwaek constantly emit; but this beast must have scaled the tower walls and managed to keep its mouth shut for the entire climb.

"Redwaek!" I shout to alert the Paders standing guard outside my door. "Redwaek! Redwaek!"

Through the deep recess of the window, the living corpse leers at me; tracks of blood tears stain his face and a tangle of thorns grows from his head.

The Paders pound on the door, which I'd locked from the inside when I decided to ignore the lockdown horns and leave a shutter open to make my reading experience more enjoyable.

The gap would be too small for the redwaek to squeeze through, and the walls were well over an arm's length deep, which is why I'd risked leaving it open; even so, my pulse is beating thick and furiously as the creature pushes his arms through the gap and starts trying to drag himself through the window.

I edge myself across the bed, away from the window and towards the safety of the Paders.

The redwaek goes limp. He's managed to drag himself halfway through and now seems to be stuck. His arms are sticking straight out of the recess, with his grey sinewy fingers interlocked as if in prayer.

I pause to watch the creature in his defeat, assured that the threat is over. But his arms suddenly spring back to life, and snap unnaturally back against the wall to give himself more leverage. His face emerges as it squeezes past his dislocated shoulders. He opens his elongated mouth and emits a chilling wail. I hear a squelching, crunching sound as he pulls himself forward.

Blood starts to ooze down the wall.

I jump out of bed, only to get caught up in the cream netting which hangs between the bed posts. I claw clumsily at the drapes, finally finding the gap and make to run for the door, but my foot catches in the net and I fly forwards, landing sprawled over the floor.

A long Pader sword strikes through the thick dark wood of the door as the redwaek pulls himself free of the window and falls to the floor, wings ripped from his body and sides scraped away to organs and bone. He writhes like a bloody worm, all the while, looking right at me, holding me in his gaze, twisting his head from side to side. He slowly gets to his feet and cackles.

I grab the carved bedpost and pull myself to my feet. The redwaek and I stare at each other; the bloody stumps of what is left of his wings flap, spreading blood over the rough-hewn ochre walls. A large crash comes from behind me as a Pader's sword slices through the door again.

My guards are still trapped outside.

The redwaek lurches towards the largest window. I run to the door and grab the large iron key. I try to turn it, but the Paders' attempt to break the door down has shifted the locking mechanism and the key won't move.

The sword cuts through the door again, the pale blade narrowly missing my shoulder. "I'm at the door, don't strike it again! The key's stuck!"

Behind me, I hear the wooden bar, which keeps the shutters closed, being lifted. The shutters fly open and bang against the wall, and several excited redwaek begin howling and screeching.

I bash the key with the base of my palm, sending painful shocks up my arm. The key moves a fraction. I force it round by hitting it repeatedly and finally the lock disengages with a satisfying clunk...

An arm clamps firmly over my chest and I'm swung round to face the army of redwaek coming through the window.

I never imagined a redwaek could be as large or sexually charged as the one stood in front of me. He's covered in ornate patterns of black and red ridges which accentuate his muscles and other bodily features. His nipples are a waxy bright red, the right one pierced with a black peg. A long black umbilical cord snakes up from his stomach and wraps around his neck. His double headed penis is covered in barbs and doesn't look anything like the descriptions of the male anatomy I'd read. His blood-filled eyes stare at me, ensuring every inch of my body feels violated.

Behind him lies the redwaek that pulled himself through the window. He twitches and flails in a pool of blood whilst a small, wingless redwaek in a ragged black cloak prods him with a long stick and hiccoughs, "No harm. No harm. No harm."

Two redwaek flank the black and red beast, another has just landed on the window ledge, and more are jostling to be the next to come through the gap.

The arm over my chest suddenly releases me and I'm pulled backwards. I look at a Pader guard with her stony yellow face, blackened eyes, and the streak of blood drawn from forehead to chin. Beneath the mask of Pader, she looks at me with pale green eyes and issues the order: "Run."

Three Paders begin the attack on the redwaek army as I exit through the splintered door, leaving them to save the day and defend the Compound against the redwaek I let in.

With my left hand flat against the newel and my right brushing against the outer wall, I control my headlong descent down the spiral staircase. I'm running away from danger, but with every rotation I make, I'm closer to having to explain to Asana how, once again, I have done something stupid. She's going to be furious when she hears that I left a shutter open during a lockdown.

I stumble into the staging area that separates the three Kaetian towers from the rest of the Compound. Splinters of light from the harsh Kaetian sun blast through cracks in the lockdown shutters and land in scorching white lines on the panels boarding up the entrance to Kasaman's old tower. They hurt my eyes to look at, so I focus on the dark blue curtain at the bottom of the stairs leading up to Asana's tower. Between the entrances to these two towers is a table which always has a jug of water and two beakers on it. Two simple wooden chairs rest either side of the table, as if Asana and I were likely to hang around here having a friendly chat.

No one ever sits here. Maybe the Paders drink the water, or laze about when no one can see them, but I doubt that.

I walk over to the table, pick up the jug, and pour myself a wooden beaker full of warm, gritty water. I collapse onto one of the hard-backed wooden chairs and take a sip. Relief swims through my body.

At the sound of footsteps descending the staircase of Asana's tower, I jump to my feet, ready to face my judgement.

The curtain is thrust aside, and three Pader guards prowl forward in attack formation, their long pale swords held across their bodies and their short black daggers out from their sides. I throw my hands up and back away; the wooden beaker drops to the slate floor spilling the precious liquid.

"Tushenta, run into the Compound." One of the Paders instructs.

"But I don't have my cloak." I reply, horrified they would have me expelled in just my undergown.

Then I turn to see what the Paders are focusing on.

The black and red beast is strutting down the stairs, his long, red tongue lolling out of his mouth, the head of the green-eyed Pader in one hand, her long sword in the other. More redwaek follow him, carrying various body parts of my Pader guards.

"I be Pader." *He grunts.*

Right now, I would run through the town naked.

Charging through the ornate archway that marks the entrance to the Kaetian Quarters, I enter the Compound unescorted for the first time in my life; not wearing the hood of my cloak up like a demure deity, but careening, uncloaked, like a common Merdiant. The long cream cotton layers of my gown billow out behind me in an ostentatious spectacle.

Thankfully, being lockdown, no one is around to witness my shame, and if they do see me, hopefully, it'll be too dark for them to see who I am.

"I chase cloud. Kyuaaaa."

Turning sharply to the left, I enter unknown territory and plunge down a dark, narrow staircase. I come out in a corridor decorated with red curtains. As I run, I scream: "Redwaek attack! Run, everyone run! Help me! Run! Redwaek attack!"

Ahead of me, an old man in a red cloak quickly retreats into the room he was coming out of, slamming the door behind him.

I reach the door and try to push it open, hoping to find safety behind it, but he's locked it.

I press on into the Compound, passing doors which are, either already closed as I approach, or slam and lock on hearing my warning, and windows which are either in lockdown or covered by permanent grilles.

The corridor turns sharply to the right. As I hurtle around the corner, I see a young man in a red cloak coming towards me, his chestnut brown hair spilling in ringlets from his raised hood.

"Help me, please!" *I scream as I crash into him.*

He pushes me roughly behind him, grabs a flaming torch from an enclave in the wall, and smashes my pursuer over the head.

The redwaek falls onto his back and the man bashes the base of the torch hard into the creature's groin.

He steps back and, pulling me close to him, instructs: "Keep going down this corridor; there'll be steps to your left. Go down them and take the first right you come to."

The redwaek is now on all fours and is growling at us. Saliva cascades from his black mouth.

"Go!" *The man shouts, pushing me away from him.*

The creature pounces and locks his jaw firmly on the man's upper arm. As I run down the corridor, I hear my saviour screaming.

11: MULL'AMAN

"S*teps to my left. Steps to my left." I repeat to myself as I run down the corridor. I come to a narrow opening and take the steep flight of stairs. The steps veer off to the left when they reach the curved wall of a tower, tracing what would have once been an outside wall. Then my escape route divides in two; if I continue down the stairs, I'm still taking the steps to my left, but to my right, there's a dark corridor.*

Did he mean for me to go to the end of the stairway and then take the first right, or take the first right turn I came to? Darn this labyrinth! I read a book once about how new towers were built on the outside of the existing Compound to create more space. It made it sound like a lot of planning went into the design and the result was logical and spacious. This is certainly not what I'd imagined when I read that text.

I take the dark passageway. It snakes around the edge of a couple of towers, and then turns sharply into a bright corridor which ends abruptly with a locked wrought iron gate. The sun shines full on through the bars of the gate. I'm at the edge of the Compound, looking out from the mountain: a little exposed cloud waiting to be spotted by any redwaek that happens to be flying past. And if they can't rip the gate off the hinges, they can screech until one of the infiltrators finds me and rips me to pieces.

I must hide. There's only one door in the corridor. I try the solid wooden door and it is locked.

Something is coming down the passageway and I have nothing to hand to use as a weapon. The only thing I have is my undergown. I pull up the skirt, use my teeth to gnaw a tear into the hem, rip a long strip off the bottom, and hold the material tightly between my hands. I have little chance of overpowering a redwaek, but I will have a go at strangling the fiend.

A loud shriek comes from behind me; I swing around to see a redwaek at the iron gate, clinging to the bars screaming. She wedges her feet on the brickwork at either side of the gate and starts trying to pull the gate from its hinges. The smell overwhelms me, and I fight the urge to be sick. I'm torn between running towards a possible attack around the corner, and staying here to let the attack come to me from both sides, and possibly being rendered unconscious by the obnoxious smell.

Thankfully, the young man in the red cloak, and not a redwaek, limps clumsily around the corner. His hood has fallen from his head, his cheek is badly grazed, and he's holding his arm against his body, but his vibrant green eyes are shining with adrenalin and victory.

He stumbles towards me, reaches into the top of his tunic, and pulls out a key on a chain.

"Quick." He gasps, holding the key out for me.

I grab the key, as he falls against the wall. I unlock the door to our sanctuary, and we slip into the dark room. Finally, it's me locking the door to keep myself safe from the attackers.

I look around the room and see an elovetta. "Help me shift this in front of the door." I say, throwing my weight behind the large base of the instrument.

He helps me move the elovetta in front of the door before slowly sliding down against it. His head falls loosely to one side.

"Are you okay?" I whisper.

He raises his right hand slightly. "Just coming to terms with the fact that I'm not dead... And that smell."

"Thank you for risking your life to save mine."

"Well, at least, if I'd died, it would've been for a pretty lady." He lifts his head and smiles at me. "Whoever knew I was so gallant!"

He stares at me for a few moments. "You know, you kinda look like Our Supreme Kaetian, Tushenta."

I turn my head away from him, so he won't realise how right he is. Whilst looking in the other direction, I examine the security of the grilles across the windows which look out onto a dark corridor. It seems to be locked at both ends, and the grilles appear to be strong enough to protect us.

There's little light in this small, circular room, which is crammed full of musical instruments and piled high with props and regalia for court performances. In the dimness, I hope that any resemblance between myself and Tushenta can be put down to a trick of the light.

The young man groans and leans forward. The bite on his upper arm looks deep. I still have the piece of material I ripped from my gown in my hands, so I kneel by him, take his arm, and attempt to tie a bandage to stop the bleeding. As this is the first man under seventy I've met in many decades, let alone touched, I'm shaking quite a bit. However, one thing I do have a lot of experience of, is reading, and my favourite topic is anything to do with the Pader warriors, including battlefield first aid, so I know all about the theory behind bandaging wounds.

Finally getting the opportunity to put my knowledge into practice fills me with a sense of euphoria. Carried away with my successful attempt at bandaging the bite wound, I examine the arm he's holding close to his body.

I prod his forearm and try to feel the bones. He winces when I prod a certain point; so, convinced his arm is broken, I decide it needs a sling.

I rip a bit more material from my gown, and construct a sling, just as described in Mairma's Medical Guide.

"Any chance you could bandage this hand?" He says, holding up his other hand.

I reach out and take his hand delicately in mine. I examine it for abrasions and damage to the bones. It only seems to have a mild scrape on the knuckle. However, this man has just saved my life, so if he wants his hand bandaging, I will bandage it.

I rip a bit more material off my gown which causes me to briefly reveal my leg. His eyebrows raise.

I take his hand in my hands and carefully wrap the bandage round and round, tucking the end in to fix the material in place.

"And my foot?"

I look at his sturdy boots. "What's wrong with your foot?"

"Nothing, but could you rip a bit more off your dress for me?"

"Oh my! You rascal!"

He laughs, a gaspy, exhausted laugh, and I settle down on the floor in front of the plinth bearing the triangular Kaetian motif, carefully hiding my legs under the shortened hem.

"We should be safe in here." He says. "You're lucky you were in the Compound when they attacked: much safer than down in the town. I can't believe the redwaek are attacking during the day. All those false alarms we keep getting were starting to get on my nerves. I need my light, and trying to do everything by candlelight in the middle of the day is just torture, especially when the attacks never come. Well, until today."

He looks at me intensely, so I turn my head away to focus on the silence drifting through the corridors.

The occasional shriek of a redwaek can be heard, and at one point, I hear the scuttling of a Pader patrol passing nearby.

It feels so safe and quiet in this dark little room, that I can't believe redwaek *are roaming freely about the Compound.*

The young man breaks the silence.

"So, who were you visiting?"

"Huh? Oh, it was a private meeting."

"I understand: discretion."

He smiles uncomfortably, looks around the room and starts tapping his fingers on the floor.

I don't want to get dragged into a conversation whilst pretending to be a Merdiant. I've never met or seen a Merdiant, and they're not a topic that comes up much in my designated reading. All I really know about them is they're the only people in Kaetia who can get permission to trade certain goods and services for the benefit of our wider society. That they've had this permission bestowed upon them is marked by the prominent display of their service medallion worn around their necks.

Thankfully, the man I'm sharing this small room with seems to be less familiar with Merdiants than I am, as I don't know where he thinks I'm keeping my medallion. I get up and look out of the grilles again, hoping that will stop any conversation.

He tries again.

"Whereabouts in the town do you live?"

I try to recall a map of the town. It's been a long time since I looked at one, and each time I do see a map, they've moved the streets around.

"In the centre." I say in a voice that I hope is both casual and believable, whilst flat and discouraging of any further questions.

"I've been there a few times. Nice market."

I cast a glance over my shoulder. He's still slumped on the floor but looking at me intensely and thoughtfully.

"Do you belong to a group, or a company?"

"What? Oh... Yes."

"Do clients approach you directly, or do interested parties contact an overseer or something?"

"Excuse me?"

"Well, I was just thinking that, you know, having just nearly died tonight, I may be interested in exploring a bit of 'Merdiant culture'." He winks at me.

"What aspect of Merdiant culture? I can't imagine trading practices are that interesting?"

He sighs. "Let's forget it." Finally, he lapses into silence.

I perch on a stool and look around the room. The concert regalia is comfortingly familiar to me. The dark blue banners of the Supreme Kaetians, the red banners of the Higher Kaetians, and the green banners of the Lower Kaetians. Instruments, props, Kaetian motifs, and… a full-sized portrait of Asana and myself in the corner.

"I'm Mull'aman, by the way; I'm the Guardian of the Nineteenth Tenet, which means I'm the head of music and celebrations."

"I thought Heshrik was the Guardian of the Nineteenth Tenet?"

"He retired… You know my father? Please don't tell me he, erm, is a…"

Worried I may be betraying my identity, I quickly cut him off. "I have heard of him. I heard he's a wonderful and gentle man. But no one ever mentioned his son."

"I'm sure your colleagues were just hiding the news of me, so they could keep me to themselves." *He laughs and struggles to his feet. He pulls at a panel on the elovetta.*

"Careful! You'll damage it!"

"And what do you care about a Kaetian instrument? Do they sneak you in for performances?"

"Out of all the instruments in this room, that instrument is the most exhilarating to play!"

He removes the panel, fishes around inside the instrument, and retrieves a bottle.

"And how would a Merdiant know that?" *He looks at me much more closely now, pulling the bottle's cork out with his teeth.*

"Is that what I think it is?"

"Are you who I think you are?"

I turn away from him.

"Tushenta?"

"You are mistaken. And I will not be in the same room as someone drinking the red weed."

"The red weed? Well, you've just proved you're not a Merdiant…" *He's silent for a few moments.* "Oh Fuck! You really are Our Supreme Kaetian, Tushenta, aren't you? I'm so sorry I thought you were a prostitute. Please ignore everything I've said to you."

"What's a prostitute?"

He takes a step back, his eyes darting around the room, looking in every direction but my face. "Erm… a person who… has the right credentials… to trade physical… sexual… favours for money."

"You thought I was here to perform sex acts for money?" *I stand up slowly and turn to face him, digesting the fact that such a trade exists, trying to decide what I think about it, and whether it's an insult or compliment.*

"How else can you explain the fact that you're running around the Compound half dressed?"

I pull at the top of my gown to try and cover up more of my chest.

"The redwaek came through my window; I couldn't exactly ask them to *postpone their attack whilst I dressed appropriately for my station, could I?"*

"How did they get through the window? Did they rip the shutters off?"

"I... Uh... I left the shutters open. You said it yourself! How many times do we get a warning of a daylight attack, and nothing happens? They only ever attack at night. I'd finally been given a copy of 'An Account of the Crimes of Kasaman', and the Council have rationed my candles, so I've been trying to save them up. I was sure the window would be too small for a redwaek to fit through, but I didn't know they were willing to die to get in."

A wave of devastation hits me, and I collapse. It's my fault that Pader with the pale green eyes is dead, and I'm sure others will die in this attack. The tears come too quickly for me to find my breath, and the tsunami of everything I've held inside throughout my life is let loose on Mull'aman.

"Everything I do is wrong. I am a shame to Kaetian society."

I hit the floor with my fist and then hold my hand up to stop Mull'aman from talking.

"I try so hard to be what I'm told to be, but I just keep getting everything wrong. I can never live up to what Asana expects of me. I know she can see the darkness in me, she can see what I really am."

"Tushenta, no..."

I hold my hand up again. I have the authority to shut him up and have no intention of being interrupted.

"I'm the centre of the debate of the age: will this corrupted vessel of Kaetian blood be the ruin of our society? Will Asana and Kasaman's child save or damn us all? Will I be good or evil?"

Mull'aman didn't dare to respond.

"And so, every little thing I do is scrutinised, looking for evidence that I've inherited the evil of Kasaman; that I'm rotten. It makes me so insecure, that I get all nervous and do stupid things. Or maybe I tell myself I keep messing up because I'm trying to hide the fact that I'm evil inside. Maybe I am just like Kasaman. A Pader is dead because of me. You nearly died!"

I turn my tear-filled eyes towards the man who saved my life, the man I nearly killed. "I wish you hadn't risked your life to save me. I can't die, you know? Not now the Blade of Sett has been destroyed. Oh, how I wish I could! Maybe then Asana could have another child, one with pure Kaetian blood, one who wouldn't be such a let-down or a risk."

I choke on my tears and saliva, and stare at the stone floor. "You could have died. That Pader did die... Because of me."

The bottle of fermented red weed is thrust in front of my face and Mull'aman joins me on the floor at a respectful distance. "Here, have a swig of red. You already *let the redwaek in, you might as well fuck up again!"*

Tentatively, I take the bottle from his hands. I've read about the dangers of fermented red weed. Water is in such short supply everyone lives with constant thirst. 'Red' is supposed to, not only quench that thirst, but quench the thirst for all the other needs of body and mind, at a cost to the soul. It's also said to quicken the redwaek's descent into deformation and derangement.

Fuck it.

I take my first taste of the red weed. It feels warm and smooth and does indeed take away all my thirst. For the first time in my life, I don't feel like the back of my throat is dry and cracked. I lean back against the plinth. And take another sip.

And another sip.

I let my head fall back against the Kaetian motif of the Blazing Court: The Courtyard of the Arcane at sunset with twenty-two stars in the sky.

After a while, Mull'aman politely coughs.

I look over at him.

"Our Supreme Kaetian, Tushenta," From the floor, he offers a devotional bow, "the view from the Higher Kaetians is that you are, well, unbelievably talented and beautiful, if I may say so."

"Yeah right. I'm no good at anything." I take another sip of the red weed. I could get a taste for this stuff. Asana would just love that! "Look, Mull'aman, I'm not your god. I'm just a messed-up girl in a ripped gown. Look elsewhere for your salvation. Have you not heard? Kasaman's my daddy."

"Tushenta, don't say things like that. I know you are exceptionally talented and an amazing deity."

I laugh at my delusional subject. "I'm glad to see you've swallowed their publicity so well! What you know is an image, not the real me, not even close. You love some carefully constructed story about the ultimate Kaetian who would easily triumph at the Blazing Court, save Kaetian society, and still have time to write a sonnet before bedtime. The genuine article is this idiot who doesn't have a clue what she's doing, never chose to be a Supreme Kaetian, and keeps making stupid mistakes, like leaving a shutter open during a lock down!"

That shut Mull'aman up.

I continue: "You know the reason behind the breach of the lockdown will be covered up? They have to do everything they can to protect the freaks at the top of the hereditary chain of power."

Mull'aman reaches out and takes the bottle of red from my hand.

Taking a drink to compose himself, he turns to face me with a deferential expression: "Well as a ranking Higher Kaetian, whose father taught you music, and who has personally seen you perform in the Courtyard of the Arcane, I can tell you that how you see yourself is not how we see you."

"I've just told you that's because you've been sold an image which has nothing to do with who I am. You're reciting these platitudes because I'm a Supreme Kaetian, not because you mean them."

"So, it wasn't you playing the elovetta at the last Celebration of Kaetian Society? Your paintings aren't displayed in the Gallery of Sett?"

"Well, yes; but how does my ability to play music or paint pictures have anything to do with my abilities to be a good leader?"

"Because you're an amazing artist; you really understand people and what speaks to their hearts. Your last composition moved me to tears; I've spent hours walking around the Gallery of Sett absorbed in the colours and textures of your artwork. How can you be such an amazing artist and yet say you're worth nothing?"

"Because I wasn't born to be an artist! I have to be so much better than that!"

"What's better than being an artist?"

"I was born into the role of Supreme Kaetian, and that involves judgment, decisions, and ruling, which will affect everyone's lives or their deaths. I wasn't born to create pretty things that will never have any impact or save anyone's life. Did you forget we live in a world with diminishing resources and almost no water, with thousands of people arriving every day, most of whom get turned away to die painfully in the Lethian Plains. And when the time comes, it'll be me who must decide who we save and who we condemn to death. Me! The whimsical artist! You can say being an artist is worthwhile because you're not part of the system."

"I'm a Higher Kaetian! How can you say that I'm not part of the system? The top tier has two people in it: you and Asana, and you're yet to assume your role. I'm in the tier below you, which has only twenty-one families in it. I may be new to my role, and some may say my family's tenet is a bit flowery, but don't tell me I'm not tied up in the system! I have politics, obligation, and codes of morality penning me in from every side. You can think what you like, but when I tell you that listening to your compositions on the elovetta move me, I mean it. Listening to you is the only time I feel free."

Humbled by his attack, I take the bottle of red from him. "The only time I'm free is when I'm playing the elovetta."

"That's because you're an artist: a worthwhile artist. Why do you have to adhere to their way of doing things? If anyone can change the system, it's you. Why can't you make decisions inspired by music, art, and love?"

"Because, if they ever let me in the vicinity of a mortal, and the Council disapprove of my judgement, or if I can't do that phronesis thing where I'm meant to strengthen the spiritual essence and end up sucking it out of them like Kasaman does, they'll decide I'm evil like my father and imprison me. I can't rewrite the rules; I have to do it their way."

He shuffles over to sit next to me.

I feel my palms grow hot and sweaty.

"Tushenta, don't let them crush you with their power games and dry politics. They make up the rules to keep themselves in power. You literally have the power in your hands; only you can succeed Asana. You don't need to bow to their rules, what you need is more people on your side, people who understand you, people who aren't manipulating things to maintain their privileged positions."

He pauses, his eyes resting on the painting of Asana and myself in the corner of the room. "Is there any way you can get to the music rooms? We could use the excuse that you want to learn more about advanced composition, and I could arrange your tuition. We could use that time to discuss strategy and how to set you free from their world."

He takes my chin in his hand and forces me to look into his beautiful green eyes. "I will show you how to shine."

I lean in towards him. My fingers reach up to touch the bandage that I'd carefully wrapped around his injured hand.

And the harsh sound of the Pader horn splits the air.

I jump to my feet and listen to the Paders' call as they sweep the Compound.

My fingers poke through the gaps in the iron grille, as I strain to hear the announcement. "The Compound is in secure lockdown. Will Our Supreme Kaetian, Tushenta, or those who know of her location please report to the nearest patrol."

I turn to look at Mull'aman. He's slumped on the floor and suffering from his injuries, but pleads with his beseeching, dopey, emerald-green eyes.

"I need to go." I tell him.

I start to push the elovetta from in front of the door.

Mull'aman looks up at me. "You need to stay here. I will free you."

"I cannot be freed."

He drags himself to his feet. "Find me. Come to the music rooms; I'll be waiting for you. Whatever you do, don't let them win. You are music, art, and love; hold on to your sense of self. I believe in you."

Feeling bold with the red in my veins, I pull Mull'aman towards me and kiss his red weed-stained lips. Electricity surges through my body and my palms start to itch. I take one last look into his eyes, before I unlock the door and run out into the twisting corridors.

Later, I sit in the recess of the large window in my small room. I knock the new shutter back and forth with my foot and feel Mull'aman's velvet voice surround me. He tells me how 'they' make up the rules, so they can stay in power; how 'they' engage in power games and dry politics; and how we hold witness to a magic 'they' could never understand.

His words speak of music, art, and love.

"Tushenta!" He whispers. "Believe in yourself. Believe in us. They don't understand, but together we can get through anything. You have a gift, and even if they can't see your worth, I do. Come and find me. I will show you how to shine."

And I realise I can do it.

I am music. I am art. I am love.

I am Tushenta and I can be a force for good.

He says: "You have to find me."

I promise him that I would.

With my left foot I flick the shutter towards myself, catching it in my hand. Using the knife I kept back from dinner, I carve M onto the edge of the wood. Flipping myself around in the recess, I carve T onto the edge of the other shutter. Smiling at my handy work, I jump down and secure the windows for the night. From now on, T and M will rest side by side at night.

Forever.

12: HANDS OF HELIOS

I finished setting up my keyboard and launched into a gothic rendition of the Arrival of the Queen of Sheba. "Rent-a-freak has landed, care of Becca's express taxi service."

Becca was poking around the small stage, examining the broken drum kit and the threadbare red curtain, unimpressed with everything in the room: especially me. "Kerella, try not to be a freak, okay?"

"It was a joke."

"Maybe you should avoid those too." She stomped down the steps at the side of the stage and arrived in front of the keyboard.

I scowled at her and let my notes descend into an angry puddle of disjointed chords. "Am I allowed to do anything?"

"Just play the keyboard, emphasise that I was at yours last night drinking detox piss-water, and try not to talk about things that aren't real."

She turned the volume of my keyboard down to erode my protesting notes, leaving the sound of fingers banging on plastic and the creaking of the keyboard stand.

She hit the off button.

"In fact, try to say as little as possible." She fixed me with her kohl-lined powder-blue stare. Then she placed her foot on top of my foot. "And none of that jiggling; it makes you look like you've got a condition. I've told you this a thousand times."

I sighed and looked around the room.

The walls were a pale olive green; they were cracked and the paint was peeling. Someone had tried to disguise the barracks-like quality of the room by sticking up three large display boards with yellow, orange, and red borders. These contained the artwork entered into the 'Summer Scenes' competition.

I cast my eye over the thick lines of poster paint and wax crayon; free of inhibitions and judgement; simple, bold, and beautiful. 'Katie: Aged 6' had even put fairies dancing on the sand. I bet no one told her off for that.

"I'll be back in about an hour."

"What? You said you'd stay for the audition!"

"I lied. I need to get out. I'm fed up with being cooped up, and I'm not your fucking babysitter."

Becca pushed through the swinging double doors, leaving them banging behind her. I was alone to face the ordeal I'd been dreading for the last four days. Even though she was being a total moody bitch, having her sulk in the corner of the room was better than leaving me on my own. Now I really would fuck up.

In fact, why was I standing in this empty room waiting to humiliate myself? I could just leave now, by-pass the torture, and move straight on to the failure.

But I knew I wouldn't run out of the door. I knew, because Mull'aman kept whispering in my ear: "Come and find me; I will show you how to shine." And because Becca said this would help her.

Mull'aman's lips brushed against my neck and the sun spilled into the room casting an arch of Kaetian gold onto the polished wooden floor. I was in his warm embrace and that gave me the strength to get through this.

The double doors crashed open, and a short explosion of America reversed into the room, engaged in animated discussion with her peroxide-haired companion. She spun round to face me. Her pink and black hair was coiled in tight spirals, and she had a relaxed, friendly smile. In one of her hands was a pile of papers, and in the other, a mug of coffee.

"Oh, hi! I'm Mannie, and you must be Kerella." She thrust the papers under her arm and dived forward, catching my hand in a sudden handshake, leaving it hanging in mid-air to be intercepted by the young man floating in behind her for the aftershock.

"And I'm Fus." He shifted the white cardboard box he was carrying to his other arm and gave me a holiday camp smile. "What an amazing dress, so original! Did you make it yourself?"

I tugged at a section of the black lace I'd sewn onto a blue velvet dress. "I just adapted an old dress I had."

"Impressive!" Mannie cooed. Did you make this as well? She reached up and pawed at my thick black velvet choker with its blue topaz centrepiece.

I took a step back.

"Yes. I wanted something to help strengthen my Vishuddha chakra."

"You know about chakras? You so have to teach me! They've always seemed too complicated for me to get my head around!"

"Well, the base chakra, the Muladhara chakra, is located here." I pointed to my crotch. "It's red and..." I remembered Becca telling me that when people ask questions like this, they're just being polite and don't really want to know. "I... I... You know, I doubt I'm the best person to ask, all I've done is read some books." I stared at my feet.

"You know, Kerella, you strike me as someone who doesn't give yourself enough credit." Fus patted me on the back, before heading towards the stage, balancing the white cardboard box on one hand and doing a silly walk which made Mannie laugh. He deposited the box on the stage and headed to the far end of the room, twirling a large collection of keys on his finger. He unlocked the storage room doors and threw them wide open.

As Fus dragged a drum kit into the centre of the room, Mannie sat down on the stage, put the papers down by her side and took a sip of coffee. She quietly observed me for a few moments, her large dark brown eyes taking in the image of this bizarre interloper that had crashed into her presence.

Nervous at the attention, I blurted out: "Your music is very powerful. It feels genuine, like you had to write the songs, or you would die."

Becca was right. I shouldn't say anything at all.

"I'm glad to hear it!" Mannie said, breaking into an easy smile. "So, which of our write-or-die songs do you like the best?"

"I can't decide between Hands of Helios and Into the Dark."

"Ah! Chris's songs. What did you think of Porcupine Fairy? Chris and I wrote that together."

"I found it uplifting."

"Uplifting? Well, that's certainly a unique first impression!" She looked over to Fus for his reaction.

He put his hand briefly to his lips, narrowing his eyes thoughtfully. "I can see Kerella's point there." He said, his finger pointing into the air. "I guess because we all know it's about Abbie's suicide, we'll always see it as a song about a sad loss. Now, Kerella coming in from the outside is probably tapping into the immortality of the memory she left behind, which is uplifting. Good observation there, Kerella."

My mind flitted back over the song. In my defence, Mannie's vocals were not always that clear, but as I listened to it with this new knowledge, the suicide angle seemed obvious. I had thought it was about escaping a horrible situation and flying to freedom.

Mannie interrupted my internal rendition of the song. "How are you finding the keyboard solo in Into the Dark? If you think it's too much to learn in the time we've got, Tyler used to do a guitar version, I'm sure we could go back to that."

"No need for that. I may have worked out something a bit more interesting."

Mannie jumped down off the stage and clapped her hands. "Oh! I can't wait to hear that!"

"Your lip looks better." A male voice came from my right.

And the possibility of a successful outcome to the audition was no longer an issue.

"Oh... My... God..." I managed.

"Not quite." Fus interjected. "This is Chris. But do feel free to worship; he is quite impressive."

"How did you come in?" I looked around, trying to work out how he'd come up behind Mannie without me seeing him.

"The door." He motioned towards the double doors.

My early morning phantom, right in front of me! Here, with the band I was trying to impress.

Oh god! I'd knocked him over!

I took a step back and looked towards the door.

He put down his cello case.

I stared at the man in the fedora hat standing in front of me. Definitely a real person and not a figment entangled with my imagination.

Fuck it. I fled from the humiliation that was the audition, leaving the doors slamming behind me as I scuttled down the corridor.

Around the corner, I saw a ladies' sign and sought refuge in a locked cubicle. Resting my head against the cracked creamy-white partition, I assessed my options. Stay in here for a couple of hours, then try to retrieve my keyboard when they'd all gone away; or leave now and send Becca to get my keyboard and face her wrath.

I stared at the floor. A faint brown stain splattered across the grey tiles. Blood had been spilled here. Maybe the band wasn't really all it pretended to be.

After half an hour of thinking about all the horrific scenarios I'd saved myself from by running away, I heard the band starting up and decided the risk of running into Mannie, Fus, Chris, or the other one, would be minimal while they were rehearsing. Escaping now and facing Becca later was the best option.

Outside of my blood-stained sanctuary, the walls of the corridor oozed normality and community spirit: this freak did not belong here. Feeling the urge to reject me from its interior, the corridor rippled and contracted. Tears welled up in my eyes and humiliation burned in my cheeks. The corridor gave one last push and propelled me forcefully towards the outside world.

Breaking into a desperate run, I slammed into a wall of flesh. Suddenly stationary, with scalding liquids sinking into my thighs, I tried to understand what had happened. I was trapped in a pair of tanned arms, and a broken mug rocked slowly by the wall, a small reservoir of tea still caught in its fragmented shell.

He smelled of aftershave and washing powder. My wet dress clung tightly to the skin of my right leg, which throbbed in time to my heartbeat. He held my arms firmly, preventing further escape attempts and my pale arms looked fragile underneath his fingers.

We stood in the corridor, with broken mugs at our feet. He didn't speak, and I wouldn't look at him. I could feel his breath on the side of my face, and Mull'aman whispered in my ear that he'd found me.

After a few moments, I looked up into the face of my human cage. An uncertain smile and unnatural pondweed-coloured eyes stared down at me.

"Kerella?"

The name 'Mull'aman' nearly exploded from my ever hopeful and delusional chest.

He emitted an air of schoolboy insecurity, laughing nervously as he pushed my tangled hair out of my face. Then an intense look crossed his face, causing a crease to form in the centre of his forehead. "I was hoping I'd bump into you. Mannie sent me out to scout around. Chris explained how he scared you whilst walking Tris before work the other day. Not really surprising. I don't call him the Lord of Darkness for nothing."

My focus skittered off to a patch of mould on the wall. "It was really dark. H-he could have been anyone, a-a-and then that big dog came running up to me."

"Tris scared you?"

"Well, it was dark, and he's a big dog."

The pondweed-eyed boy laughed pleasantly, patting my upper arm reassuringly as he did. "You're the first person I've ever met to be scared by Tris; you'll be good for his ego!"

He let go of me and took a step back.

"I'm Tyler." He smiled. "I've been looking forward to hearing you play ever since Becca told us about you and your supernatural musical abilities. I'm just sorry about the trauma with Chris. It isn't the first time he's scared people off. Trust me though, there's nothing to fear. Okay, when you look at him, just remember that he likes ice cream, plants, dusting, and, even though he'll never admit it, he plays the flute! How can you be scared of someone who plays the flute?"

I laughed at the image of Kasaman the flautist.

"Is your leg okay? Do you need to run any cold water on it?"

"No, it's fine."

"Are you okay to come back in?"

How could I say no? He was my Mull'aman. I didn't care if it was real, he was my Mull'aman, and he'd come to find me.

I closed my eyes as I mustered the strength to respond. "Yes."

He gave me a light thump on my shoulder; then, looking at the broken mugs, added: "Come on, we'd best clear this mess up before Mannie makes me fill in a health and safety report!"

Lumps of damp blue paper towels and shards of broken mugs were deposited in the kitchen bin, and I was dragged back into the lion's den. The doors banged behind us to draw attention to my return and I wished I were elsewhere, preferably with a bottle of white wine and loud music.

I did not want to be here.

I did not want to be here.

"Forget the caffeine, I come back with girl. Much better! And it's okay, I've explained that Chris is a serial killer, but won't lay a finger on her as long as she doesn't run away again."

He locked one arm tightly around my waist and pulled me close to his side.

"Now Tyler, behave yourself." Fus ordered, banging on his drums. "Kerella, I'm sorry for this misunderstanding; you have no cause for concern."

Chris tapped the end of his bow on the floor a couple of times, before turning his dark eyes towards me. "I start work at seven, and Tris likes to have a bit of a run in the morning, so we often walk along that path first thing. Sorry if you thought I may have been there for other reasons."

I looked at the floor. "I... I... I'm sorry. I'd had a bad experience and was not in a trusting mood."

"Well, I'm glad that's all behind us now." Fus said.

I darted to the safety of my keyboard and firmly hit the on button.

"So, let's get things started, shall we?" Fus banged on his drums a few times and waited for Tyler to put his phone in his pocket before he continued. "Kerella, welcome. We are The Casa Martyrs, and we're looking to recruit a keyboardist who's prepared to put in a shit load of unpaid work over the next month, because we have an impending gig with our arch-rivals, Angel Waste."

I coughed. 'Thanks for not mentioning that, Becca.' I thought.

"No one can accuse us of being 'recreational rockers' in the local press and get away with it. A man's reputation is his castle: attack that, and it's war."

Fus laughed, "Ty, you take everything too personally. I keep telling you it was a publicity tactic to get us on the same stage as them, because they need us there to get enough people to turn out to one of their gigs." He turned to face me, a bastion of seriousness. "Which doesn't mean we don't want to wipe their smug smiles off their little arses. There's also the issue of the prize money, which we hope to secure to save this beautiful centre of excellence."

Tyler chuckled at Fus's description of the community centre.

Fus ignored him and carried on. "But, for today, we want to see if our musical styles mesh and give you the opportunity to get to know us. Kerella, do you have any questions so far?"

"Nope." I shook my head nervously, wondering if I should ask if sleeping with the opposition's drummer, then breaking his index finger and giving him a black eye, was going to be an issue.

"Okay. Well, as you said you liked Hands of Helios, how about we give that a bash?"

"Sounds good to me." I said.

"Okay, are we ready?" Mannie jumped up, got a nod from everyone, and started to make the mournful "Nya nya n-yas." of the introduction.

I flowed naturally into the music. This was what I could do; it felt instinctive and intoxicating. At that moment, I was grateful Becca had talked me into joining the band, that Mull'aman had given me the courage to be here, and that he was standing in the same room as me, with his magical eyes, and that reassuring smile.

Mannie's voice flowed over the lyrics:

Persephone
> has been taken from me.
> down the River of Acheron
> and now she's gone.

Barren is my land
> and empty is my hand.
> A winter that never ends
> has come.

The mistakes I make are mine to bear.
The lies they tell are my shroud.
I plant seeds, carry death underground,
hoping Helios will tell me where.

He-eee-lios.
My loss.
Like Demeter,
I'm on my knees.
He-eee-lios.
My loss.
Please.

With my life, I would pay.
Raise your hand and show the way.

During the interlude, whilst Chris let the cello sing out, Mannie bounced over to the keyboard. She raised her thumbs and mouthed the words "Fantastic." at me.

The sun rises on an empty space.
I close my eyes and see your face.
You will be here one day.

I will find a way.
Helios will show me a way,
A way.

Persephone
    has chosen the earth.
    So I plant seeds to bring on spring:
    to prove my worth.

Fertile is my land,
    but empty is my hand.
    A daughter that can't be found,
    yet on I search.

The mistakes you make are mine to heal.
The lies you hear will fall apart.
Saplings of love for the God of sun,
hoping he'll tell me where you've gone.

He-eee-lios.
My loss.
Like Demeter,
I'm on my knees.
He-eee-lios.
My loss.
Please.

With my life, I would pay.
Raise your hand and show the way.

As the song concluded, cheers erupted from Tyler, Mannie, and Fus.

"Well, thank god you came back." Chris said as he unwound his bow.

Fus picked up a clip board and a marker pen and wrote something. He then held up a piece of paper with 10/10 on it.

"I've a good feeling about this, Kerella, I really do." Fus said. "What I really loved was the way you took the section about the river and played something which sounded like running water. What do you think, Mannie?

"I think that was our best performance ever. I'm shaking! Look, I even have goosebumps. The only change I would make," she said, coming over to my keyboard, "is this." She turned up the volume.

"Tyler, how did you find that?" Fus asked.

"You've had our music, what, five days? Becca said you'd never heard us play. Are you sure you're not a secret fan, hanging around waiting for an in?

I can't believe you could just pull that out of the hat!"

"Tyler," purred Mannie, "that's because Kerella here is a musical genius. You're just a boy who likes to... strum it." She said, making a masturbation gesture.

"You'll regret saying that when I write us a song that takes us viral. But I will say this: Chris, you talking Simon into following his girlfriend to Australia was the best thing for the band. I finally forgive you!"

Fus hit his drums for attention, then paused for dramatic effect before he spoke. "Well, I think it's safe to say The Casas enjoyed Kerella's performance, but we need to ask Kerella, did you enjoy playing with us?"

"Yes, thank you, I did."

"And what did you like most about it?" Fus asked.

"I really liked the bit in the bridge with the key changes, it makes me feel sad that Persephone is lost, yet hopeful that Mannie'll be reunited with her daughter, as she's clearly a devoted parent."

"Well, thank you, Kerella. I think that's the nicest thing anyone's ever said about my song."

I smiled at Chris, feeling stupid that I ever thought he could be the Devil.

"I wanna hear Porcupine Fairy! I wanna hear what you did to that!" Mannie let out an ear-piercing squeal, which wound down into a segue into the introduction to Porcupine Fairy.

I hit G several times to ground myself, before exploding into the new and, even if I do say so myself, much improved introduction.

I am Tushenta. I am music. I am art. I am love. I am the notes I have under my command and music is my magic. I nearly cried with the beauty of the tune and finished with an even more ornate flourish than I'd originally prepared.

Addressing the group, Tyler declared: "And she gets better and better!"

Mannie clapped her hands in the air, and then set about arranging a circle of chairs in the middle of the room. Fus went over to the stage and opened the white cardboard box, Chris leant against the 'Summer Scenes' display, and Tyler vigorously checked his phone.

"Kerella, I made this to celebrate you joining our ranks. I just knew it would work out; sometimes I know these things."

Mannie slapped his arm. "Be honest."

"Okay, Kerella, I bought this to celebrate you joining the band."

Mannie pulled the sides of the box down and started cutting the cake into slices. Tyler quickly swooped in and grabbed the largest slice whilst Mannie was laying out five napkins.

"Tyler!" She chastised him. "That was rude! You should let the guest choose the first slice. This is just so typical."

"So typical of what? She's not a guest; she's one of us now." He spoke through a mouthful of chocolate icing. "Mmmm, good cake. Although next time, can we have ginger? I'm not that big a fan of chocolate."

Mannie threw a chocolate button at him. "You are despicable! You always grab the biggest slice or go for the shiniest thing. You are a magpie."

"And what's wrong with that? Why deprive yourself? If you can have the best, take the best: anything else would be patronising the little man. No offense, Mannie." He said patting her on the head and walking off towards the steps up to the stage.

"Now, come on you two, it's group time." Fus motioned for us to take a seat in the circle.

Chris and Mannie joined us, but Tyler walked up the steps and sat down next to the cake. He picked at the topping as he scrolled through something on his phone.

"Okay, we were going to run through all five songs before making a decision, but I think I speak for everyone here when I say, we really hope that you're interested in joining The Casa Martyrs."

Too nervous to speak, I nodded my head.

"And Becca explained to you that this is an unpaid gig?" Mannie asked. "That we're trying to raise money to top up our fundraiser for repairs to the building, and if we don't succeed, the Council are going to sell the building to a developer who wants to convert it into luxury holiday apartments, and relocate us to smaller premises which will lead to a cut in staff and funds?"

I nodded.

"Woohoo!" Mannie exclaimed and handed me a slice of cake in a napkin.

"Tyler, come and sit with us." Fus yelled over his shoulder.

"In a minute! I've just got to comment on what Ian's just posted."

Fus sighed and returned his attention to me. "Okay, we've one month until we'll be performing with Angel Waste at The Water Hole, and we really, really want to prove we're so much better than them."

I picked at the edge of the orange plastic chair, wondering if I should mention that they weren't doing themselves any favours by including me in their band, considering what happened between me and Martin, but I couldn't find a voice to tell them.

"So, Mannie and I have been looking at the rota, and it looks like we'll be able to find a room for rehearsal every Monday, Wednesday and Friday between now and the gig. On a couple of occasions, we'll have to double up with Mikey's Sugar Swords. I'm sure you'll find that an interesting experience."

"Mikey's Sugar Swords are a band of young teenagers. Lovely kids, but they all have come through some troubled times." Mannie explained.

"So, we'll start on Monday, in this room, and start preparing to wipe the floor with Angel Waste. And save our precious community centre."

"No can do." Tyler plonked himself down on the empty chair. "I'm not available on Fridays."

"Something more important than this?"

"Yes! I have a standing arrangement with Ian."

"Well, that's a shame, we'll have to cope without you on Fridays." Fus smiled at Tyler, a glint in his eye. "So tomorrow we've organised a welcome party for you, Kerella. Shame you're going to have to miss that, Ty. Chris has given us the run of The Acres."

"The Acres?" I asked.

"Garden centre out of town. Perfect venue for a party, pretty sparkling lights, chiminea, goldfish, and no neighbours." Mannie explained. "If you want, I can give you a lift."

"That sounds great, and yes to the lift, please."

"I guess I'll have to rearrange tomorrow. I wouldn't want to miss Kerella's big welcome." Tyler said winking at me.

"If you can rearrange tomorrow, you can rearrange every Friday. Playing pool with Ian is no excuse. It's only one month, Tyler, have priorities." Fus commanded.

"So, that's all arranged." Mannie declared. "How about we get back to practicing?"

Tyler was looking at the floor with a cute pout. He dragged himself out of the chair with exaggerated effort. "We're doing Dream Filled Cage." His expression changing as he looked at me, "I want to see what our new resident genius has done to my song."

I licked the remnants of chocolate cake off my fingers and wiped them with the napkin. I couldn't stop smiling; I knew Mull'aman was going to adore what I'd done to his Dream Filled Cage.

13: THE ACRES

"It's the blood. There was so much of it." Tied to his seat and distressed, Fus swung to the window to escape, but he was trapped in this metal coffin. Swinging around in the other direction, he found Mannie's shoulder and nuzzled into her smooth dark brown skin as she clung to the steering wheel.

Mannie took over the narrative and Fus poked and headbutted her shoulder. "She cut her wrists in the toilets at the centre. Made a horrible mess. Bloody handprints and finger painting all over the wall and not much skin left on her arms. The blood pooled halfway to the door. Poor Daxa found her, and she was only six at the time. You'll see her hanging around at rehearsals."

"She's the one who clings onto my Mansie," Fus added, pushing his fingers one by one into Mannie's muscular shoulder, "but has barely said two words in the last year."

Mannie shook off as much emotion as she could. "So that's why the song is called Porcupine Fairy. One year, Abbie was dancing around in pink fairy wings, a pristine, innocent thirteen-year-old. Then some prick gets a hold of her, shows her how to stick needles in her arms, and voilà! From fairy to fatality." She slammed the steering wheel.

I sank into the back seat, as the horrors of what really happened replaced the horrors that I'd imagined, leaving me feeling ashamed of the mysteries I'd projected onto those blood-stained tiles.

Mannie swung the car sharply to the right and gravel crunched loudly under the tyres. The jolt sent both Fus and I banging into the car doors, and brought a welcome end to the affectionate sharing of grief in the front of the car.

The rusty silver car came to a halt in a large carpark in front of a barrel full of red and orange flowers. Behind the barrel was a wrought iron arch covered in russet ivy, and nestled in the flaming foliage, a slate sign announced the entrance to "The Acres".

"Down the River of Acheron and then I'm gone." I whispered under my breath, before I opened the car door and sank my metal healed biker boots into the choppy sea of ochre gravel. The muffled baseline of loud music being played nearby pulsed pleasantly in the air.

The carpark was empty except one large van near the arch and two electric cars plugged into recharge points in the far-right hand corner. Beyond them was an old redbrick farmhouse with three chimneys. A large black door dominated the front of the house, and on either side of the steps leading up to the door, large fountains of ornamental red grass erupted from black glazed terracotta pots.

Mannie grabbed a box of beer from the boot of the car and loaded it into Fus's arms, before picking up a hemp bag which had fallen over and scattered its contents during the drive. She quickly restored a bottle of organic guava juice, a box of bean burgers, her phone, and some dog treats, before slamming the boot shut.

She pivoted in the gravel, linked arms with me, and pulled me in the direction of the ivy-covered arch: "Let's be social, girlfriend!"

We followed Fus as he strode off into Kasaman's lair. I stumbled awkwardly to the left, as my narrow heel slipped on a chunk of gravel. Mannie laughed as she pulled me back upright and I prayed Mull'aman wasn't watching my unceremonious approach.

At the archway, we passed a begging dog made of stone. Water poured from its mouth into a red bowl which bore the inscription 'Dogs Welcome'. We walked into the warm rays of the evening sun, a neat red brick path replaced the ochre gravel, and I breathed in the welcoming scent of honeysuckle.

Welcome to Hell, Kerella.

Fus bore right past a row of trolleys, but a rattling noise made him stop in his tracks.

Slowly, he turned round, his nose in the air as if he were following a smell. Still perched on my arm, Mannie drew to a halt and copied Fus's actions.

A man in a yellow polo shirt and green apron pulled down the shutters to the Acres café. He locked them, and as he looked towards us, Fus yelled out: "Yoohoo! Nick! How's it hanging buddykins?"

Nick sheltered his eyes from the setting sun and upon seeing us, waved. He walked down the red brick path towards us, crossing the small stream with a humpbacked bridge decorated with metalwork apple trees, and down a path flanked by pink and purple flowers, his yellow staff uniform glowing in the evening's golden light.

I stole a quick glance around the neat paths and ornate flower displays of Kasaman's floral habitat. Could the Devil really live here? I watched a group of blue tits flying between bird feeders hanging from the trees. One bird landed on the head of a water dragon statue which rose from the ornamental pool next to the outdoor café area. Amongst the rushes and exotic water flowers, the tit cocked its head and started to sing.

I turned to face Nick, resigned to the fact that The Acres wasn't going to live up to my expectation of Kasaman's earthly haunt, and tonight was not going to be full of fantastical intrigue, soul mates crossing dimensions to prove their undying love, or any battles of life and death.

This party was going to be boring.

"Hey Fus." Nick said, shaking hands with him, holding his upper arm affectionately.

Mannie lunged at him and pulled him down. "And Mannie." He said, kissing her cheek as she hung on his neck.

"And..."

"Kerella." I replied.

He nodded at me.

"Working late?" Fus asked.

"Just finishing off." Nick said.

"Chris works you too hard!"

"It's been a busy day, and I'm taking a few weeks off, so want to leave everything in some kind of order."

Mannie looked concerned. "Oh, does this mean your mother is...?"

"Final days." Nick smiled weakly. He looked tired and distant; lines deeply scored the hollows of his eyes and the amber rays from the low-lying sun cast dramatic lines over his features, making him look arid and Kaetian. He tried a stronger smile. "I haven't seen Chris this evening, but you'll find Ty playing with the chiminea in the garden."

Suddenly, the unmistakable feeling of Kasaman's presence overwhelmed me. I looked around his lair. Drunken cherubs leered out of artfully arranged recesses, redwaek morphed into stone gargoyles, and orange petals burst into flames. Against the evening sun, Chris's lithe frame stalked down a path flanked with red flowers and three silhouetted gnarled trees.

"Namaste, mate." He greeted Nick with a hardy pat on the shoulder. "Guys." He addressed us with a precise nod. "Can you give us a minute?"

"No problemeo! We're chiminea bound. Let's see what trouble Ty's got himself into." Fus skipped down a path signposted for 'Garden Ornaments and Gift Shop'.

Laughing, Mannie mimicked him and danced down the path.

Striding self-consciously in my metal heels, I followed them. As I turned the corner, I cast a look behind me and saw Nick and Chris arguing. Chris forced an envelope into Nick's hands and strode off, leaving Nick looking annoyed.

I quickly pushed through the large glass door into the gift shop. The music was louder in here. Mannie and Fus were heading past the tills to a door marked 'Staff Only', but a sign for 'Local Artists' caught my eye, and I was pulled towards a rack filled with cello-wrapped prints and original paintings in rustic wooden frames hanging on the wall.

"Ker! This way!" Mannie called.

Turning my back on my fellow artists, I hastened towards Fus as he held open the door for me.

"Sorry, I got distracted by art."

"Oh! Take your time if you want to go back and look. We'll just be through here." Mannie said.

I tore myself away from my desire to explore my competition; having only in that instance discovered my ability to be jealous that, someone I'd just met, sold artwork by people I didn't know, in a shop I'd never been to before. Which was stupid because I hated creating art solely for financial reasons.

"I'm good for now; I'm here for you guys. I can look at pretty things another time." Realising what I'd just said, I quickly added: "Not that you aren't pretty!"

Mannie laughed as we passed through the door to the staff area and into a wall of sound.

Paradise City was pounding through speakers mounted on the walls of an indoor patio area. At least I wouldn't have to worry about making conversation; I didn't think I'd be able to hear what anyone said over that.

There was a triangular mosaic decorated with dark stones and smooth red glass in the centre of the patio. Positioned around this mosaic were two picnic tables and a pool table. To the right, was a raised bedding plant display, a back-lit ornamental fishpond, a set of lockers and a small kitchen unit. In front of us, a red door led into the main house, and to the left, patio doors opened onto Chris's back garden.

Through the patio doors, I could see Tyler lounging at the bottom of the garden on a camping chair by a large clay chiminea. Tris laid at his feet. Ty wore sunglasses, khaki knee-length shorts, and a black shirt opened by a few buttons to partially reveal his well-toned chest. He held up a pair of barbeque tongues to acknowledge us.

I turned in horror to look at Mannie and Fus in their ripped jeans and T-shirts.

I'd overdressed for the occasion!

In my effort to impress Mull'aman, I'd chosen a seductive long-length black and red silk dress with an embroidered dragon pattern on the front and a high slit up the righthand side. The result was, I looked like an overdressed goth in the staff area of a garden centre.

Fus dropped the beers onto a picnic table, dug out a bottle, and threw it to Mannie.

He hopped from foot to foot, "Sorry guys, gotta pee!" He pushed through the red door and disappeared into the house.

Mannie laughed and smiled at me. "Be back in a mo, hon." She said, heading off down the neatly trimmed lawn with the bottle of beer and pack of bean burgers.

Two sparrows flew off the bird table as she passed. Tris got slowly to his feet, stretched, and took a couple of lazy steps towards her for a fuss.

I crept around the pool table to get a better view out of the patio doors. Tyler accepted the beer from Mannie with one of his coy half smiles. He raised his sunglasses and gave her a cute wink, but Mannie started waving her arms and shouting at him. They got drawn into a heated discussion, which I couldn't hear over the music.

I edged closer, peering out through the patio doors. Mannie slapped Tyler in the face, and he waved a raw steak at her, causing her to pull back. She pointed her finger at him and issued a threat I couldn't hear.

The 'Staff Only' door slammed behind me. I spun round to see Chris stride into the room; I smiled, trying to look innocent, and dove towards the table with the beers on it. I dug my fingers through the thick cardboard packaging, and tried to extract a bottle, desperate to distract attention away from the fact that I'd just been caught spying.

Chris walked up to the stereo and turned the music down.

"Kerella, you strike me as more of a red wine girl?"

I looked at Chris, "Well, white, if there is any?"

"Sorry, I only have red."

"Then, red it is, thanks."

He walked around the bedding plant display to the staff kitchen at the back of the room, retrieved a bottle from a locker and two glasses from a cupboard. He filled the glasses and placed the bottle on the side. As he walked slowly back to the patio, he kept his dark eyes fixed on me.

He handed me a glass of wine and quietly said: "Here's to you joining the Casa Mar... tyrs."

I was so sure he swallowed the last bit. Had Becca been talking to him? His eyebrows, shaded by the rim of his hat, raised inquisitively and I panicked, but chose to pretend that nothing was up. I tipped my glass a little to acknowledge the toast and perched awkwardly on the bench furthest away from him.

He walked past me and sat on the other end of the bench, stretching his legs out in front of himself and taking off his hat to reveal a dark blue bandanna tied underneath it; his straight, shoulder length dark brown hair fell slightly inside the collar of his black shirt.

Fus trotted back in, "Oh hello Chris, how are you on this lovely, and if I dare say so, magical evening?"

"Glad to finally have a glass of red in my hand after a long week."

Fus laughed, dug himself a beer out, and settled down on the bench between us. He took a bottle opener out of his pocket and flicked the bottle top off. "So, Kerella, do you play pool?"

"Not really."

"Oh, well honey, you'd better learn!"

Mannie came back in, a thunderous look on her face. She motioned for Fus to come to the patio doors. She said something to him in a low voice which I couldn't make out, but he responded loud enough for me to hear. "Just let it go Mannie, you can't control everything."

She snorted and looked angry, then shrugged and yelled out in her usual happy tone: "Ker, honey, I'm gonna grill our burgers, 'cause Ty's gotten the chiminea covered in animal fat."

"Okay, that'll be great." I smiled at her, but felt bad she was giving Tyler such a hard time. I preferred my burgers grilled, so didn't see the problem.

Fus, quickly changed the topic. "Sounds like Nick's mother's getting bad."

"I doubt she's got two weeks left. So, I told him not to come in for four or five weeks. Or whatever he needs."

"How will you cope without him?"

"Ugh. Don't ask." Chris said, rubbing his fingers over his tanned face. "Nick's the saviour of this place; we'll be lost without him. I suppose we'll have to learn how to cope. Once his mother's gone, no doubt he'll realise he can do a lot better than working here. I guess I'll get Tyler to help out again. But you know Ty: quite good at creating work." Fus laughed and Chris took a sip of wine. "You have to admit it though, he's very good with the customers. Well, the pretty, female customers. Gets them to buy twice as much as they came in for, but always finds a reason to give them a discount."

I saw him coming before they did, and flicked my hair from my face.

"And greetings to the Noob, are you ready for your initiation?"

"Ty, don't tease her." Fus said.

"You're no fun, but have a steak anyway. Chris, yours is still cooking; it won't be long. Where's Nick?"

Chris shook his head. "He's not joining us, Ty, sorry. He's really not in the mood."

"Oh. He'll miss trying my seasoned steak a la Ty-la."

"I think he's got more important things on his mind at the moment."

"Quick!" Tyler said, holding his hands in the air. "Someone change the subject before we get the 'family is all that matters' lecture."

Chris looked sternly at him. "Tyler, Nick sacrificed a lot for Elsie. I believe that kind of devotion deserves to be acknowledged."

"So, you pay for her funeral." Tyler said, with a flourish of his hands.

"Elsie isn't dead. Comments like that are not welcome. And I didn't pay for her funeral, I just gave Nick a small bonus for all the work he's been doing, to help him out at this time. I remember all too well what it was like to lose a mother when you have no other family and aren't exactly rich."

There was an awkward silence punctuated by the sound of Tris barking at a grey and white cat walking along the wall at the bottom of the garden.

A klaxon sound split the air. Tyler whipped his phone out his pocket and looked at it. A crease formed down the centre of his forehead and his lips contracted into a straight line.

He jabbed the phone. "Yep." He snapped, walking off into the garden.

Chris shook his head and looked annoyed as he watched Tyler shoot short answers to the caller.

Tris came bounding in and barked at me before sticking his head between Chris's legs and getting fussed.

I took a sip of wine, and looked over at Fus, hoping he'd start a conversation, but he was busy sawing at his steak.

Tyler trudged back to the patio area, looking downcast.

"How're the steaks?" Chris asked.

Tyler looked confused for a moment. "Oh shit!" He said running back out, returning shortly with two blackened steaks on paper plates.

Mannie returned with our burgers, which had been put in buns, and served with a side salad on ceramic plates. Looking at the lads struggling with their steaks on paper plates she laughed. "It's times like these that make me grateful I don't eat meat." She winked at me as she handed me a plate.

Sitting down next to Tyler, she gave him a mock frown, and he put his head on her shoulder. "You know you love me, really."

"I love you when you're not causing trouble."

"Love me enough to let me beat you at pool?"

"Ha! That'll be the day! Have you ever beaten me at pool?"

"I'm feeling lucky today."

"Okay, you're on, but I'm not letting you win! Just let me finish eating."

Tyler raced through his steak and was the only person who didn't seem to have trouble with it. I watched Chris feeding most of his to Tris, who then went under the table to assist Fus in the same manner.

Tyler was too distracted to notice as he set up the pool table and chalked up his cue.

"Come on!" He urged Mannie, as he finished his beer and helped himself to another.

The match got underway with mock commentary from Fus.

I finished my burger and Chris topped up our glasses.

"Thanks..." I wracked my brain for something to say. "So, Hands of Helios... it's about running a garden centre?"

He let out a dry laugh and sighed. "Erm, I suppose so. It's a bit more complicated than that."

"Complicated how?"

He let out another sigh.

"I... I have a daughter I want to make contact with, but her mother took her away from me, and I haven't been able to get in touch with her. The 'garden centre' bit of it," He said making air quotes, "is about how I lost everything except the memory of my little girl, toddling around the garden helping me plant herbs." He paused, his eyes fixed on the large oak tree at the bottom of the garden. "Anyway, long story short: now I'm here. I like to think with each plant I bring to life, I grow closer to her, even if it's just on a spiritual level."

"I'm sorry."

And then it happened. My idiot mouth opened, and the lie slid out. The lie I'd told my father to explain why I ran away from him, so I didn't have to tell him the truth. The lie I later told Becca. A lie that had been retold so many times, it'd taken on its own kind of reality and couldn't be discarded. To say it to someone who'd lost a daughter was evil. But then again, evil is as evil does.

"I… have a daughter too. Her father's family are raising her, and it was agreed she'd be better off if we cut all ties."

Chris's head snapped round, and his dark eyes stared straight into my dark soul.

"You have a daughter?" He looked as though he knew I was lying.

"Mmm hm. Yes. Excuse me, I need the ladies' room." I stood up.

His eyes narrowed a bit, but he pointed to the red door and said, "Through there and to the right."

"Thanks." And I darted away from the mess I'd created.

The bathroom was clean and white with dark blue towels neatly folded on a shelf. I sat on the edge of the bath and took sips from a glass beaker filled with cool, refreshing tap water, whilst I stared into my deceitful dark eyes in the mirror. Dark eyes that reflected my dark soul. My dark soul that reflected in Chris's brown eyes.

Wow! Our eyes looked so alike. Could I be the daughter he'd lost?

I shook my head. 'Get a grip.' I told myself. Chris wasn't much older than me, of course I wasn't his daughter.

Unless he really was Kasaman.

But why would the Devil be running a garden centre in the middle of nowhere in the north of England?

I took a few deep breaths, visualising roots growing from the soles of my feet and deep into the earth. Then, as Dr. Devries instructed, even though it felt ridiculous, I tapped myself three times on my forehead and returned to reality.

I washed my hands and crept out of the bathroom. I was about to re-join the party when a recess in the wall caught my eye. I checked no one on the patio could see me, before moving closer. A brass statue of a Buddha stood in front of a thank you card. I picked it up. It was from Nick, thanking Chris for his support and understanding. Next to this, was a Lapis Lazuli pyramid, behind which was a painting of a toddler in a vegetable garden, waving a freshly unearthed carrot in the air. On the other side of the recess, was a painted wooden tablet of a lady in a dark blue cloak and a gold halo over her head. 'Saint Laura of Constantinople' was written along the bottom. Next to the tablet, a postcard had fallen over. I picked it up, there was no message on the back, just the information about the artwork: Proserpine by Rossetti.

Then I saw what was under the postcard.

The smooth white stone with a black streak running through it which I'd rescued from North Beach, and the rough pitted ochre stone I'd found on South Beach. The offerings I'd left for the Dispossessed God.

I dropped the card back where it was and fell back against the bathroom door. "Reality, reality, reality." I told myself, but no matter how hard I willed it, reality was proving a tad slippery.

I rushed back into the bathroom and stared into my eyes. Chris's eyes. Kasaman's eyes. The Devil's eyes.

No, I was not evil. But what the hell was happening?

Again, I crept out of the bathroom, and headed back to the patio. They were all absorbed in the game of pool. I waited until I could see that Tyler was heading off to get another beer, whilst Mannie and Chris started a game.

I slipped through the door and went up to Tyler. "I've just seen something that's odd, and I'm feeling a bit shook up."

"What? In the bathroom? Are you okay?"

"I'm not really sure. I think I need to leave."

"Okay. I'll call a taxi."

Mannie came up to us.

"Are you okay?"

"We're just going to get a taxi." I said.

"She's just had a bit of an incident in the bathroom. I don't think she's feeling well. I was going to call her a taxi."

"Oh no! It can't have been the burger, not this quickly." Mannie sat me down on one of the benches.

"What's going on?" Yelled Fus.

"Kerella's eaten something that disagrees with her, I'm going to drive her home." Mannie yelled back. "Can you grab me some towels?"

"Ookelly Dookelly!" Fus yelled back and disappeared through the door, promptly returning with his arms full of towels.

I was ushered out of the Acres in a manner that made me find my concern about Mull'aman seeing me stumble on my way in, rather foolish.

"Shall I put the towels on the car seat?" Mannie asked, as we got to her car.

"Oh no, I'm just feeling a bit nauseous." I replied, deciding it best to play along, as long as it got me out of there.

"You poor thing! Well, let's get you home so you can rest up." Mannie helped me into the car.

She drove along the country roads in silence. As we pulled into the carpark of my building, she turned to me, a look of concern etched on her face. "Kerella, you seem like a lovely girl. Please be careful with Tyler, he's a bit, 'precious', and for the sake of the band, best keep things platonic, if you know what I mean?"

I pretended to suffer another wave of nausea to hide my hurt. I was delusional, not deluded! I didn't need it pointed out that, as a newbie on a temporary lease, the other band members were more valuable than me.

"I best go. See you on Monday." I mumbled, letting myself out of the car and running inside, hoping I'd moved quick enough, and she hadn't seen the tears.

14: DREAM FILLED CAGE

"So, you pooped your pants?" Becca said, leaning my keyboard against the wall by the double doors.

"What?!" I threw the keyboard stand down on the ridged dark brown carpet and checked no one else was in the corridor. "I was in the bathroom hiding from Chris! Look, I had these stones which I gave to the Dispossessed God, and they turned up in his house. That's a little bit more than odd, don't you think? I did not poop myself!"

Becca smirked, looked at her sparkly nails briefly, before flicking her gaze back to meet mine, mouth open in mock shock.

"Chris had my stones."

"I bet he did." Becca said, laughing. "You can make this about Chris's stones as much as you like, but Tyler said the bathroom stunk like a mother fucker. That's got nothing to do with Chris's stones."

"I didn't even use the toilet! I just hid in there because Chris freaked me out!"

Becca stuck her head through the swinging doors, but the kids were still rehearsing their dance routine, so she pulled back quickly.

"Did Ty really say that? It isn't true. He can't think it's true. Oh god! How embarrassing."

"Ker, I'm winding you up. Mannie was asking about you yesterday. And why the fuck do you suddenly care if some 'two-dimensional' wanker thinks your arse stinks like a septic tank?"

"Well, maybe Ty's a bit more three-dimensional."

"No, he's as two-dimensional as they come."

She kicked my ankle to stop me from tapping my foot.

"Oh, for fuck's sake! I did not see this coming. Do not fuck this one. Avoid. That's a rule, or I'll be the one who gets it in the neck from every fucking angle. The one thing I've always admired about you is that you just use guys, you don't give a fuck about them, don't care about impressing them, don't get all fucked up over them. But then you fall for the biggest womanising prick out there!"

"I haven't fallen for him."

She gave me her 'I don't believe you' look: face pulled back to double up her chin and eyes rolling in wearied annoyance.

"No, seriously, I don't have a thing for Tyler. I have a thing for a completely imaginary guy as part of that fantasy bullshit you ridicule me for, and I'm just projecting onto Ty for a bit of fun. I honestly know the difference between making up a guy who doesn't annoy the hell out of me and Tyler… I promise."

Her disapproving expression relaxed slightly.

"Okay, play with your imaginary friend as much as you want, just don't play with Tyler, got me? And don't obsess yourself into a corner and get confused between the two."

I nodded my consent. It was easy enough to do. I knew Tyler wasn't really Mull'aman, and even if he was, why would I desecrate my earthly totem to my soul mate with an act as destructive as sex?

Becca wandered down the corridor a few steps and looked out of the cracked window at the scaffolding holding up the main hall. "They should just bulldoze this place. You know you're on a fool's errand? No one in their right mind would try to save this place. Then again, Mannie and Fus are definitely not in their right mind."

She looked down the corridor and sneered. "Mr. 'I think I'm so cool cos I've got a stupid hat' is here. I'll pick you up in two hours."

I grabbed her arm. "Becca, no! Please! You promised me you would stay throughout the rehearsal."

"No, I specifically said I would stay in the building during the rehearsal. I'm going to pester Mike. See you in two hours. You're on your own. And do as I tell you."

"Hello, Rebecca."

Becca sauntered past Chris without acknowledging him, swatting at loose sheets on the notice board on her way.

"Do you always let her speak to you like that?"

"She's allowed to talk to me like that. I trust her, she looks out for me, she doesn't have secrets, or lie to me."

He nodded slightly in a way that suggested he didn't agree with me, and moved over to the door.

There were too many unanswered questions to relax in Chris's presence. Why were my stones in his house? Was he the Dispossessed God? Was that Kasaman or something worse? Why was the band called The Casa Martyrs? Why did his girlfriend run off with his daughter? Why should I give a fuck?

"Why aren't you going in?"

"Well, there are kids in there."

"You find it hard to be around children?" He gave me a pitying look and pushed through the double doors with his cello and bass, before returning to pick up my keyboard.

He motioned for me to follow him, so I picked up my keyboard stand and followed him into the squall of adolescent chaos. I tried hard not to flinch as the noise tumbled into my head like a chaotic abrasive mess.

Mannie waved to us from the side of the stage as we came in. Chris put my keyboard down by the drums and went over to join her. I remained at the back of the hall, observing the confusing dance routine, set to something I assumed was current popular music.

Mikey's Sugar Swords came to a dramatic stop in defiant poses and were treated to enthusiastic cheers and whoops from Mannie, and a series of encouraging, deliberate claps from Chris. I joined in with a self-conscious fluttering applause, but I was comfortably invisible at the back of the room whilst Mannie helped half of the troupe with suggestions for a dance manoeuvre and Chris talked to the rest of them. They nodded along to what Chris was saying, until a girl in a purple jumper snatched his hat from his head and started up a dramatic scene of being a pirate and forcing a boy in a red t-shirt to walk an imaginary plank off the stage. Chris leant back against the wall as mayhem erupted around him.

"Hey, sultry molasses."

"Hello." I smiled as simplicity walked in. My Mull'aman proxy: the toy that I could bat around and wasn't allowed to get involved with, with his beautiful emerald green… "What the hell happened to your eyes?"

"I'm not wearing my contacts. You thought they were naturally like that? That's not exactly biologically possible, you know?"

With his rather dull, grey flecked brown eyes, scratching his arse through dirty black combats, and smelling of a take-out curry from the night before, the earthly, two-dimensional Tyler came to stand next to me, laying his guitar at his feet. "Ugh! I forgot it was going to be one of the days we had to share with the brats."

"Chris seems to be enjoying it." I observed.

"Yeah. Theresa really missed out being snatched away by that bitch." Tyler grabbed his guitar and moved further into the room.

Realising he'd just farted, I bent down to pick up my keyboard stand.

"Beep Beep Beep! Bop Bop Bop!" Fus barged into the room. "It's five past and we're not ready! Do we not want to beat Angel Waste? Are we wasters?" He paused as he passed me. "Hey Angel, are we feeling better?" Tyler's toxic fumes must have reached his nose at that point. "Maybe you should try some peppermint tea?"

I cast Tyler an angry glance, and he laughed, held his nose, and wafted the air in front of his face.

I hauled the keyboard stand over to him. "Well, I hope you've got that out of your system."

"Don't look at me, you're the one who needs some peppermint tea!"

Fus leapt onto his stool and started the drum beat from Dream Filled Cage. With each round, he revved up the tempo. Taking the hint, I hastily assembled my stand and ran to drag the extension cord over to the keyboard. Tyler launched into the introduction, and right at the last moment, Mannie snatched the microphone off one of the girls, Chris's hat off the head of another girl, and jumped off the stage, dropping the hat onto Chris's head with excellent precision.

She launched into the fast-paced lyrics:

> A dream is a moment in time:
> a temporal logic that passes,
> a desire intent on a crime,
> convince me salt is molasses.
> Following the trail of breadcrumbs,
> to the object of my desire.
> Play the game 'til success succumbs,
> and the dream and the cage conspire.

Clearly familiar with the song, the kids on stage started clapping in time as we revved up the tension. Taking a deep breath, Mannie began the powerful chorus, backed up by Tyler's honeydew drawling.

> This cage is filled with dreams,
> and these dreams are my cage.
> If you play to win, pray you'll lose:
> the prize is not one you would choose.
> This cage is filled with dreams,
> and these dreams are my cage.
> Victory brought me to my knees.
> My precious dream is my disease.

The clapping stopped as suddenly as it had begun, and the kids huddled together whispering to each other during the next verse.

> Sleepwalk into the honey trap;
> dark and sticky and now I'm stuck;
> mosquito drowning in the sap;
> the door slams shut, I'm out of luck.
> The scales fall from my tainted eyes,
> I see the tempt(er)ress anew.

> The promises that morph to lies,
> the dreams that were just passing through.

As the melodramatic bridge kicked in, the plans that had been whispered during the last verse became clear. One by one the kids left the stage, following a haphazard zigzag path towards us.

> I watch them as they fade from view;
> the dreams that were just passing through.
> I watch them as they leave the stage;
> I'm trapped within my dream filled cage.

> I watch them as they fade from view;
> the dreams that were just passing through.
> I watch them as they leave the stage;
> I'm trapped within my dream filled cage.

Like an organised pack of wolves, Mikey's Sugar Swords encircled us, and were standing in a perfect ring ready for the clapping ritual of the chorus.

> This cage is filled with dreams,
> and these dreams are my cage.
> If you play to win, pray you'll lose:
> the prize is not one you would choose.
> This cage is filled with dreams,
> and these dreams are my cage.
> Victory brought me to my knees.
> My precious dream is my disease.

They stopped clapping and began collapsing noisily and with great drama for the Coda:

> Set me free.
> Release me.
> Within my hands,
>   the golden prize
>   dies.

Mannie dropped the microphone on the floor.

The tempo and jumping melody had given me a huge adrenalin high. I closed my eyes to take in the buzzing sensation throughout my body and the lightness in my head. The kids were cheering and yelling in the background. After a few long moments, I opened my eyes and Tyler was stood in front of me, staring.

"What?"

He opened his mouth but didn't say anything.

"Tyler?"

"Sorry. I know you're a genius, and what you bring to the song is totally out there, but I didn't realise what a strong presence you had. You're totally amazing."

"Oh, for god's sake, Ty." Mannie thumped him. "Firstly, don't hit on our keyboardist. And secondly," She thumped him again, a lot harder.

"Ow!"

"And secondly, never, and I repeat, never, be that cheesy again."

Chris didn't look impressed. "Tyler, that was a bit much. You walk out on Kat less than a week ago, and you're already spouting shit like that?"

Tyler shot him an angry look and walked to the other side of the room, casting a look back in my direction as he went.

Mull'aman was remembering.

Mannie ran over to the girl in the purple jumper. "Was that your idea, Gems? What an excellent use of spatial theatre!"

Tyler wandered over to Chris. "Don't you think Timmins Cave would make a great backdrop for a video of Dream Filled Cage? Let's head out there later to get some recon shots."

"Well, Tris'll need walking, so we can kill two birds with one stone."

"Fantastic! Kerella!" Tyler turned to face me. "You walk?"

"No, I levitate everywhere."

"No! Like, could you walk five miles or so?"

"I could walk five hundred miles, if properly motivated."

"Excellent! You're coming with us!"

Fus started the accelerating drum riff again, cutting off the conversation.

"Thank you." He said. "Okay, let's try that again, but this time, Ty, stop staring at Kerella's keyboard, and focus on what you're playing, and Mannie, can you give Chris a nod before you head into the bridge, so he knows exactly when you're going to start?"

As we delved once more into the Dream Filled Cage, I pictured us in a dramatic rock video, the camera filming us through the gnarled pillars of sandstone at Timmins Cave. In the background, an ominous black mountain with three twisted turrets rose out of the sea.

15: TIMMINS CAVE

Becca slammed on the brakes, making the slightest gesture of pulling over to the side of the road by the carpark. "Had I known you joining the band would involve so much work for me, I would've told them to fuck off."

"I owe you big time." I said, hooking my finger around the door handle. I paused and turned back to Becca. "Are you sure you don't want to come with us? It looks like it'll be a lovely evening."

"Do I look like I fucking walk?" Becca snapped at me and started revving the engine. I quickly opened the door and got out. The car was edging forward as my feet hit the ground, so I slammed the car door shut and waved as she sped away.

Wearing my exceptionally sensible walking boots, tight black jeans, and layered red and black vest top, I crunched my way over the ochre gravel, singing Dream Filled Cage in time with my steps.

I strolled through the large glass door into the darkened gift shop. Had Becca not dragged her feet and made me late, I would've taken the opportunity to look around the art section and bask in my tortured ambivalence of feeling jealous of the artists Chris had chosen, whilst distrusting him and wanting to keep my artwork as far away from him as possible.

I hurried through the gift shop and into the staff area. I paused briefly to watch the shimmery fish in the pond, then pushed open the red door into Chris's house. As I closed the door behind me, Tyler sauntered out of the bathroom, pink and raw from the shower, a dark blue towel tucked around his waist.

Letting out a sound like a slurry, inebriated cat, I turned to the wall. "Sorry!"

"Is that the time?" Tyler casually asked. "I guess I should throw some clothes on." As he walked away, he untucked the towel and opened it wide behind him, before wrapping it back around his waist as he turned. He gave me a wink, then ran up the stairs, disappearing around the corner.

I took a deep breath to calm the burning sensation running through my lower torso, and diverted my attention to more important matters. I descended on the alcove, to lay eyes once again on proof that Chris could not be trusted. Three fir cones now encircled the brass Buddha, the Lapis Lazuli pyramid had fallen over and was now pointing at a rose quartz tumble stone, and the Saint Laura icon and the Proserpine postcard stood upright behind a smooth oval red stone and a shard of quartz with black flecks in it.

Had I imagined that my stones were here last time? I pulled out my phone and took a photo of the alcove, even though it was too late to capture any incriminating evidence. Why had I not thought to photograph the stones last time?

Dejected and confused, I wandered past the stairs towards the red settee and armchairs in Chris's living room. The walls were filled with artwork: red, orange, and yellow; abstract, dry, fiery, and angry. Grooves scratched into the canvases; stains dripped down into the depths. Then, I turned the corner and I saw a scene I never thought I'd see again. Familiar, calm waters pooled over smooth sand, and from the sea rose the selkie I painted last year, her dark longing eyes staring up from the white gold sand.

The cool blues of my long-lost masterpiece lured me in. I stepped closer, drinking in every sedate ripple, each water droplet on my selkie's breasts, the way the light faded into the distance, and the imprint on the horizon of a mountain my selkie could never explore.

"You like it?" Chris asked, putting his mug down next to his hat on the coffee table and coming to stand by me. "I got it from Shambles. Becca told me the guy who painted it lived in Almwood Hospital and killed himself shortly after completing it. But I get the impression she was bullshitting me. Look here:" he moved towards my selkie, "See how the artist's use of blue on this sea bound creature mirrors the use of colour on these distant mountains. It has such a strong pull, dragging you from the depths of the sea to the heights of the land."

"I just love the look in the nymph's eyes." Tyler added, as he jogged down the stairs, Tris bounding after him. "You know you're in for a good night with that one. She's been in a few of my late-night fantasies, I can tell you!"

"Becca lied to you." I snapped. "It's my work. See here." I tapped the K signature. I thought my father had destroyed the paintings he'd confiscated that day. Had Becca known about this deception all along?

"Whoa! There's no way I'm believing you painted that!" Tyler said.

"I don't care if you believe me."

"Let me see your work then. What's your website?"

"I don't have a website."

"Social media?"

"I don't do social media."

"No one that good has no online presence."

"How does being online affect the quality of my art?"

"Clearly no one has shown you the wonders of online marketing yet. How about I come over to yours some time; you can show me your artwork and I'll create a website for you. If you really did paint this, you're missing out on a goldmine by not monetising your online presence."

Chris picked up his hat and placed it over his dark blue bandanna. "Tyler, this is not a marketing seminar. Get your arse out the door and let's get to Timmins Cave before night fall, okay?"

Tyler grabbed his camera from the sideboard and led us out of the house and through The Acres. We walked up the red brick path, following the course of the stream, past rows of neatly arranged plants categorised by preferred growing conditions, listening to the gentle trickle of the watering system, until we reached the back, where a wrought iron gate set within a high red brick wall blocked our way.

The grey and white cat was sauntering along the top of the wall. When it saw us, it jumped down in front of Tyler and rubbed up against his leg, before heading off to explore the fruit trees.

"Maybe time away from Kat will be a good thing; you'll get to spend more time with Isolde." Chris said.

"I'll never get over the irony of Kat being allergic to cats."

Chris pulled out a set of keys and unlocked the gate as Tyler knelt down and started taking photos of Isolde weaving in and out of the pots of the tall fruit trees.

"Ty, I'm not holding the gate open for my health."

Tyler jumped up. I followed him and Tris through the gate, and Chris closed it behind us. We were now on a narrow woodland path. Tris led the way as we walked in single file. After a couple of minutes, Tyler bent down, picked up a stone, and put it in his pocket.

As we reached the coast, the path widened and split in two. The fork to the left led to my secret ledge, but we turned to the right and followed the steep descent towards a rocky beach. Chris walked next to Tyler, and I trotted along behind them. Tris ran off ahead and examined various items on the beach, before returning with a large piece of knotted rope, which he dropped at my feet. I threw it onto the beach for him to chase.

Chris bent down, picked up a stone, examined it, and put it in his pocket. "So, are you going to tell me what happened, so I can deflect Mannie, or do you want to face her interrogation?" he said to Tyler.

"Oh god! Spare me that!"

"Well give me something I can tell her."

Tyler lowered his voice so I had to discretely pick up my pace and walk as quietly as I could to hear what he was saying.

"It's been getting really bad for months. She won't go out. She just sits in front of the computer all day and night. I do all the shopping, the cleaning, and the bills. She barely says anything to me, and then, when I invite my mates over, she flies into a rage and screams at me for no reason. I did everything I could, but when she told me to get out of the house, after everything I'd done for her? There's only so much flagellation a man can take!"

"Well, you're not crashing at Ian's anymore. Bring your stuff over and you can have your old room until you sort things out. You're too old for staying up all night drinking and playing computer games."

"I'm not too old, I'm only twenty-four; that's a perfectly respectable age for gaming nights, dad."

"You're twenty-five in a fortnight."

"Oh my god! Me too!" I blurted out, for I am the master of eavesdropping and subterfuge.

They turned around and stared at me, as though they'd forgotten I was even there.

Tris started barking at the rope he'd returned to me.

Then Tyler's broad grin returned. "Wow! When?"

"Eighth of August."

"Hey! That's my birthday too! We'll have to have a mega party after the gig." Tyler did a little dance, then bent down and picked up a stone, looked at it, and put it in his pocket. "Chris, what did you do to mark your quatercentenary?"

"Tyler, you are aware that means four hundred years?"

"Huh? Oh. Quarter century?"

"I'll let you know in February."

"No, I mean when you turned twenty-five."

"Yes, Ty, I know what you mean. I will let you know what I do in February, when I turn twenty-five."

"But aren't you nearly forty?"

"Thanks, Ty. No. I'm nearly twenty-five. I've just spent my life working a lot harder than you."

"Stop winding me up; no way is that true. So, I met you, like four years ago and you'd already, not only had a child, but lost her by the time you were twenty-one? That's not possible."

"You do know how reproduction works?"

"Of course I do! I've had a lot more practice at it than you have!"

"Clearly not the actual reproduction part."

"So, what, you were, like, seventeen and got a girl knocked up?"

"Eighteen, and can we change the subject please."

"Alright, but one day, you will tell me the full story." Tyler bent down and picked up another stone.

"Okay, what is it with the bloody stones?" I yelled.

"Duh!" Tyler responded, before jumping up on a rock and singing:

"I'm a Skimmin Timmin champion:
I know where it's at.
He's in, she's in, they're in,
but I will win the hat!
Skimmin Timmin, Skimmin Tim,
make sure your stone is flat!
Skimmin Timmin, Skimmin Tim,
spin it low, spin it fast,
but I will wear the hat!"

He held his arms up as he finished, as if his performance was an explanation.

"You want to wear a hat? Well, I'm sure if you're nice enough to Chris, he'll lend you his."

Chris laughed, picked up the rope to throw for Tris, and continued along the coastal path.

"No! We're off to skim stones. Why else would we go to Timmins cave? That's why it's called Skimmin Timmins Cave!" Tyler said before jumping off his rock and following Chris.

I paused for a moment to take in the absurdity. Tyler could not be further from my refined, courtly Mull'aman. I set off after him. "It's called Timmins Cave after Mary Timmins who used to walk out here every day to participate in illegal religious services until her husband snitched on her and she got hung from the big arch back in the seventeenth century." I replied, hoping I was reciting my mother's history lessons correctly.

"Shit, that's not fun."

"No, being persecuted for your religious beliefs or being betrayed by your spouse is not fun, Tyler." Chris said, "But, Kerella, that's not why I'm picking up stones."

I fell into step beside him to hear his explanation.

"Nick suggested I try this as an exercise to help me let go of some things from my past. I'm supposed to imagine the events that I keep replaying in my mind are in the stone. I then throw the stone into the water and let the past go, so I can make space for the present. If I'm honest, most of the time, I imagine I'm throwing the stones at a certain person's head, which probably defeats the point, but the guy really deserves it. So, less Buddhist forgiveness and acknowledging impermanence, and more cathartic imaginary revenge."

We walked down the path in silence. I imagined throwing stones at all the people who'd treated me badly, Tyler picked up large flat stones when he saw them on the path, and Tris, having lost interest in his rope, had run ahead on the path, and was sniffing around some bushes.

Chris suddenly stopped and pointed inland. "Look at that redwaek in the field."

I jumped behind Tyler, who was looking confused in the direction Chris was pointing.

"Wow! It's not often you see red kites here!" He lifted his camera up and started snapping away. "I could photoshop it between you two standing under the arch of the cave and make it as tall as both of you. Hashtag NewBandMember. Should get a few shares."

"I'm not posing for you." Chris said and strode off round the final corner before the caves.

Tyler looked at me, raised his camera and took a photo.

I gave him the middle finger, but he just took another photo, so I turned round and walked away.

The elegant arch of Timmins Cave came into view. Carved by nature into sandstone, the grainy surface of the cave walls held the imprint of ancient tides, hands, and beliefs. Growing up I heard tales that it was haunted by smugglers, double crossed and left for dead by their accomplices; by women accused of witchcraft, brutally tortured then buried in the larger crevices; and of course, by Mary Timmins herself, roaming the earth to find her duplicitous husband and exact her revenge.

For me the ghosts were more recent. The ghost of childhood: the family picnic when I explored the small narrow cave which required you to crawl in, arse in the air, front trapped in the tapering space, where I first felt my uncle's wandering hands going up my skirt. The ghost of adolescence: a fun walk with school friends that turned nasty when it turned out they weren't collecting dog shit along the coastal path out of civic duty, but to pelt me with, before running off and leaving me crying and stinking, hiding from the other walkers in the back of the larger cave. The ghost of romance: The moonlit lover's walk that ended rather roughly with the guy ticking off a new fuck point on the grid before joining his cheering mates who had secretly filmed the act, and ran off congratulating him on dipping his chips in Tommy K. It was the first time I'd heard anyone call me that, but I've heard it many times since then.

I scrambled up the incline to stand on the grassy top of the caves. I looked down at Chris and Tyler, wondering what was going to happen this time.

Tyler threw a stone which bounced fifteen times and threw up his arms in celebration, starting the Skimmin Timmin dance again.

He tried to give his camera to Chris, but he shook his head and walked away.

"Oy! Kerella! Get down here! I need you to film me skimming!" Tyler yelled.

I smiled. I didn't know what I was doing right this time that I'd got so catastrophically wrong on previous occasions, but I seriously hoped I wasn't about to mess it up.

I climbed down the embankment and walked over to Tyler.

"It's easy, all you have to do is press this button, and it'll start recording, and press it again when I've finished. Have you got that?"

I nodded, lifted the camera up and hit record.

After nine attempts, Tyler had failed to recreate his Skimmin Timmin success, and had run out of stones.

He turned to Chris: "If you'd bloody well filmed me when I asked you to, I'd have the perfect clip to upload tonight."

He snatched the camera from me, and I took a few steps back in case he started blaming me for jinxing his performance.

"What about the photo of the red kite?" Chris suggested.

"Do I look like a fucking twitcher? You think my followers want pictures of birds of the avian variety?"

"Life is more than social media approval, Ty." Chris said, fussing Tris who'd turned up proudly toting a piece of driftwood.

Tyler gave Chris a scornful look. "Yah, yah, yah. You know, I put up with this whole tortured Grandpa Martyr routine of yours when I thought you were a grumpy old man, but now you're claiming to be younger than me, I'm going to impart my wisdom on you for once. You've sacrificed your life for some fantasy perception of home that you're never going to find because you're fixating on the past. Life is online now. It's my social media activity that brings out the fans to see your precious 'Martyrs'. Sign up for online dating, meet some woman and knock out a new kid to get obsessed about. Hell! Theresa probably has an online profile somewhere. Although do be careful how you go about searching for young girls on the internet. Just leave the fucking martyrdom in the songs, it'll never get you anywhere."

Tyler suddenly turned his focus to me. "So, newbie, while we're on the topic, here's your initiation; I'll save Chris the effort of asking you himself. What Casa are you the Martyr for?"

"Huh? I… I'm sorry. I don't understand." I felt things start to unravel. I had no idea what was going on. This was the end. It always fell apart like this.

Chris laid a hand on my shoulder. "That's because Tyler isn't making sense." He walked to the water's edge, shaking his head, before turning back to me. "If you'll excuse a preachy, grumpy old man lecture, from someone younger than you," Chris tipped the brim of his hat in Tyler's direction. "'The Casa Martyrs' was my first song. I wrote it with Fus, back when he still worked at The Acres. It's inspired by the fall of Constantinople. When I was studying the event at university, I kept thinking, this is so like contemporary social movements. People come together for different reasons. For example, in Constantinople, you had those who lived in the city, mercenaries, and people who came because of friendship, religious affiliation, or politics. Where they came from didn't matter, what mattered was the bond that formed, which was almost like family.

"One staff social with a lot of very nice red wine, and poor Fus was cornered as I bombarded him with my ideas about how the same patterns are still around today. People join certain groups because they believe in them, or because they look good to post about on social media," He looked at Tyler as he said that. "or for many other reasons. When they find their cause, they find their place. It becomes part of their identity, and they fight to protect it.

"By the end of the evening, the guitar was out, Fus and I were writing lyrics, and Mannie was singing for us. And we were celebrating the amazing people who come to defend a cause, or a city, that may not be theirs by birth or identity, but because they care, and they're willing to make sacrifices to protect others. That night, The Casa Martyrs was born, to respect those who stand up for a worthy cause."

Tyler made a big show of yawning before interrupting Chris. "Someone needs to define the meaning of 'worthy cause' to Mannie, and point out that wreck of a building doesn't fit."

Chris sucked in his cheeks. "Tyler, the fight to save the community centre isn't about the building, it's about the people who have found their home there. Uproot them, send them across town to a smaller, shared, multi-purpose building, with less funds and staff, and something valuable will be lost."

"Some things should be lost."

"Wait until the fight is to protect somewhere you think of as home." Chris turned to me. "So, Kerella, what is home to you? Where does your heart belong, and what would you sacrifice for it?"

I had no answer. Home to me was pain, fear, and feeling that I was never good enough. I stared at the ground trying to think of an answer that would be right for the situation.

"Sorry, clearly home hasn't been an easy place for you. Think about it and tell us your answer when you're ready." Chris fussed Tris and turned to follow the path home.

Tyler patted me on the back. "Don't worry, you're a Martyr now, you belong with us." He followed Chris up the path, leaving me with too many thoughts.

Where would I say was my home? Obviously, it was my flat, but that wasn't the answer Chris wanted. The closest thing I had to a 'home' by his definition, was a small room with three glassless windows, an arch nemesis who may want to kill me, and a maternal figure who seemed disappointed in me. And Mull'aman. And none of it was real. What would I sacrifice for that fantasy? Maybe I had to sacrifice the fantasy to find a real home.

As exciting as The Casa Martyrs may be, I didn't feel ready to let go of the Kaetian world for them just yet.

16: KAETIAN GARDENS

I lift myself into the central window. After the infiltration, grilles have been installed to prevent redwaek pulling the shutters from their frames again. Although I could never have gone anywhere through the windows, I miss being able to lean over the edge, imagining the lives of my citizens, far below in the hazy streets, huddled around the base of the mountain, safe in the shadow of the Kaetian Compound.

I trace my fingers over the metalwork. The detail is exquisite. Sett is depicted with a dark blue cloak of glistening sapphires. She was the original Supreme Kaetian, chosen at the first Blazing Court to lead society out of the darkness which cursed this land, and towards the perfect society which, when attained, would lift the curse. She and her family were granted a lifespan of three thousand years to work towards this end; an obligation, blessing, and curse, that passed down the generations until, somehow, all our hopes came to rest with me.

Tears well up in my eyes as I jump down from the recess. How can anyone with the deaths of four Pader guards on their soul be able to save themselves, let alone a whole society?

I head over to the next grille. This one pays homage to the original twenty-one Higher Kaetians, picked to rule over the most important aspects of Kaetian life and society. They were endowed with a lifespan of three hundred years, so they could learn the Tenets of Sett, implement her teachings, and pass on this knowledge to the next generation, who would continue their good work.

I play the same game I've played all week since these grilles were fitted. I go through each of the twenty-one stars of the Higher Kaetian families in order, feeling my heart flutter when I trace Mull'aman's family, whilst not letting myself hover any longer over that star than any of the others.

I asked Asana if I could have some more music tuition. She laughed at me, saying there was nothing anyone in Kaetia could teach me about music. I tried again with the suggestion that I could get involved with the planning of the musical side of the Celebration of Kaetian Society. She said she would ask the Council but doubted they would be keen on me spending my time on 'decorative frills' when I had more important matters to think about. Considering how little I was told about anything important, let alone involved with it, and how much time I was left alone in this room with pre-approved books I'd read a hundred times, I really couldn't see why participating in something to promote Kaetian society wouldn't be for the greater good.

I walk over to the grille protecting the smallest opening. The wall under the window is now stained brown with redwaek blood. I look over the fifty-six-star pattern celebrating the Lower Kaetians, those who ensure the minutiae of society are attended to, so the Higher Kaetians can get on with the more significant work. The sight of the ugly brown stain makes me feel sick, so I force myself to look at it a little bit longer.

Even though the air still gently drifts through the grilles, the small room feels more like a prison than ever. This is what I deserve. I have four deaths on my soul. The redwaek must have ripped the shutters off at some point during the attack, so my culpability was never revealed, but my heart has been blackened. After the intoxicating effects of the red weed wore off, the guilt sapped all my energy and the only thing that could motivate me was the hope that, one day, I would see Mull'aman again.

I press my hands against the rough stone, imagining Mull'aman is also touching a wall somewhere in the Compound, and through the rocks, we're somehow connected. And then, my arms drop, heavy with the realisation that he'll spend the rest of his short life within a mile or so of me, and I may never see him again.

I pace around the room, dragging my fingers against the rough stone as I go. Past the waist high mosaic of the Blazing Court decorating the wall beside the bed, past the table on which sits my designated reading material for this month, past the brown stain where redwaek blood forever stands witness to my secret guilt, past the shutters with T and M in their secret union, and through it all again. From one end of my home to the other. This isolated little room: a part of nothing, and the heart of everything.

The only rooms in Kaetia which are higher than my little prison are Kasaman's ghost quarters and Asana's tower, where I imagine her candles burn late into the night as she deals with things too important to include me. I try to believe that one day it'll be me sat in that tower, scratching out my thoughts on rough paper, raising the next Supreme Kaetian, who I won't keep locked up in this tower. I hoped Mull'aman would be there by my side, trying to somehow lift the curse from this *land by getting right what had been gotten wrong for so many millennia.*

A loud knock on the door halts my frantic pacing.

Time for the monthly Council meeting.

I grab my blue cloak from the bed and swing it around my shoulders, pull the hood over my head, and shove wayward strands of hair out of my face. I collect the pile of books from the table and make my way out of the newly fitted door, which no longer locks from the inside for my own safety. I nod briefly at the Pader guards standing by the door, hand one of them the pile of books, and head down to the staging area.

Asana is standing by the ornate arch leading into the Kaetian Compound. Her hands are clasped demurely in front of her, and her hood drapes around her face in the desired way I've never managed to emulate. She waits like a statue of Sett between two Pader guards.

A benevolent smile gently touches her face as I approach. She turns to the Pader stood next to her: "Melingad, we shall go via the gardens today."

I recognise her code for, 'I have something private to tell you', and fall in step behind her. Two Paders walk in front of us, and two Paders follow.

It's the first time I've been out of the Kaetian Quarters since the invasion. The procession moves through the corridors. We pass the turning I took during the redwaek attack: the dark, narrow opening that had changed my life. Of course, we don't turn into the chaotic depths of the Kaetian Compound but continue down the wide authentic Kaetian path; one of the same paths Sett would have walked; a route Kasaman would have followed. I wonder if Mull'aman is permitted to be in this area of the Compound, if his footsteps have fallen on these stone slabs.

We descend one level and arrive in the gardens. I don't get to come here very often, even though it's one of my favourite places. As we enter, an army of old women in green cloaks fall to their knees. As Asana greets them all by name, I let my senses savour the delights the garden has to offer.

The swooping arches of the ornate metal lattice work, which let the air and sunlight in, whilst keeping the redwaek out, create an optical illusion. If you sway slightly, they crash into waves, cascading out in all directions. In the heat, the herbs release a spicy fragrance, and the trickle of the water through the irrigation system reminds me of a song I'm yet to hear.

There is an echo of Kasaman in this garden: he loved it here as much as I do. I can see him working on the irrigation system to ensure that more water got from the only source of water in Kaetia, the fountain in the Courtyard of the Arcane, to these gardens and then down to the lower levels. I can hear him telling me of the importance of reforming water rations to make them fairer and talking with Asana about how to prevent illegal syphoning.

But all the books say he deliberately sabotaged the irrigation system and diverted the water into a secret supply for himself. Decades later, and no one has worked out where the water is going, or managed to undo his actions. Because of my father, we all suffer additional thirst, and fewer mortals can be saved.

It's odd how memory lies to us. I put my hand on the metal lattice work and I'm so sure I can recall a conversation my father had on the steps in front of me, with an old man in a red cloak, about how the water pooling in the decorative ponds was unjustifiable when people were thirsty in Kaetia. My dysfunctional mind remembers these ponds, yet there's no record of them, and where I thought they were, is a bed of culinary herbs, established by Sett herself when Kaetia first started to crawl its way out of darkness.

Asana dismisses the Lower Kaetians, and they return to their duties, tending to the plants that will nourish us all. It's wonderful to behold such a bustle of activity. I'm sure if the Blazing Court were to judge Kaetian society on the zeal and activity of these women alone, the curse would be lifted by night fall. But it's all aspects of Kaetian society which must be judged worthy for the curse to be broken.

Instructing the Pader guards to wait in the gardens, Asana opens the gates that lead onto the balcony and motions for me to follow. It's the only space we can go where we can talk quietly without being overheard, and the only time she goes out there is to warn me about my behaviour, or correct bad habits I've picked up.

I hesitate by the gates, another false memory teasing me with the ridiculous scene of Asana and Kasaman in lively, animated discussion. They're smiling freely and there's a glowing feeling that the curse will be lifted within a generation. It's so simple; they've worked out how to save us all, and before we know it, water will flow freely again. They embrace with genuine tenderness, before opening their loving arms to me. Asana laughs as I toddle clumsily over to them.

She isn't laughing today. She never does. Maybe she never did. It's not like I can trust my memories; there's so much I get wrong. I guess it's the torturously long Supreme Kaetian lifespan, or it could be Kasaman's blood spreading deceit through my veins. I remember a loving, warm, animated woman, but she's a careful statue. Nothing is out of place; everything is correct. She is Sett in stone. I am Kasaman in a messy, fleshy package.

I pass through the gates, ready to hear today's litany of what is wrong with me, whispered to the air, lip movements hidden from anyone who could report my failings to the Council. To everyone else, we're just quietly admiring the view. And it is quite a view. Beneath us is a tiered sequence of descending gardens, and far below that, is the town I've dreamt about visiting so many times. I can just about see the idyllic red rooftops, lined up along the neat little streets.

Asana lifts her arm and points to the ridge of the Crater of the Dead and sweeps her fingers down the conduit back to the Compound. Her words bare no relation to these gestures; they're barely audible, hurried, and don't follow the movement of her lips, which smile in serene reverie.

"What was all that swaying? Tether your whimsy. Exercise control. You're the second oldest person in Kaetia: act like it." She pauses, giving me a stern look with her eyes, whilst the gentle smile remained painted on her face.

"Keep your leg still."

I calm my leg, letting my anxiety settle in my chest instead.

"The Council approved your request. You're to lead the musical tribute to Kaetian Society at this year's Celebrations. You will be observed more closely than ever: be very careful. Watch out for Mull'aman…"

One of the Pader guards has stepped through the gates and is leaning in our direction. Asana looks round and casually instructs: "Melingad, could you help Gestrick with that box, she's not as young as she thinks she is."

Asana looks at me: "Be on guard and observe the fourth tenet." Turning back to the gate, she waves an old woman in a green cloak past the Paders. "Yuescret, the beans are looking healthy." She and the Lower Kaetian launch into a quiet discussion about beans, so I wander off to think about the fourth tenet.

Obviously, I've never seen Sett's actual tenets, only a select few Kaetian Elders are permitted access to the text, and only after years of spiritual preparation. Translations, interpretations, and discussions abound, and all pretty much agree on the meaning, especially for the less difficult lessons like the fourth tenet. I've read all the discussions and consider myself well versed in their complexity. However, I always return to the rhyme I learned as a child when faced with matters to do with the Tenets of Sett.

> *"Higher, lower: know thy place,*
> *Kaetian order, we embrace;"*

The fourth tenet states that the hierarchy in Kaetian society is as it ought to be. Unless an individual is found guilty of heresy, or is elevated through a union with a higher-ranking individual, they should be treated as worthy of the station they were born into and the roles they've been assigned, no matter their abilities or disposition. Kaetian order depends on us all working towards being the best we can be as a collective, and not descending into a milieu of people vying for power. The collective is above the individual, as it is the collective that will lead us to salvation.

It's an odd tenet for Asana to highlight. As it's so rare for me to be around other people, maybe she's reminding me to act aloof like she does. Or maybe she's pointing out that Mull'aman could be a potential suitor as he has the attributes of a Supreme Kaetian.

I turn around to see if further questions are possible and see her pull her hand back from where it had been resting on the old lady's fingers.

I couldn't remember the last time Asana touched me, yet she let some dirty woman in a green cloak pollute her divine fingers? I barge past the Paders and wait impatiently by the gate, as Asana had done for me many times before. No doubt we're late for Council, and the hurried way she comes to meet me, gives me a rare sense of satisfaction. I hope one of the many people who are cataloguing my every incorrect thought and behavioural indiscretion are making a note of this. But, as I look around the garden, I can't see anyone writing anything down, or paying any attention to us.

17: LAESCENNO

As our procession heads off, I find the children's version of The Tenets of Sett stuck in my head. I try to recite it silently in time with my footsteps as we ascend back up to the Council Chambers:

>*Act on thought and think on act;*
>*I am not an acrobat.*
>*Not to juggle or create;*
>*it's our world we celebrate.*
>
>*Seek no secrets, hear no lies;*
>*only truth before my eyes.*
>*Greater good before my heart,*
>*body mine shall play its part.*
>
>*Higher, lower: know thy place;*
>*Kaetian order, we embrace.*
>*Let's obey the word of Sett,*
>*so the curse we can forget.*
>
>*And accept her blessing true;*
>*divine love, she gave me you.*
>*And the path to walk along,*
>*with you as we sing this song.*
>
>*Our strength is our society,*

it's not you and it's not me.
Let Kaetian light lead the way;
Kaetian rule will save the day.

"Shhh." Asana tugs sharply on my cloak. I must have started to sing out loud.

"Oh, don't be so hard on the child; I often find that rhyme stuck in my head too." From the dark corridor on our right, Laescenno emerges and gives me a playful wink. He puts his hand gently on my shoulder. "Come on Tushenta, sing the rest with me!" His pink, rheumy eyes shine with enthusiasm as he bursts into song and dances down the corridor in his unique rickety way. I daren't join in but smile as I follow him.

"Nothing shall be left to chance.
Respect those who lead the dance.
Understand their judgement fair;
greater good is in the air.

Sacrifice brings freedom close,
for those who devote the most.
With their help we keep alive,
hope that Kaetia will survive."

He breaks from his singing to open the grand double doors for us, bowing reverently as Asana leads the way through, but lifting his head slightly to smile at me as I pass. I grin back at him and follow Asana up the steps to take our place on the thrones at the front of the room. There are six thrones: a monthly reminder of the missing members of our family. We take the central pair and Laescenno resumes his singing.

"Be it less or be it more,
we give thanks for what's in store.
And resist the urge to take,
or to give, with what's at stake."

A man with a face etched into a permanent scowl slaps his hand loudly three times on the table. "Laescenno, that's hardly appropriate behaviour for these chambers."

"Oh, don't worry, Syreme, it's all in Sett's name."

But with three verses and six tenets left, Laescenno abandons his performance.

I'm quietly relieved that I don't have to be scrutinised through the nineteenth tenet, in case I blush, and reveal my secret affection for that tenet's Guardian.

With the lack of ceremony and casual authority only Laescenno can pull off, he flops into the First Seat of the Council, at the far end of the table, directly facing Asana and myself.

I shift nervously as the eyes of the sixteen members of the Council turn on us. All male, all old, all cloaked in red.

Asana picks up the ceremonial blue-cracked-glaze pottery sphere from the arm of her throne and holds it out in front of her for a few moments as it fills with the solemn blessings of Sett. Then she lifts it up into the air and slams it down onto the floor beneath us. A spicy citrus fragrance rises from the broken shards, and Sett's wisdom passes from the Supreme Kaetians through the air to the Council. One by one they sniff and nod as the fragrant wisdom reaches them, and they turn to Laescenno to begin proceedings.

All attention rests on Laescenno as we wait for the mystical scent to reach him. His face is set in reverent composure. His grey eyes are concealed behind his eyelids; the criss-cross pattern in their thin skin shines in the blue, red, and green light dancing through the gem adorned grilles. Around his eyes, the lines grow deeper, darker, and more erratic, revealing two hundred and thirty years of jovial expressions. The skin on his cheeks droops softly, etched with fine vertical lines, and gathers in a sac of uneven pale flesh hanging under his chin.

I raise my hand to my smooth face and wonder how many centuries I have to wait before it has that much character on its surface. I hope I can somehow get approval for my match to Mull'aman before he grows too much older, so we can be ceremonially united, and his life span and aging will mirror mine.

Asana has a saying: 'They grow old in a day and go in the night.' I never understood her fear of aging until now.

Finally, Laescenno twitches his large, pore covered nose, and his eyes burst open. "Ah! Thank you, Sett, for this wonderful blessing."

"You know what came to my mind during that sacred experience?"

He looks around briefly, not actually expecting anyone to venture an answer.

> "Be it less or be it more,
> we give thanks for what's in store.
> And resist the urge to take,
> or to give, with what's at stake."

He looks at me. "Now, Tushenta, I don't know if you remember, when I was a child of about seven, I got the pleasure of meeting you: my whole class did, in fact.

It was a great honour, and we were all so excited to meet a direct representative of Sett in the flesh. It was a bit of a disappointment, when you shuffled in looking more scared of us than we were of you, but you calculated to cover up your poor deportment by bringing with you a small pot of honey.

"The Council had just presented it to you as part of a carefully managed distribution plan, where this scarce resource was assigned according to worth and need, and you got it into your head that the best way to handle this gracious gift, would be to disperse it amongst a gaggle of children, gathered together from all over the Kaetian Compound. You snuck it in and asked us not to tell on you, of course, appealing to a child's desire for secrets, conspiracies, and coteries.

"The chaos this caused for months afterwards! We would nag our teacher, I forget her name, some Greeny, for her to give us something she'd never experienced herself. And any poor visitor we had! We were all over them, trying to find a fix of something sweet. Having set us such a bad example, you never came back, leaving us feeling cheated out of a personal connection to you and robbed of a sweet taste we didn't know was such a rare thing in this world."

I drop my head in shame, fixing my eyes on my hands which I clasp tightly in my lap. I remember that day, it was impossible to forget. Because of my actions, I was never allowed around children again, and I was never given another ration of honey, even before all the bees died.

I also remember Laescenno that day. He'd been first in the queue for the taste of the honey, and had done such a cute funny dance around the courtyard as he savoured the sweetness on his tongue. It had felt so good to watch the children enjoying themselves, that it hurt me all the more when Hyrensus, Laescenno's father, dragged me into the Council Chambers and declared me heretical for giving away what Sett had bestowed upon me. He suggested dismemberment, to see if I could be killed without the Blade of Sett, which would allow Asana to have another child, no doubt with himself lined up as the Council's chosen partner now that Kasaman had been exiled.

As the Guardian of the Sixth Tenet, responsible for arranging matches between couples when they reach a certain age, Hyrensus had originally chosen himself as Asana's best match. My grandparents overturned the engagement in favour of a mortal whose soul had been declared the purest and most beautiful in over a thousand years by all ranking Supreme Kaetians. Such a heretical disregard for the Guardian of the Sixth Tenet was rewarded by the emergence of redwaek in the land, and, as it turned out, Kasaman was completely evil.

I wonder if this was why Hyrensus hated me so much and made such public demonstrations of the evil in my blood. No doubt we'd all have been better off if Asana had obeyed the Council and accepted their partnership. The curse may have *already been lifted.*

Thankfully, Laescenno is much kinder when dealing with my many flaws, even though I have the power that should have been his.

He finishes his lecture on the drier points of the fourteenth tenet. Reth'satar, the Council member to his right looks uncomfortable. He's the Guardian of the Fourteenth Tenet. It is poor manners to trespass into another's area of influence, and a slight on their capabilities. But Laescenno is the Head of the Council, and I get the impression that he's treated like the third Supreme Kaetian in Kasaman's absence, so he rambles on wherever his mind takes him.

There's quiet for a moment, and Syreme opens his mouth to say something, but Laescenno launches into another speech. "I know this will be a bit of a controversial thing to say, especially in these chambers where we have to deal with things in the harsh glare of the Kaetian sun: I honestly believe that you, Tushenta, are a blessing."

I hear the sharp intake of breath from the other members of the Council.

"Tushenta, you give us an opportunity to react to your transgressions, and in doing so, we learn about ourselves and demonstrate to the Blazing Court our dedication to the twenty-one tenets. Asana," he turned to my mother. "you were always so perfect, so diligent and pious. Well, until your insistence on choosing a mortal soul for your partner, a wicked mortal soul, at that. But before then, you personified the Tenets of Sett so well that you made us complacent. Tushenta is shaking us out of our torpor and maybe that's what we need to appease the Blazing Court. The Higher Kaetians have let Kaetia down by not reigning in the wandering notions of one family. Supreme Kaetians, or not, we all must abide by Sett's rules.

"Don't worry, Tushenta, when the time comes, we'll find you a suitable match; someone to temper your impulses. And when you've learned how to be a more obedient Servant of Sett, you can spend more time around people, and you'll need fewer books."

He places his hands on the table and pushes himself to his feet, picks up a book from the table behind him and totters over the tiled floor between the Council table and the thrones.

Looking up at me, he asks: "But you do like books, don't you, Tushenta?"

"Yes, knowledge and exploring Kaetian culture are the only ways we shall move forward and break the curse. The more information we can digest, the better our chances."

Laescenno chuckles and pats the book in his hands. "Well, hopefully this book will help you explore yourself to better our chances. The transcribing was completed last week, and you shall be the first to read it. Your mother helped me write it, so she already knows most of what's in it, but I do hope you both discuss it and share with me what you think."

He walks over to the door. Picking up on the signal, Asana rises from her throne and glides down the steps to meet him.

Laescenno bows deeply. "Thank you, ladies, for your time. We have the authority of Sett, and won't bore you any further. I'm sure you have more important things to attend to."

Asana heads out of the door. I pause by Laescenno, wanting to linger a little longer in the presence of someone who smiles at me. He hands me the book and cups my hands. "Read well, my little bookworm."

I nod as I imagine Asana would nod, and follow her through the door, glancing down at the book in my hand: 'A Treatise on the Supreme Kaetian by Laescenno'.

As the grand double doors are closed behind us, Asana sighs. Imbuing the ceremonial sphere with her essence must be very tiring. She waves vaguely in my direction and informs the Paders: "We shall offer our devotions in the Courtyard."

Great! Just what I need. Staring into running water for an hour or so whilst not being able to drink anything. I also think I need to pee, although I'm not sure I needed to before Asana declared that we were going to pay our devotions.

The Pader guards open the gates to the Courtyard of the Arcane. Asana walks into the centre of the courtyard and turns back to look at me. The sun is setting, and behind her, the three gnarled columns of sandstone rock are silhouettes, casting dramatic red and black shadows over the smooth courtyard floor. The pattern it forms looks like the stripes on the Paders' cloaks.

Asana's gaze flits briefly to the window leading into the Council Chambers before she walks over to the fountain, sinks to her knees, and presses her palms together in front of her devout murmuring lips.

I hand Laescenno's book to the Pader who's carrying my new supply of reading material and traipse over to the fountain. Thousands of years of devotions have left smooth depressions where the knees of the faithful have perched before us. I slot my knees into the grooves and stare into the spluttering water, imagining what it would be like to stick my tongue into the fountain.

I mouth my way through the usual prayers, trying to keep my eyes off my new supply of books. My palms have started to itch, but I force myself not to scratch them; fidgeting during devotions is a serious offence.

Through the window which connects the Council Chambers and the Courtyard of the Arcane, I can hear that the atmosphere has changed a bit since we left. I can't hear everything that's said, just the odd phrase that floats across the Courtyard.

"Heresy? Been a while since we've had one of them."

"Always trouble when we mix the cloaks."

"Ungrateful Greenies."

"From the North side?"

"Dirty."

"Objects to increased rations?"

Suddenly Laescenno's voice carries over the muffled conversations and the sound of the flowing water. "She should be grateful to don a red cloak. Keep an eye on her; if she doesn't alter her attitude, she can wear a black and red cloak."

At this, there's laughter. Asana's eyelids twitch.

I stare at her. Could it be possible that she isn't here out of devotion, and she's eavesdropping? In direct contravention of the second tenet of Sett?

I can feel the evil of Kasaman making connections that shouldn't be made in my mind.

As Asana mouths the words to silent prayers, I start to think that, perhaps she isn't infinitely better than me, she's just better at playing their game. Maybe that's why everything she does seems so perfect, and I fail again and again.

I won't survive if I keep trying to become the person they think I should be.

They'll always find something wrong with me.

It's time I stop believing that lifting the curse is my main objective, and start learning to separate the role they want me to play, from who I really am inside.

18: INTO THE DARK

I slipped quietly through the double doors and sat down on one of the orange plastic chairs at the back of the practice room. I pulled out the jar of honey I'd bought on my way over, unscrewed the lid, dipped my finger into the rich orangey-brown coloured gloop, and savoured the sweet taste. As Mikey's Sugar Swords gyrated and ran around to some gimmicky synthetic pop, I imagined a young Laescenno dancing in the corner.

One of the doors behind me started to wobble, and then slowly opened. A young girl crept through the door, closing it silently behind herself. She waited a few moments before tiptoeing around the edge of the room, until she was stood directly behind Mannie, who was engaged in a discussion with Gems about a dance manoeuvre.

"Look, this is what I mean." Mannie said, taking two steps forward and then two steps back, colliding with the little girl.

"Oh Daxa! Sorry darling. Are you okay?"

Daxa nodded her little head, her long black hair falling over her face. She reached into her pocket and slowly pulled out a daisy chain necklace, holding it up towards Mannie.

"Is this for me?"

Daxa nodded her head more enthusiastically and a shy smile lit up her face.

"Is that about the age your daughter would be?"

I spun round. Chris had sat down next to me.

"I guess." I said shrugging.

"If you ever need to talk about it, I'm here."

Here we go again. I was bobbing in the ripples of the lies I told when I was seventeen and the police delivered me dirty and confused back into my father's possession. I'd burst into tears and told him I'd been pregnant and run away with my imaginary boyfriend, rather than the truth, which was that I'd run scared after overhearing him talking about sending me to the US for 'corrective therapy', and googling what they planned to do to me.

Back then it had saved me from admitting I'd deliberately sabotaged his plan to 'cure' me, and thankfully, he had no interest in chasing down his lost, fictitious granddaughter. What I didn't know was that the lie was a parasite, burrowing out confusing patterns in my mind. Whilst it had to live on to prevent the truth getting back to my father, it also became a useful tool to repel people who didn't want to invest time or energy in a fuck up with issues, an excuse to push people away, and an explanation for my commitment phobia. It had served a purpose, but now it was jumping around with no control, trampling on other people's pain, and sending their shit my way.

I shrugged at Chris. "Probably. It's not like I was a real mother. I made the choice to walk away. You have all these memories of your daughter. You had the experience of her first words, her first steps. You got to know a real little person and she was taken away from you. My situation doesn't compare to that."

Chris was still for a few moments. Then he took off his hat and rubbed at his temples through his bandanna. "I guess it's impossible to know what's going on inside someone else's head." He stood up and headed over to our instruments, which Fus had set up for us in the centre of the room.

The children started to pack up and were draining out of the room, getting louder as they left. Fus settled behind his drums and Chris checked the wires on his bass. I slipped the jar of honey back into my bag and headed over to my keyboard.

As the last of the kids filed through the doors, Tyler slouched in wearing dark sunglasses and holding a cone of chips. Ignoring the fact that we were about to start, he headed to the stage, sat down, pulled a can of coke out of his pocket, and proceeded to eat his lunch at a leisurely pace.

Fus gave him a withering look. "Let's start with Porcupine Fairy." He suggested, and we launched into the song without Tyler. We were halfway through Hands of Helios before he came over, picked up his guitar and began to play. However, his guitar was slightly out of tune, so he dropped back out and started to tune up in the background.

When the song was over, Fus said: "Nice of you to join us, Ty."

"I can't play on an empty stomach, I get dizzy."

Fus sighed. "Well, if you're not too dizzy now, shall we try 'Into the Dark'?"

As the guitar riff for the introduction formed a wall of sound, Mannie started jumping up and down. Chris moved slightly off to one side and out of my eye line. As the drums burst onto the scene, I took my cue to start banging out the theatrical chords. Mannie stopped jumping and threw all her vocal power into the dramatic tune.

A shattered timeline;
    fragments by the side of the road.
Piecing together what was mine;
    what was taken.
        What was owed.

A deviation;
    lines that shift, blur, and decay.
Footsteps in the wrong direction.
    What to hear;
        what to say.

And so we go.
And so we go.
Into the dark, dark, dark, dark.
Into the dark, dark, dark, dark.
Into my heart, heart, heart, heart.
Into my dark heart, dark heart.
Into my dark heart, dark heart.

And so we go.
Into the dark.
    Into the dark.

A survivor's guilt.
    A life that cannot be restored;
a life that cannot be rebuilt.
    Sever the tie.
        Cut the cord.

This profit and loss:
    can it bring back my family?
Lines of callous calculations.
    Death for you;
        but what for me?

And so we go.
And so we go.
Into the dark, dark, dark, dark.
Into the dark, dark, dark, dark.
Into my heart, heart, heart, heart.
Into my dark heart, dark heart.

Into my dark heart, dark heart.

And so we go.
Into the dark.
    Into the dark.

What drives us,
    past where we are willing to go?
Who drives us,
    when we have said no?

What drives us?
Into the dark, dark, dark, dark.
Into the dark, dark, dark, dark.
Into my heart, heart, heart, heart.
Into my dark heart, dark heart.
Into my dark heart, dark heart.

And so we go.
Into the dark.
    Into the dark.

And I am in the dark.
    Faces haunt me from the road.
Events I bury leave their mark.
    What I build,
        they erode.

Memories tell lies,
    of the things I most held dear.
Loosening of former ties.
    What I love,
        and what I fear.

And so we go.
Into the dark.
    Into the dark.

The end of the song felt damp. It was wrong. I didn't know why.
Mannie frowned and walked over to Chris. "Hey hon, are you okay?"
He was pale and a sheen had spread over his face. He looked in Mannie's direction, but didn't seem to focus on her.
"I'm not sure."

"Shall we talk about it in the office?"

He nodded slowly and she led him out through the doors.

"What's up with him?" Tyler asked Fus.

"I don't know, and if he wants us to know, he'll tell us." Fus headed up to the stage and started to tidy up the mess left by Mikey's Sugar Swords.

I walked over to Tyler. "I think I might've said something to upset him, although it seemed to be the song that triggered him."

"Maybe he's had another run in with Mike. It's coming up to the anniversary of the crash, and Mike tends to go overboard with the mea culpas round about now."

"What's Chris got to do with Mike's accident?"

"He was in the car, got knocked up really bad."

"Clearly not as bad as Mike."

"He didn't lose any limbs, if that's what you mean, but he had a really nasty head injury. Fucked up his memory, especially anything to do with his daughter."

I slapped my hand over my mouth, realising why he'd reacted the way he had done.

"And whilst he was recovering, Anna up and left with his kid. The bitch even went through all his things and took every photo he had of Theresa. Chris thinks it was because he had to drop out of his prestigious Oxford history degree and was no longer likely to be the success Anna's family wanted from her future husband. Still, he got off better than Stuart."

"Stuart?"

"Did Becca not tell you anything? Stuart was Chris's cousin who died in the crash. Although it was Stuart who grabbed the steering wheel and caused the crash: so instant karma, really. Stuart and Mike were tormenting Chris because he didn't want to get in the car with them, but they insisted on driving him to the station after his aunt's funeral, even though they were in no fit state to drive."

"Oh no! Becca never mentioned any of this. I knew Mike was in prison when I met her, but I always assumed he was alone in the car. I didn't realise someone had died."

"On the plus side, Chris's uncle took him in, and when he died a year later, Chris inherited the Acres."

"Hey! You know, instead of gossiping, you two could help me tidy up this mess." Fus shouted from the stage.

Tyler mouthed "Anal." at me and we headed over to the stage.

Fus passed me a box. "Kerella, could you please fill this with any recyclables you can find?" Turning to Tyler and handing him a black bag, "Ty, fill this with any non-recyclables, thanks."

Whilst we got on with our litter picking, Fus went over to the storage cupboard. He returned with a step ladder and climbed up to fix the curtain, which was hanging loosely where it'd been pulled off a hook.

"Hey, Ker!" Tyler called over to me, "Why don't you come over for dinner tonight? Chris could use a distraction from all his paperwork, and you can save me from the boredom of being in a house with no games console. I mean, what kind of uncultured hell hole has no console?"

"Sounds good." I made a mental note to pick up a console in case Tyler ever came to my flat.

Chris and Mannie returned. They slowly walked back to the instruments.

"Seriously, we can leave 'Into the Dark' out, if that'd help." Mannie said.

"No! You can't do that!" Tyler yelled out from the stage. "It's our strongest song, and I've worked really hard on the introduction!"

"It's okay, Mannie. I think you've helped." Chris tapped Mannie's shoulder.

"Speaking of helping, I've invited Kerella over for dinner." Tyler called out as he walked down the steps.

"And what will you be cooking?" Chris asked.

"I thought you could cook that minty-limey-quinoa dish you made last month?"

"Oh, you did, did you?" Chris shook his head and picked up his bass. "Mannie, Fus, would you like to join us? It's the least I can do."

"Sorry, we already have plans tonight, but do feel free to give me the recipe, it sounds delicious."

"Of course, Mannie." Chris said with a half-smile and a tip of his head.

Tyler returned to his guitar and started picking out the introduction to Diametric Destiny. "When you guys have finished your love-in-athon, we have songs that need attention."

I saw Mannie wink in Chris's direction, and we delved into the twisted logic of Tyler's masterpiece.

19: REVERBERATE

Three sparrows pecked at the seed scattered on the bird table. The trickle of the irrigation system watering the plants throughout The Acres merged into the buzz of insects. It hadn't rained for over two weeks and the heat was pressing in. I finished setting up the patio table for dinner and wandered back through Chris's house to the kitchen.

Tyler looked up from his chopping and smiled at me, his vibrant green eyes shining. "Kerella, I was thinking that after dinner I'd take Tris for a nice long walk. If I head along the coastal path towards town, do you want to join me? Save you getting a taxi."

"I'd like that, thanks."

He added the last of the tomatoes to the salad bowl and threw the knife into the washing up bowl. The frothy water flew up and splashed Chris.

"Thanks Ty."

"Sorry mate."

"Any chance you could head over to the café garden and grab me some sage, oregano, and mint? Just a handful of each will be fine."

"Really? There's no way we'll be able to taste all of those."

"And this is why you ask me to cook. Of course, you're welcome to cook your famous tin of tomatoes with dried oregano, but I won't let you call it arrabiata sauce in front of our guest."

"Kerella! Come on!" Tyler said, grabbing his phone off the black marble countertop and heading out of the door.

We walked through The Acres towards the café.

Tyler tugged playfully at my long hair. "So, are you a natural blonde?"

"Yes."

"Hmm." He stood to one side to allow me to cross the ornamental humpbacked bridge, then followed behind me and asked: "How did you get that scar on your cheek?"

I covered my cheek with my hand and let my hair fall over my face. I walked slightly off the main redbrick path and stared into a display of lavender plants.

He came up beside me and slipped his hand over mine, worming his finger underneath my palm and slowly moving my hand away from my face.

I looked at my feet as he ran his finger down my scar.

"It got cut on broken glass the night my mother died falling out of a window." I forced out, pushing his hand away and covering my cheek again.

"Shhh." He said quietly, "Don't hide it; it's beautiful."

His face lingered close to mine and I thought he was going to kiss me.

Suddenly, he walked off, up the steps to the café and through a tall green wooden gate with a staff only sign nailed onto it. He left the gate open behind him.

After a few moments, I followed.

The garden was bigger than I'd expected. Backing onto the café was a long greenhouse, next to this, was a green shed. A slate sign hung next to the shed door on which 'Nick's Office' was written in chalk pen; the door was protected with a large padlock. Rows of raised wooden beds contained a variety of vegetables. At the back, fruit trees and bushes backed onto the red wall which ran around the perimeter of The Acres.

Tyler was in the heart of the herb section, trying to locate the plants he needed.

I walked over and ran my hands up a branch of rosemary, bringing my fingers to my nose to inhale the spicy scent.

"Wow, if the apocalypse comes, Chris'll be well fed." I said.

Tyler began tackling the sage bush. "It's been a bit of a project of his. It was only finished last year. I think it comes from growing up a poor city kid, or maybe that story he tells about his daughter in the garden. I thought he was off his rocker, but it's actually been really popular. The café's gone from a pointless hut serving chips and sandwiches, to somewhere old ladies 'do lunch'."

He finished harvesting the herbs and looked at me with an intense focus. "Crazy ideas sometimes pay off."

We headed back through the green gate. "Speaking of crazy ideas which may pay off: I've started writing a graphic novel. It's very early days. I began getting loads of ideas a couple of weeks ago, and I'm still trying to wrangle them into some kind of shape. The working title is 'Reverberate', or 'Reverb'. It's about a musician taking on a corrupt political elite with his super sexy, dark haired, backing singer and muse. By day, they change culture through their music, and by night, they foil evil plans and uncover political lies." He paused before adding: "I wanted to ask your permission to give the backing singer your scar?"

I turned my back on him as I crossed the bridge, a rock sinking in my stomach. That was an intimacy too far, even for my earthly Mull'aman.

Knowing I was risking all I'd been hoping for, I answered without looking behind me. "I'm really not comfortable with that. But the comic sounds fun. Although 'sexy sidekick'? Why not make them equal partners?"

"Because he's the main character, it's all about him. She's just there to bounce the story off. And it's a graphic novel, not a comic." He sounded stroppy.

"Sorry. I'd really love to see it. It's a great idea."

He seemed appeased.

"I'll show you a few sketches after dinner. I'd show you my earlier work, but that's still at Kat's. I've a whole shelf full of notebooks I filled during lectures. They're a goldmine of ideas."

"If you need help picking your stuff up, just ask."

"It's not that important right now."

He opened the door to Chris's house, put his finger to his lips, and mouthed: "Hey, take a look at this." He led me past the stairs and opened the door to the dining room. "Welcome to Chris's den of obsession. All he's missing is a wall of crazy, bits of red wool forming a web, and stalker photos."

There were notes spread all over the dining room table. I picked up the nearest piece of paper to me. On it was writing in several different languages which finished with a list of names: 'Demetrius, Giovanni, Veronica, Katherine?'

I put the sheet carefully back where I found it and cast my eye over the rest. Amongst the foreign scribblings and weird symbols, were some pen and ink drawings, most of them of a dark-haired young girl with wide, innocent eyes. If that were his daughter, it looked nothing like me when I was younger.

On the piano in the corner were piles of books on topics ranging from 'Leonardo da Vinci' and 'The Fall of Constantinople', to 'Discovering Past Lives' and 'The History of Tarot.'

Sheets of paper were all over the floor next to the printer. I walked over and stared down at holiday rentals in Milan, newspaper articles from five years ago, documents on the Hagia Sophia, and print outs from a Greek Myths website.

It hit me how my flat must've looked the day my father walked in and saw my notes on Kaetia. This looked crazy enough, and Chris was researching things that existed. My floor had been full of things that weren't even real.

And then it hit me.

They
Weren't
Even
Real.

And I knew it.

Maybe it was time to grow up and leave the madness behind before I started creating my own wall of crazy.

"What's he doing?" I whispered.

Tyler shrugged. "To start with I thought he was trying to piece together what happened in the couple of years before his accident. Maybe find a new lead on Theresa. He seemed to get focussed on Milan and Istanbul, so perhaps she was taken abroad? But then he was looking at dates back to the fifteenth century, so who bloody knows? And Kat has nothing to do with his daughter." he said picking up a drawing of an attractive woman of East Asian appearance and waving it at me. "She didn't know him back then."

He thrust the drawing back on the table and we snuck out of the room and returned to the kitchen.

"Ah, thanks, guys." Chris said, taking the herbs off Tyler. He tossed the herbs in a colander and rinsed them under the tap. "Ty, could you fish out that bottle of Sauvignon Blanc from the fridge and pour three glasses for us?"

Tyler retrieved three wine glasses from the cupboard, the bottle from the fridge, and poured the wine. "Any news from Nick?" He asked.

"I told you earlier: Elsie passed away this afternoon." Chris said, throwing the chopped herbs into the frying pan and stirring them into the quinoa. "I'm going over there tomorrow to help him sort a few things out. Could you hang about here, so if any of the staff have a problem, you can call me to let me know?"

"Of course. Pass on my condolences to Nick." Tyler said as he got three bowls out and lined them up on the counter.

Chris distributed the quinoa, we each took a bowl, and filed out of the kitchen. As we walked through the lounge, Tris jumped down from the settee and followed us out to the patio.

Sitting down at the patio table, I took a taste of the quinoa. Chris was right, the combination of herbs really gave the dish an earthy depth, and with the lime, it was the perfect zingy dish for an evening like this.

"I can't believe the gig's only a week away." Chris said, as he gently tossed a tennis ball across the lawn for Tris to trot after.

"I hope the weather breaks before then. I don't want the smell of sweat to be the one thing people remember from the night." Tyler replied.

"I doubt that." I said. "They'll be too blown away by your amazing music to even notice the smell."

"I think you mean 'our' music?" Chris said.

"'Our' music." I corrected.

Tyler's klaxon ringtone split the air. He slipped his phone out of his pocket and headed to the other side of the garden before answering it. He kept his back to us throughout the phone call.

When he returned, he ate with diminished enthusiasm. Eventually throwing his fork down into a half empty bowl. He pushed himself back from the patio table. "I best go finish that blog post. Gotta keep pushing the gig! Kerella, check it out: it'll all be about you tonight. See you Monday, molasses."

He disappeared into the house.

Chris shook his head. "Don't worry, you'll get used to the winds of Ty. He blows one direction, and then he blows another."

"He seems changeable." I added quietly, taking my final bite of quinoa, and pushing the bowl to one side.

"He just gets caught up in things and forgets what he was doing from one minute to the next. He's harmless, you just have to keep your head when you're around him." He stacked the bowls. "I guess that means I get the pleasure of an evening stroll with you?"

"His loss, my gain." I smiled at Chris, hiding my hurt. I gathered up the glasses and followed him into the kitchen.

I discretely pulled my phone out and faked a text alert. I pretended to read it whilst Chris filled up the dishwasher.

"Oh! Becca's going to be passing in the next few minutes. She says if I head to the end of the road, she'll pick me up. Thanks for the lovely food; Tyler was right, you're a great cook. Sorry, gotta rush. See you Monday!"

I grabbed my bag from the settee and ran through The Acres, over the carpark, and then cut across the field which would connect me with the coastal path.

I shot off a text to Becca telling her Chris had weirded me out, so I walked home, but told him she picked me up, to make sure she didn't contradict my story. Still, I couldn't shake the feeling that Chris would know.

I shook my head. Did I want a wall of crazy? Of course, Chris wouldn't know. He wasn't Kasaman with magical powers of perception: Kasaman wasn't real.

I felt his eyes on me as I ran towards the sea. I joined the coastal path and continued at a brisk pace until I came to my secret ledge. I clambered over the rocks and slumped back, recovering from the exertion.

I was angry with myself. Had I not decided, less than an hour ago, that I was going to let this foolishness end? Maybe more drastic measures were needed. I thought back to what Chris had said about the Casa Martyrs. Maybe I had to make a sacrifice to really find my home. Deciding to give up the Kaetian fantasy was one thing, actively destroying it would really show my subconscious that I was ready to move on.

I looked out over the sea. What was I willing to sacrifice to find peace?

20: BEETROOT

I read Mull'aman's words for the last time, taking every flourished pen stroke to heart. The wind has finally picked up and the time to let go has arrived. I tear the page into pieces and slip the first fragments through the grille, just to the right of Sett's sapphire blue cloak. Over the next hour, I slowly feed all the pieces into the breeze. Finally, Mull'aman's words are gone, and we are safe. No one will ever find the correspondence that will condemn us, but I remember every word, every devout promise, every flowery compliment, and all his brutally honest secrets.

He has not held back during the exchange we've been secretly conducting during rehearsals; billowing cloaks and loud crescendos have their uses.

I know that his mother was declared a heretic after being killed in a redwaek attack on the town. She was found to have been illegally redistributing vital Kaetian resources to Merdiants for personal gain. I understand Heshrik's sadness and early retirement a little better now. Such a shame would have been hard to live with: her actions will have extended the curse and affected us all. I remember the music he played in the last few years we worked together. The sound was so sad. I had no idea. I wish I'd known, although I understand why this knowledge was held back from me.

Mull'aman says I've inspired him to give up the red weed. He'd turned to it to cope with the scrutiny of growing up the son of a heretic and traitor. He knows this is a shadow of what I must have experienced as Kasaman's daughter, but it gives him some insight into what it feels like to know everyone is judging me all the time.

The thing that worries me the most is, he has told me of his involvement with a secret group which likes to share old scraps of paper and items which have been passed down through the generations. They call themselves 'The Historians', after the quaint lower realm pastime of collecting old objects and telling stories about them.

I will admit, my first thought was I should report Mull'aman to the Council. Surely such activities are in direct contravention of the second tenet of Sett, which strictly rules out seeking information which has not been distributed by the Council. What if these artefacts contain lies, or fantastical dreams presented as truth? What if some poor individual receives a fake relic as a joke and believes they've received a message directly from Sett? Who can control such a haphazard spread of misinformation? There's a reason Sett explicitly decreed the Librarians should have the responsibility for archiving all information, and the Council should be responsible for its dissemination. The spread of fake ideas could condemn us all to an eternity of the curse, or hurt people in other ways, by sowing discord and tearing families apart.

I would not participate in anything that could bring harm to any of my subjects, and I passed my misgivings onto Mull'aman in a missive, rather than reporting him to the Council. His next message, hidden amongst the provisional lyrics for the opening number, said he would show me why the Historians were necessary, if I'd just give him a list of the books I'd been allocated this month.

I made some revisions to the lyrics. I held back on the changes more than I'd have liked. Although I was officially the head of the musical side of the Celebration of Kaetian Society, I'd noticed that Mull'aman was sensitive of people encroaching on his tenet's domain and preferred to have his vision for the Celebrations accepted without challenge. However, I also have a responsibility to Kaetian society to ensure the Celebrations, as the annual apex of our collective attempt to lift the curse, are as powerful as they can be. Mull'aman's quirky approach to Kaetian grammar, while endearing on a personal level, won't pass in a formal setting. I returned the manuscript with a two-page letter explaining my changes. Within these notes I referred to the books I'd been given this month. I passed this to him at the last rehearsal. During the exchange he handed me a letter where he first made explicit his feelings for me, and I've been floating ever since.

I watch the last pieces of Mull'aman's letter disappear from view and sit down at the small table to eat the salad the Lower Kaetians of the North Side have prepared for me. It's a nutritious dish of root vegetables and beans, floating in a red puddle of flavoured beetroot juice. I eat most of it but keep pushing the beetroot to the edge of my plate. I dislike its musty scent; it feels wrong that something that smells like it's mouldy, is edible.

Just as I'm about to put the first slice of beetroot in my mouth, there's a light tapping on the door. I put my fork down. No one ever comes to my door unexpected, except occasionally Asana, but her knocks aren't dainty. I rise to my feet, smooth my hair down and grab my cloak from the bed. Could Mull'aman have possibly *found an excuse to come to see me in private?*

I open the door to a Lower Kaetian wearing a triangle brooch with the point at the bottom, indicating she's from the West side. I recognise her from rehearsals; Mull'aman gives her more responsibilities than someone with her musical proficiency deserves, but she seems an assertive young lady, and Mull'aman has a kind heart and finds it hard to say no.

She smiles at me, a smile that takes up most of her face, yet feels more ornamental than an expression of conviviality. A long strand of blonde hair has worked its way out of her hood, but she seems too distracted to tuck it back; instead, she flicks it away with her hand every few moments.

"Mull'aman asked me to deliver this to you, Our Supreme Kaetian, Tushenta." She dips into a rather paltry curtsy, which is undermined by the gleam in her eyes as she mentions Mull'aman's name. The poor girl has no idea she doesn't stand a chance, no matter how many errands she runs for him.

I take the parcel from her, nod vaguely, and give her a dismissing wave of my hand, hoping that's how I'm supposed to behave in these circumstances. I take a quick look to see which Pader is on guard. It's Melingad, so the Council will be aware of this unorthodox transaction in no time. I give the parcel the tempered look I've been practicing and retreat into my room, leaving the door ajar. I place the parcel at the foot of my bed and return to my lunch, slowly leafing through a book on the Scouts of Kaetia. In the corner of my eye, I can see Melingad observe my actions for a few moments before she quietly closes the door.

I place my fork back on the wooden plate and tiptoe over to the bed. Throwing myself onto the sheets, I make myself a little nest and pick up the parcel. It's wrapped in red fabric, tied together with dark blue twine, and fixed with the wax seal of the Celebration of Kaetian Society. Thankfully, the secrecy and hype around the Celebrations accord the planners some privacy and mystery, yet Mull'aman is taking a risk.

I carefully break the wax seal, examining it for signs of tampering, before slipping out the revised plans and two slim books. One book is incredibly old and almost falling apart, the other is well read, but not yet disintegrating. They are both copies of 'The Castes of the Lower Kaetians' and are exactly like the one on my table, although much older. I flick through the pages of the oldest one, wondering if Kasaman had held this very book.

Finally seeing the old objects Mull'aman was making such a fuss about, I feel much calmer. I can see that the Historians are just harmless and misguided. If all they do is share benign information like this, which had already been approved for dissemination by past Kaetian Councils, what damage to our society could they do?

I carefully turn the pages of the oldest book, admiring the ancient penmanship.

Writing was more ornate back then. I pause at a rations table that doesn't look quite right. I jump up and fetch my copy of the book. Either I've remembered it incorrectly, or there was an error when the Librarians were transcribing the new copies, as the guidelines for the Lower Kaetian rations are much higher in the oldest book.

With all three books open at the same rations table, I see that it's neither my faulty memory, nor a mistake. With each reproduction of the book, the Lower Kaetian rations have been reduced by exactly the same amount. I leaf through the pages to see if I can find other discrepancies. In the oldest book, The Lower Kaetians were represented on the Council, and there were no rules preventing women from taking on leadership roles; in the second copy, only men were eligible to represent our society, and by the latest version, only male Higher Kaetians.

Then I realise that these books must be fakes. There's no way the Librarians would alter the rules laid out by Sett in such a drastic manner: that would make the curse impossible to break. Unfortunately, I'm back to the quandary of whether to report Mull'aman and concerns about how dangerous the Historians are.

Trying to decide what I should do, I turn another page and my heart stops. Right in front of me, in sepia and off-colour white, is a drawing of the decorative ponds in the gardens and a footnote saying that the ponds originally contained golden fish that survived the curse, but once these died, the ponds were retained, so when the Higher Kaetians visited the gardens, there was something pleasant to look at. They're described as reflecting the glory of Sett.

I reach for my copy and open it at the same section. The text states how Sett decreed that all elements of the garden should be functional, and the illustration shows the tiered herb bed established by Sett herself.

I've never mentioned my false memories to anyone! How could this cult of Historians be playing such a horrendous joke on me? Unless it really is the Librarians who can't be trusted to accurately store and preserve the knowledge of Kaetia?

I throw myself back onto the bed. I think about all the new books I'd been so excited to lay my hands on, even if it was a book I'd read before. That feeling of holding a newly transcribed book, the smell of it, the feel of the stiff, thick pages. How, sometimes, I felt so stupid when I read it, because I'd remembered what was in the book so badly. But what if over time, the Librarians had been changing the texts? Does the Council know? Does Asana know? Is it one rogue Librarian, or are they all in it together?

I feel like I can trust no one.

Except Mull'aman.

He has risked so much to show me the truth. He could be tortured, expelled, or executed for such an act of heresy. But what is heresy if the true word of Sett has been distorted? Is it heresy against Sett, or heresy against the Council, or the Librarians' false version of the Word of Sett? How can we ever triumph at the Blazing Court when something as simple as the truth has become something those in power can make up as they go along?

Mull'aman.

He's the only person I can trust. I must speak to him: truly speak to him, not drip feed words in codes and whispers. He's the only one who has never lied to me. With his beautiful green eyes and sweet grin, the way his forehead creases in the middle when he's thinking. I rub my hands over the sheets as I think about how, in this harsh world of heat and lies, I have found him and he has been brave enough to, not only reach out to me, but rip the blindfold from my eyes.

Everything I think I know is shifting around me. The only thing that remains constant is that I need Mull'aman. He warned me about power games that no one had ever mentioned to me before. He's been honest with me like no one else has ever been in my whole life. He promised he'd help me before I even knew I needed help.

Mull'aman.

There's a rehearsal tomorrow.

I get to see him tomorrow.

I stroke the sheets, feeling my palms grow warm. I hear the crackle of my excitement as I think of him. I feel the fire of my passion pulsing through me. I move my hand over to my leg, and a searing heat scalds my thigh.

I sit bolt upright and stare in shock at the scorch marks where I've been rubbing my hands over the sheets; a blue light is dancing across my palms.

Oh no!

I stare at the sheets and the burn marks that will betray me.

Once a Supreme Kaetian sparks, the Council has twenty-two days to announce the partner they've chosen for them and to arrange for the new couple to 'walk in the lower realm'. There's a ritual which will erase their memories and send them to be born as lower realm mortals. They'll live full lives in the lower realm, so they can better understand the people they'll be judging, prove their love for each other, and reveal their true character.

I'm not ready.

Once the marks on the sheets are seen, the Council will marry me off to someone they choose. What if they don't understand the connection Mull'aman and I have? I'd planned to lay the groundwork with the successful delivery of the musical side of the Celebrations, to prove what a great team we made, and show how our partnership would be in Kaetia's greater interests.

I clamber out of bed, go over to my cloak, and unpin my brooch. I could stab it into my wrist and cover the sheets with blood. That way, they'll think it's my period, and I'll be safe. I hold the pin over my skin, but I can't puncture my flesh. Then I realise the Paders know my cycle and I'm not due for two weeks.

I look at the beetroot on my plate, sitting in that horrid smelling red putrefaction. I hide the old versions of the Lower Kaetian book in my cloak, and rewrap the manuscript Mull'aman sent, puffing up the package, so the size is about the same as when that Lower Kaetian girl handed it to me. Then I take my lunch to the bed and let out a little shriek as I 'accidentally' spill the contents all over my sheets. As expected, Melingad comes rushing in.

"You really will do anything to avoid eating beetroot won't you?" She says, giving me a disapproving look before heading down the stairs to fetch someone to clean up the mess.

Okay, I'm breaking the third tenet by not eating everything I've been allocated, but something bigger is going on here. I must protect my future with Mull'aman.

At the thought of him, my palms start to spark again. I take a deep breath and try to calm myself. Hiding this is going to take some work.

I sit down at the table and try to remain calm. I fill my mind by reading 'The Scouts of Kaetia' whilst my sheets are changed. The sweet Lower Kaetian finishes the job with a scattering of nervous curtsies before running off, and I'm alone again.

I sit on the floor, carefully away from anything that could get scorched or ignite. I must admit I'm excited. If an unseasoned mortal were here right now, I could send out my light and know everything about that person, and if I judge that person worthy and useful to Kaetia, through a process called Phronesis, I could strengthen that person's spiritual essence, so they'd survive in our world. This is the whole reason for my existence.

I open my palm and will the blue light to flow.

Nothing.

I don't know whether I'm relieved or disappointed. At least it'll be easier to hide if it's only going to happen once or twice a day.

I can't wait to tell Mull'aman; he'll know what to do. At the thought of Mull'aman, the blue light audibly crackles across my palms. Hmmm. So that seems to be the trigger. It'll be hard not to think of Mull'aman during rehearsals whilst he's right next to me. At that thought, a blue light shoots across the room, nearly as far as the bed.

I spend most of the night practicing thinking of Mull'aman and not sparking. I find wrapping a piece of fabric around my hand and clenching my fist works well, but that'll be of no use whilst I'm playing the Elovetta. Finally, I discover that if I conjure up the image of Laescenno in my mind, that seems to calm the light down.

I imagine the different ways I'll tell Mull'aman. I want it to be perfect, as it'll *be the moment he knows that, within a month, we'll officially be together. We may even be walking in the lower realm, proving our love is genuine.*

By the time the morning comes, I feel as though I can get through rehearsal without betraying my status as a soon-to-be-fully-fledged ranking Supreme Kaetian.

21: BETROTHAL

I slip the Historians' books into the secret pocket I've fashioned at the back of my gown for the purpose of smuggling my correspondence with Mull'aman. I pull on my cloak and take time to arrange my hood, carefully pushing back my dark brown hair. An odd thought hits me: what if Mull'aman likes that Lower Kaetian's long blonde hair and large smile more than he likes my features? Although I can't imagine Mull'aman wanting to marry someone from a Lower Kaetian background, I can imagine the relaxed scrutiny of such a pairing would have an appeal.

My palms start to spark again, so I fix my mind on Laescenno's neck, the way the skin hangs loosely under his chin.

I follow a Pader I've not seen before to rehearsals. She looks quite young and a bit nervous. Her face is painted plain yellow, showing she has not been tested in battle and is yet to claim her first kill.

She opens the doors to the practice room. The noise isn't right. The usual cacophony of people tuning their instruments, singing, talking, and furniture being dragged across the stone floor, has a brittle quality, like something is about to break.

One of the two lower realm mortals Mull'aman chose to perform with us, as a symbol of our united society, is screaming in her own language. I look around the chaos in the room. Some people are tuning their instruments as normal. Some are crying, some are sat staring into space. No one is making a scene like the lower realm mortal. They're so undisciplined. I hope I'll have more self control when I'm walking among them.

I use the disruption to pretend to check the elovetta's tuning, whilst carefully slipping the books from the back of my dress into the secret compartment Mull'aman and I have been using for our exchanges.

The lower realm girl is still screaming, so I look around for the other lower realm mortal to ask him if he'd translate for me. I like him; he plays very unusual but soothing music.

I see Mull'aman standing by the pretty Lower Kaetian having a serious conversation. I head over to them.

"What's going on?"

"Ling's been executed." Mull'aman said, looking at his feet. "He was found with the written word, and it wasn't in Kaetian. I think he was translating our music into his own system, but the Paders wouldn't have known that. I wish they'd consulted me before they acted, yet the rules are clear."

"Rules?" The lower realm girl screams at us. "Rules? Do you have any idea who Ling was? You stupid cosplay fantasy rejects!"

Mull'aman walks over to her and takes her hand, leading her to a chair and sitting her down. He sits down next to her. "Birgitta, you must calm down; you know it isn't safe to display your lower realm passions in this setting."

She sucks in her breath and thrusts out her chin. Her hair is arranged in a strange lower realm fashion under the hood of her brown cloak, causing it to jut out on either side of her head.

She cries silently. Her anger doesn't look like it's abating, and I'm worried her eyes may pop out of her head.

Mull'aman gently pats her hand. "I know you and Ling were close but dying for his memory will achieve nothing. You must think about your future."

She lets out her breath in a long noisy stream and looks like she's calming down. I'm so impressed that Mull'aman can control a lower realm mortal with so few words. I feel compelled to have a go myself.

I pull a chair over and sit at the other side of her.

"Did you know Ling from the lower realm?" I asked.

She looked at me confused. "He was Chinese."

"I'm sorry, I don't know what that means. Were you in different castes?"

"He was from China. I lived in Denmark."

"So, you didn't mix when you were on your earth?"

"No, we did not mix! He was almost on the other side of the fucking globe!"

What she's saying makes little sense to me; she doesn't speak Kaetian very well. "Still, it must've been nice to hear your own language. I can see why you'll miss him."

"He was Chinese, I'm Danish."

Mull'aman gives me a discrete shake of his head. I guess she's in such a state that she isn't making sense.

"He died at Tiananmen Square, you know?"

"Is that the lower realm concert hall?" I asked.

"He died protesting for basic rights, and then you freaks kill him again for having a piece of fucking paper with music on it you asked him to fucking write. What did we do so wrong that we ended up in hell?"

"No, this isn't hell. You're lucky: you were chosen to come to Kaetia." I correct her.

She fixes me with her puffy, red eyes. "You're, like, 'God', right? Aren't you supposed to know everything? How are you so fucking stupid? This is hell. Hell! Hell! Hell! There's no joy, no animals, no relief: just heat and pain and torture." She has started to raise her voice again, and Mull'aman's hand on her arm isn't having a calming effect any longer.

She jumps up and points her finger at me. "You have the power; you have to change this place. It's your fault. You torture us, starve us, eat us like we're meat, and then force us to sing about your glory. Well, I've had enough!"

She lunges at me, and I raise my hands to protect myself. Out of nowhere, my new Pader guard jumps down and slices through Birgitta's neck with her long pale sword. I feel the hot splatter of blood across my face. The head rolls and comes to a stop by my feet.

A blue light crackles across Birgitta's face.

The room is silent for a few moments before the rest of the musicians react. There's a suppressed scream and some muffled sobs, before one of the Lower Kaetian vocalists breaks into the traditional coming of age song to welcome the Supreme Kaetian to their new status. A song which hasn't been needed for over five hundred years since Asana first sparked.

Others start to join in with the ugly, inappropriate song, until Mull'aman signals them to stop, and the background noise returns to a suitable din to frame my disturbed state.

"Don't move." Mull'aman says.

He uses his cloak to remove the blood from around my mouth and eyes. I look into his green eyes and say as quietly as I can. "I sparked."

"I saw." He nods.

I burst into tears and thrust my face into my hands, struggling as hard as I can to regain my composure.

I hear the scuttle of a Pader patrol coming down the corridor.

I grab the edge of my cloak and rub it over my face. Putting on my stone mask, I stand up tall and aloof, as though death cannot touch me.

The Paders burst through the practice room doors and, with military efficiency, remove Birgitta's body. As they're leaving, they instruct the musicians to pack up, informing them rehearsal is cancelled for today.

Amidst the chaos, Syreme has entered the room.

He slowly claps. "Well, Mull'aman, you certainly know how to control a group of people planning a party. I hope you now see how ridiculous your idea of including lower realm mortals in your little ensemble was?"

"What do you want, Syreme?"

"I've come to deliver the Council's verdict."

Mull'aman stands up and clenches his fists at his sides. "Now is not the time."

"Well, rehearsal has been cancelled; now seems the perfect time."

"Okay, let's go outside."

"Here will be fine; it won't take long." Said Syreme, waving his hand through the air.

"No…"

Syreme cut Mull'aman off. He's the Guardian of the Fourth Tenet and commands a lot more authority than Mull'aman.

"The Council has reviewed your accusations of heresy against your fiancée and has decided that, although her expression of discontent about the distribution of rations to the Lower Kaetians was misguided, it was more out of concern for her elderly parents, rather than an attack on the Kaetian system. Your union will proceed as planned, and the Council has decided it will make an excellent finale for the Celebration of Kaetian Society. A merger between a red and green cloak is always a good opportunity to bring Kaetian society closer."

Syreme gives Mull'aman a smug smile, and then his hard brown eyes land on me. Although my heart feels like it's being wrenched through my lower body with a hook, I paste a passive look on my face. "The Council will be most excited to hear the news of your condition, Our Supreme Kaetian, Tushenta. Maybe the romantic celebrations will be two-fold this year." He gives me a sharp nod, before following his Pader escorts through the door.

I stare at the blonde Lower Kaetian. From the look on her face, she's not the fiancée Syreme was talking about.

I sink deep into my reserves and wave my hand nonchalantly. "This has nothing to do with me." I declare and indicate to my Pader guard we're leaving.

Mull'aman moves to grab my arm, but the young Pader gets between us. I hear the pretty Lower Kaetian hissing angrily at Mull'aman. "I gave you something precious, and all the time you've been lying to me."

She will learn soon enough that everyone will lie to her. Mull'aman will find her precious books in the elovetta and return them to her, but neither of us will get those beautiful, deceitful green eyes.

Mull'aman runs up to me as I reach the door. He waves a sheet of blood-stained manuscript paper at me. "I've made some changes, Our Supreme Kaetian, Tushenta. Please could you consider them and let me know your thoughts."

I brush him away. "We can talk about it at the next rehearsal, I've other things that require my attention right now." *And in a cool manner that would make Asana look like a West side nurse maid, I glide down the corridor on the rails of my rage.*

The Council is in charge. They have access to all the information and control it to protect us against ourselves.

I fell prey to misinformation, and it will not happen again.

At least now I know Mull'aman's silly artefacts are fakes, and he cannot be trusted.

The time has come to let this delusion die.

22: THE FACELESS KEYBOARDIST

So much for burning Kaetia on the bonfire of my subconscious so I could move forward with Tyler. I wished my brain would behave. Now I was pissed off with Tyler for something that wasn't even his fault.

I rolled over and grabbed my phone. There was an email telling me the console I'd ordered was going to be delivered today, and a text from Becca telling me she was coming to mine for lunch. I hoped she'd be happy with stale bread and waxy cheese, as I didn't have much else in my kitchen.

I dragged myself out of bed, showered, and settled down on the settee with my tablet to see if Tyler had finally got around to doing the blog post about me. I hit refresh and the photo of me giving him the middle finger came up. I cringed at the weird droop of my lower lip, but the wind was blowing my hair over my face, so it wasn't obvious who I was. The caption under the photo read 'The Casa Martyrs will be performing on Saturday with their new keyboardist'. There was no mention of my name. I guess with my reputation, I can't blame them for not wanting to make a big thing about who I was.

The rest of the post was about Tyler's work on some new material, and how he was looking forward to 'holding his guitar up next to Jenny and settling once and for all who is the better musician'. There was already a comment from Jenny which read: "If last night is anything to go by, I don't think there's going to be much competition. You may as well just admit defeat now!"

I did an online search for Angel Waste. The band banner photo on their website contained one female; she had long, ingot-smooth, dark red hair, and was leaning forward in a tight black dress, which drew attention to her full, perfect breasts. She was sticking her pierced tongue out suggestively at the camera.

Compared to the unflattering photo Tyler had posted of me on his blog, I can see why Jenny was getting his attention.

The intercom went and I absent-mindedly retrieved the console I'd bought so when Tyler came over, he'd see we had things in common. The image of Jenny and Tyler bonding over the gaming experience flitted through my mind, so I threw the box, unopened, into the hall cupboard.

I went over to the keyboard and started to play how I was feeling. I'm not very good at experiencing my emotions the way I think normal people do, but I find creating musical patterns and writing songs helps me get to grips with what's going on inside. Sometimes, I feel my fingers lead me to where my head should be at. Sometimes, I think they know things that even normal people wouldn't be able to piece together.

Today my fingers danced over the keys in prophecies: they warned of anger, betrayal, and rejection. The dark was coming home, and I would choose my sacrifice. Maybe I was still working through some residual anger from the dream, but I felt a destructive force running through me and the feeling of control this gave me was exhilarating. It felt like a power that would…

Buzz through my head like Becca interrupting my thoughts.

I let her in, and she thrust a brown paper bag at me as she came through the door.

"Brie, salad, olive, and houmous baguette." She said.

"Seriously?"

"You think I'd entrust you with lunch? You'd probably try to serve me jam on cheese. I know you couldn't keep a stuffed toy alive." She walked past me and threw herself onto the settee.

"Luckily for us, you're not that complex." I shot back at her, as I pounced on my unexpected treat.

"Do you know this 'Jenny' that plays with Angel Waste?" I asked her, sitting down.

"Yeah." She said biting into her ham and cheddar baguette, dripping mustard onto her sap green vest top. "Total slut. Not too bad at the guitar though."

"Do you think she's prettier than me?"

Becca slapped her baguette down on the table. "Oh shit, I never thought." She wiped the mustard from her top and stuck her finger in her mouth. "Look, Ker, Martin tried to rape you: that's not the kind of guy you want to get fixated on. He and Jenny may have an on-again, off-again thing, but that has nothing to do with you. And if that bastard pulls any more misogynist crap, or tries to stick it to you on Saturday, you fucking do more than stick your elbow in his eye and bend his fingers back, right?" She pulled out her phone. "I'd better tell Mannie to get Fus to keep his eye on you." She burst out laughing. "I guess I got that the wrong way around, I know who I'm more afraid of!"

"Leave it. I can look after myself." I said.

"Okay, but tell me if he tries anything, and I'll rip his fucking nuts off."

"I appreciate that."

I sank my teeth into the baguette, pulling the sandwich slowly away, as my teeth worked through the tough bread and into the creamy mix of brie and houmous. I hit the sudden salty tang of an olive and then the crisp earthy flavour of the iceberg lettuce.

The real world does have better food than Kaetia.

Becca finished her baguette, screwed up the brown paper bag and tossed it into the bin at the other side of the room, leaving a trail of crumbs across the floor.

"Would you like a cup of tea Becca?" She said, pretending to be me. "Why of course I would, how nice of you to ask… You stay there, I'll get it for you. Care for a biscuit while I'm at it? … Well, that would be just lovely, thank you."

I motioned to my mouth to indicate I was still eating.

She huffed and went into the kitchen.

I heard the tap running and the kettle being thumped down. Then a lot of banging of cupboard doors.

"What are you looking for?"

"I don't fucking know."

There was a clatter of stones falling on the tiled kitchen floor.

"Oh! Bloody hell! Crap!"

"What's up now?"

"I broke the fucking jade bracelet Mike gave me last week, that's what the fuck is up. And the damn beads have rolled under the sodding fridge."

"I'm coming." I said.

My phone pinged. It was a text from Tyler.

"Hey molasses! U got any pro artist marker pens? I wanna try em before I buy em. bring tonight?"

I shot back a text telling him I would, then remembered I'd no idea where I'd put them, so headed to my art supply cupboard.

"Thanks for your help, Kerella." Becca slammed my tea down on the table as I crawled out from the depths of my supply cupboard with a set of markers and a bleed proof sketch pad.

"Shit. Sorry Becca. I needed to find these for rehearsal tonight."

She arched her right eyebrow and sat down on the settee. "Do you ever clean your kitchen? The amount of crap on your floor." She threw a piece of paper at me.

I caught it and looked down into Asana's sombre golden eyes.

I felt light-headed.

"Where was this?" I stammered, struggling to find words.

"Down the side of your fridge. It's just one of your dream thingies right? Why are you acting like I've given you the answer to the meaning of life?"

"I... I... I..." I stared at the painting in my hands, looking into the reverent face of the most majestic lady I'd ever known. "Asana." I touched the painting, and my eyes filled with tears.

"You getting all religious on me Ker? 'Cause I don't think I could cope with that. Your recent happy chatty state is enough of a head fuck, but 'Hosanna'? Jeez, I'm getting out of here."

"No, no. Not 'Hosanna', 'Asana'. It's her name."

Tears were streaming down my face. There was no way I could explain this; no way I could tell Becca that holding a picture I'd painted of a woman from a dream could fill me with such emotion. I didn't even feel this when I looked at photos of my mother, but I'd never lost them. Then I remembered I was supposed to be growing up and letting this Kaetia crap go, so I slipped the painting under a large artbook lying on the bottom shelf of the coffee table.

"From your dreams?"

"Yes. I thought I'd lost it." I wiped my eyes and tried to act normal. "I think I have some elastic somewhere; do you want me to fix your bracelet?"

"Nah, I'll get me mum to do it. She's got all that jewellery making equipment for the shop."

She dunked a biscuit in her tea.

I was trying hard, but my mind was slipping back to Kaetia.

"You know it's really weird, in my dreams I have dark hair..." Becca took a sip of tea and didn't respond. "Don't you think that's strange?"

"Nothing about your dreams surprise me."

"But it's weird. I mean, I've never had dark hair, so why would I dream about it?"

"Dye it then, if it bothers you."

"Maybe I will. Do you ever dream you look different than you do?"

"Why would I, when I'm this hot?" She slapped her thigh. "I'm getting a headache. Could you just go play something on the piano and we'll worry about your image issues another time?"

Happy to return to my music, I went over to the keyboard and slipped into the song I'd been working on. I continued to improvise, and the tune and the lyrics started to come together.

"Oy!" Becca yelled, clapping her hands loudly to get my attention during a dramatic passage I was working on for the bridge.

I turned round to see Chris stood next to Becca.

"So, you sing as well? That was very impressive."

"I don't sing in front of people." I snapped defensively. "How did you get in?"

"You ignored the intercom, so I let him in. Anyway, Chris: tag, you're it.

I'm off to get on with stuff."

"Bye, Rebecca." Chris said.

"Yeah, yeah." She said heading out of the door.

"What can I do for you?" I asked.

"You asked me to pick you up for rehearsal."

"Oh, yes. Is Tyler with you?" I said, trying to look behind him.

"No, I dropped him off at Kat's. They've got some stuff to sort out." He looked towards the French windows. "That's the reason I'm a bit early; I thought we could have a quick chat."

I motioned to the settee, and we sat down.

He took off his hat and looked uncomfortable. "I was a bit worried about the way Tyler was leading you on the other day. He and Kat may be going through some trouble, but they're meant to be together. It's hard to explain to an outsider. They're from a similar background and they will end up together."

I drew on Tushenta's ability to push her emotions down and waved my hand vaguely in the air. Unfortunately, my voice came out squeakier than I'd hoped, but I managed to say the words without bursting into tears. "I don't know why everyone thinks I have a thing for Tyler: I really don't. I prefer men who are more focused and a bit less flighty." I took a deep breath, and in my desperation to change the subject was probably a bit more forward than I normally would've been. "Anyway, what's Becca's problem with you?"

He looked down and turned his hat slowly around on his knee. "She propositioned me when she was drunk one night, back when Mike was still in prison. I turned her down, and she didn't handle the rejection very well."

"She's not your type?"

"No, I prefer my women a bit more focused and a lot less flighty." He looked at me with his intense dark eyes and gave a brief half-smile before standing up. "Right, shall we get your keyboard to the car?"

23: DIAMETRIC DESTINY

I hit the final chord of Into the Dark. The song ends with a little drum solo. Each time, Fus does something a little bit different around the theme of a meditative heartbeat. Today, he plunged into an energised and dramatic riff, which came to a very loud, abrupt end.

As the cymbals faded, Ty said: "Well, that woke me up!"

"I should bloody hope so. Four days left, and you're playing as though this is the most boring thing you've ever done. I know it's stuffy as hell in here, and you're going through some personal things, but a performer needs to be able to fake it for thirty minutes. Let's see if you can muster some enthusiasm for Diametric Destiny?"

"Give me a break. We don't have an audience and I don't have to fake it for you guys. Anyway, what's the point? Angel Waste announced their charity; there's no way we can win if they're giving the prize money to the Bayview Animal Rescue Centre."

Mannie glared at Tyler. "I think you underestimate the support we have in the community. Everyone knows how important this place is."

I took a step back. Yeah, we were going to lose. But we still had to perform, and I hoped I was a better faker than Tyler was. I'd always thought Diametric Destiny was just a clever play on words, but with what Chris said, I now realised it was about Tyler and Kat's relationship.

Tyler shrugged at Mannie, closed his eyes, and started playing the introduction. Mannie took her cue, and nodded at Fus, so they started at the same time.

What pulled us together, tore us apart.
What pushed us away, brought us back home.
What felt like the end, was really the start.

What made you stand still, forced me to roam.
Drawn to the centre and flipped to the side.
My lodestone is charged and you push away.
To the circumference, we pin our divide.
In our polarity, we start to stray.

I wanted revelation; you gave me revolution.
I wanted change, you kept turning it around.
I thought we'd come together heading in the same direction,
but as we traced this circle, we knew where we were bound.
I said it's a fictitious force,
you said dissociative state.
And we'd find each other if we stayed on course,
because it was written in our fate.
Diametric destiny: no escaping our polarity.
Diametric destiny: you are part of my reality.

Spinning our web, getting caught in the reel.
Whirling around as the dance became true.
From opposite sides, you snapped at my heels;
that didn't make me go faster than you.
In this centrifuge, it all became clear;
we went too fast, now we're pushed to the brink.
Running in circles to never get near;
rival combatants with an endless link.

We are tied to opposition,
through the knots of definition.
Good is bad, dark is light.
Young is old, wrong is right.
True is false, trapped is free.
Up is down, you are me.
Diametric
Destiny.

I wanted revelation; you gave me revolution.
I wanted change, you kept turning it around.
I thought we'd come together heading in the same direction,
but as we traced this circle, we knew where we were bound.
I said it's a fictitious force,
you said dissociative state.
And we'd find each other if we stayed on course,
because it was written in our fate.

Diametric destiny: no escaping our polarity.
Diametric destiny: you are part of my reality.

Follow the lodestar to what shall be found,
both of us on the verge of the path.
All we encounter, becomes common ground,
but you're only there for the aftermath.
The friction builds and you tear through my mask,
leaving your mark like the circles in crops.
Yet, in all this time, we do not ask:
what happens to us when the movement

    stops?

Tyler usually watches me as I perform. Today, he'd barely looked in my direction throughout the whole session. During Diametric Destiny he walked off to the other side of the room and stared out of the window for the entire song. His performance was a little better than it had been, but still lacked its usual spark.

I also realised that the song was a verse too long. Why had I not seen that before? Was my obsession with Tyler warping my mind that much?

"I think we should give it a rest for today." Mannie said, fanning herself with a pile of fliers she'd had printed to promote Saturday's gig. "They say the weather's going to break tonight; so let's all take the evening to regroup and cool down."

Fus opened the storage cupboard. "Anyone leaving their instruments here, get them in tout suite."

I took my keyboard over and tucked it away in the corner of the cupboard. Heading back to fetch my keyboard stand, I saw Mannie and Tyler having an intense discussion. I fiddled with the screws longer than I needed to, but I couldn't hear what they were talking about, so took the stand to pack it away with the keyboard.

On my way back out of the cupboard, I bumped into Tyler. He dropped his guitar in the middle of the doors and grabbed my arm. "Come on, we're out of here."

"Don't forget, everyone must take a pile of fliers and put them out wherever you can!" Mannie called after us.

"We'll grab them tomorrow." Tyler yelled over his shoulder.

"Ty, you're hurting my arm." I said as he dragged me out of the front doors, past the scaffolding, and onto the street.

"Sorry, molasses. I just had to get away from Mannie; she's doing my nut in."

He paused and looked up and down the street, face set in a frown as he pulled at the neck of his grey T-shirt. Dark circles had formed under his armpits. I felt a trickle of sweat drip down my spine and hoped my choice of black vest top, loose-fitting thin black cardigan, and patchwork black, cream and sepia patterned long flowing skirt, would hide any patches of gathering moisture.

Without a word, he headed off down the backroad into town. I trotted after him.

His pace picked up and he showed no sign of knowing I was there. I started to wonder if he wanted me to follow him.

"Ty, what's going on?"

"I just need some space."

I stopped walking. "You drag me out of the community centre and then tell me to give you space? Make up your fucking mind."

He stopped, turned around and came back to me.

The clouds were starting to get very dark behind him.

His face softened as he looked into my eyes. "I meant space from everyone else. You're the only one who isn't telling me what to do right now." He reached out and ran his finger over my cheek before pulling me close to him. He held me tightly for a while, then pulled back slightly to kiss my forehead. I lifted my hands up to feel the heat of his chest. Maybe I didn't want to know what was going on; I just wanted to stay like this forever.

He sighed deeply, his breath stirring my hair, then turned to walk into town, this time with his arm around my waist.

I floated along beside him as we walked up to the Victorian shelter. We stood for a while looking out over the bay. I watched a flock of seagulls, and Tyler fixed his eyes on a small red fishing boat making its way back to the harbour.

Suddenly, he thrust me back into the shelter and drew me into a deep kiss. He pushed his body firmly against mine and I felt his penis start to grow hard. His hands rubbed up and down my back, and he pulled our bodies even closer.

It was both exactly as good as I thought it would be, and absolutely awful. Emotionally, I was swept away with dreams of Tyler, Mull'aman, music, and fantasy. Mentally, I was listening to Chris telling me Tyler and Kat were destined to be together. Physically, I was a chemical quagmire rushing towards an explosive reaction.

The smell of his sweat was unpleasant, and I had to fight the urge to pull away from the sticky damp patches under his arms. I turned my head towards the sea to grab a breath of fresh air, but he forced my face back to his squishy lips. His hand slipped inside my vest top and started to clumsily grope my breasts. To my own surprise, I pulled away and walked down the hill leading to the concrete-rimmed sea bathing pool.

Tyler followed me. He didn't ask what was up. He probably knew better than I did why I was crying.

I sat down on the steps and watched the water slap and gurgle over the edge of the pool wall. Ty sat down next to me and put his arm over my shoulder. I leant into him.

I wanted to kiss him again. I wanted to ignore all the confusing messages and jump into his arms and stay there. That idea was huge and scary: I'd never had such a possibility dangled in front of me.

Eventually, I sabotaged that hope myself.

"How did your talk with Kat go earlier today?"

I felt him stiffen, but he didn't pull away.

The sound of the waves breaking on the shore breathed into the gap where no words were spoken.

I heard a rumble of thunder in the distance and a warm breeze picked up.

"It's such a complicated mess." Tyler ventured into the abyss. "Kat's a friend of Mannie's, and everyone just keeps pushing and interfering. And they all take her side and think she's totally perfect and innocent. If only they knew."

He stopped, searching for the words to explain the complexities of the situation, but I'd grasped it. He had such a docile heart; I could see how a relationship with a clingy ex would be trouble for him, and friends pushing him where he didn't want to be, would tear him apart.

"Tyler." I reached out and laid my hand on his arm like Mull'aman had done to Birgitta in my dream. "It's not up to them. You are your own person, and they need to accept the relationship is over. They need you in the band; they can't throw you out over this."

He kept staring out to sea, pulled his lips into a taut line, and snorted. "It's not that easy."

"Yes, it is. If they throw you out of the band, I'll quit too, then they'll lose their precious community centre and maybe their jobs."

"Kerella." He turned his contact-lens adorned eyes to me and ran his fingers through my hair. The breeze was starting to get stronger, and the waves were crashing at the bottom of the steps.

This was the beginning of the best moment of my real life.

I met his gaze for what felt like the longest five seconds ever.

He looked back out at the clouds on the horizon. A bolt of lightning hit the sea and about twenty seconds later, the gentle roll of thunder shrouded the land.

"It's just that, she... was in an accident and she lost her hand."

"Okay... That doesn't mean you should lie to her by pretending you feel something you don't."

He turned to face me, and I saw his true eyes; they were soft and vulnerable, and filled with despair.

"You'd be doing the wrong thing if you went back; you have to live your own life." I added.

The ambiguity had been lifted; finally, we were on the same page. He moved closer, staring intensely into my heart. My pulse raced and hormones pumped around my body leaving me drunk and dazed. I moved forward to kiss him.

He stood up abruptly. "Stop being so clingy and manipulative."

I fell over, catching myself roughly on my right wrist, grazing it on the concrete steps.

"What?" Then I twigged: he still wasn't being honest with me.

"Look, I can't do this. Not with someone like you. I'm moving back in with Kat tomorrow. I've made up my mind. This was a mistake."

A loud crack of thunder caused him to duck. He cast one last look down at the pathetic, crumpled heap that was me, before striding up the steps.

A thick drop of rain hit me on the forehead where I could still feel his kiss from earlier.

I doubled over on the steps, crying as the rain came down in large heavy drops. The thunder ripped through the sky again as I sucked in the storm air between my hysterical sobs, and I thought: why is there never an open bottle of wine in your hand when you need one?

24: A MATCH MADE IN KAETIA

I flick the shutter towards myself with my foot and trace my finger over the letter 'M' that I'd carved on the edge not so very long ago, when my heart was still young and naïve. I take the knife I'd kept back from dinner and start to score the duplicitous letter away.

Once Mull'aman is erased, I collapse on the floor and cry for the loss of Ling and Birgitta. I've never known anyone who's died, and I'm totally confused by the things I'm feeling. I remember their music most of all. Ling's music was light and made my heart feel like it was floating. Birgitta's music felt more alien, but I would laugh, duck, and bob with Mull'aman, as she played her slapping, whooping melodies. She told me it was 'pop' music, and it did make me feel like popping bubbles: I would jump up and down and pretend to burst them with my fingers. Mull'aman laughed at that.

I doubt I'll ever feel that euphoria again.

I've been summoned to the Council today. They'll be telling me who I'll be partnered with for the next two thousand, seven hundred years. Who their new God will be. Chosen by those sixteen old men, in that musty smelling room, with all its crevices and tiers.

I must not cry.

No matter what they say, I must not cry.

I won't know the boy, but it'll be okay. I trust Laesconno's judgement.

It won't be Mull'aman, and I'm both glad and devastated by that. All along, he knew he was to be married to someone else. And with all his heretical activity, his talk of the Historians, injustice, and reform, he reported his own fiancée to the Council for heresy!

It's probably a good thing the Council are picking my partner, as I clearly have no judgement.

I wonder what my partner's laugh will sound like.

I wonder if I'll hear him laugh today.

He will be there today.

In my refusal to let the memory of lower realm mortals disperse as easily as their bodies turn to dust, I never even thought that I'll be meeting my future partner today. It feels so wrong to even think of love when my heart hurts this much.

I pick myself up off the floor and begin my hollow preening, fixing my hair back with twigs I'd gathered throughout the years during my trips to the gardens, and shaping the drape of my hood with wires I'd saved from broken things I came across and stored for a special occasion. And today is as special as it will ever get.

I run through several repetitive prayers to induce an air of elevation suitable to my station, and by the time the knock on the door breaks my concentration, I'm so detached from my body, I might as well be dead.

Not that I can die.

The Pader who'd snubbed out Birgitta's quirky candle waits for me outside the door. She leads the way down the steps of my tower. At the bottom, Asana, Melingad, and two other Paders wait for us.

Asana nods at the young Pader. "Thank you, Nuihue."

Hovering outside the gates to the Kaetian Quarters is a group of young Lower Kaetians. Their cloaks are bedecked in foliage; the girls are holding pomegranates and the young boys are holding staffs.

I've read about this ridiculous fertility procession in books, but I never thought I'd really have to go through with it. Why couldn't the Librarians have scrubbed this silly nonsense out of existence?

I walk through the gate and see the blonde Lower Kaetian who delivered the Historians' books to me. Her cloak is draped in the most foliage, and she's positioned right behind me in the parade, showing that she's from the highest-ranking family. Despite the honour, she really doesn't look like she wants to have the privilege of following me to hear who our next God is going to be.

I know I should mention her visible disinterest in a holy duty to the Council, but I feel a strange sympathy towards her. Maybe, had I been better behaved when I was growing up, I might've been friends with this girl; we could've spent nights discussing books and the tenets, giggling over clever compositions on the elovetta, or whatever it is that people with friends did when they spent time together.

The younger girls dance along before us, sweeping the path with their branches. I do hope these weren't trimmed unnecessarily from our trees, and that we won't lose any vital resources because I couldn't control my hands and triggered a load of archaic rituals.

As we get to the doors of the Council Chambers, the Lower Kaetians fan out around me. The blonde girl comes to stand in front of me, and with a pathetic dip, drops a ring of leaves on my head. She positions it so a leaf is right over my eye, but I hold off correcting the placement, so as not to ruin the moment. I assume the Lower Kaetians are getting more out of this spectacle than I am. This is my duty: to be their entertainment; the focal point for their pageantry.

The Council Chamber doors have been decorated with an arch of flowers, leaves, and pomegranates. Over the door hangs a veil of red material. One of the young boys passes Asana his staff, and she knocks on the door three times. From the other side, four knocks sound in reply, and the doors slowly open.

The couple at the back of the procession drop their cloaks, revealing outfits of strategically draped red cloth and vines. There are gasps from the Lower Kaetians, and some of the younger children giggle. I avert my eyes as the semi-clad duo walk past us. The young man and woman each take one side of the veil and draw it aside to allow us to pass through the door. This is certainly an addition to the original ceremony.

I race through the door, using the opportunity to rearrange my foliage crown so a leaf isn't poking into my eye, and, forgetting about poise and ceremony, I charge up the steps and throw myself into my usual throne. I take a few deep breaths and look out at the sixteen old men who know my fate.

Laescenno smiles at me, and I smile back, knowing he would never give me to a boy who'd harm me or be bad for Kaetia. I relax a bit as the formal ceremony begins.

The Higher Kaetian representatives file in. I see Mull'aman. He doesn't look in my direction. I'm not pleased that his eyes rest on the ceremonial young woman, but I guess he isn't my concern anymore.

I look at each of the men and wonder who will be walking with me in the lower realm within a month.

Asana sits down next to me and lifts the blue-cracked-glaze sphere from the arm of her throne. She holds it aloft slightly longer than usual before slamming it down to the ground. The scent takes longer than ever to reach Laescenno, and the people behind him have reacted long before he twitches his nose.

He pushes himself to his feet and staggers over to stand in front of our thrones. He reaches out and takes my hand, smiling up at me. "Congratulations my child, this is a wonderful and exciting time for all of us."

He turns to face the Chambers and gestures to the partially clothed pair to come and stand either side of him. "No point in having such pretty decorations standing at the back." He says to the audience. There's a polite ripple of laughter, and a lot of uncomfortable shuffling. The displaying of flesh isn't allowed by Sett's decree, so no one knows how to react to such a thing, especially in the second most holy place in Kaetia.

"Well, here we are." Laescenno raises his arms in the air to welcome the pair, and, as he lowers them, it looks like his hand briefly slips over the young lady's buttocks. I hear Asana let out a quiet disapproving "Hhn." sound.

"Young love is a precious thing." Laescenno begins with a sigh and a wistful look in his watery eyes. It's going to be one of his long rambling speeches and I can see many members of the audience are already looking bored before he's even got going.

"Upon hearing the glorious news that our little Tushenta here has reached the age to be married, I took a few days with the original Tenets of Sett to meditate on how I, as Guardian of the Sixth Tenet, could best serve Kaetia at this crucial time."

I feel a twinge of jealousy. Because of me, Laescenno has been reading the original Tenets of Sett. I wonder if I'll be allowed to see them when I get back from the lower realm.

"The last time Kaetia was in this position, the Council were swayed by considerations of the heart over the good of the realm, and we have severely paid the price in the years since. We shall not be making the same mistake again. As such, the Council have reviewed all aspects of the ceremonies and guidance of Sett, and an omission has been corrected. This is why these two fine symbols of fertility have been included in these proceedings."

He gestures at the man, and whilst turning around, accidentally brushes his hand across the lady's breast. She takes a step back, but he holds her arm, steadying himself as he loses balance, his face lingering close to her chest.

"Ooo, dizzy spell, do excuse me. Anyway, if you'd all join me in thanking these two lovely new arrivals from the lower realm for helping out Kaetia with such a gallant sacrifice."

I look up, startled. Surely he's not going to have them executed for their public indecency if the Council specifically requested them to dress in this ridiculous fashion for the ritual?

Laescenno leads a spluttering round of applause.

"Ah, young love." He continues. "When I was younger, I was lucky to be paired with an exceptional lady. She was beautiful, witty, and smart. Well, it was not luck, the Guardian of the Sixth Tenet, together with the Council, knew what they were doing. As they do today. It's such a crucial role for Kaetian survival: ensuring the right men are paired with the right girls, so they can produce the next generation to fill the robes of their fathers."

I scan my eyes over the crowd to see what Mull'aman is up to. He has his hand over half of his face. It looks like he's trying to disguise that he's staring at the half-naked lady with his mouth hanging open. *Does he care about my fate at all?*

"And, so it was, that I filled the robe of my father. I'm sure that all of you know that back in the day, my father was supposed to be Asana's partner. He stepped to the side to allow Asana her romance with... well, we won't mention his name today, even though he still threatens our skies with his redwaek and sorcery.

"I have found my decades spent helping Kaetia's young ladies find their hearts' home truly rewarding and fulfilling, and it is with great sadness, that this pairing will be the last in my role of Guardian of the Sixth Tenet, as I hand over the responsibilities to my beautiful daughter, Melisia, and her husband, who is showing such promise in his role.

"Do stand-up child." He waves at her.

A rather solid, stern looking woman, holding a baby, half rises in her seat and gives the room a brief nod before she sits back down.

"And, as you can see, my dear friends, that's my granddaughter, Khora, who arrived with us just a couple of months ago. Such a blessing. I am so blessed."

He wipes a tear from his eye and starts clapping. A few others join in.

"I have enjoyed my vocation, serving Kaetia in this capacity, and I do believe myself to have executed my duties admirably. In fact, our records show that I have been the most successful 'Guardian of the Heart', as I like to call myself, since records began. We've had fewer rejections than ever before, and it's got to the point where we've had to seek alternative sources for our Pader Guards, as fewer rejected lovers choose to take up arms to protect our sacred society.

"Unfortunately, this success rate also means that there are no available young men hanging around waiting for our beautiful little goddess to shine her blue light on them."

He pauses, looking to his right. "Well except this young stud here, but mortals of the higher and lower realms are no longer permitted for Supreme Kaetian consideration, for the sake of Kaetia.

"My dear Supreme Kaetian, Tushenta." He turns around to face me. "Let us be honest, you are not just any eligible filly in the stable of Kaetian society. We cannot deny that you are a tricky, sticky, picky mess, and not just any man would have you, as you do have evil mortal blood running through your veins, and that will stain your future husband's reputation.

"My wife and I were so lucky, it was uncomplicated, and we had many decades of mutually supportive bliss. We helped each other and she was my everything. She died last year and didn't get to see the fruit of her daughter's union. Our little Khora.

"Now I've achieved so much, and I had planned a quiet end to my days. But in this last case of mine, I'm reminded of my own personal connection with you, my *darling little bookworm. Although I'm old and can barely stand without a cane…"*

He pauses, holding on to the lady's arm again and casually casting his eyes over her lower body.

"I remind you that I am in fact younger than you are. There was a time when we were considered the same age, and I will confess, I had a bit of a crush on you. Remember my first Council meeting, when I dropped my books, and you jumped down from your throne to help me pick them up? And that time we both sang 'Under the Kaetian Sun' together, in the Courtyard of the Arcane? I have so many memories of you, as I am sure that you have of me.

"Now, whilst I was reminiscing on these memories and affections, the Council raised an unusual, albeit technically valid avenue, that I, as a widower, hadn't even considered. As a single man, I am probably the most eligible Kaetian with the capabilities to handle such a temperamental lass as you."

Syreme and Reth'satar are shaking their heads and don't look happy with Laescenno's portrayal of the Council's discussions.

I take a moment to process what he means.

Then it hit me.

"My darling Tushenta, although I took some convincing, I have accepted your proposal, and look forward to walking with you in the lower realm, where we shall meet in physical bodies more congruent with our passions. Don't worry, I may not be as handsome and spritely as I once was, but you will fall in love with me in the lower realm, where we will be of the same age, and not divided by status, or the baggage of your infamous father."

Asana's hand shoots over to my arm and she digs her fingers into my wrist. I stare down, shocked that she's touching me, and I focus on the fact that my mother is actually touching me, as the rest of my life melts away.

The room bursts into applause, and Asana uses the noise to hide her voice as she hisses at me: "Do not react."

My eyes swing round and I try to find Mull'aman. All I see is the fertility couple flanking my fiancé, who coughs and trips, accidentally pushing his hand down the woman's abdomen and pulling her leaves down as he totters. He turns around and raises his arms to the crowd.

I can't see Mull'aman, but he was long gone before this moment.

Asana drags me down the stairs. My body feels numb.

She bows to Laescenno.

"What an immense honour you've shown us. What a great service to Kaetia. Your honour knows no bounds. We shall go and prepare my child to walk in the lower realm."

I look at Laescenno's face. A face I'd looked up to in friendship; a face I'd trusted more than any other face in Kaetia; a face I'd considered paternal; a face that now leers at me in a suggestive manner.

I look at the floor and see his yellow toenails sticking out of his sandals.

Asana's fingers dig into my wrist harder. I manage to draw myself up and declare: "You honour me too much sir. I need to go and... prepare."

Asana pulls me through the door, and we escape the thumping applause celebrating my doom.

25: BLACK

I fell into Becca's flat, giggling.

"What's so funny, Ker?"

I leant against the wall, as my balance was a little off that afternoon, and slid down to the carpet. I continued to laugh, unable to form words. By the time I'd calmed down, I'd forgotten what was funny.

"Oh wait! I have something for you." I grabbed my bag and pulled out the console. "This is for you for being such a great friend." I held it up for her.

She took it from me and said "Thanks Ker. Now I'll have something to play when my niece comes over. I'm surprised you didn't get it in pink."

But she smiled and put the box down on the sideboard.

"So, have you got any wine?" I asked her.

"It's four o'clock."

"Do your cupboards have time locking mechanisms?"

Then I remembered what was funny and started giggling again.

I have a black sense of humour because it wasn't at all funny. I was laughing because it was all so crap, I had to laugh.

"Well, I didn't sleep with anyone in the band, that should make you happy!"

"Glad to hear it, Ker. Is that what you're laughing about?"

"Yes." I announced proudly. I could laugh at my situation: that was how strong I was.

"Why is that funny?"

"Because it isn't." I said, bursting into tears.

"Oh. So, you heard about Tyler's engagement?"

"Actually, no. But nothing surprises me right now." I started pawing at the carpet.

"Ker, what are you doing?"

"This is the floor. There isn't any more down. I just didn't know I'd ever be down here."

"Oh, fuck this shite." Becca said. And it was so comforting.

She sat down next to me, and I latched onto her. I didn't want to tell her I thought I was losing my grip on reality and even my subconscious thought the best I could do was a lecherous old man with a neck that looked like a pair of testicles were wedged in his throat. I didn't want to explain why I felt like I wanted to jump into the sea and never come back, and thankfully, she didn't ask.

She stroked my hair and let me whimper for a while. She was my constant in this world: if I could keep hold of her, I'd be okay.

"Kerella, honey." She tapped me on the head, "I need to get as drunk as you are if I'm going to spend the whole evening cheering you up. West End?"

I sat up and nodded. The idea of a pub sounded great, and The West End was a three-minute walk, so that was even better.

"You're on fruit juice."

"Bitch."

"Until I catch you up, or you'll be unconscious by six, and that's my evening screwed."

She had a point. She was clever like that.

I bought us most of the bar menu and stuck it on dad's credit card. Well, this counted as an emergency, and the chips tasted so good.

I put my head on the table and pushed grains of salt around the varnished wood whilst Becca told me that one of the bitches I'd been at school with was knocked up and her boyfriend had dumped her because it wasn't his and her parent's wouldn't let her move back in as she'd stolen from them. I knew this was the sort of thing I was meant to take pleasure in, but I wasn't wired properly. She'd been mean to me, she beat me up and took my money, and she'd taken photos of me changing for P.E. to give to the boys in my class. Still, I couldn't bring myself to be gleeful at her pain like Becca. I hate to think what she'd done to make Becca so happy that her life was falling apart.

I reached over to stroke Becca's hand to swish away the nastiness that must've happened. She pushed my hand away, so I played with my hair, moving it around the table, forming patterns out of the long pale loops. 'Who's got long straight blonde hair now!' I sent out across the universe to Miss-Pretty-Massive-Mouth-Lower-Kaetian who didn't get Mull'aman and didn't exist anyway.

"Hey! You still want to dye your hair dark brown?" Becca said. "We could grab some dye on the way home and stain your bathroom the fuck up tonight."

"Let's dye it black. I'm black now. I'm all black. Black. Black. Black."

"That we can do. I think it'll look pretty cool."

"Black, black, black, black." I sat up. "Yes, this is just what I need. I need a change. Everything will change tonight. There'll be no going back, and I shall not regret this day."

"Yes, dear. It's just your hair. We ain't gonna fix you that easily."

"No, it's this song I'm writing, it's called Regrettable Day, and it's all about how I'm going to forge a new day by burning everything down."

"Are you planning something stupid? Like, real arson?"

"No, metaphorical Armageddon, all the way! My glass is empty, bitch. It's your round."

"Pace yourself, I don't want to be carrying you home in a body bag."

Then Tyler walked in with a group of friends.

I died.

Well, not literally. I ducked under the table and hid.

Becca pulled me up, knowing if she pulled my clothes, I'd have to follow, rather than let her ruin the fabric.

"Stop it! I'm trying not to draw attention to us."

"And hiding under the table is not going to look strange, because?"

"Tyler's just walked in."

"Right, it's time I gave that fucking wanker a piece of my mind."

"No Becca, don't."

"Why?"

"I just, want him to not exist. Can you do that instead? Make him disappear?"

"He actually looks depressed, Ker."

"I don't fucking care. I don't want to see him. We need to get out of here."

"They're standing right by the door. You'll have to say something to him; we can't get out any other way."

I jumped up and sat down at the other side of the table. Thankfully, we were in the end stall, and the back of the booth was high enough for me to hide behind. As long as he didn't decide to play pool, we'd be okay.

"Chris has seen me." Becca said.

My heart was racing. Not in the fun way either. "Let him know somehow to piss off."

"Oh! Larry's at the bar." She jumped up and went to talk to him. I could've killed her. Okay, killing would probably not be an option, so I drank her beer instead.

A glass of white wine arrived in front of me.

Chris followed.

"Hello Kerella."

I ducked down and looked behind him.

"Don't worry, Ty's talking to Ian; he doesn't know you're here."

"Get him out of here."

"Kerella, what happened? You both missed rehearsal and Fus is not happy. Tyler won't talk, and that's the first time that's ever been known to happen."

"Fuck off. And don't think I don't wish you were dead as well. Why the fuck didn't you just tell me straight out that he and Kat got back together? And Becca told me they got engaged, so don't pretend you don't know."

"Oh. Becca told you that?"

I wanted to scratch his black eyes out of his head and strangle him with his own silly blue bandanna.

I glared, seething beyond being able to talk.

"Look, they were always meant to be together. No one, not even you, could change that. None of this reflects on you."

I replayed what Tyler said in my head. "Not with someone like you." That was what he said. Chris was lying to me.

"Kerella, I'm sorry, but it was Tyler's responsibility to tell you, not mine."

"I know. It just hurts, Chris, and I feel so goddamn stupid. I know you warned me; I should've listened. I just thought you wanted to get me in bed."

He laughed.

"Okay, I was wrong about that too."

Not-with-someone-like-you-not-with-someone-like-you-not-with-someone-like-you.

He stood up and came to sit down beside me. He knocked me lightly under my chin. "Look after yourself, okay? I know you, how you feel things, Kerella. You have emotions other people can't understand, and they will consume you. Write your music, paint your pictures, live the experience, but remember to stop. I don't want to lose you to the darkness."

I was shocked by his observation.

"I won't get lost."

"Kerella, look at me."

"No."

He was scaring me; he seemed to know me. No one was allowed to know me, but I'd let my guard down with Tyler and created vulnerabilities I wasn't expecting.

I could not crush without being crushed.

Not-with-someone-like-you.

I started to cry.

Chris pulled me to his chest and patted my back. "He's the first person you ever let close to you, isn't he?"

A squeak was all I could manage in reply.

"Look, don't let him scare you out of the band. It wasn't all bad, and it's not like he doesn't care for you. No one meant for you to get hurt."

I'd regained control of myself, so pulled away, grabbing at my glass of wine as a safety net.

"Are you going to be okay?"

"I have someone I can trust." I smiled at him.

He smiled back.

"And she's bloody wonderful."

Becca sat back down in front of us.

"Hello Chris."

He nodded.

"You see you're wrong, Chris. Becca here, she's the bestest, bestest, bestest person in the world, and she really knows me. Tyler, you know," I took a sip of wine. "Ty," I shook my head, "didn't even scratch the surface."

"Is that so?" Chris raised an eyebrow.

"Okay, he scratched, but not the real surface."

"And what's behind the real surface?"

"Black. Black. Black. Black. Black. Black. Black."

I think my turn for the drunk frightened Chris off. He returned to Tyler and Ian, and managed to talk them into going to another pub. I'd tell him later that I appreciated that. If I remembered anything about tonight.

I took a sip of wine.

Becca suggested we headed to The Bull.

I took a sip of wine.

I couldn't find Becca.

I wasn't sure how I got to The Bay.

I had a glass of wine.

I was sat in someone's gateway. Two lads were stood over me.

"Hey, go on." One of them said. "Dip your chips in Tommy K."

"Seriously?"

"I dare you."

"Look, I don't know you. Please, leave me alone." I managed to say.

"Ha! It'll be good for a laugh…"

"Get up, darling: you're coming with us."

They tried to pull me up, but there was a swoosh of a midnight-blue cloak and a dark shape got in the way.

"Leave the lady alone."

"No, you got us wrong. It's just Tommy K. It's fine."

"Go home."

"Jeez, you must be desperate."

As they walked away, I heard the shorter one say: "He must have a load of chips on his shoulder."

The other one took a moment. "Ha ha! Yes, 'cause he's desperate for Tommy K."

Chris held his hand out for me. "Where's Becca?"

"She said she'd be back, but she left me."

He helped me to my feet. "It's okay. I'll get you home."

"She left me."

"You're safe now."

"I don't deserve to be. I am evil."

"I very much doubt that. You're just a bit drunk."

"I lied to you."

"Let's just get you home."

"I don't have a daughter. I lied. Do you hate me now?"

I felt him tense up, but he kept steering me in the direction of my flat. "I'm sure you had your reasons."

"I did. I really did. It was the only excuse I could think of to stop my dad locking me up in a psych ward."

"Well, you had a good reason then."

"Maybe I belong there."

"I think most of us probably do."

26: THE CHOICE

I feel faint and can barely stand. Asana steers me down endless corridors. I'm sure I'm going to fall over. Everything's blurred.

I feel faint and can barely stand. Asana steers me down endless corridors. I'm sure I'm going to fall over. Everything's blurred.

I hear the scuttle of the Paders rushing to catch us up. I'm pushed to one side as a Pader hurries past me to take the lead and they assume their usual protective formation.

The corridor is devoid of colour.
And dark.
So very dark.
It's almost black.
Black. Black. Black.
Is it later than I think?

And then the familiar gates of the Kaetian Quarters are in front of me. I'm seated on a chair in the staging area. I reach over and pour myself some water. I don't care if I've exceeded my rations today, it's this or a bottle of red weed, and I doubt my mother is about to offer me that.

"Ah, Melingad!" Asana says, turning with her usual poise to address the Head Pader. "I'm concerned that Kasaman may use this turn of events as an excuse to endanger Kaetia, and act on his long-held vendetta against Laescenno and his family. I know you're assigned to us, but I'd feel so much better if you'd lend your expertise to Laescenno, and help him and his entourage review their protective arrangements. I would hate for any harm to befall him due to his pending union with our family."

"I'm sworn to your protection; leaving my post would be a dereliction of my duty."

"With the grilles on the windows, we'll be safe in the tower with three members of your team guarding us. I mean look at this one, with her new blood-mark after valiantly defending my daughter against that lower realm insurgent. Right now, we won't be the target, but my daughter's beloved may be. Please, for the sake of her delicate heart, Laescenno is probably not aware of the danger he's in."

Melingad takes a bow and runs down the corridor, her black cloak with the red streaks flowing behind her as she disappears around the corner.

Asana looks at Nuihue. "Please forgive the boring task of guarding our door whilst a mother explains certain indelicate things about conjoining and life to her daughter."

I look at her. The line of blood down the centre of her yellow mask reminds me that she cut Birgitta's head off, leaving me splattered in warm blood. I'm starting to believe Birgitta was right: this is what the lower realm mortals call 'hell'.

Asana motions for me to get up and climb the stairs. The time for contact is clearly over, but the welcome sanctuary of my little room beckons me, so I run up the steps and throw myself, with no decorum, onto the bed, and cry into the pillow.

Asana doesn't shut the door when she follows me into the room. Then, much to my surprise, she sits down on the bed with me and strokes my hair.

"We don't have much time. I play their game so, when the need arises, I can catch them off guard by going off script. They'll regroup quickly enough. Although, if they catch us, it's hard to think of a worse punishment than what Laescenno's just announced."

I sit up, confused, looking through the open door at Nuihue.

"She's one of mine." Asana quietly says, casting her a warm smile, the likes of which I've not seen on Asana's face in two hundred years. "She's the daughter of a dear friend."

Who is this lady sat on my bed?

Then she surprises me further by drawing me towards her and holding me tight against her bony body.

"Oh! I've wanted to do that for over two centuries. I'm so sorry we had to descend to such lows before I got the opportunity."

She pulls away. "Now, we must be quick. Are the rumours true?"

"Rumours?"

"You and Mull'aman."

"No!" I pause to think for a moment. "Well, yes. But no." I take a deep breath. "How do people know? We were so careful."

"Not careful enough, apparently."

"But now, definitely no. He reported his own fiancée for heresy!"

"She told him to do that."

"Why on earth would she do that? She could be expelled or forced to be a Pader."

"That life would suit her better than being traded into the Higher Kaetian hierarchy. She's an exceptional woman. I'm…" Asana pauses and bobs her head. "close to her mother, Yuescret."

"So, they're not romantically involved?"

"Well, they probably were when they were younger; there aren't many women in Kaetia Mull'aman hasn't been 'romantically involved' with."

With that revelation, I feel like dealing him another blow. "He's involved with this group that call themselves The Historians."

Asana stands up suddenly, and stares at me with her usual severe authority. "Never betray the identity of a Historian!"

Then she looks thoughtful and walks off to the small window, running her fingers over the brown stain. "I'm shocked: I never thought the boy had any depth. At least he has one redeeming feature." She shakes her head. "But do you think he'd be a suitable partner? Well, more suitable than Laescenno? Our choices are beyond dire at this juncture."

"You're the one who said he had potential! You said observe the fourth tenet!"

"When?" She looks confused. "Oh! In the gardens!" She laughs. "I said that because he's such an obvious buffoon! I was worried you'd forget to tip-toe around the fragile Kaetian ego and treat him with the respect he really deserves!"

She paces back and forth across the room; her back is straight, and her hands are clasped in front of her, but there is a relaxed flow to her movements I'm not used to.

"There have been no decent Kaetians in such a long time. I'm sorry, this is why you've been kept so isolated; to delay the biological inevitability of your sparking for as long as possible. Or at least that was my reasoning. I'm sure Laescenno's motive has something to do with the hope that his blood line would eventually produce a male heir he could marry you off to, but now he's done something worse. I'm sure this is what he planned all along: I was so shocked when the Council agreed to your involvement with the Celebrations. That odious little worm man." She sighed. "It's a shame mortals are off the table now."

"Because a mortal match worked out so well with Kasaman!"

"Not all that happened was his fault."

"He murdered our family!"

"I don't believe he did."

"He created all the redwaek."

"That one's a bit harder to explain or forgive. Anyway, my darling daughter." She turns to face me, reaching forward and stroking my face. *"You have a choice: Laescenno or Mull'aman."*

"Mull'aman is engaged."

"To someone far too good for him. She'll be relieved to escape that fate."

"But he's good enough for me?"

"Compared to Laescenno, yes. That family is corrupt to the bone. He's not remotely as nice as he seems."

Mull'aman's green eyes shine in my mind. I could look into them for two thousand years.

"Mull'aman." I whisper and a blue light crackles over my palms.

"Agreed."

Asana is animated. *"I think it'll be an interesting time to walk in the lower realm; you're going to love it. My days in Milan will always be the best of my life, it was lovely to be insignificant and surrounded by so much beauty. You'll come back different. No Kaetian will ever understand. I do hope you end up in Italy, but that's not one of the variables we can control."*

"There are some that you can?"

"Oh, many. There's no point in sending you off into the lower realm with no control or boundaries. And no parent would risk sending their child into a warzone or a life of abject poverty. There are protective spells that can be cast to ensure you're safe, that you fall in love with who you're supposed to, that you have a good level of comfort and affluence, and so forth."

"I have some skills in this area: Laescenno has more. His resources far exceed mine, and he will be out for revenge."

"Why are we even discussing this? It isn't possible to go against him. He won't allow Mull'aman and I to go through the portal."

"All you need to open the portal is the blood of the highest ranking Supreme Kaetian and the fountain in the Courtyard of the Arcane. I have some control over who has access to what flows through my veins. Once the portal is open, anyone who adds their blood to the water will be born into a lower realm body and their fate tied to every other Kaetian currently walking in the lower realm. I won't be able to control who goes through after you, but we can make sure you and Mull'aman go through in such a public way that Laescenno will be deterred from losing face and following you.

"We'll need a certain act of theatre to help maintain my cover. I'll be in a better

position to protect you over the next few decades if they believe I'm their obedient servant. Whilst your body is here and your soul is in the lower realm, you will be vulnerable. If they know I helped you, I won't be able to get close to you to check for counter spells placed around your body.

"What we need to do is ensure that Mull'aman is the darling of Kaetia, and, as a key figure in the Celebrations, we have a chance to make him seem much more suitable than he really is. Laescenno will not want to look like a fool competing with a younger man, or jump into a battle in the unknown, where he won't be in control or able to draw on his network of allies and those indebted to him."

Nuihue discretely taps the door with her long sword, and we hear footsteps coming up the stairs.

This strange meeting of mother and daughter is over.

"I will put plans in place." She says and her posture morphs into the deity I always knew; she grows taller, her movements become precise, and the colour leaves her face. She stands in front of the largest of the windows, the blue sapphires of Sett's cloak in the grille casting a halo around her.

"You're so lucky, Laescenno has so much experience and knowledge. He will be an asset to our band of Supreme Kaetians. I certainly look forward to sharing my daily walks with him."

Melingad arrives at the top of the stairs.

"Ah, Melingad, I hope my future son in law was well? You can inform me of the new arrangements for his welfare on our way to the Crater of the Dead; those souls won't judge themselves, although, I'm sure some of them would rather it that way." Asana casts a look in Nuihue's direction. "Can you ensure my daughter has something special for her dinner? I may have been a bit harsh with my warnings about the temptations and dangers in the lower realm."

And with that, she is gone.

27: BLACKER

What if Laescenno had followed us through the portal and was in the lower realm with us? It makes more sense than Kasaman walking up to the fountain in the heart of Kaetia and leaving his body unattended to follow us through. Maybe Chris was Laescenno? Would that be so bad? Had I made a mistake when I told Asana I chose Mull'aman?

My stomach churned and my head felt raw. I moved my arm. I wasn't in my bed, but I recognised the protective smell of my mother's black and red crocheted blanket, and the soft texture of the badger cushion Becca gave me last year for my birthday. I was on my settee.

I opened my eyes a crack; the light from the French windows was too much.

I groaned and thrust my face down into the cushion.

Why could I not let this stupid Kaetian shit go. I was the biggest fucked up fuck up that ever fucking lived.

I heard the kettle being switched on in the kitchen.

Oh shit. I brought someone home last night. Then why was I still clothed and on the settee, not in my bed?

"Becca?" I tried calling. It came out a raspy whisper.

"Peppermint." I croaked, the thought of black tea causing my stomach to turn on itself.

Chris came through from the kitchen carrying a tray.

"Oh god!" I mouthed and pulled the blanket over my head.

"Don't worry. I brought you home and stayed to check you were okay. I would never take advantage of you like that."

He placed the tray down on the coffee table. I grabbed the glass of water and gratefully eyed up the plate of dry crackers and mug of peppermint tea.

"Thank you, and I'm sorry to put you through this trouble."

"I've got to look after our keyboardist." Chris said, sitting down in the red armchair with a cup of tea.

"What about Tristan and Isolde?"

"Ty's at mine sorting out the last of his stuff."

"Where's Becca?"

"I don't know. Last night you told me you lost her."

I felt in my pockets and then looked at the table. "My phone?"

"It fell out of your bag. Don't worry, I picked it up. It's over here." He retrieved my phone from the bookcase and placed it in front of me.

I picked it up and there were two texts.

The first was from Tyler: "I want you to know I miss you."

The second was from Mike: "Tell Becca to phone or get her butt home now."

I texted Becca. "Where are you? Mike's texting me, he must be mad – if you need to get away, my spare bed is always yours."

I looked at Chris and smiled awkwardly. I was grateful that he'd looked after me, but now that I was okay, I wondered how I could get rid of him.

He smiled awkwardly back. "I was hoping we could have a little chat about what you told me last night."

"Oh god. What did I say?"

Had I told him I thought he was Kasaman? Were we waiting for the authorities to come and pick me up to lock me away forever?

"I wanted to let you know, I understand why you lied about having a daughter, and to not feel guilty about it around me."

"Oh shit, I told you that?" I sighed, relieved I hadn't said anything stupid about Kaetia, and worried that I broke the fabric of my lie for the first time in eight years. "I know it's a lot to ask, but could you please not tell anyone. You're the only one who knows. I hate to think how angry everyone would be with me if they find out I lied."

"I will keep your secret." He nodded.

"I…" He picked at a loose thread on his shirt cuff. "I was hoping I could tell you something?"

"Of course."

"I…"

His phone rang. He looked like he was going to ignore it, but when he saw the caller ID, he changed his mind.

"Hello… Mannie? What's wrong? Slow down… Say that again."

He stood up and walked over to the French windows.

"In the woods?"

My heart began a deep, uncoordinated thumping in my chest. It was clearly bad news, and if it involved Mannie and Chris, it would be about Tyler. He must've had an accident walking to the Acres through the woods last night.

"I'm actually there right now… No, not like that… I can't believe this… Should we cancel Saturday?"

Oh god! I picked up my phone. I needed Becca; whatever the news was, I couldn't face it alone. I texted her: "Becca where are you? Can you come over?"

In my mind, I made a deal with the universe. 'Make Ty be okay, please? I promise I won't feel this way about him anymore. Just make sure he's okay.'

Chris ended the call and sat down opposite me.

"Kerella, I have some bad news to tell you." He paused. "It's about Becca."

"Becca?"

"She was found in the woods a short while ago. It looks like she overdosed. I'm sorry, she passed away."

"No, that's not possible. Becca wouldn't go to the woods; she hates the outdoors."

"Well, when people are doing drugs, they don't always act like you think they will."

"But she wasn't on drugs. She had quit. Seriously, I know her; there's no way she'd do that. She'd quit, I promise you."

"Clearly not."

Chris came over and sat next to me. I pushed my face into my hands and cried. I felt his arm rest gently on my back. I fell towards him, and he held me close.

"This is my fault. I dragged her out. It's my fault."

"No. It's not your fault."

"If I hadn't lost her, she'd be okay. She was going to help me dye my hair."

I slid down onto the floor, into the darker dark that I hadn't known was there. I clutched onto Chris's legs and buried my face into the faded black denim of his knees. He gently patted my back.

"She's all I have. I can't be alone. She can't be gone."

"I'll make sure you're not alone." Chris said.

And the devil's hand stirred in the undergrowth.

28: REGRETTABLE DAY

The sun fell on the rickety stage in the community centre. I watched the dust particles whirling in the shafts of light, remembering the first time I'd been in this room. I could still see Becca rummaging around the stage.

All she was now was memories.

My silly Kaetian fantasy fell apart when I realised that, if Kaetia were the afterlife, it wasn't where I believed Becca was. This was real. Becca was real. And now she wasn't. I didn't know where she'd gone, but I couldn't imagine her as one of the ghostly lower realm mortals slowly taking corporeal form in the Crater of the Dead, waiting to be held in Asana's blue light and have their soul judged.

I stood in the middle of the room holding my keyboard stand, an incorporeal shadow, staring at the stage, hoping to see Becca's ghost come out and roll her eyes at me.

Chris put his hand on my shoulder.

"Are you okay? Do you need help with the stand?"

"Sorry, I zoned out there." I nodded at my keyboard, which he was carrying. "Thanks, just put that there, I've got it."

Chris left to go back to his car.

Mannie came through the double doors and bee-lined straight for me, pulling me down into a big hug. "Are you okay, hon?"

I felt awkward and fought to free myself. "I just need space."

"I understand. Fus is talking to Mike in the office. He's a wreck. They both are. I couldn't cope with all the tears, I had to get out." She took a step back and a deep breath. This seemed to reset her emotions and she smiled. "The makeover looks great! I love your hair that colour! It's going to look great on stage."

I'd taken the plunge and died my hair black in memory of Becca. I was wearing her chunky metal plated boots, which I'd borrowed two weeks ago, and a tight black jumper of diagonal gauze layers and ornamental safety pins she'd given me. I wanted something to remind me of her, and something devoid of colour. I hoped I could get through tonight merged into the black curtain at the back of the stage; to fulfil my promise to Becca and then disappear into the darkness. No more fantasy, no more real world. No more Mull'aman, no more Tyler. And no more Becca.

I wasn't worried about seeing Tyler. I'd gone beyond that. I was shards of broken glass. Ready to cut. Unable to feel.

Becca's death had put things into perspective: nothing mattered.

Now Tyler was here, joking around, green contacts in, hair gelled up in silly look-at-me spikes, a crisp new black shirt tight over his chest. He smiled at Mannie and ignored me, as he carried his guitars into the room.

Chris returned with his cello and came over to me.

There was a loud crash as Tyler's music stand fell over. We looked over and he glared at Chris, but Chris wasn't going to give that child any of his attention right now.

I finished wiring up my keyboard and rested my forehead on the keys.

"Kerella, are you going to be okay?" Chris placed his hand on my back. "You're grieving. We can always go on without you if it's going to be too much."

"Oh, for fuck's sake, Chris! Grieving? That's a bit strong! Stop milking the situation so you can get laid. Just 'cause it's too late to make it with Kat, doesn't mean you have to hit on my other girl."

Chris's eyes hardened. He sucked in his cheeks and took his hat off. He fixed Tyler with a serious look. "Becca died, Tyler. Will you just get over yourself and realise not everything is about you?"

"And I'm not your other girl." I threw in.

"Shit! No one told me. Look, Kerella, I'm sorry. How am I supposed to know if no one tells me anything?" He walked over to Mannie. "What the fuck happened?"

Chris carried a chair over. "Now I've got the cello here, how about we run through that song you've been working on?"

I nodded. I needed to fill the space with something. There were only four hours until the big 'Battle of the Bands' and if I could just play the keyboard for as much of that time as I could, I might just make it through.

I charged full throttle into the rumbling low notes of the introduction and didn't care who was in the room as I started to sing.

> Hot: like the due
> in your eyes,
> that burns
> into my head,

        the dark
          coming home
    into my bed.

Bring in the rain
   to wash you away
      from me.
Let it all drown.
I won't save you now.

Feeling nothing but the rhythmic changes of the season and another branding iron making its mark upon my head.
Hating every need of nothing, counting days and wanting more.
Never to be satisfied, by the pain or by the whore.

But I am not to be had.
I am not to be found:
   not here,
      not in this desert amongst men.

I can feel it,
I can hear it,
   but I won't regret this day.
I can feel it,
I can fear it,
   but I won't regret this day, this day, this day.

Caught up in a little game of trusting blind emotion. To the
ends I hope I satisfied and proved your foul devotion. In the
mask that I will always wear to cover this deception, scratching
T from M and life from limb, a memory that never was inside a dream of self-creation, tore my cloak in hesitation.
Self-destruction reigns supreme: you cut my heart, I cut my dream. And
where I find you, burn it down, block you out of sight and sound.
I call the storm to feel the rain; I see the wretched pain.

You're an echo
   in my eyes,
      and deceit
   set you free.
     And now,
      I wish that you
would lie to me.

Betrayer with a smile.
    Me, a fool and a dog.
        Game ends,
throw me away.
That is how you play.

Feeling nothing but the rhythmic changes of the season and another branding iron making its mark upon my head.
Hating every need of nothing, counting days and wanting more.
Never to be satisfied, by the pain or by the whore.

But I am not to be had.
I am not to be found:
    not here,
        not in this desert amongst men.

I can feel it,
I can hear it,
    but I won't regret this day.
I can feel it,
I can fear it,
    but I won't regret this day, this day, this day.

Need to bring it crashing down, remove all hope of a tomorrow.
Taking what was your domain, to where you'll never want to follow.
Sticky fingers leave their mark, a stain a prize, a deadened heart, which hides behind the consolation on the path of my creation.
For the friend now bonds are broken, games of pawns and I have spoken: let the black and red decide if blood should ever condescend. And tear at me and fall apart, this story line is getting hard.
I feel his touch, I hear his breath, I see the hollow

Pain.
In your eyes.
Closing in.
It's not you.

Regrettable Day.

If you could see
    where I am
        in this space,

>   my choice
>   would be one
>   I could not face.
>
>   I believe in your tears:
>   pain,
>   brought on yourself.
>   Pity (less) sympathy.
>   Revenge
>   will set you free.
>
>   But I won't.
>   Regrettable Day.

After Chris and I finished there was silence for a few moments before Mannie exclaimed: "Oh my god! Oh my god! Oh my goddesses and more! I guess we don't have to worry about finding new material after tonight! That was absolutely amazing! I can't wait to get going on that! You'll have to join me on vocals; I couldn't hit those high notes for the life of me."

I didn't mention that there would be no 'after tonight' for me. I was done with the band. I was done with people. I was going back to my art and my gravestones. My life would be full enough with my father and Ergle the graveyard demon.

Fus came in and Chris went to talk to him.

Tyler came over to me. "I'm sorry about Becca."

I nodded politely and made some notes about a new pattern for the introduction to Regrettable Day.

"Kerella, please. Look at me. I really care for you, more than anything. Everything's just complicated."

"No, Tyler, it's all very simple. Like you."

He grabbed my arm. "Kerella, you're the only person I've ever felt this way about. I can't live without your friendship."

I shook him off. "Don't live then. Life. Death. There's no difference anymore."

"Kerella, you're scaring me."

"Don't concern yourself with me. You gave up that right."

"I'm sorry Becca's dead, I really am. But this isn't just about her; you're still angry with me. And what's going on with you and Chris? You know he's got a huge obsession with Kat, right? You shouldn't use him to make me feel jealous. That's not fair. I still care about you, and you know this is hurting me."

"Tyler, shut up."

He did.

"There's nothing going on between me and Chris. It's just that Chris and I are now the friends you and I are not. My best friend has just fucking died. I have my first ever gig tonight, and if I fuck it up, a good person, maybe two, might lose their jobs and a community they really care about. And some idiot is in my face telling me he's the centre of the universe, and that he cares for me, but he's not even bothered to mention that, in the middle of all of this, he's decided to get married to someone else."

"Come on now, you're misrepresenting things for attention. But I get it; this is hurting me too. You kind of have this power over me…" And then he added in an almost inaudible whisper. "I think I love you."

He walked over to his guitar and started to tune it.

"Take that back." I whispered to my keyboard. I felt my defences crack and Mull'aman found a little niche to worm his way back in.

I pulled myself up and looked over at Chris. What I needed was to sacrifice something so Tyler would never want me, so I could never be tempted. Something that would prove to my stupid imagination that I knew Kaetia wasn't real. If I burned all of this down, then maybe I could find a new home somewhere else.

And Chris was the key.

29: PORCUPINE FAIRY

The stage floor in The Waterhole was covered in scuffed black paint. I stood between two black curtains, which smelled of stale beer, and watched Fus and the singer from Angel Waste set up the instruments. The singer pulled up some photos on his phone and showed them to Fus, who cooed over the singer's three-month-old baby girl. So, that was how Fus behaved around his nemeses.

Tyler and Jenny were at the other side of the stage. Tyler ran his fingers through her hair and said: "I'm writing a graphic novel called 'Reverberate'. It's about a musician taking on a corrupt political elite with his super sexy, dark haired, backing singer and muse. I wanted to ask your permission to give the backing singer your hair?"

Jenny shook her hair and thrust her hips to the side, sliding her hands down her black velvet dress. "Super sexy, huh? I can live with that."

Martin came up behind them. "Yo, Ty. I hear you have Tommy K playing the keyboard for you? You guys are really dredging the gutter. Couldn't you do any better than that? It doesn't seem a fair contest, you may as well pull out now."

"Yeah, you should pull out now, Tyler. Come on: do it for the puppies." Jenny said, leaning forward to show off her cleavage.

Tyler shrugged and Jenny laughed, patting his chest.

Martin pulled her hand away. "No fraternising with the enemy until after we win, Jenny."

"Seriously though, Ty, what's up with that? Is her father sponsoring your band, so you have to include her, or what?" Martin asked.

"Why would he do that?"

"'Cause he's loaded, and the rich have more money than their children have social skills. I hear he used to pay that dead bitch to pretend to be her friend. If he's paying you, get out while you can: the girl is cursed."

"So, she's rich?"

"Tomlinson and Co. duh!" Jenny said. "About her only redeeming feature. I know someone who went to school with her. They say she's got autism, like really high on the scale. They shouldn't let those kinds of people in places like this. I mean, I want to relax and enjoy myself, not be a fucking care worker for the night. How can I unwind when I know there's some mental patient walking around?"

"Ignore them." Chris said, coming up behind me. "You have more talent than they will ever have, and you're here because you're an exceptional musician and we like you."

"Your fiancée is here." Martin said to Tyler.

Tyler pushed Jenny roughly to one side and went to the front of the stage.

"Look what you escaped." Chris said.

"His true colours have certainly been made clear." I said, watching Tyler jump down from the stage and embrace a beautiful woman wearing a stylish black and cream striped dress, with an expensive looking cream coat draped over her arm. She had shoulder length sleek black hair and shining ebony eyes.

"Just for the record, I dyed my hair because it was the last thing Becca and I talked about. This is the first time I've ever seen Kat. I wouldn't change my nail varnish for that prick."

"Duly noted." Chris said.

Tyler led Kat to a reserved table, before running to the bar to get her a drink. I watched her settle down and chat with Mannie. Her manner was easy and confident. She said something to Mannie, who laughed until she had tears in her eyes. Then, Kat shifted her coat and I saw her arm.

"It was a boating accident." Chris whispered in my ear, having moved closer as I watched what would have so recently torn me to pieces.

"I know. Tyler actually managed to tell me that bit."

"Did he tell you it was his fault?"

"No. He missed that bit out."

"They were messing around on her dad's boat, and he dropped her. She went over. Very messy. But could've been worse."

"Poor girl."

"She handled it remarkably well. I think Tyler had more of a problem with it than she did."

"Why doesn't she ever come out then? I got the impression she never leaves the house and Ty has to do everything for her. He said he pays all the bills and does all the shopping."

"Try the opposite way around. Kat's a workaholic, and one of the most in demand computer programmers in the country. She pretty much keeps Tyler. His 'social media empire' isn't as successful as he likes to make out, and most of his income comes from working at 'Sal's Seconds'."

"He's never mentioned that."

"It doesn't fit with his image." Chris put his hand on my back. "Looks like they're getting ready to begin. Will you be okay?"

I looked at my keyboard, lost and lonely on the cold, empty stage. I remembered the image of Kasaman on stage with a bass guitar, and couldn't believe how far away that scene felt right now: how lost Kasaman, Tushenta, Asana, and Mull'aman were. I gave them up for this. And soon I'd have nothing.

"Let's get this over with."

Someone from the local radio station walked onto the stage and began a warmup spiel. The members of Angel Waste convened at the other side of the stage and The Casa Martyrs gathered around me.

"So, who's going to come out for the coin toss, or has either side chickened out already?"

Tyler and Jenny walked into the middle of the stage and began mock posturing: Jenny patting her behind, and Tyler performed mock kung fu kicks in her direction.

"So, what will it be, heads or tails?" The host asked Jenny.

"I think I'll let the lesser musician pick." Jenny answered, sticking her tongue out at Tyler.

"In that case," Tyler said, taking a long look at her curvy figure, "I'll choose tails."

The host tossed the coin, caught it, and slapped it down onto the back of his hand. He showed it to Jenny, who smiled. "Heads, baby. Heads. We'll go on after these amateurs warm the audience up for us."

I felt Chris push me gently and I tripped awkwardly towards my keyboard.

Mannie bounced to the front of the stage and grabbed the microphone.

"Welcome everyone and thank you, thank you, thank you, for coming out to support The Casa Martyrs tonight. Now with every drink you buy you'll get one of these little green token thingies, and remember, they go in the jar labelled 'The Casa Martyrs'. We pledge to donate the prize money to the 'Save Our Community Centre' fundraiser, so a vote for us, is a vote for the future of our town."

A moderate applause rippled through the room.

"Now, we lost one of our own this week, so I'd like to dedicate our first song to the memory of Rebecca Edwards. And this is, Porcupine Fairy."

> Silver stars on net and wire;
>   innocence parading through.
> A precious soul on fire:
>   the world wasn't kind to you.
> Hiding your hurt under bluster

  and spikes, jutting in and out.
Your shine, diminished lustre;
  your world filled up with doubt.

Now you can fly without the need
  of ripped net sequined wings.
Now your quills have made you bleed,
  but the child inside still sings.
Now the world that hurt you,
  has let go and you are free.
Now we say goodbye to,
  our Porcupine Fairy.

Your wings that now are broken,
  lie forgotten in a draw.
Harsh words that once were spoken,
  cannot hurt you anymore.
Too young for what you lived through.
  Too young for how you died.
Your song, it shall continue,
  your spirit immortalised.

Now you can fly without the need
  of ripped net sequined wings.
Now your quills have made you bleed,
  but the child inside still sings.
Now the world that hurt you,
  has let go and you are free.
Now we say goodbye to,
  our Porcupine Fairy.

Now you truly shine.
Now you are carefree.
Cross the line.
Forever be.
Porcupine
Fairy.

  I tried to resist them, but tears rolled down my face. As absurd as it was to think of an innocent Becca pratting about in fairy wings, the song had a strange poignancy. I quickly wiped my face before we launched into Dream Filled Cage.
  After our final song, I ducked off the stage whilst the rest of the band

were still taking bows and sucking up the applause.

At the bottom of the steps, I bumped into Jenny. "Have you seen your face? If you're trying for emo, you just look like a freak."

I pushed past her, and she yelled "Retard!" at me as I ran into the toilets.

I walked up to the large mirror and leant on the dark wooden plinth, staring into the sink. After a few moments, I lifted my eyes to see the humiliation that had paraded on stage in front of a hundred judging eyes.

Jenny had been right to laugh at me. I had mascara streaks down my face, and where I'd rubbed my tears away, I'd left ugly black smudges. I grabbed some paper towels and scrubbed the marks until my cheeks were pink and naked, and the black around my eyes had been tamed.

That would be enough for scurrying home in the dark.

On my way out of the toilets, I bumped into Nick.

"Oh hi. You're Kerella, right? We met a few weeks ago at The Acres."

"Hi. Yes. I'm sorry for your loss."

"Thank you. I'm sorry to hear about Becca. I hear you two were close."

We both nodded politely, like those silly dogs you get in the back of cars.

"You were great up there. So brave to go on so soon after such a tragedy."

"Thank you. Will you be joining us?" I motioned towards the bar.

"Oh no, I'm not ready to be social just yet; I just popped in to show my support." He dropped his token in the jar for The Casa Martyrs.

"Well, good luck and see you around."

"Yes, goodnight."

Angel Waste were well into their first number. I could see The Martyrs assembling at the table where Kat was seated.

A generic-boy-in-black-jeans passed in front of me carrying a couple of pints.

For a second, I scanned the bar for Becca. Then her absence slapped me in the face again. I turned to leave, my promise to her fulfilled, but Chris was stood between me and the exit, a glass of white wine in one hand, a bottle of beer in the other. He walked up and handed me the wine and the token that came with the drink.

"Come on. I know this won't be easy. One drink, and then we can go. Deal?"

I nodded, then took a large gulp of wine.

We arrived at the table and Fus and Mannie pulled over a couple of stools for us to sit on.

"Ah, Chris," Kat said on seeing us. "I owe you a huge thanks for taking care of Ty whilst I finished that contract. You know how difficult it is to work with Ty and Ian running their all-night gaming sessions. You'd think by now Ty'd know how to use a vacuum cleaner or that when you knock over a bottle of coke, you clean up the mess before it dries on the carpet." She nudged Tyler in the ribs, and he stared into his drink.

Mannie looked like she was inflating with rage, but no one pointed out that Tyler had said they'd broken up and that was why he'd been exiled.

"So, does that mean you've some free time on your hands?" Fus asked. "'Cause, if you have, I was hoping we might be able to wangle a little charitable donation of that good ol' brain of yours, Katty?"

"Well, I do owe you for babysitting Ty. Name your price, and don't forget to include the danger money." Fus and Mannie laughed, and Tyler got up and headed to the bar.

Fus continued his sales pitch. "You know the Council is trying to use the Abbie incident, the dip in attendance, and the repair work as an excuse to move us to a smaller and less central location, and to cut our funding. So, we're fighting back by trying to show that the community is behind us and that our centre has a future, is the future for our children. But it's really difficult to appeal to the youngsters of today without money and tech, so we were hoping you may have an idea of how to get us, well, computers. Free computers. And the publicity of a firm wanting to give us computers."

"Well, it's not exactly my area of expertise, but it shouldn't be too hard. You'd just have to develop more of an idea of what kind of computers you want, and exactly why you want them. Draw up policy documents and plans for social engagement, skill development, tutors, buddy systems, etcetera. Pair them up with funding opportunities, and you should be able to get a few donations and press releases. I'll help you write the applications."

"Are you okay?" Chris whispered in my ear.

I turned my face towards his. "Thanks. Just coming down from the set. It was good. One of our best performances."

"The new keyboardist really made the difference."

I smiled and took a sip of wine.

"Yes! Here's to our new keyboardist!" Tyler lifted a shot glass, downed the contents, and slammed the glass on the table. "Hey Chris, shift up." He dragged a stool over and squeezed between us. He looked over at Kat, who was discussing business with Fus and Mannie.

He drank half of his pint in one go.

The song finished, and I joined in the clapping, although I hadn't paid any attention to the music.

"Do you think Regrettable Day is finished, or are you going to work on that idea you had for the overlapping whispers in the chorus?" Chris asked, leaning over Tyler to speak to me.

"I think it still needs to find its shape; a few more run throughs should help that."

"Please, guys, don't do this." Tyler interrupted.

"Do what? Talk about writing songs?" Chris looked at him.

Ignoring Chris, Tyler addressed me. "I don't expect you to remain celibate; I know I can't expect that, but not Chris, please. Someone I don't know, maybe. Just don't sleep with him."

Chris stood up. "Let her do what she wants to do, Tyler. Go back to Kat, and don't make a scene."

"Look mate, I'm telling you to back off."

"Grow up. She's not your toy. You just want everyone to want you and you have to face the fact that you can't have everything. In fact, you certainly don't deserve what you've already got."

Tyler looked at Chris. He put his beer down on the table and slowly stood up. Then he punched Chris right in the face, sending him flying backwards into the group behind us, his hat flying off onto the dancefloor.

"What the hell, Tyler?" Kat bellowed.

Chris was pulling himself to his feet. I ran to his side.

He was shaking his head. "You were never much of a thinker, were you, Tyler? Make up your mind, do you want Kerella, or do you just want her to hang around mooning after you?"

The blood rushed to my face and I started backing away, scared Kat would attack me.

Everyone was staring at Kat as she pieced together what was happening. Her focus snapped to Tyler. "Well?"

I jumped in between them. "Nothing's going on."

Kat looked at me like I was dirt. "Shut up." Then fixing back on Tyler. "I would like to hear Tyler explain."

Why was I protecting him? I stepped towards Chris.

Tyler started grovelling. It was a pathetic sight. "I'm sorry, okay? I just got a bit of a pathetic little crush, and never acted on it. When it came down to it, I realised there was only one woman I loved. I love you. I always will do." He gave her the pleading look he'd given me only hours earlier. "I may have misled Kerella a little bit, but Chris is trying to use the situation to get her into bed, and she's a bit special needs, so I was trying to warn her she was being used." He hastily added, "As a friend, nothing else."

Kat looked at me. I backed into Chris, and he put a reassuring arm around my waist.

"Tyler, we're leaving."

Tyler looked at me; I looked at the floor. I felt Chris let go and move away. Tyler picked up his jacket and ran after Kat.

Mannie came up and gently held on to my arm. "Ker, are you okay?"

I was digesting being described as a 'pathetic crush' and 'a bit special needs', in front of Tyler's perfect little fiancée.

"I won't be the one with a black eye in the morning."

"Take him home and look after him." Fus said, passing me Chris's hat, which he'd retrieved from the dancefloor.

I looked around to see where Chris had gone. He was sitting at the bar, giving me space to make my decision. I turned his hat around in my hands.

I wished Becca was here.

I walked over to Chris and placed his hat back on his head. I held out my hand.

"Take me home."

30: THE CASA MARTYRS

We didn't talk in the taxi on the way to The Acres, and Chris led the way in silence through the gift shop to his red back door.

I felt like I was making a huge mistake, but I didn't want to go back to my flat and collapse into a lonely pit of emptiness, wallow in the loss of Becca, and the death of my stupid crush on Tyler. I knew that would lead to emptying my drinks cupboard and a horrid hangover tomorrow. An awkward early morning cross-country walk-of-shame was a marginally better option.

"Make yourself at home." Chris said, taking off his hat and gesturing towards the red settee Tris was slowly vacating, pausing to have a good stretch on his way down. "Wine or tea?" he asked, heading into the kitchen.

"Tea, please. Any chance you have peppermint?"

"Coming up."

I sat down on one of the armchairs, not yet ready for the intimacy the settee signalled. I looked into the eyes of my selkie hanging on the wall. What did she think about what I was going to do tonight?

I put my bag on the coffee table next to a fruit bowl containing several fresh red apples; the lights reflected bright and white off their smooth skin.

I stood up, turned on the standard lamp in the corner, and switched the ceiling lights off. I dimmed the lamp until I'd chased most of the light out of the room. Whatever was going to happen tonight was for the shadows alone.

I returned to the armchair, checking out of habit for a text from Tyler. Annoyed with myself, I put my phone back in my bag and reminded myself why I was here: to put Tyler behind me once and for all.

Chris came back, put the mugs on the table and sat down. Tris settled on the rug by his feet. Chris moved an icepack from under his arm to his eye, which was already starting to discolour, then he lifted his arm in an invitation for me to come over.

This stoical mystery of a man. And I'd broken down his doors.

I had cost him his best friend. And he wanted me to give him comfort.

I went over to him, handing him his tea to stop things going too quickly. I slipped under his arm and my body tucked neatly against his. For a while, I rested my head against his chest, listening to his heart beating. I couldn't think of anything to say. Chris wasn't talking either, so I took that to mean the silence was okay for him. But I didn't feel comfortable, and needed to move, or talk, or do something.

I lifted my head to look into his dark, Kasaman-like eyes. His uncovered eye observed me from the shadow of his dark blue bandanna. I got up onto my knees and lifted the icepack from his face, so I could see both of his eyes. He still didn't say anything: we just held eye contact and it didn't feel too weird. I gently touched the cold skin with its burgeoning purple-blue mottled stain, and he winced, so I rested the icepack back against his eye and he placed his hand over it to keep it in place. He closed his other eye and leant his head back.

I took the mug from his hand and placed it on the coffee table before I slowly leant towards his slightly parted, cinnamon lips. I brushed my lips gently over his, savouring the sensation of the soft skin.

The threshold of intimacy had been crossed.

I straddled him, without putting my weight onto his legs, and ran my fingers slowly over his face, feeling the stubble which was starting to push through his skin. I moved my fingers up, lifting the bandanna from his forehead. Although I knew he must have been scarred from the car crash, it was a shock to see the thick red lines radiating across his pale forehead. I shot forward, and pressed my cheek against his neck, so he wouldn't see my reaction to seeing his true face.

He let the icepack drop to the floor and moved his hands to my back. The hand which had been holding the mug was hot and moved slightly under my black jumper, stroking the skin of my lower back. Suddenly his ice-cold fingers teased my senses as they skimmed the skin on the other side.

Caught up in the moment, I placed my hands along his jawline and pulled his mouth to my lips, lowering my weight onto his legs.

My phone burst into a recording of Dream Filled Cage, the ringtone I'd assigned to Tyler. I jumped up, grabbed my phone from my bag, turned it to silent, and threw it down onto the armchair.

But the moment was over.

I took my time looking at the artwork on the walls before picking up an acoustic guitar and handing it to Chris. "Play me that song you were talking about the day we went to Timmins Cave, the one the band is named after."

He looked up at me. "What? Now?"

"Yes." I said, moving my phone to one side, noticing I had a voicemail, and sitting down in the armchair.

"Okay, if that's what you want." He said, plucking at the strings and tuning the guitar up a little bit, before strumming a few chords.

I'd never heard him sing before. His voice was quiet and understated, letting the tune and the lyrics do the work.

> We create ourselves from the building blocks of experience.
> We are defined by the categories of our audience.
> We exist within constellations of affiliations.
> We are trapped by obligations and negotiations.
> We are stretched between our roots and defining our own space.
> We strive to find a family, a cause, a bond, a place.

> They're coming through the Circus Gate
>   to spread lies that would bring down Rome.
> On the walls, the martyrs wait
>   to fight to protect their home.
> And the friends that made such promises,
>   sit at home with all their gold;
>   they discuss it in their palaces:
>   the demise that was foretold.

> This is all I have ever known; I will fight to protect it.
> Some travelled until they found us, now we're interconnected.
> Our brothers overseas tell us we are always in their hearts,
> but it's our household in danger and the cracks in our ramparts.
> They said if I prayed their way, they would come and help me.
> We thought our icons had the power to assure our safety.

> They're coming through the Circus Gate
>   to spread lies that would bring down Rome.
> On the walls, the martyrs wait
>   to fight to protect their home.
> And the friends that made such promises,
>   sit at home with all their gold;
>   they discuss it in their palaces:
>   the demise that was foretold.

> Fated friends who came for the end,
>   to stand with our family.
> The Catalans and Italians,
>   defending our casa with me.

> The moon grows dark, and the fog takes the prayer from our breath.

> The battle is here: those that are gathered wear the mask of death.
> We could have chosen capitulation, humiliation.
> But for our home, this sacrifice is our oblation.
> The casa martyrs stand up to die on these three walls with me.
> And the history books talk of inevitability.

Chris plucked out the most heart-breaking tune to wrap up the song, and I struggled to hold back tears.

It was such a beautiful and emotive song, but I couldn't find the words to express what I felt, so I grabbed the first thing that came to me. "Wow! You do like history!" I said, and immediately regretted my lame reaction.

Chris looked odd without his bandanna; there was too much light coming from his face, and there was no hiding from his eyes.

"Yeah... I think it's important that we know what really happened in the past, and not cling without question to the versions that are familiar to us. Even if addressing these false perceptions is painful." He took a deep breath and stared into the bowl of apples. "I was hoping to tell you something the other day, but with everything that happened, I never got the chance."

I remembered the moment that I made a deal with the universe for Tyler to be okay and was promptly punished by having Becca torn from my world.

"You were very honest with me about... the protective falsehoods you fostered, and I feel I ought to try and explain my own experiences. I had an accident a few years ago, and it affected my memory. Whilst I was recovering, I thought my girlfriend left with my daughter, and I've never been able to track them down. Over the last month, I've been remembering some really odd things, and I'm starting to think that maybe they didn't leave, maybe I imagined them, and they never existed in the first place."

"How is that even possible? Surely your friends and family would know whether you had a daughter or not?"

"My mother was my only close family, and she died when I was sixteen. I've never been good at making connections. I find it difficult to trust people, and I think I scare most people away. Except for the memory of a family that may not even exist, I never really had anyone I would call a friend until I moved here and met Ty."

"How did you end up here?"

"I came up for my aunt's funeral, even though we weren't close. But family is family, especially if you have so little of it. Stuart and Mike drove me to the station, and there was 'the accident'. Stuart died, and his father took me in whilst I rehabilitated. I stayed to help him out, and when he died a year later, I found out he left me The Acres."

He sighed and rubbed his hands over his face. He picked up his tea. "I haven't been coping very well lately. It got to the point where I asked Mannie to get me the phone number of a psychiatrist friend of hers. I haven't been able to face making an appointment yet. It would be a waste of everyone's time, as I don't think I can explain what I'm feeling. It makes no sense. I'm sure I have a daughter, but I can't find any evidence that I do. I don't believe in past lives, yet I feel so connected to Constantinople in the fifteenth century. And there's a whole lot of stuff which is even more ridiculous than that." He looked at his reflection in the patio doors, and then his ghostly double made eye contact with me. "I do really like you Kerella, but this month has been a bit crazy, and I'm not sure I'm in a good place to start a relationship."

I looked at Chris without the cloak of Kasaman I'd placed around him. He was someone who may be just as messed up as me.

I stood up, walked across the room, and settled down next to him. I picked up his hand and laced my fingers through his.

"So, let me get this straight: we both may have lied about having a daughter; we both have scars on our faces and probably a lot more in our souls; and both need to see a psychiatrist. I think, we may be more suited than we both realised." I smiled up at him. "But there's no rush to go anywhere." I said, lifting his arm up and snuggling up against his side.

"You're different from anyone I've ever met." He said. "I think that's a good thing."

31: LEAP OF FAITH

Asana had some very strange ideas for the Celebrations. I was reluctant to follow her advice, as I thought it'd make Mull'aman look stupid and conceited, but he was very keen to enact her suggestions.

In the weeks leading up to the sacred event, we stencilled Mull'aman's likeness onto parchments with the phrase 'Celebrations brought to you by the Golden Sun of Kaetia'. The Lower Kaetians of our troupe then placed these icons around the Compound and even hung some in the town.

I didn't see the point of this. Attendance was compulsory for all who lived in the Compound, so there was no need to let them know the Celebrations were taking place, and it was Mull'aman's job, as Guardian of the Nineteenth Tenet, to organise the musical entertainment, so why tell everyone something they already knew? Also, as they are a symbol of our unity and what our society achieves together, implying one person is bringing the Celebrations to Kaetia felt wrong. When I raised this point, Mull'aman pointed out that we weren't saying he was bringing the Celebrations to Kaetia, rather they were coming from the Kaetian Sun everyone had inside of them. If people interpreted the words incorrectly, that was their fault.

For the week of the Celebrations themselves, Asana said we needed to come up with a short phrase that Mull'aman would use regularly and a musical riff to follow each conveyance of this sentence. I thought that would make him look like he couldn't think of new things to say. Asana said as people grew familiar with the phrase, they'd feel a sense of belonging, and associate Mull'aman with the positive message.

I proposed 'Sett is in our Hearts', but Asana said the phrase ought to suggest Mull'aman himself is taking action combined with a vague promise of something good yet intangible. In the end, they settled on 'Bringing you to a brighter Kaetia', which was to be reinforced by a light ringing of bells and an uplifting sweeping crescendo from the woodwind section.

Tonight is the finale of the Celebrations, and I am shocked to have been so wrong about Asana's ideas. It's been completely surreal. All week, Lower Kaetians, and even the occasional Merdiant, have been walking the corridors trying to bump into Mull'aman, and when he is spotted, people have been asking for the strangest things. What seems to be the most popular is for Mull'aman to press his nineteenth tenet brooch into a putty mixture, so the devotee can create an impression of it as a souvenir.

All the icons we distributed have disappeared. Some were pulled down by the Paders, but one of the Lower Kaetians from the choir told me that the Merdiants were selling them in the town for a high price. I asked Asana if she'd cast a spell to influence the behaviour of everyone in Kaetia, she shook her head and said: "No. It just goes to show how similar Kaetians are to lower realm mortals."

After the first couple of days of the Celebrations, Laescenno started repeating the phrase 'Leading for Kaetia's own good' in his lecture series. By the fourth day, he even had a group of musicians on stage with him to follow each repetition with a little upbeat jig to which he danced in that funny manner I used to find so endearing. Parchments with his likeness and the phrase, 'Glorious Leader, Benevolent Ruler' appeared throughout the Compound, but they only disappeared when they fell down and got trodden under foot.

The finale of the Celebrations takes place in the Courtyard of the Arcane so the twenty-one Guardians of the Blazing Court can hear Kaetia's devotion and lift the curse if they are pleased. Asana suggested we place the two elovettas either side of the fountain, facing the audience, so our hands could not be seen and Mull'aman would get the credit for my performance. Around the elovettas, the musicians, instruments, decorations, and holy relics were arranged in a complex labyrinth, so each musician needed a map to navigate the way to their seats.

Laescenno insisted that we involve him in an integral way, so we told him we've arranged a special surprise for him, something that will make him the most popular man in Kaetia. During the finale, he's to wait in the Council Chambers, and after our duet, he'll be brought in by palanquin to a great fanfare.

Once the Celebrations are officially concluded, the dual union of Laescenno and myself, and Mull'aman and fiancée, Miareanas, is scheduled to take place in front of everyone who lives in the Kaetian Compound.

By which time, I hope, I'm so far away, that I'll never see Laescenno again.

The orchestra is building up from the tranquil introduction to a section inspired by Birgitta, which I call 'The Bubble Interlude'. Mull'aman and I are hidden in a tower in the corner of the Courtyard, waiting to make a dramatic entrance before our elovetta duet.

He reaches over and squeezes my hand. "This is it, there's no going back now."

I take a quick look around. No one can see us and as the music gets louder with the lower realm style thumping, no one can hear what we say. "Have you sewn the stones Asana gave you into your outfit?"

"Every single one of them. We will be rich, we will be pretty, we will live charmed lives, and we will prove our love to all of Kaetia."

"I'm scared." I say in a small voice. A blue light fizzles around my clenched fists.

He takes my face in his hands and pulls me close. "You'll be safe, as long as you remember to fall in love with me in the lower realm. Take that into your heart: you must fall in love with me, and only me. If there's any ambiguity, when we get back, I will be executed, and you'll be locked away for the rest of your life and forced to procreate with that repulsive son-of-a-redwaek."

"I'm hoping he'll die before we get back. He can't have many more years in him."

"I'll drink to that." Mull'aman says, winking and pulling out two small bottles. He hands one to me. "For courage?"

I shake my head. He shrugs, drinks both bottles, and pushes them through a hole in a grille to drop down the side of the mountain.

And then we hear our cue.

We walk out of the tower and into the maze. We follow the twisting route towards the centre, our progress marked by coloured lanterns being raised, and different sections of the orchestra picking up the main melody. As we reach the fountain, the music grows louder and more frantic, before suddenly breaking off. The crowd begins cheering loudly and a chant starts up: 'The Golden Son! The Golden Son!' Mull'aman raises his arms into the air and the clapping intensifies. I've never witnessed such passion at a finale of the Celebration of Kaetian Society. I wonder if this may be the key to lifting the curse.

I look around at the twenty-one stone statues that loom over the central courtyard. They remain dormant, their left hands still outstretched, palms facing to the sky as they always have done, the barely legible symbols and arcane words etched into their gowns still mostly obscured by their sandstone cloaks.

I shift my gaze to the tiers of Higher and Lower Kaetians. From the top of a tower behind us, a multitude of coloured lights are being shone so that they sweep over the audience. The people start to get to their feet, stamping, screaming, and waving their arms at Mull'aman. Far back in the darkness of the higher tiers, special guests from outside the Compound are waving banners in the air. The atmosphere is so charged, I feel that whatever happens here tonight will be divine.

Mull'aman and I sit down at the elovettas and let our music weave through the gnarled limestone columns. I play with my entire soul, praying to Sett that our plan goes smoothly.

We finish the duet, and Mull'aman leaps up to take a bow. "And that, my friends, is bringing you to a brighter Kaetia!"

As the bells ring through the air and the woodwind swoops through the crescendo, the crowd claps with increased enthusiasm. Mull'aman lifts his hands to quieten them, and they respond immediately.

He commands the audience's attention. They hang on every twitch of every facial muscle. And Mull'aman is drawing it out to maximum effect.

Whilst he's toying with the audience, Asana moves quietly between the elovettas in preparation for the closing rites. She looks like the perfect Kaetian deity: posture correct, eyes devout, hood framing her inscrutable face.

Mull'aman breaks his silent posturing. "You honour me Kaetia. And tonight, I have been doubly honoured. In light of the success of these Celebrations, and the bond I've formed with my Supreme assistant during the process, our glorious leader and benevolent ruler, Laescenno, has agreed to let matters of the heart sway the Council, and I will be your next Supreme Kaetian."

The crowd starts thumping and chanting: "The Golden Son! The Golden Son!"

The dazzling coloured lights begin to swoop and dive again, making it hard to see what's going on. Behind us, the orchestra launches into The Bubble Interlude, but this time with even more volume. Through the chaos, I see the Paders start to head our way, but our labyrinth is hindering their progress.

Mull'aman pulls a knife out of his cloak, spins around, grabs hold of Asana's hand, forces it over the fountain, and drags the blade across her palm.

She feigns shock so well, I panic, thinking things aren't going to plan. This is what she suggested we did, wasn't it?

A bright magenta sparkling light bursts forth from the fountain and projects up into the sky.

The coloured lights from our production suddenly stop, and the normal lighting returns. I see a body fall from the tower where the lights were being coordinated.

Laescenno bursts through the Council Chamber doors, his face a deep red. He grabs a sword off a Pader and heads towards us.

My hand is pulled over the fountain. Mull'aman smiles at me, his emerald-green eyes reflecting the pink glow from the fountain. "We love each other: what can go wrong?" *He says as he draws the blade over my palm. As my blood drips into the fountain, I feel like I'm fading. A warm tight sensation wraps itself around my head and I hear screaming.*

Then everything goes white.

And I think: "What can go wrong?"

32: THE FALL OF CONSTANTINOPLE

I strode along the coastal path, the sea breeze cool and pleasant on my face. It was nice to be moving after the weird limbo of the last couple of days. With no band, no gig, no Becca, and no to-and-fro texting with Tyler, my life had come to a dramatic stop. My father had phoned several times, but I was not in the mood to talk to him. Becca's funeral was on Tuesday. I'd see him then, no doubt.

It had been a welcome quiet. I lounged on the settee and let my thoughts wander. All my life I'd been told what to do and how to think. It was always made clear what was expected of me, and I tried so hard to be who I was told I should be, I never really formed any opinion of what I wanted, or who I was. Maybe that was why I filled my head with silly fantasies. But now Kaetia was as dead as it could be, I started thinking, what if I put all that energy into creating my real life?

Chris sent a bouquet of flowers the day after we'd fallen asleep together on his settee, with an invitation to come over for dinner today. No one had ever sent me flowers before. There was something unobtrusive and tranquil about Chris. I'd been sucked into Tyler's drama and not really noticed how much I enjoyed my time with Chris. He didn't make any demands on me, and around him I could be my own creative strange self and he offered support, rather than trying to bring the attention back to himself.

Tyler hadn't phoned or texted since he left me the voicemail on Saturday. Anytime I felt myself growing weak and my feelings for Mull'aman creeping back in, I would just hold the phone to my ear and listen to his last words to me.

I did it once more on the walk to Chris's, just to remind myself I wasn't the only one burning bridges.

"I left Kat for you tonight. I told her I made a mistake and that I wanted to be with you. I come over to your flat to tell you, and where were you? Fucking that freak, that's where. You make me sick, and I never want to see your manipulative scarred face again."

Well, Mull'aman, I'll make sure there's no ambiguity over our relationship.

I bent down by the path and picked up a stone I thought Chris may like. Then, I saw one I liked. I put my bag down and stood for a while as I looked out to the sea, imagining Tyler saying he couldn't be with someone like me, calling me a pathetic little crush, telling me I made him sick, asking me what could possibly go wrong.

And then I took the stone and threw it with all my strength, right into the face of an imaginary Mull'aman, hovering in the air above the sea. It made me feel a little bit better, but I'd need a lot more stones to really make any difference.

I picked up my bag; the stones I'd gathered clinked against the bottle of red wine. I'd walked into someone else's life. I didn't do polite meals where you turn up clutching a bottle of wine and have pleasant conversations about the weather. I did disconnected drama and running away. What on earth would I talk to Chris about? "Hey, by any chance are you the Devil, or some really lecherous old git? And how do you feel about losing the Battle of the Bands, the community centre being sold off to developers, Mannie losing her job, and Fus quitting in protest?" But this was part of the new future I was creating; I was going to have to step out of my comfort zone.

Chris said he'd meet me at his after he'd finished with work, and to just make myself at home until he got there.

I freshened up in the bathroom, swapped my walking gear for the knee length dark blue dress and heels I'd got for Becca's funeral, and ran a comb through my black hair, noticing the roots were already starting to show. I felt like a little girl wearing her mother's clothes. I missed the layers, decorations, lace, and safety pins I usually hid behind: anything to stop the eye looking at the scared girl underneath the material.

But it was time to take my cloak off. I wanted Chris to see me.

Heading through to the living room, I picked a red apple from the fruit bowl and slumped into the armchair. I pulled out my phone and started to scroll idly through the local news. The two boys who drowned last week looked familiar. Maybe they were the guys who tried to make me go home with them before Chris swooped in to save me, but I couldn't be sure: they all looked alike to me. Bloody lower realm mortals.

I took a bite of the apple.

The back door opened, and Tris ran into the room, sticking his nose into my lap for a brief fuss before running into the kitchen. "Chris?" Nick called out.

"He's not here at the moment. Shouldn't be long."

"Do you mind if I wait for him?" Nick said, coming down the hall, folding

Tris's lead carefully and laying it down on the coffee table.

"Of course not. Don't mind me."

"I just wanted to have a quick chat with him about coming back to work."

"He said he'd be here not long after seven."

Nick nodded politely and looked around the room.

He walked over to the bookcase and picked up a photo of Tyler, Chris, Fus, Mannie, and himself.

"Sorry about the Battle of the Bands. People are saying if it weren't for Tyler's outburst during Angel Waste's set, you guys would've won it."

He put the photo down and ran his hand through his floppy dark blond hair. "It's a shame. I mean, I know they couldn't be more different, but they've pretty much been family since Chris caught Tyler sleeping in his car in the carpark and dragged him inside. Do you know what happened to make Ty so angry?"

"It was just Tyler being Tyler."

"Well, Mannie'll talk it out of him."

"So, he's staying with Mannie and Fus."

"They took pity on him after Kat kicked him out."

I laughed quietly to myself. The truth always followed a few days behind Tyler's mouth.

Nick pointed his finger with enthusiasm at my selkie. "Chris said this is your work?"

I nodded.

"You are so talented. This painting is magical."

"Thank you." I said, blushing.

"I wanted to be an artist when I was younger, but never really had the patience with it."

"It's never too late to start."

"Nah, that phase died years ago. If I were to take my life in a new direction now, I think I'd be a nurse after what they did for my mother. I got totally caught up in it all last year." He gave a little snorty laugh. "I read so much about nursing and hospice care, Mannie staged an intervention." He sighed. "I have to be realistic; that kind of training costs too much. Anyway, I'm not complaining. I love working here."

"I'm glad to hear that." Chris said, rubbing Tris's head. "So, you're coming back to work?"

"I was thinking next week, if that's okay with you?"

"Any chance you can start on Saturday? Lucy's off on holiday, and Tyler was going to cover her shifts, but I doubt that'll be happening now."

"Even better. I'm going a bit crazy rattling around the house on my own."

See you then. Nick ruffled the fur on Tris's back. "Lovely talking with you again, Kerella. Have a nice evening."

Chris lifted his hand slightly in a wave as Nick left. His eye didn't look as bad as I thought it was going to look, just a fluffy pink cloud lining the socket. He turned to me. "Wine?"

"Yes. Please." Then, remembering the wine I'd brought with me, I tipped the contents of my bag on the floor. "I brought you this." I said handing him the bottle. "Oh, and these." I said, getting down on my knees, scooping up the stones, and holding them up towards him.

He looked at me for a few moments, lips slightly parted, eyes quizzical, his left-hand hovering in mid-air.

He put the wine on the coffee table, then cupped my hands with his to retrieve the stones, examining the treasure in his hands. "Thank you, Kerella, this is exceptionally thoughtful of you."

Wow. If he reacted with this much gratitude to a handful of stones I picked up on my way over here, I should've given him the console. He'd probably offer me up his first born. Although, that might be me, and I already have one of those.

I reached under the coffee table to retrieve the bottle of water that had rolled out of my bag and shoved it in the side pocket. Chris placed the stones in a small wooden bowl on the bookshelf, and I followed him into the kitchen.

"I hope you don't think this is cheating, but I made up a pomegranate salad for us earlier." He said, retrieving two bowls and a bottle of white wine from the fridge.

He poured me a glass of Chablis and poured himself a glass of the red I'd brought with me, and without needing to say anything, we picked up our bowls and walked out to the patio to enjoy the meal in the evening air. Chris closed the patio doors behind us. Tris pawed at the carpet a couple of times, then went to settle on the settee.

As I got to the table, I saw a small parcel decorated with a dark blue ribbon.

Chris gave me a half smile. "I hope you don't mind. Happy Birthday."

I was shocked he knew it was my birthday. Not even my father had remembered.

He handed me the parcel. "It may be a bit odd. I took a gamble."

I put my bowl down and picked up the present. I pulled the wrapping away to reveal a facsimile of the Visconti-Sforza Tarot deck.

"I saw you had a few Tarot decks on your shelf when I was at yours. This was always my favourite, so I thought you may like it."

I opened the box and ran my finger over the gold edges of the cards. This was probably the most thoughtful present I'd ever received. "Wow. I love it. Thank you."

I took a sip of the wine Chris had picked out for me. It was probably the nicest wine I'd ever tasted. I took a bite of the salad, bursting the smooth pomegranate jewels one by one, letting their juices mingle with the creamy goats' cheese.

The evening breeze carried the scent of clover, and I looked around the warm tones of the flowers in Chris's walled garden.

Until Dream Filled Cage broke the mood. I grabbed my phone out of my pocket, hit reject call, and threw my phone into the bushes.

I looked into Chris's dark eyes and stood up. As I passed his chair, I held my hand out behind me. Our palms met and he followed me to the evening shade under the oak tree.

I turned to face him, reaching my hands up behind my back and pulling down the zip. My dress slipped down to the grass and I stepped out of it.

He moved towards me, kissed my neck and ran his hands gently over my back, sending shivery sparks through my body. I unbuttoned his black shirt and worked it slowly over his shoulders. His skin was soft and warm.

Under my fingers, his belt slid through the buckle and the buttons of his jeans popped through their holes. His fingers ran through my hair, down my back and rested lightly at the base of my spine.

I pushed his jeans down and he kicked them to one side, then he pulled off his socks.

We moved close, so our skin was touching, my head filled with his musky scent. He cupped the back of my head with one hand and kissed my shoulder. I grabbed at his buttocks, feeling his erection rise against me as his hands slid over my back and unhooked my bra.

As one, we lowered ourselves onto the grass and I gazed into his brown eyes.

The loud rumble of the staff area patio doors caused us both to pull away.

"Tyler! What the hell are you doing here!" Chris yelled, jumping up.

"Who the hell is Asana?" Tyler shouted, running towards me. I fumbled with the pile of blue material on the floor next to me, trying to find the bottom of my dress, then quickly pulled it over my head.

Chris ran at Tyler, grabbed him by the neck and thrust him up against the wall. He hissed in an unearthly voice. "What do you know about Asana?"

"Only that the bitch cut into my head and told me to tell Kerella that Kasaman's here." Tyler managed to croak.

Chris slowly lowered Tyler to the ground and turned round to fix me with his devil-eyes. Even in just his black underpants, Kasaman was intimidating in his human form.

He stalked towards me. "And who are you? Why is Asana sending you messages?"

"I don't know." I said, falling back down onto the grass, holding my arms above my head.

He pulled me up roughly and threw me against the wall next to Tyler. "But you know Asana?"

"I don't know. I don't know. I don't know." I shouted.

I looked at Chris and squeaked. "Who are you?"

The question seemed to confuse him.

He took a step back.

"Demetrius." He finally said.

Tyler took a step forward. "So, you're not Kasaman?"

Chris looked at Tyler. "Where is Kat? Is my daughter safe?" Then he looked at me. "Does that make you Miareanas?"

Tyler took another step forward, and I could see that he was holding a rock behind his back. "Are you Kasaman?"

Chris's jaw dropped in devastation and he looked at me. "You can't be Tushenta?"

And the rock came down on his head.

33: INTO THE WOODS

"You can't hit someone with a head injury!" I shrieked at Tyler, as I ran onto the lawn and grabbed my shoes.

Chris lay sprawled face down on the patio.

He didn't move as I tiptoed back past him.

"Oh my god, you killed him!" I slapped Tyler's arm.

"I doubt the Devil dies that easily. Come on!" He said, grabbing my hand and pulling me towards the gift shop.

"We need to call an ambulance. My phone's in the bushes, have you got yours?" I said, pausing to slip my shoes on.

"I'm not calling a fucking ambulance. What part of this are you not getting? We are running away from the Devil who wants to kill us. Now move." Tyler pushed through a fire exit, and an alarm started to go off.

I stumbled across the ochre carpark as quickly as I could whilst Tyler charged on ahead.

"Will you hurry up! What's taking you so long?"

"I'm not exactly dressed for this."

"Why are you wearing such stupid shoes?"

"Because tonight's plans didn't involve running over gravel with an annoying prick whilst trying to escape the Devil." I shouted at him. My ankle twisted sharply to one side. "Ow!"

"Yeah, I could see what your plans were for tonight. And I could just fucking leave you here, but that's not the kind of person I am. Look, hold on to my arm, and lose the shoes when we hit the road."

"How did you get here?"

"I walked over."

"With no kind of escape plan? Jeez, what a great strategic thinker you are!"

"Hey! Today was meant to be about recon; I didn't know you were already in bed with the enemy."

"We should have taken Chris's keys and stolen his car."

"It's a bit late to suggest that now, unless you want to go back to see if he's still unconscious?"

"Or dead." I said sadly. I really hoped he wasn't dead.

We reached the road, and I slipped out of my shoes, picking them up in case we met any more rough terrain in the course of our escape. The alarm stopped.

"Shit! He must be awake." Tyler said, looking panicked. "He's going to be pissed I hit him."

"Are you sure he wants to harm us?"

"Do you want to go back and check? And if he didn't want to hurt us before, he probably will now. I, for one, don't want to risk it."

I thought about the thousands of people Kasaman had turned into redwaek, all the stories of murder, torture, and sorcery. We couldn't risk it. "This way." I said, starting to jog down the road. "There's a footpath in the next field which'll take us up to the woods; we can hide in there."

"What kind of powers has he got? He might know where we are, no matter where we hide."

"I think if he had those kind of powers, we'd have seen evidence of them by now."

"What if he uses Tris to sniff us out?"

"You have to train sniffer dogs, but if you keep dawdling, he'll be able to see you with the magical power of his eyes."

"Well, if you had sensible shoes on, we'd be in the woods by now."

"If you'd not come barging in, we wouldn't be running for our lives right now. Here's the footpath." I said and started to climb over the wall.

Tyler put his hands on my arse to give me a lift.

"Get your hands off me."

"I'm just trying to speed you up; you're taking forever."

"It's not exactly easy to climb in this dress." I clambered down the other side. "And don't start the whole, 'Why are you wearing such a stupid dress?' thing."

Tyler jumped down into the field. "Well, it is a stupid dress." He winked at me.

"Fuck off."

"Shit! I hear a car!" Tyler said.

I threw myself down onto the grass and rolled up against the hedge. "Quick, lie down. If it's him, he may not see us." Tyler copied me.

As the car drove past, Tyler lifted his head up a bit. "Yep, that's Chris's car."

I sat up. "Give it a moment, then pelt it up to the trees in case he comes back when he doesn't see us on the road."

"The idiot really shouldn't be driving after being hit on the head."

"*The* idiot shouldn't have hit him on the head in the first place."

"I was saving your life, remember? And it was more helpful than squealing: 'You can't hit someone with a head injury.'"

"I do not sound like that."

"Come on, let's run! Now!"

The run up the grassy bank was easy, but the path through the woods was uneven and stony. I paused to put my shoes back on. "He didn't say he was Kasaman, he called himself Demetrius. Who the fuck is Demetrius?"

"Yeah, 'cause the Devil would never lie to confuse us. Will you hurry up, we're not far from the back gate of the Acres."

Tyler set off at a brisk walk and I limped painfully on for about an hour until we got to the edge of the reservoir.

"I need to stop here." I said, slipping clumsily down into a depression by the path. I carefully removed my shoes to see how bloodied and blistered my feet were.

"I guess we're far enough away and it's getting dark. He won't find us here tonight." Tyler said. He took out his phone and used the torch to have a look around.

"Do you think he'll call the police?" I asked.

"Nah, Chris wouldn't do that."

"So, you think Chris wouldn't call the police, yet you made me run all the way out here because Kasaman would kill us?"

"Well, better safe than sorry?" Tyler replied, sounding uncertain. He shone his torch down at me. "You left your bra behind." He said, resting the light on my nipples.

I wrapped my arms around myself. "It's cold and I wasn't planning to be sitting in the woods at night with a pervert."

He climbed down to sit next to me, slipped out of his jacket, and draped it over both of our shoulders. "I may be a pervert, but I'm also a gentleman."

He put his arm around me, and we leant into each other for warmth.

"By the way," he whispered into my hair: "happy birthday."

"Right back at you. I guess coming through the portal at the same time meant we were born on the same day."

We were quiet for a while.

"What are we doing here?" I asked the aether.

"We're hiding from Chris."

"This is ridiculous; none of it's real."

"Well, I didn't really believe any of the stuff I've been dreaming, but if Chris really is Kasaman, and you really are Tushenta, I really must be Mull'aman."

"So, you really are Mull'aman."

"I really am your Mull'aman. Your fiancé, the man who saved you from that redwaek, and now Kasaman. I am the Golden Son of Kaetia."

"And the biggest disappointment of my life."

"Hey, that's not fair." He was quiet for a moment, then laughed. "I knew you were my sidekick."

"I am not your bloody sidekick."

"No, I mean the character in Reverberate. I knew it was based on you. My backing singer, muse, and lover. Taking on a corrupt political elite, and it doesn't get any more corrupt than the Kaetian Council."

"Why did Chris ask if I were Miareanas? Is she down here as well?"

"I think she might be Kat. But I left her for you. Before I knew any of this, I made my choice. We really do belong together."

"Nick said Kat threw you out."

"Only because I broke it off with her and it is her house."

"I just don't believe anything you say anymore."

"Please, Tushenta, you must believe me: had I not already been with Kat when I met you, we wouldn't be in any of this mess. Would you prefer me to be the kind of person to drop someone he's been in a relationship with for six years for a girl he's just met, no matter how amazing that girl is?"

"I'm not Tushenta."

"Yes, you are."

"Here, I'm just Kerella."

"Okay. But you are Tushenta, and this is really real?"

"Yes."

"Jeez, what a head fuck."

"What do you remember?"

"Just weird bits that come to me in dreams. Like earlier today, I fell asleep, and this psychotic bitch called Asana cut into my head to get my attention. She asked me to tell Tushenta, who is Kerella…" He paused and pointed at me. "You."

"Yes, I know who I am."

"To tell you, that they think Kasaman got someone to sneak his blood into the portal, so he'd be down here with us. Becca was with her."

"Becca's with Asana?"

"Well, she was in my dream."

"There's a meeting of opposites."

"Who is Asana, anyway?"

"You don't remember?"

"Things are a bit fuzzy. When I dream about them, they feel real. Then, when I wake up, after about an hour, I've forgotten most of it."

"I used to write down the dreams when I woke up, but I stopped when I convinced myself I was going crazy."

"So, you know who Asana is?"

"She's my mother."

"The one who died when you were young?"

"No, the Kaetian one. She's also, sort of, God."

"And what does Kasaman want with you?"

"He's my father."

"So Chris is also the head of Tomlinson and Co.?" He said with an odd chuckle.

"Ty, you can't honestly be this thick? Kasaman is my Kaetian father."

"It was a joke. Jeez, I thought you had a pretty good sense of humour." He punched my arm gently. "So, God and the Devil had a child, and that's you? Hold on, I'm remembering something. God... Asana... Isn't she sleeping with Mia's mother?"

"What?" I exclaimed. "I know nothing about that."

"Well, Mia and I were close. I'm sure she told me that."

"Well, fuck me. I'd never have guessed. She always seemed so... stiff."

Tyler lapsed into silence for a bit.

"So, when we get married and do the whole ceremonial 'conjoining of essences' thing, I'll be an immortal God too."

"How about we get to me not hating you first?"

"You don't hate me." He said kissing the top of my head.

"Maybe it's more pity than hate."

"Conjoining of essences." Tyler said slowly, ruminating on the sound. "Kaetians really suck at naming things. They should call it something like 'The Ritual of Consummation', or 'The Night of Rising Miracles'."

"I think it sounds better in Kaetian. And it's certainly not the first thing I'd change about that place." I muttered, feeling rather sleepy.

"Yeah, I'd get rid of the no sex before marriage rule."

"From what I hear, that rule never stopped you."

"You're one to talk! You've hardly been a puritan saint since you've been down here!"

"Look, can we try to get some sleep? If we have to fight the Devil tomorrow, it'd be nice if we're not yawning our heads off."

"Okay. Good night, Tushenta."

"It's Kerella." I corrected him. "Goodnight, fuckwit."

"Hey!"

34: DEMETRIUS

A fluttering sound woke me up. I slipped carefully out from under Tyler's arm and crept up the embankment. I watched as two swans and four cygnets walked down to the water and swept away on the calm water.

Tyler let out a snort and slept on.

It was starting to get light and would soon be time to jump back into the madness that was whatever the hell was going on.

I decided I wanted to face it alone. I didn't feel comfortable with Tyler's decisions, or the assumptions he was making. I picked up my shoes and headed to the edge of the reservoir. There was no way I could walk far in my heels today, but it would be quiet enough at this time of the morning to walk barefoot along the road back into town. I couldn't phone for a taxi, or go back to my flat, as my phone and keys were at Chris's house. So, my only option was to turn up dishevelled at my father's office and beg to borrow the spare key. It wouldn't be the first time, and no doubt he'd make me pay for it.

Until the office opened, I would just have to hide, and I knew exactly where I wanted to be.

I found a service road and carefully picked my way along the grass in the centre, hoping I was heading towards the main road. For the first few minutes, each step stung and ached, causing me to hobble about as though I were drunk. Eventually the pain blurred into a permanent dull throb, my skin found a compromise between healing rigidity and functional flexibility, and walking became easier.

I'd been on the main road for about twenty minutes before I heard a car coming, and to be safe, ducked down in the verge, but it wasn't Chris's car.

As I got closer to town, I took a backroad to the coast and limped out to my secret ledge.

I lowered myself gently down from the rocky outcrop, and slowly took the weight off my feet, gasping as the pain shifted form.

I pulled one of my feet close to my face, assessing the damage. Well, if Chris doesn't kill me, I won't be able to walk anywhere for a week after this.

Oh god. This can't be happening.

Had I imagined it all? Had I had a psychotic episode, hit Chris on the head myself, and run around all night?

Either way, I was going into hiding after this.

I watched the sky morph from pastel dawn to belligerent day. A group of seals were basking on the rocks below and a heron flew past in a long arc. If I wasn't so hungry, I would stay here all day. I should probably start keeping a box of snacks here. And maybe a mini fridge with a good stock of wine. And some books.

I kept imagining footsteps on the other side of the rocky outcrop. I told myself that, even if Chris were there, he'd walk right by and never know I was here. Still, every few moments, I checked he wasn't perched on top of the rocks, ready to swoop down on me.

And then I did hear something.

To start with, I didn't dare move. Then, slowly, I turned my face up to the heavens.

Perched, Pader like, at the top of the rocks, was Kasaman; a devilish silhouette against the bright blue sky. He was looking down at me, although with the shadow of his hat and the sun behind him, I couldn't see his face.

He was holding something behind his back.

I started to edge backwards.

"Stop, you'll fall." He said, breaking the silence.

"You won't hurt me?"

"Of course I won't hurt you."

His voice was different: deeper, slower, travelling right from the depths of hell itself.

"Tyler hit you, not me. I wanted to call an ambulance, but we were scared and ran away."

"Where is Mull'aman?"

"I left him sleeping in the woods. I needed some space to think."

Kasaman shifted his weight and started to climb down. I edged back further. He stopped, then moved the object from behind his back and slowly lowered my bag down to me.

I couldn't trust him, but I was thirsty. I fished out the bottle of water, checked the plastic tabs were still intact, twisted the top off and took a long satisfying drink, letting the water spill down my chin.

"How did you know I was here?"

"I remembered seeing you here that morning I took you by surprise before we were introduced. Then, that night you told me Rebecca was taking you home, I was walking Tris, and saw you here again. I figured this place had some special meaning for you. I will confess, I explored the rocks a few times after that."

I looked at him, trying to get a clue about his true character from his face, his eyes, his heart. But it was all shadows and darkness, and the bright sky behind him was hurting my eyes.

"Please believe me, Tushenta, I'm not going to hurt you."

"Kerella. I'm not Tushenta. I am Kerella. Kerella. Ker rell a, Ker rell Ah."

"Okay, Kerella."

"But you are Kasaman?"

"Yes."

"You said you were Demetrius. Who's that?"

"That is who I am. Demetrius. Later, I was Giovanni. And now, I am Chris. Kasaman is what the Kaetians call me, and I am not Kaetian."

"You're the Devil."

"No. That is a narrative the Kaetians created. I was born human, Demetrius, here on earth, in 1427. I lived and died like any other mortal."

"Did you murder Asana's family?"

"I was falsely accused of that crime. I believe Hyrensus framed me. Asana knows it wasn't me, but I fled for her sake: for your sake. If we challenged the Council's version of events, they'd have brought us all down."

"And the redwaek? How do you explain them?"

He stared over the sea; his eyes fixed on the horizon.

After a long while, he spoke. "I can make excuses. I can explain what happened. But I cannot say I am innocent in this."

"Not quite the comforting answer I was hoping for. So why are you here? What do you want from me?"

"To get to know you. To get to know my beautiful daughter."

"Well you certainly did that!"

"Yes, well, thank god Mull'aman turned up when he did."

"Yes, I shall thank Asana when I see her, and for once, Tyler did something right."

"Remind me to send him a fruit basket."

"Fruit basket from hell."

"I'm not the Devil. This is why I'm here. I heard that you and Mull'aman came to walk in the lower realm, and I used the opportunity to try and get close to you while you were away from Kaetia. I want you to get to know the real me, not the monster Kaetia makes me out to be."

"Did you know who I was?"

"Clearly, I did not. Initially I thought you may be Kaetian. Kaetians have a certain magnetic pull towards each other. People from the lower realm seem somewhat…"

"Two dimensional."

"That works. I kept dropping hints, but neither you nor Mull'aman reacted. I thought Kat must be a Supreme Kaetian as she excels at everything she sets her mind to." He paused. "I also thought I was going crazy."

I looked out at the horizon.

Crazy.

Crazy.

Crazy.

Of course this wasn't happening. I started scratching at my face, hoping the pain would somehow bring me back to reality.

My hands were shaking and I couldn't quite get enough breath. I kept trying to suck it in, but it wasn't working.

I felt a presence by my side. It must be my imagination.

My hands were pulled away from my face and down towards my legs.

It can't be the Devil. It can't be the Devil.

"Shhhh." Still holding my hands firmly away from my face, Chris gently put his other arm around my shoulder.

I sobbed into his chest.

"What have you done to your feet? You were that scared of me?"

"I thought you were the Devil."

"I'm just your father. That is all I will ever be. I will never hurt you."

We watched the sea for a while, and I let my perception shift and settle into the new normal. The wounds to my reality were severe, but I had no choice: I had to keep moving forward.

"I don't know if you remember, when you were younger, I asked a Merdiant to fashion you a small Pader cloak. Such things are not approved of in Kaetia, but you loved it. You refused to take it off. I can see you so clearly, pretending to be my personal Pader guard whilst helping me build the herb bed in the Kaetian Gardens."

"After they removed the fishponds." I interrupted him.

"After they removed the fishponds." He repeated after me. "So, you remember?"

"Not really. But they changed the books to say the fishponds were never there in the first place."

"Bloody Librarians." He said.

"Bloody Librarians." I echoed.

"Please will you let me take you somewhere to clean and dress your feet?"

"Is your car nearby. I don't think I can walk far."

"It's at home. I'll go and get it and bring it as close as I can. Do you want me to carry you to the road?"

"I'll get to the road, but can I ask a favour?"

"Anything."

"Can you take me back to mine and stop on the way to pick up a brie, houmous, black olive, and iceberg lettuce baguette?"

He smiled and was Chris again. "I wasn't expecting that."

"You have a lot to learn about me." My stomach gurgled loudly at the thought of food.

Chris started to get up.

"Chris?"

"Yes?"

"Promise me you won't go off on Tyler when we see him."

He looked stern for a few moments. "I promise. He'll probably be at The Acres, so I'll bring him back with me."

"No. He'll be in the carpark of my flat, pretending to be a hero."

"We'd better get three baguettes then."

We pulled into the carpark. I opened the car door and slowly put my feet on the gritty tarmac. I was clinging on to the three baguettes.

Chris came round to help me. "Do you want me to carry you?"

"No, I'll be okay."

"Get away from her!" Tyler yelled, running at Chris waving a big stick in the air.

Chris walked up to Tyler and punched him in the face. Tyler fell backwards onto the floor.

"You bloody hit me, man!"

"Chris! You promised you'd let him be!"

Chris shrugged. "He hurt you. He has also hit me twice this week and I refrained from hitting him back. And, as apparently I'm the Devil, I let myself see red."

With a devilish smirk, he held his hand out for Tyler. "Even?"

Tyler looked at him sideways, then looked at me. I held out a Pork baguette for him. "He's safe."

"But he's the Devil."

"He's not really the Devil, he's just, like, really fucking old."

Tyler took Chris's hand and let him pull him up to a standing position.

I thrust a baguette at each of them.

Chris tried to pick me up; I swatted him away.

"Look, this is what's going to happen. Tyler, you're going to move in with Chris. Some things are just so weird, you have to keep them in the family, and our shit, is as weird as it gets."

"Seriously?" Tyler said. "You expect me to move in with the Devil?"

"I'm not the Devil."

"You hit me."

"You knocked me out!"

"Shut. Up. Now, I'm going to limp upstairs, soak my feet, put some music on, and maybe paint some shit. And neither of you are going to text, or phone me, until I get in touch with you."

They both stood there staring at me.

"Do you understand?"

They nodded.

"Now go! Allez, allez!" I said, clapping my hands.

Without looking back, I hobbled over to the door, and let myself and my baguette in. I pulled myself up the six flights of stairs to my flat and was back in my nice normal home.

The only indication that things had changed was that I locked all the extra bolts and moved a chair up against the door.

35: THE MISAPPROPRIATION OF THE BLOOD RED ROSE

I held a blood red rose in my hand.

It was an empty, gimmicky gesture. Becca wouldn't care what I held or what I did. I let her die. I was so wrapped up in my own drama, I hadn't noticed her drug problem was getting worse. If I hadn't lost her that night, she would be here to tell me that Chris and Tyler were winding me up. If she were here, Kaetia would still be just a figment of my imagination.

But she was dead. And cold. And rotting. And apparently, with Asana taking a knife to Tyler's head.

I'm sure she would find some happiness in that last bit.

Socially prescribed attendance at this lower realm ritual, throwing flowers on a wooden box, and listening to three songs in a borrowed room, before the conveyer belt moved on and changed the corpse and the grievers, would not change anything. Becca was dead. We let her down. She needed us, and we weren't there. Maybe now her addiction made her bleed, she can fly without the need…

I looked around for Mannie.

I wanted to hear her sing Porcupine Fairy. But we were being fed tinned music and a stranger was telling us God loved her.

Because we didn't love her enough.

Mannie was shrouded in black net. A dark cloud in a crowd of grief. It was not her stage to perform on today.

She was leaning on Fus's shoulder. He held her tight, his lower lip trembling.

The Devil sat next to them, not so discretely looking in my direction every few moments.

Mull'aman was in the row behind, his headphones hanging over his shirt collar, not quite as hidden by his jacket as I'm sure he believed they were.

I slid out of the uncomfortable chair with the red velvet seat and headed out of the nearest door.

Despite the heatwave, the grass was green and inviting. I carefully made my way across the carpark, my feet still tender. Upon reaching the grass, I kicked off my sensible flat black shoes, and walked a few paces out onto the soft manicured lawn of the funeral home garden.

There was a small slope leading to a stream. Four trees on either side of me created a conduit down to the water. I leant against the nearest tree and watched a group of ducks swim against the current.

"I thought I told you to stay away from me?"

"You said not to phone or text you."

"And you think that means chase me away from a funeral?"

"Kerella, please."

"Chris... Just leave me alone."

He took a few steps back, but the other mourners were spilling into the carpark, and my solitude was over.

Becca had been packaged up and sent on her way; now we could get back to normal and pretend nothing had changed.

I watched my father convey his sympathies to Mrs. Edwards before looking around for his next target. His grey eyes landed on me, and he methodically strode through the crowd gathering in the carpark.

"They were placing the roses on the coffin."

"I wanted to keep mine."

"That is not the correct behaviour."

"Becca would want me to have it."

He shook his head and sighed. "Put your shoes back on; you're a grown woman for god's sake."

My earthly father, disappointed and burdened with me, stood by the nearest tree. My Kaetian father leant against the next tree. Mull'aman kicked at a rock in the background, one ear bud discretely distracting him.

"You've not been answering your phone."

"I've been busy."

"I can imagine." He cast a look behind him, realising we had an audience, and started walking towards the stream, indicating I should move ahead of him.

"I have made a lot of mistakes." He said, turning to face me. "I always acted in your best interests, but I've failed you."

I stuck the thorn of the rose into my thumb. He had failed me in so many ways, but I doubt we'd ever agree on that list.

"Did you pay Becca to be my friend?"

"I reimbursed her for certain expenses and inconveniences." He dismissed my upset with a wave of his hand. Then turned to face me. "You got Rebecca involved in drugs and that was what my money paid for. I should've seen it, and I'm sorry for my negligence."

"Wait. I don't do drugs. And Becca wasn't on drugs when she died."

"Kerella, enough! I thought giving you space would make you grow up, help you learn to take responsibility for yourself, but that was a fatal error."

"Becca didn't die because she was on drugs!"

"I can understand your denial, but your activities have led to some serious consequences. And I'm sorry, it's time you faced up to the problems you caused."

"She was not on drugs." I repeated.

"Look, Kerella, I've seen your credit card bill. The night Rebecca died you spent sixty-five pounds in the West End. How do you think that makes me feel? That I paid for the orgy that led to her death?"

"Okay, I probably shouldn't have put all that food on the credit card, but it was just food! And one round of drinks. I was a bit drunk and needed sobering up. But that didn't kill Becca."

"Kerella, I know what happened, don't lie to me."

"It was just food."

"It wasn't, Kerella, and you know it wasn't." He looked at me. "People talk. Do you really think the rumours wouldn't get back to me? You had an affair with a married man, broke up a successful band, and caused the community centre to shut down. All of this right after that irresponsible pregnancy scare, which someone else had to deal with because you wanted to stick your head in the sand. Then you dragged Rebecca out, racked up a huge bill in a pub and she died because of your actions. Don't you understand? You are destroying everything you touch."

"That's not true."

"It is. And I won't sit by and let you ruin anyone else's life. Do you know how upset Margaret is? Can you honestly look at her and tell me your actions have no consequences?"

I looked at the ducks in the stream.

What would he say if he knew the truth? I would be locked up before I could draw breath.

"And you haven't learned anything. I've seen this dress before, so if the eighty pounds you put on your credit card wasn't actually for funeral clothes, what did I really pay for?"

"I did spend it on funeral clothes. I just got in an accident and they got dirty."

"Look, you're not mentally well. It's time we stop pretending you can ever be normal. I've come to a decision. I'm going to rent out your flat and you're moving back home. I've cancelled your credit cards. You will obey my rules and you will not hurt anyone else."

"What? That's not fair! I never took drugs! I never hurt anyone! You can't do this because of rumours."

"I should've done a lot more a long time ago, but I won't hold you responsible for my mistakes. I'll give you a week to pack up your stuff." He walked away.

I sat down on the grass and looked up into the unforgiving blue sky. Then I threw the rose into the stream and watched it float out of my life.

Chris sat down on one side of me, Tyler on the other.

"I told you guys to leave me alone until I said otherwise."

"I think things have changed." Chris said.

"Jeez, your dad's a piece of work." Tyler said. Then looked at Chris. "I mean, your other dad."

"He thinks I killed Becca."

"You didn't." Tyler said.

"He paid her to be my friend."

"She cared about you. No money could fake the bond you two had." Chris answered, then added: "Are you going to come and live with us?"

"How many ways can I say no and mean it, but say yes in the end?"

"As many as you want." Chris stood up and held his hand out for me. "Want a lift?"

"I'm going to say no."

"But mean yes?" Chris finished my sentence.

I nodded. "I just want to…" I motioned in the direction of the carpark. "See Mannie."

"We'll be by the car."

I didn't know how to interrupt Mannie, or why I needed to see her. Thankfully, as I got close, she pulled away from Fus and came over to me.

I stood awkwardly in front of her, clasping my hands behind my back to keep them still. "I'm sorry I messed up and lost you your job."

"Don't be stupid! The Council have wanted us out of that building for years and they finally got their way. Let's face it, the building really was a dump, we just got caught up with having a stage to perform on. But life's about more than a raised platform, and we have other things to think about now."

I stared at her and began to cry.

She pulled me down into a firm hug and let me sob it out for a bit, before pulling away and doing her usual reset.

"I'm surprised to see you three getting along so well. I'm impressed Tyler's handling the whole 'you and Chris' thing so well."

"There's no 'me and Chris' thing. It didn't happen."

"What? Seriously?"

"Yes. There was no sex spark. At all. No sex. No spark. Absolutely no sex. Not even a little bit of spark."

"Well, that's a shame. I thought you two would make a great couple."

"No, we wouldn't. We realised we were just friends, and try as we could, we couldn't cross that line."

"Well, these things happen. Hopefully, Ty'll learn a few things from this. But I doubt it."

"I wanted to tell you: I didn't do it. I didn't kill Becca. It wasn't my fault."

"Oh my word! Why would you even believe I would think that?"

"Well, other people told me they thought I was to blame. I didn't want you thinking that."

"No, honey. You didn't do anything wrong."

I felt myself starting to cry again, so took a step back. "Well, hopefully I'll see you around?"

"Yes, of course! I mean, we've put The Martyrs on hold for a bit, I'm sure you understand, and next week we're off to America for a month or so, bit of a road trip and family visit now we're free from our employment obligations. But when I get back, we'll meet for coffee."

"Have a nice trip and thank you."

I felt like blessing her with whatever Kaetian power I had. Instead, I turned and walked back to Chris's car.

Controlling my crazy was getting harder, and now I was going to be living with Kasaman and Mull'aman, there would be no escaping the madness.

36: DRIZZLE

I dropped the box on the picnic table and sank onto the bench. Chris, Tyler, and Nick filed past carrying the bric-a-brac of my life into Kasaman's lair to save me from one lousy human.

I loved that flat. I loved that space. I loved that height.

I was adrift: a confused powerless deity, who'd been bested by a pathetic lower realm mortal in a stupid grey suit, and evicted from her own home.

It was hot and I was sweating into my practical clothes; damp patches spread from under my armpits, and I didn't care.

I missed Becca. I didn't mind that she was only my friend because she was paid to be. She was still my friend. She was uncomplicated.

Now, things had passed complicated a little while back.

Tyler rushed through the door with a peppermint tea. "This is for my Supreme Kaetian." He said putting the mug in the middle of the table.

"Never, ever call me that again. Look, you need to calm down. We don't want everyone knowing that… people thinking that…"

I couldn't say it.

"That you're God." He said, sitting down on the bench and putting his hand on my thigh.

I picked his hand up and dropped it onto his crotch.

"I'm not God."

"Yes, you are."

His forehead creased down the middle.

I slipped into a previous weakness and ran my finger down the line.

"You're an arsehole."

"Hey! I brought you your favourite tea!"

"Sorry. I'm just still really pissed off with you."

"Not very God like of you."

"I'm clearly a work in progress."

"Well, I'm happy to work you as much as you need." He gave me a wink. "Anyway, you have to see what Chris and I have been doing! Give me a few minutes to set up, then come through."

I picked up my mug, bounced the tea bag up and down on its string, and inhaled the earthy fragrance.

The red door opened and Nick came through, his dark blond hair sticking to his sweaty forehead.

He'd put on a bit of weight since I'd first met him and was looking much healthier.

Not seeing me, he walked straight over to the lockers and opened one. He pulled off his T-shirt and rubbed it over his face and chest. There was a series of chakra tattoos down the centre of his back.

I coughed to let him know he had company.

He spun round, clutching his discarded T-shirt in front of him.

"Oh, Kerella! I didn't know you were there!"

He grabbed a fresh T-shirt out of his locker and pulled it over his head. The design on the front read: 'This two shall pass...' with a cartoon of an empty number two bus speeding past a busy bus stop.

"I barely know you, and you spent the whole morning helping me out. I don't know how I can pay you back, but thank you, for everything."

"I didn't do it for a reward. You needed help, I had time on my hands. It was nothing."

"Well, I owe you. If I can ever do anything for you, just let me know."

"In a heartbeat. Well, welcome to the family." He said, gesturing to the red door.

We both nodded at each other.

"See you around." He said and headed towards the gift shop.

I blew onto my tea and took a sip. It was still too hot.

I picked up the mug and delved into Kasaman's lair.

"Hey Tu-Kerella." Tyler said, waving me into the dining room. "Look what we've done!"

I stared around the room. This was like my research into Kaetia on steroids, with a whole dollop of crazy and chaos thrown in. Since I'd last been in this room, the notes and drawings had spilled onto the floor, and several sheets were stuck to the wall with blue tack. Stones were everywhere: in bowls, in piles, standing on ceremony in their own space. Some looked like they'd been picked from the path or the beach, some were more exotic gemstones, some had been polished, some were dirty, some had been engraved, and some had symbols drawn on them with marker pen.

"Is it safe to have all this stuff laid out like this?"

"No one comes in here but us, and when we've finished, we'll burn it all." Chris replied. I couldn't tell if he was joking.

A large whiteboard was propped up against the wall by the door and looked like the safest place to begin. In the centre, contained within a wonky blue cloud, was a list titled 'Kaetians in the lower realm'. Under this, in Tyler's barely legible scrawl, were listed the four Kaetians that we knew of, and their earthly names:

- Tushenta – Kerella
- Mull'aman – Tyler
- Kasaman – Chris
- Katherine – Miareanas

"Is Mannie Kaetian?" I asked.
Tyler shrugged and looked at Chris.
"Well, we don't know anything for certain, but I don't think she is."
"Then, why do I care what she thinks?"
"Because she's a nice person?" Chris suggested.
"But she's not two-dimensional."
"That's because you've taken the time to get to know her." He paused, took off his hat and tapped his fingers on the table. "I think Kaetians in the lower realm act a bit like magnets, attracting other Kaetians. Maybe it's a familiarity, or the spells. And I get the feeling lower realm mortals sense that Kaetians have an other-worldly presence. But just because they emit a certain intensity, doesn't make them deeper or better than the mortals. In fact, in my experience, they're a lot worse."
"Hey!" Tyler interrupted Chris.
"They're also deluded about their own worth and treat others with a callous disregard. As Ty is good at demonstrating."
I cut in before an argument broke out.
"Should we tell Katherine?"
"Oh god, no!" Tyler responded swiftly.
"Are you sure about that, Ty? We could get her to move in with us, and you can grovel at her feet and tell her how I'm just a pathetic little crush. Yeesh, no wonder she'd rather have been a Pader than marry you."
"Wait, hold on. This is information we don't have." Chris said, grabbing a pen and a pad of paper. "Tell me everything."
"I had a dream where Asana told me that Miareanas asked Mull'aman to report her for objecting to the Lower Kaetian rations, so she'd be found guilty of a minor heresy and get to be a Pader, rather than marry this fool." I sighed, feeling a bit bad that I was attacking my new roommate. "Look, I've got a notebook filled with all this stuff, I'll dig it out for you later. I've no idea how accurate the information is, some of it is embellished half-forgotten dreams, some of it I may have just imagined, so maybe Asana never even said that."
"It was a mutual thing you know." Tyler said, picking at a patch of blue

tack on the wall. "I wanted to be with you, she wanted out of the Kaetian Compound. Everyone twists everything to make me look bad. It's not fair."

"You want to complain to me about misrepresentation? Seriously?" Chris said.

"Hey! We're all Historians here." I said. "We will get to the truth, even if we have no way of knowing what the truth really is. But there are no Librarians in the lower realm to manipulate the facts and feed us fallacies, so it may be easier here than in Kaetia. And when we get back, we really will know, and then we shall be beacons of truth in a Kaetian world of spin and lies. We shall usher in a new era where those who lead can be trusted and books do not tell lies."

"Hear, hear!" Tyler said, banging the table.

Chris looked uneasy.

"What?" I snapped at him.

"Well, there is one little lie we need to stick to."

"Seriously? Are you a closet Librarian? We need to lead by example."

"Yes, but if the romance between you and Mull'aman doesn't come across as real, it won't matter how honest or virtuous our message is, you will be married off to Laescenno and Mull'aman will be tortured and executed."

"And how will they know?"

"How does Asana know your lower realm name?"

"I don't know. Magic?"

"Did you ever mention any of this to Becca?"

"I may have mentioned Asana's name and she saw some paintings of Kaetia."

"And that's all it took for your lower realm identity to be betrayed. Normally walking in the lower realm is completely anonymous. If Asana knows, I wouldn't be surprised if the Council doesn't work it out before too long. Then they'll be able to interrogate any mortals they find who witnessed anything you did or heard any gossip about you. You'll have to work hard to make it look like your romance is real in front of everyone, all of the time, and for the rest of your life on this plane."

"What's not real about us?" Tyler said turning his artificial green eyes to me. "I love you. And you clearly love me, as no woman can be so annoyed with someone they don't have feelings for. The Librarians were just really sneaky by sending Mia down and making sure I met her years before you. Had I met you first, then bam! We'd be married and knee deep in babies by now."

"The Council." I snapped at Tyler. "The Council controls events; the Librarians fake the books."

"And how do you know you're right and not me?"

"Because Chris also remembers the Council being the Council and the Librarians being the Librarians, you are a fucking idiot, and when it comes to women, I don't believe you're the marrying type, so that's another lie."

"You 'know', or are you imagining things again? Because I see a whole lot of making stuff up going on here. Remember, I was engaged to Kat, right, engaged! That means going to get married."

"Are you trying to make my point for me? You chose Kat over me, and then lied about it over and over again. And engaged is not married. I'm sure you would have weaselled out of it before you were trapped in a fucking Dream Filled Cage!"

"I only lied because you wouldn't believe me."

"I wouldn't believe you because you were lying!"

"I was wrong, clearly you two are in love." Chris said, leaning against the piano and sipping his tea.

"Enough of the fucking sarcasm, 'Dad'." Tyler snapped at Chris. "I love Tushenta, that's so obvious."

"Is it?" Chris asked him. "Kat threw you out, and you only came for my daughter when you found out who she was."

"I left her a voicemail before then."

"Yeah, telling me how I made you sick and that you never wanted to see my manipulative scarred face again."

"I was angry you chose this prick over me." Tyler took a deep breath. "I'm sorry I said that. But you have to let me prove that I do love you, above all the other women in this world… and Kaetia."

I looked at him. There was no solid ground. I couldn't believe him. "Okay, I cannot believe I'm agreeing with the Librarian here."

"Not a Librarian." Chris interjected.

"Let's start our noble crusade on the corrupt political elite and their legacy of fake history, by lying our arses off, and pretend we're in an unambiguous passionate love affair."

"Why pretend?"

"Because I don't trust you."

"Can we have this discussion when your father, AKA 'the Devil' isn't looming over me?"

I looked at Chris. He picked up a box of stones from the table. "I'll get back to my project and leave you two love birds to fight this one out."

"What is with these stones?"

"Chris is going to make it rain."

"What? No chance! The forecast is wall-to-wall sunshine for the next week, at least."

"If rain were forecast, the experiment would be a little pointless." Chris answered, on his way out of the door.

Tyler ran his fingers through my hair and moved to kiss me.

"Get off me." I swatted him away.

"Tu-Kerella, please. We have to be together; we both know it. My life depends on it."

"We need to *pretend* to be together; that's not the same thing."

"But you still have feelings for me, and we do need to talk about us."

"There is no us. You can't be with someone like me. You decided that when you called me special needs; I decided that when I nearly fucked Chris."

"Nearly fucked? I thought we were being honest here? We both know you gave him the sympathy bone the night I punched his lights out. There are no lower realm mortals around here to lie to."

"We did not have sex."

"Well, you certainly were going to that night I caught you two at it."

"Yeah, I've been meaning to thank you for interrupting us."

"No need to be snarky."

"No seriously: thank you." I said, patting him on the arm. "I'm genuinely glad you interrupted the incident which we need never speak of again."

"You don't still have feelings for him?"

"No, I do not have those kind of feelings for Chris! Supernatural parental lineage, even if it turns out we're all having a group hallucination, which I still haven't ruled out, pretty much a mood killer!"

"I never thought of that! Holy shit! That's gross!"

"Yes. So, thank you for making it not happen, and for never mentioning it again."

"Okay."

"Anyway, what's he been like?"

"What's who been like?"

"Chris, Kasaman, The Devil, Demetrius, the guy you've been living with for the past two weeks."

"More intense than he used to be. Very focused on his stones."

"Yeah, what's he doing with all these stones and how will they make it rain?"

"Stone magic!" Tyler beamed.

"And that is?"

"Well, Lacey Mo casts his spells on us by placing stones close to our bodies that are still in Kaetia, right? So we can fight back by holding our own stones and thinking really hard. At least now I know why my graphic novel proposal keeps getting rejected and why I can't hold down a job. That wanker cursed me."

"Do you think Chris is safe?"

"Hold on. You told me to move in with him, and you weren't one hundred percent sure he was safe to be around?"

"He isn't going to murder you here."

"Where is he going to murder me?"

"This is still Chris... you know. Everyone thinks you two are best friends. If anyone knows him, it's you. Do you really think he's the Devil?"

Tyler leant against the table and looked at me. "In your dreams, in the back of your mind, how do you feel about him?"

"Truthfully? Shit scared."

"Exactly. Maybe we should run for it?"

"But Ty, it's not that simple."

"Yes, it is that simple. We have to get out of here. You think our Kaetian crusade will be helped by our association with Kasaman?"

"Tyler, think. Why are we so scared of him? Why, even here with our memories erased, have I always had nightmares about a demon in a dark cloak with supernatural powers who wants to hurt me? Because the Kaetians told us to fear him, over and over, until it was written into the fabric of our souls. It's all myths, stories, propaganda, and fake history books."

"And redwaek." Tyler added.

I sighed. "He still hasn't explained them."

"Well, there's time yet. But let's keep our wits about us. I can't exactly afford a hotel room at the moment."

"I'm going to get a jumper, it's getting cold." I said.

Tyler's jaw dropped.

"What?"

"Look!" He said, pointing out the window.

I turned to look outside.

"Oh. My. God." I said, and we both ran for the door, colliding with each other on the way. Tyler pulled back and let me go through first.

We charged through to the garden and stared up at the sky.

Chris was in a trance, sat cross legged in the middle of the grass, a stone in each upward facing palm.

"Holy fuck man, you made it drizzle!" Tyler shouted as he danced around the garden. "I guess this means we have some serious power on our side against Lacey Mo."

"Laescenno." I corrected him.

"Whatever. I mean, look at that!" Tyler said, laughing uncontrollably and pointing at the sky. "We have the power, and we are Gods. Bow down before us, mere mortals."

Chris slowly came out of his trance and stood up.

He looked at Tyler, gyrating and dancing around, pretending to zap the flowers with his invisible Kaetian sparks.

He frowned. "Seriously? That's what you chose to bring to this realm?"

"It was him or Laescenno. Pickings were a bit slim."

"Kaetia is doomed."

"Nah, you can make it rain, this will change everything."

"I could never get this spell to work in Kaetia. No matter how much power I absorbed." Chris shook his head as he looked at the glistening grass.

"Well, when we get back, you can absorb even more power. I'll absorb power with you. Seriously: rain! Now we can win." I raised my arms into the air bound droplets.

"I'd better get back to the protection stones. If Rebecca is talking in Kaetia, we have no idea who is listening to her. Laescenno might be gathering information to cast stronger and more specific spells." Chris left us and went inside.

I laughed at Tyler as he paraded around. If we could make it rain, surely, we could bring down the Council and their Librarians.

For the first time, I actually felt like we could do this.

37: MATHEMATICIANS EAT BABIES

I assembled the things I thought would be of use to our Kaetian information gathering exercise and carried them downstairs to the dining room.

Tyler was lying on the grey couch in the corner, his legs draped over the armrest. He was wearing the same clothes he'd been wearing yesterday; his hair was sticking up unevenly and was starting to get a bit curly at the back. His head was stuck in Machiavelli's 'The Prince', which he'd been reading all week.

I dropped my collection on the table and threw a ball of red wool at him.

He looked down at his stomach where the wool had landed. "Hey! Great idea!" He said, missing the joke, and starting to unravel the wool.

Chris came in with a flipchart stand and set it up next to the whiteboard.

"Thanks." I said. "I found the notebook. Do you have any preference what order we cover things in?"

"Probably best just to throw it all out there, see what things more than one of us remembers, and try to work out what's real." Chris said, passing me a flipchart marker.

I picked up the notebook and opened it at a random page.

"Okay, here's a map of Kaetia I tried to draw."

I turned to the flipchart and copied the map I'd drawn a couple of months ago, when I still believed I was making up a fun world to escape to. Now, I was drawing up military strategies with the Devil who liked plants and long walks on the beach, and a court jester who thought he was a political genius because he'd read half a book on the subject.

I turned to Chris for his input before I committed his mountain to the page. "Is the Black Mountain about here?"

"Those who live there call it the Red Mountain, as the rock is filled with veins of red."

"Well, it's called the Black Mountain by everyone in Kaetia, so that's what we shall call it."

"Typical Kaetian arrogance."

"Should I put it here or not?"

"It's a bit further out than that."

"Are you sure? It can't be that far away."

"I should know; I brought it forth into existence."

Tyler loomed up behind us. "You created the Black Mountain?"

"Yes."

"Why?"

"I was hoping that, by creating a mirror of the Kaetian Mountain, a second source of water would come into existence, one the Kaetians did not control."

"And did it?"

"No. Its fountain spits out lava."

"Cool." Tyler said, walking off, cutting off bits of wool and tying them together in clusters. He kept scratching his head.

I went to the window and opened it, trying to get rid of the ripe smell he'd traipsed over to our side of the room. "I'd go with hot, and not very useful."

Chris looked at me. "If we're going to win this fight, you're going to have to see the world outside of the Kaetian mindset. We'll need all the people of the higher realm on our side, not just those tucked away in the Kaetian Compound."

"He who obtains sovereignty by the assistance of the nobles maintains himself with more difficulty than he who comes to it by the aid of the people." Tyler pronounced from the other side of the room, where he was climbing on the couch to attach a clump of red wool to a photo of Chris. He then started to connect the other strands to the pieces of paper stuck on the wall which had anything to do with Kasaman.

"Will you stop quoting Machiavelli at us?"

"He has useful things to say about taking power."

"I do not need to listen to the advice of someone who is younger than me, parroted at me by the Guardian of the Sing Song Tenet."

"It's that kind of disrespect that got you exiled, and Machiavelli is older than you! He was born in…" Tyler picked up 'The Prince' and flicked through a few pages. "1469."

"By which point I'd already been born into the lower realm twice."

"Whoah?" Tyler stared at Chris, his jaw hanging open.

"Anyway, if you place the mountain up here, then the Crater of the Dead goes here, and the ridges go like this." Chris drew the details with his red pen.

"You see how it mirrors the Kaetian Conduit?"

Tyler started laughing.

"What? You think you can draw a better map?" I asked him.

"No, I was just thinking: Chris, what did you do for your quatercentenary?"

"Birthdays aren't exactly marked in Kaetia, and, as I was living in exile with a load of redwaek, it wouldn't have been much of a party."

Chris ripped the sheet we'd been drawing on from the flipchart stand, stuck it to the whiteboard with a couple of magnets, and continued to expand the map, filling in detail I never could have imagined. He drew the Lethian plains in detail, and then rivers crossing them.

"Wait! There are rivers in the Lethian plains?" I asked, excited.

"Rivers of lava." Chris responded as he moved on to draw mountain ranges, gorges, even the names of some settlements.

"Who on earth could live all the way out there?"

"A mixture of exiles, lower and higher realm mortals, Merdiants, and the descendants of the Ratwe people."

"Rat wee." Tyler echoed from the other side of the room, giggling.

I looked at Chris. He looked at me. Then we both looked at Tyler. We were starting to worry about his behaviour.

"How far have you explored? Might there be water somewhere out there?"

"I've explored it all. If you trek for about four weeks in any direction from Kaetia, you hit oceans of lava that not even the most determined of winged-redwaek has managed to reach the other side and return to tell the tales."

I sighed. "I guess we have to somehow take control of the Kaetian Compound." I went back to my pile and slipped the notebook underneath the protection stones Chris had made for me. I didn't want the boys to read it and see my childish love notes about Mull'aman, or unvarnished thoughts on Kasaman.

I handed Chris the painting of Asana that Becca had found down the side of the fridge.

"Oh my." He said, sweeping his bandana off his head, and sitting down on one of the dining chairs.

He placed the painting on the table and ran his fingers over her face.

"That's Asana!" Tyler exclaimed. "I recognise her from my dream. Doesn't looking at her make you angry?"

"I may not agree with how she handled everything, but, except for my amazing daughter, I love this woman more than anything, and I always will."

"Yeah, whilst she's busy loving other women."

"Tyler! Shut up." I snapped at him.

Chris propped the painting up on the bookshelf.

"Whatever our relationship is, or has been, we will need her. We need a figure head people can get behind."

"Surely, I'm the best candidate for that." Tyler said. Jumping up on the couch and sitting on the back. "I am 'The Golden Son of Kaetia'." He flung his arms in the air.

Chris slipped his bandana back on. "Tyler, that was twenty-five years ago and for one month. Do you really think Laescenno won't have undermined your reputation whilst you've been away?"

"What about her?" Tyler said pointing at me.

"No one will trust me. I'm half evil."

Chris stood up and came over to me. He placed his hands on my shoulders and looked straight into my eyes. "Never believe what they say about you. You are one hundred percent pure, and innocent, and good. There is no evil in you."

"Well, I've not made a redwaek yet, or any big fuck off mountains, but I haven't been tested. What happens if I get into the Crater and start racking up redwaek like it's Halloween?"

"I'll make sure what was done to me, never happens to you."

"What was done to you?"

"I was trying to help."

"Because nothing's more helpful than a load of rampaging, rotting, evil mother fuckers." Tyler chipped in.

"Tyler, shut up."

Chris walked to the window and looked outside. "Hyrensus claimed he'd found a formula that would bring rain to Kaetia. It was risky, and a sacrifice was required. For the sake of Kaetia, I made that sacrifice."

He turned to face me. "When a Supreme Kaetian judges a mortal as worthy, they put part of themself into that person so they'll thrive, mentally and physically, in the tough Kaetian world. It's exhausting and drains the Supreme Kaetian of their power. It's also very confusing to step inside so many minds, empathetically feel what it's like to be them, and then return to oneself. That's why there's meant to be six ranking Supreme Kaetians performing their holy duty at any one time. The fact that Asana's coped all these years on her own is a miracle. It just goes to show how amazing that woman is."

I looked at my feet and thought about all those times I'd gotten so angry at Asana for being tired, cold, distant, or absent. I never thought what her life must've been like.

Chris continued. "Hyrensus suggested that instead of putting part of myself into the mortals, I pulled their sacred energy into myself. It would sacrifice a few souls, and we only picked the most evil. With that power, I was able to exert some control over the elements."

He looked to the ceiling. His eyes glassy and unfocused. "I sacrificed my sanity, my wife, my daughter, my reputation. And I never made it rain."

"Not to juggle or create; it's our world we celebrate!" I blurted out.

Tyler laughed. "You and that bloody rhyme."

"No, seriously, the Council made you break the first tenet. If something as simple as making glass is forbidden because it's considering meddling with the elements, what on earth were they thinking having you play alchemical games with the power of mortal minds? So the redwaek were their fault, all along!"

"But I didn't stop… I couldn't. I felt I needed more power. I kept trying to make it rain. I became obsessed. And I took all the evil and the anger of those souls into myself. Here I can control myself. Over there, it takes a lot more effort."

"The Council were highly reckless. The Word of Sett is clear on these matters, and it protects us."

Chris let out a snort of laughter.

"What could possibly be funny?" Tyler asked.

"I have no idea. I just find the notion of 'The Word of Sett' amusing for some reason." He continued making a strange chuckling noise in his throat.

After such a dark revelation, I found his bizarre laughter uplifting and turned to the whiteboard to write:

Word of Sett = funny

I looked at the section on the whiteboard above where I'd just added the new note and started giggling.

"What's so funny, Tu-Ker?" Tyler asked.

"I was just thinking…" I burst out laughing and doubled over. I took a deep breath. "The Librarians are the bad guys, as they rewrite history, and the Historians are the good guys as they try to re-establish the truth…"

"Yes." Tyler said.

"So, what do the Mathematicians do?" I said, thumping the table, amused by my own punchline.

Chris smiled and nodded.

Tyler jumped up on the back of the couch. "Oh, I know this one! Mathematicians… Mathematicians…" He narrowed his eyes. "Mathematicians live in the walls and eat babies!"

"Ha ha! Good one!" I laughed.

"Well, write it down."

I continued laughing.

"Why are you not writing it down?"

"Oh, you're serious?"

"Of course I am. Why don't you ever take me seriously? If you say something, or the Devil says something, you write it down."

"Will you not call me that?"

"But if I remember something you laugh at me."

"Oh, okay, I'll write it down." Not sure if he was winding me up, or being serious, I wrote in small letters in the bottom right-hand corner:

Mathematicians eat babies.

38: INSIGNIFICANT

Using a palette knife, I manoeuvred the yellow, red, and blue across the sweep of the petals, watching the layers of oil paint form complex patterns on the canvas. I wiped the knife clean, reapplied the paint, and repeated the motion.

"That's not as life-like as it could be. There's not really any blue in the petals." Tyler said, putting his can down on the patio table, pushing his chair back, and coming over to peer closely at my progress.

"Thanks for your tutelage, Ty. If I wanted an exact replica of it, I'd take a photo."

"You know what you should do? Paint another selkie. You do the female form really well."

"I feel like painting flowers right now. They have women in Kaetia, but not so many flowers."

"You could paint me, you know. I'd pose for you however you want."

"I'm happy with my sunflowers, thank you."

"That's all you've been doing lately. Can't you take a break for a few hours? We could go for a romantic walk through the woods."

"Ty, you know Chris has given me that space in the gift shop; I want to be sure I make the best use of it I can. It'll look stupid half full."

"Come on, it's not like you're a real artist! What am I supposed to do whilst Chris is working and you're out here playing with your paints?"

"Why don't you work on that graphic novel you were talking about?"

"You said you hated it."

"I didn't say I hated it. I just said it sounded a bit sexist. Anyway, what does it matter what I think?"

"Because my entire reason for existing whilst I'm stuck in this stupid realm is to please you."

"Don't be so melodramatic. You're here to learn about this thing called being human. Go out. Have some fun. Get laid. Have a shower."

"I can't get laid."

"Why not?"

"Because they will know." He whispered, pointing at the sky.

"Well, just say we have an open relationship. Perfect excuse for commitment free sex. I thought that'd be right up your alley."

"Everything's just so pointless now. Why are we even bothering? We could just go back to Kaetia now and get on with our real lives."

I put the palette knife down. "Ty, seriously, are you okay?"

"No, I am not fucking okay! The meaning of my whole life has been reduced to which woman I shack up with and you act like you don't care."

"Well, currently you're shacked up with Chris."

"You know what I mean."

"Do you know what Asana said to me before I came down here? She said her years in the lower realm were the best in her life. To be insignificant and have no one know who you are. She described it as a blessing."

"Well, I feel insignificant enough alright."

"Tyler, in about fifty years, we're going to die and get sucked back to Kaetia. A place where there are no computer games, very little alcohol, and the likes of Laescenno breathing down our necks making up the rules as they go along. Make the most of this world while we're here."

"How can I enjoy it with all the curses flying about?"

"Are you doing the things Chris told us to do?"

Tyler pulled a stone out of his pocket and showed it to me.

"And you did the meditations and said the mantras?"

He nodded and stuck the stone back in his pocket.

"Then you've nothing to worry about."

"But the curses are still working. How else can you explain my life?"

"What's wrong with your life?"

"Well, my fiancée won't have sex with me for starters."

"Oh Tyler, don't start this crap up again. I said when I feel ready, we'll talk about it."

He jumped up and dragged me to my feet, knocking the pot of sunflowers off the patio table.

"Tyler! What the fuck are you doing?"

"Come over here. You like it alfresco: I know that."

"That was when it was consensual, and everyone else had gone home for the day."

He pulled me towards him. "Come on. You let every guy in town dip his chips in Tommy K, but not me. Why?"

I slapped him in the face as hard as I could.

"Because you're an arsehole, that's why!"

I picked up the sunflowers. Their petals were crumpled, and the stems broken. The paint on the canvas was smudged.

"Get out of my fucking face." I snapped at Tyler. "And until you learn to fucking respect me, do not talk to me. Now go inside and have a fucking shower, you stink. Consider that an order from your fucking God!"

I stormed off through into the Acres to pick out a new pot of sunflowers.

I rifled through the display, trying to find the perfect plant for my painting, but having already picked my favourite, none of the others felt right.

I slammed one after another down.

"Hey, hey!" Nick called out to me. "Easy on the merchandise. What did these little beauties ever do to you?"

"Sorry. I just had a spat with Tyler. I shouldn't be taking it out on your flowers."

"Don't worry about it. I understand your circumstances are a bit stressful right now."

I looked at him, shocked. How much had Chris told him?

"With your dad kicking you out of your flat so he could make some extra money, forcing you to move in with someone you'd only just started dating."

"Oh, those circumstances." I let out a long sigh and suppressed the urge to cry.

"You know what?" Nick said. "I need a cup of tea. Care to join me?"

I hadn't spoken to a normal person since Becca's funeral, so I nodded, followed him up the stairs, and through the green gate to the café gardens.

The door to the shed was propped open, revealing a chaotically cosy space crammed full of personal effects. A rickety upholstered chair covered by an old, crocheted blanket squatted in the centre, taking up most of the space in the shed. On a shelf at the back was a small radio, a little buddha statue, and a collection of smooth wooden carved shapes. On the unit by the door was a tin kettle on a gas-powered travel stove, and, propped up by the window, an old teddy bear with one eye kept watch.

The walls were decorated with inspirational quotes and posters. The one that caught my eye was a framed needlepoint which said: 'Whatever you do in life will be insignificant, but it is very important that you do it. ~ Gandhi'. I wished I could drag Tyler up here and smash his face into that one.

Nick filled up the kettle with water from a reusable bottle and lit the gas. He pulled out a folding chair and motioned for me to take the upholstered one.

I sat down carefully and ran my fingers over the blanket. "Is this your mother's work?" I asked.

"Well, yes and no. We made it together when I was little." He smiled at me, picked up one of the smooth wooden shapes and started twirling it around with his fingers. "I think it's obvious which squares I did and the ones she snuck into the pile to make sure the blanket was completed before I lost interest."

"I have a blanket my mother made. It's one of my most treasured possessions."

"I gather she's no longer with us?"

"No, she died when I was twelve."

"I believe the people we love never really leave us; they remain imprinted on our hearts, and in our crocheted blankets."

He handed me a chipped cat mug of foamy far-too-milky tea.

"How are you doing since your mother passed?"

He pulled the folding chair a bit closer and sat down, running his hand through his floppy dark blond hair. "To be honest, I've been feeling a bit down lately."

"Do you want to talk about it?"

"I suppose. But I don't want our first proper chat to be me moaning about things which in the grand scheme, don't really mean anything."

"I'm sure I'll have heard a lot worse. I can guarantee I've said a lot worse."

He smiled and took a slurp of tea.

"I feel bad that the memories I associate with my house are the recent ones of all the care equipment, the pain and the suffering, the tiredness that got into my bones, how things seemed to drag on forever, yet she slipped away far too quickly. I want to walk in the door and remember her as she was before the cancer, hear the laughter that used to fill the house. But all I hear is whirring and slow beeping, and all I feel is the painful sting of death."

"I'm sorry."

"I thought time would make everything okay. I mean, I don't want things to change, but they already have, and I know they need to change more, so now I'm starting to think about selling our family home, and I can't even believe I'm considering that. My mother was born there, and I want to walk away because she died there."

"Well, as you said, the people we love are imprinted on us, not our houses. You can move and take your blankets and other knick-knacks with you, and she'll be there in the new place, without the bad memories."

"I like the way you put that." He said, smiling at me. "Now, it's your turn. What upset you to the point that you had to attack a load of defenceless sunflowers?"

"Oh, just a silly lovers' tiff."

"I think it was more than that. Come on, I shared with you, bare your soul to me."

"He brought up my past..." I took a deep breath and decided to be as honest as I could with this lower realm mortal. "I have a bit of a reputation for being easy pickings. I never used to know how to say no to someone who wanted to sleep with me, and much of the time, it was the only time I had any meaningful contact with anyone, so I'd just go along with it, because if someone wanted to have sex with me, it must mean they cared about me, right? It was a tangible sign someone actually gave a fuck about me, right? But I'm in a proper relationship now, and the things that people used to do to me are supposed to be in the past. I managed to change things. I don't have to do those things anymore. I'm someone else now. They can't do that to me. But Tyler brought it up and he clearly thinks that's who I still am. Who I really am." I felt my cheeks burn with the shame of the confession and the guilt of the half lie.

"Have you explained any of this to him?"

"And I feel completely trapped." I rushed on. "I'm so used to having my own space: I need my own space. But everywhere I turn now, there's someone in my face demanding something from me."

He nodded. "Do you have somewhere you could go for a night or two?"

"I suppose I could phone Mannie and see if she'd let me stay at hers."

"Mannie and Fus are in America at the moment. When they get back, I'm sure they'd let you stay over for the occasional night, but I don't think that's a long-term solution."

"I suppose my father wants me to move back in with him. But he can get really overbearing and controlling. I don't want to move back there and be powerless again. On the other hand, he's barely ever there, so I would actually have my own space."

"Is there a way to keep an escape route open when he's around? So you never feel completely trapped."

I thought for a few moments. "I could ask Chris to pretend to give me a job here; that way I could come and go as I feel I need to."

"If you want a real job, I'm sure we could find you one. Save you from having to lie to your father."

"I already have a real job!" I snapped, fed up with everyone telling me I wasn't a proper artist. "I was making a little money selling my art at Shambles. And now Chris has given me space here, I should be able to make a bit more." I took a deep breath and the anxiety flooded in; I ran my finger along a line of red in the crocheted blanket. "Anyway, I doubt I'd be of any use to you guys here, plants and paint: not the same thing."

He held his hands up. "I wasn't implying your art isn't a real job, I was just suggesting a way to not lie to your father. But I've seen you helping Chris around the place; you're a natural when it comes to nurturing. So none of this 'I won't be any use to you' crap. Why not get paid for the work you're already doing? Even if you turn right round and hand it back to Chris as rent."

"I suppose that might be a good idea, as long as it's part time, but I don't think I'm up to facing my father. I doubt I could even walk through the front door."

"Would you like someone to come with you?"

"You would do that?"

"Of course!"

"Seriously?"

"Yes." He drained the final bit of tea from his mug. "Anyway, I need to start closing up. Fancy giving me a hand, learn the ropes?"

"If you really think I could be useful?"

"I wouldn't ask if I thought you'd just get in the way!"

I smiled at him and jumped to my feet. The thought that I could be useful to Nick's work at 'The Acres' made me feel like I was moving forward again, really learning what it was like to be a human being. I wouldn't let Tyler hold me back from making my time 'walking in the lower realm' the best life I would ever have.

As I followed Nick through the green gate, I saw Chris watching us from the other side of the Acres. I waved to him, but he turned away and strode off into the gift shop.

39: PANDORA'S BOX

I had vowed never to set foot inside this house again. But needs must as the Devil propagates and my soul mate drives me up the wall.

So, here I was, standing on the doorstep, ready for my scheduled meeting. After we'd stood there a while, Nick reached past me and pressed the doorbell.

I shot him a mock scowl and he shrugged.

A few moments later, the father who scared me the most, opened the lid of Pandora's Box.

He cast Nick and his 'Budding Buddha' T-shirt a worried glance and led us through to the kitchen.

The house was just as it had been when I was last here six years ago, and yet not at all like I remembered it. The colours were brighter. There were no mysterious shadows which moved when you held them in the corner of your eye. The walls were flat and perpendicular to the floor, not bulging and unstable. It was smaller than the house I'd carried in my mind all these years; I didn't feel like a little lost child in a giant's castle. I wondered if it was the house that had shrunk, or my confidence that had grown.

My father made a pot of loose-leaf Ceylon Orange Pekoe tea in the blue teapot he and my mother had always used. He'd taken off his tie and suit jacket but was still wearing his pressed white shirt and grey suit trousers. He placed three teacups on the kitchen table and moved the teapot to Mum's green trivet. I'd forgotten all about the trivet, but suddenly, it was the most precious thing in the world to me.

We sat down for the conference.

"Margaret tells me she's almost out of your artwork and hasn't been able to get hold of you for replacements."

"I've been selling my paintings at The Acres. I seem to be able to get a much better price there than what Mrs. Edwards was charging for them at

Shambles."

"I asked Margaret to do you a favour and I wish you would respect our arrangement. Just because your new paramour is happy to inflate your prices doesn't mean you should neglect your existing commitments. Please do get in touch with her."

I bit back my anger at his attitude to the value of my art, especially since he kept me begging for handouts. "Well, I'm trying to fill a big display space at the moment... but I'll see what I can spare."

"I went by the Acres last week. That boy runs a tight ship. Although I really don't feel comfortable with your bohemian lifestyle."

"I'm just staying in his spare room; there's nothing bohemian about it. But that's part of the reason I asked to see you."

I reached over and poured the tea into the cups, steadying myself for the speech I'd practiced and perfected over the last couple of days.

"I have a part-time job there now, in stock management. I'm starting to feel working and living in the same place may not be the best fit all of the time, so I was wondering if your offer to move back home was still on the table? Only for a couple nights a week, as most of my shifts start really early, so I'd sleep over there on those nights."

I saw my father's face soften in a way I hadn't seen in years.

"I'd like that very much." He said.

"Chris has been teaching me how to cook some international dishes, so I could make dinner for you when I'm here and you've been working late." I wasn't sure why I was deviating from my planned script, but seeing my dad look vulnerable in such a way, I felt the need to pile on the good daughter vibes.

"That would be nice. So, are you going to introduce me to your gentleman friend?"

"Oh, sorry, yes. This is Nick, he's a colleague of mine."

"Colleague?"

"Yes. He's the Deputy Manager at The Acres."

"Nice to meet you." My father said, nodding in Nick's direction, before all awareness of the-assistant-of-something slipped from his radar, and I became his primary focus. "What subject matter are you concentrating on for your art these days?"

"Well," I said, turning the blue, art deco teacup round in front of me. "As I have an unending supply of exceptional plants available to me," I smiled at Nick, "I'm going through a bit of a botanical phase."

"Oh, that's wonderful!" My father exclaimed. "And such attention to your route to market! Of course flowers will sell well there. That's my girl."

I smiled and nodded, pretending to have put thought into my business model, rather than being influenced by what was in front of my face and the dearth of flowers in Kaetia.

"Is there a problem?" My dad shot at Nick.

"Oh, nothing, really." Nick gestured with his hands and looked at me.

"I'm sorry, I don't know what you mean." I said.

"I was just wondering where the milk was?"

"Dear boy!" My dad slapped the table. "In front of you is one of the finest teas you'll ever taste. You don't want to be sullying the taste with milk!" He let out a laugh I knew he meant to be humorous, but it sounded very pompous and patronising.

I chipped in. "Do try it, it was my mother's favourite tea. You won't miss the milk."

My father's phone began beeping from the worktop, and he went to retrieve it, then left the room to make a call.

I mouthed "Sorry." at Nick, worried that I'd dragged him here, and he'd been insulted.

He looked really angry for a moment, then pulled a face and burst out laughing, quietly slapping the table and saying, "Dear boy!"

I joined in the quiet mockery of my father.

"And don't forget your route to market!" I added, sending us into a fresh wave of giggles.

By the time my father returned, we'd laughed ourselves out, finished the tea, and were gathering up our things to leave.

"Sorry about that, Chaddy just needed some figures for tomorrow's meeting. Anyway, your room will be waiting for you; just turn up when you're ready."

I smiled, thought about hugging him, but settled for knocking on the table twice. He returned the gesture, like he used to, and I felt part of my happy childhood come back to life.

On the way out of the house, we passed the music room.

I'd spent most of my younger years in that room. When my mother was touring, I was pretty much left on my own, so I'd play the piano for hours, often skipping school to creep back to the empty house and practice more. I wanted so badly to be like my mother, and I thought if I worked hard enough, and became good enough, she'd take me on tour with her.

I looked around the room and the intense hope that one day I would escape my life and tour the world with my mother came flooding back, and I realised it was never the touring or performing I'd craved, but to be close to someone who cared about me, and away from this place.

In the centre, where it had always stood, was my mother's grand piano. I'd forgotten that amongst all the horrors and pain, this house also contained so many nuggets of pure joy. I stopped, open mouthed, staring at it. I could see my mother behind the keys as though she'd been playing it only yesterday.

"Do play it if you want." My father said, coming down the hall. "I keep it tuned, but the tuner always chastises me for not exercising the keys enough."

I hesitated for a moment, before my feet carried me over to the rosewood piano stool. I closed my eyes, took a deep breath, and Silver Stream flowed through my fingers.

When I finished, I looked up. My father was leaning in the doorway. "You're so like your mother. I'm happy I'll be seeing more of you."

I think part of me was happy too.

I drifted out to Nick's dark grey car and slid into the seat without noticing I was moving.

"That could not have gone better." I sighed, rolling my head back on the head rest. "Step one of my escape plan is complete."

"Step one?" Nick asked as he drove the car around the red brick drive and out onto the road.

"Yes, step two is get the fuck out of this town."

"And where are you planning on going?"

"I've no idea yet. Maybe Edinburgh."

"Why Edinburgh?"

"I don't know. It always looks pretty on TV, and there's that big hill I could walk up. Where would you go if you were planning to escape?"

"Oddly enough, probably Edinburgh! I've some lovely memories of the city from family holidays, and it's close to some really pretty countryside."

"Well, let's go right now! Do you have a map in here?"

He laughed. "Yes, but I also have a shift in the morning, so maybe we should leave the great escape until another day."

"What would you do in Edinburgh, if you'd just won the lottery and money was not an issue?"

"I'd probably train as a nurse."

"Seriously, if you didn't have to work, you'd be a nurse?"

"I can't think of a better way to spend my life."

"Say, if you knew that your life wasn't going to be judged on anything you did, and nothing mattered: would you still be a nurse?"

"In a heartbeat."

I looked out of the window and wished Tyler had a fraction of Nick's enthusiasm and focus. But I knew I had to make do with what Sett had bestowed on me.

And accept her blessing true;
Divine love, she gave me you.

Oh Sett! I know it was an honour to have even been given a choice of partner, but seriously? Laescenno or Mull'aman? What kind of blessing is that?

"Thanks for the lift and for coming with me." I said, closing the car door and watching Nick drive away down the small country lane.

I turned and walked through the archway to The Acres.

"Where've you been?"

Chris's voice came from the dark path behind me.

I spun round, my heart beating in my throat.

"Nick just took me to see my father. My other father."

"I was worried."

"Hey, Chris, it's only nine, and I've been out later than this walking on my own plenty of times in the last month. It's no big deal."

"Why did you need to see that man?"

"I went to ask him if I could see a bit more of him. Maybe stop over the occasional night. I get the feeling Ty needs some space from me and a bit of normality in his life. This is all driving him crazy. It's driving me a little bit crazy."

"We need to be careful. You didn't tell him anything about us or Kaetia, did you?"

"I was careful. You think I want to be locked up? Of course I didn't say anything."

"I'm sorry. I just worry. You know I trust you."

"I know." I smiled at him, trying to work my good daughter vibes on him. "Fancy a glass of red and a game of Kaetian Stones?"

"I'll follow you in, I just need to finish up this display." He said, lifting up a tray of plants.

"Oh, okay!" I said, scurrying off, relieved he'd been working late and tired, rather than hanging about waiting for me to get home because he was angry. Still, to be safe, I would open the expensive bottle of Bordeaux I'd bought as a surprise for him.

I sighed. My life had become a balancing act, trying to keep those who had power over me happy, whilst they tried to trap me in the image of the ideal family they held in their mind. And while they treated me like a prop in their diorama, all I wanted to do was quietly exist as my authentic self, and they were making that impossible.

40: IMPRINTS AND ECHOES

Nick was waiting for a text from me to tell him I'd packed the boxes I was taking over to my father's house, then he was going to drive over and pick me up. What we were really waiting for was Chris's suppliers to turn up for their meeting and Tyler to take Tris for their afternoon stroll through the woods. I'd packed the three boxes I planned to take with me last night and they were discreetly stacked in the wardrobe in Chris's uncle's bedroom.

Chris had never removed his uncle's presence from this room, and his uncle had never erased his wife's touches. Her mottled turquoise glass perfume atomiser was still on her dresser, embroideries that oozed with this stranger's imprint were still hanging on the wall, a knitted blanket created by long silent hands was neatly folded on a rocking chair no one went near.

This was the end of the line for that family. No one remembered them with affection, so the pieces they left behind morphed from treasured possessions into clutter. I wouldn't be the one to break the chain of preservation: to forcibly evict the lonely imprints and their echoes through time.

Both Kaetians and lower realm mortals were only here temporarily. I wondered if everyone else felt like they were perpetual foreigners in this world, dressing up their surroundings to make themselves feel like this was where they belonged, trying to convince themselves they had some divine connection to the dirt beneath their feet, even though tomorrow, a stranger would be standing in their home, calling it theirs.

I'd always be a squatter whilst I tried to play happy Kaetian families in this house. I would never belong here. I could balance the entire contents of my life on the varnished surfaces of someone else's antique furniture, but this would never be my home.

Maybe, by moving back to where I grew up, where I could be on my own at least some of the time, I would find a piece of this world that was mine. That 'home' may be in a house I'd long ago decided was a realm of evil, but having spent the last month tiptoeing around the doilies of the deceased in the Devil's lair, I was ready to take the risk. It was the best option I had at this moment in time. If I took my crocheted blanket and all my knick-knacks with me, I'd be safe.

The bay window curved around Chris's aunt's dresser. Beyond the coloured glass bowls and kitsch figurines, lay the open view of fields and sea. Far to the left, were the muted tones of the town. But today, I was watching the comings and goings in the ochre sea beneath me.

Even though most of Chris's business associates dressed casually, they always stood out from the customers pulling into the carpark to claim their little piece of the pre-packaged natural world.

After I'd been looking for what felt like hours, a couple got out of a car. Their body language screamed that they were here for business, not pleasure.

I ran through to Chris's bedroom.

The small room was mostly taken up by a double bed. There was a built-in wardrobe with mirrored doors, the blanket at the bottom of the neatly made bed was covered in dog fur, and a framed photo of me and Tris stood on Chris's bedside table, between his alarm clock and a bowl of stones.

The room didn't feel like Chris had imprinted on it in anyway, but the large window held a wonderful view of the entire sweep of the Acres, which was Chris's true passion in this mortal diversion from our real lives.

Hovering at the side of the bed, I bounced around by the mirrored wardrobe to keep an eye on all the goings on, whilst hopefully, not being visible in the window. As it was the middle of the week, the Acres was quiet. The couple I'd seen in the carpark came through the arch and were greeted by Chris. That'd keep him occupied for the next hour or so.

I watched a bored older lady being escorted around the redbrick paths by an overly enthusiastic younger man, and a new mother showing brightly coloured flowers to her baby who waved their chubby arms from the pram.

Finally, I saw Tyler and Tris head up through to the back gate.

I sent a text off to summon Nick and brought my boxes out of hiding, piling them up by Chris's seldom used front door. I opened the door a crack and kept an eye out for Nick's dark grey car.

My plan was perfect. My father was out of town today, so I could slip in, drop the boxes off and be back before the boys even noticed I'd gone. Then when I needed to escape, I had everything just a cross country ramble or a short taxi ride away, easily disguised by dinner with daddy: they wouldn't even know I was moving out.

Nick pulled into his reserved spot in the corner of the carpark closest to the house. I picked up the first box and carried it over to him.

"Thanks so much for your help." I said, passing the box over to him.

"There are two more, I'll just run back and get them."

I balanced one box on top of the other, and carefully walked back to the car, peering around the side to see where I was going.

"Is Ty not helping you?" Nick asked, as he loaded the boxes into the boot and slammed it shut.

"No, he's out walking Tris. He really needed some exercise and space."

"I understand. Exercise is really good for depression."

"He's not depressed." I said, getting into the car.

"Are you sure? He's definitely not his usual self."

I thought for a while as Nick drove. When I found out Kaetia was real, I felt validated, like I had a purpose for the first time in my life. I still had my art and my music, and life now had an extra layer of exciting. Tyler had things in his life he'd lost. Kaetia had cost him his fiancée and his home. He'd already rejected his 'soul mate', and now she'd turned round and rejected him. He no longer saw his friends, or played computer games, or posted on social media, losing him the dopamine hits of click-bait-validation. Then he was thrown into a quiet existence with two introverts who found him a bit annoying and hadn't really tried to understand what he was going through.

"I think you may be right." I eventually admitted to Nick, as we got close to my dad's house.

"Well, make sure you look after yourself as well as Ty." Nick said, smiling over at me. "People like us aren't always so good at making sure other people don't sap us dry, and being close to someone with depression can be challenging, especially someone like Tyler."

"People like us?"

"Sensitive-emotional-sponge-people-pleasers. Feel free to correct me if I got it wrong."

"Oh! Erm… No, I think you got it right."

"Anyway, make sure you set clear boundaries and remember you have needs as well. You can't pour from an empty cup and all that jazz."

"Oh, I'll make sure he knows what I want." I let out a dry laugh.

Nick pulled into the drive.

"That is so typical of my father." I said gesturing at his car, which was parked blocking the entrance to the house. "He knows I'm coming today but he has to leave his car right in the way to assert his authority."

"Maybe he was in a rush?"

"Do you always have to think the best of people?"

"I try to."

"Well, my needs right now are that I want to rant and have you nod along like I'm right, even if you don't think so."

"Communicated loud and clear." He said, laughing as he got out of the car and we each picked a box out of the boot.

"So where are we taking these?"

I unlocked the front door and opened it to let him through. "Head up the stairs and go left." I put my box on the floor and entered the code into the house alarm.

Nick climbed the stairs, but stopped by the window at the top, and looked down at the patio. He stood there, motionless, staring through the large glass pane that had replaced the antique stained-glass window that had been broken all those years ago.

The box fell from his hands and all the objects I'd brought with me to keep me safe started to tumble down the stairs.

"Kerella, go and wait for me in the car."

"What is it?"

"Please, just do as I say. Go to the car and wait there."

I ran up the stairs to see what he was staring at.

My father was lying face down on the patio. His blue tie curved into the arc of scarlet draining from his head, his grey suit jacket flung open like wings. Not far from his left hand was a large stone that looked like it'd fallen out of his hand when he fell.

Imprint of home.

Blood stains on stone.

I sank my hands into my pockets. I'd left my stones at The Acres. I couldn't remember if I'd said my mantras that morning.

This was my fault.

I scrambled for high ground.

I needed to be somewhere safe.

I rocked and repeated the mantra Chris had given me over and over and over and over.

> With golden light, these threads I weave
> into a bright, protective dome.
> Love and blessings, I receive,
> I am safe within my home.
>
> My-home-my-home-my-home-my-home:
> I'm a God without a home.

Voices were breaking through, so I put my hands over my ears and sped up my recitation.

"How did she get up there?"

"She climbed the trellis. I tried to follow her, but it came away from the wall."

> My-home-my-home-my-home-my-home-my-home.

And then Kasaman was on the garage roof with me.

The night Becca died, I told him how important she was to me.
She was a threat.
The day my father died, I was moving in with him.
He was a threat.
And there were the two boys who'd tried to take me home against my will and drowned shortly after.
Could I really trust the Devil?

41: THE UNRAVELLING

Chris eventually punched through my protection spell.

"Come back to us, Kerella, come back to us."

A police car was now parked behind my father's car. Nick and Tyler were talking at the far side of the drive. How safe were they from the Devil?

"Good, you're back." He said, putting his hand on my hand. "Now can you do something for me?"

I looked briefly into his black eyes, then stared at my boots. They were black with a red fiery pattern along the bottom. I called them my Pader boots. That was stupid. I was stupid.

Chris had asked me a question. He wanted me to obey him.

I didn't dare say no, so nodded my head slightly.

"Can you climb down and sit in my car? Then when the police are ready, you'll need to answer a few questions. Then I'll take you home. You must hold it together, or they may take you in to check you out, and we can't risk that. We must protect our home."

"How far would you go to protect your home?"

"As far as it takes. Come on. There's a ladder here now, so the climb down should be easier than the climb up." He said running his finger down my arm, which was badly scratched from the rose bushes on the trellis.

He led me to his car and once I was safely stowed away, shut the door, and went over to Tyler and Nick.

I stared into the vent: those smooth plastic strips which led into the darkness. Did they protect the world from the darkness, or the darkness from the world? Which side did I want to be on? Did I even have a choice anymore?

Eventually, the two police officers went over to question Nick. They spoke to him for a while before Chris led them to the car.

He opened the door and knelt beside me. "Are you ready to have a quick chat with these officers?" He asked.

I nodded. He stood up and let the female officer take his place, but he didn't go far, and Tyler came over to stand next to him.

"Hello Kerella, this shouldn't take too long, your friend Nick has already told us most of the details, I just have to double check a few things with you."

I nodded, unsure that I'd even be able to talk.

"What time would you say you arrived?"

The words were thick, my tongue was clumsy, and my mouth full of cotton wool. My brain wasn't retrieving what I needed, so I imagined myself typing the words, and once the words were there, my mouth became an automated narration device. "Half two." I managed to force out, looking at the ground just in front of her knees.

"And, in your own words, could you describe for me what happened?"

"We pulled up. Took the boxes out the boot. I opened the door. Nick walked up the stairs. He dropped the box." I remembered the contents of the box cascading down the stairs. "He dropped the box. He dropped the box. Then he told me to go back to the car, but I followed him. And then I saw my dad... like that." I looked at the gaping black hole of the open front door.

I did it. I opened Pandora's box and now, just a few metres away, my father was lying dead on the patio.

The police officer nodded and wrote a few things down. "Now, Kerella, you said you were carrying boxes inside, could you tell me why you were here?"

I looked up at Chris and Tyler; they were staring straight at me. Their eyes saw into every part of my life; there was no hiding. My perfect plan had unravelled. I moved my focus back to the red bricks of the drive. "I was bringing some stuff over. So I could stay over sometimes. I was sort of moving in." I mumbled.

I looked back up to see how they took the news. Tyler was furious.

Chris turned his back to me and said something to Tyler. They moved away.

Everything became blurred with tears.

"Thank you, Kerella. And you're staying with Mr. Houghton at The Acres? We can contact you there?"

I nodded, thinking that of all Chris's names, Mr. Houghton sounded the most bizarre. I wanted to laugh, but instead, the tears took over and I ugly cried.

Alone.

She returned to her colleague. They spoke a few words to the lads, and then Tyler and Nick got into Nick's car and drove off. Chris exchanged a few words and a handshake with the officers, then walked over to me. He got in the car and pulled off without saying a word. The muscles in his jaw line were tight and they flexed as he stared at the road ahead.

Eventually he said. "I'm sorry you had to go through that. Are you okay?"

My eyes hurt and kept leaking. I was living on quicksand and nothing I built would ever survive. I wasn't stupid, but somehow, everyone was always three steps ahead of me. And people where dead because of me.

Dead. Dead. Dead.

Because of me.

> A survivor's guilt.
> A life that cannot be restored;
> a life that cannot be rebuilt.
> Sever the tie.
> Cut the cord.

> And so we go.
> Into the dark.
> Into the dark.

Chris had asked me a question.

I just nodded, too scared to make a sound.

"I wish you'd told me you wanted to move out. You didn't have to go behind our backs."

"It was only going to be for a night or two a week. I needed some space from Tyler."

He didn't respond.

"What's going to happen now?" I croaked.

"You're going to have a nice long bath and try not to think about what you saw. And I'll deal with everything. We're your family now."

"Is Nick safe?"

"Why should Nick not be safe?"

"You promise me you won't hurt him?"

He pulled into the carpark and slammed on the brakes. He slowly turned to look at me, and his black eyes cut deep. "Why on earth would I hurt Nick?"

"Anyone who gets in your way seems to die." Then panicking I quickly added: "Maybe it's the curses."

"I had nothing to do with what happened to your other father. The police don't even think it's suspicious. And I certainly don't go around hurting my friends." For the first time ever, he looked angry with me.

I burst into tears. "Every time I feel like I reach solid ground, someone seems to die."

He let me cry it out in silence for a while. No comforting hand on my shoulder. No kind words.

"Well," I said, throwing my head up and wiping the tears from my face. "It looks like I'm not going anywhere now. I guess I'll go and have that bath and pretend this is my home."

"If you really think I did this to trap you here, there's something you haven't thought of."

I looked at him. He stared straight into my eyes, but I couldn't work out what he was thinking.

"What?"

"You'll get your flat back now."

42: WHEN GODS ROLL DICE

It turned out my father had hit his head on the wall whilst collapsing in the middle of a heart attack. Why couldn't I have just kept my suspicions to myself until I at least knew the cause of death? They even pinned the time of death down, and Chris was with Tyler setting up a display of pansies when my dad clutched his chest and lurched sideways to his death.

I knew that Chris would forgive me sooner or later. Probably long before I forgave myself for accusing him to his face of being a murderer. Since I'd said those hurtful words, he wouldn't look at me, found work to do in the evenings, and didn't even come with me to the funeral.

Tyler had escorted me, and quietly held my hand as I watched the coffin that was too expensive for this little seaside town get lowered into the ground next to my mother. The man in the grey suit would lie parallel, organised, and appropriate until my time came to fill the empty space next to him.

Well, I wasn't ready to crawl into the earth just yet. Despite my shaky start, somehow, I was going to make something of this life. I would look back on my time 'walking in the lower realm' with pride. I wish I knew what I wanted to do as clearly as Nick did. I still didn't mix well with other people, so nursing, or something like that, really didn't appeal to me. But I didn't want to tread water until the day I died and returned to my Kaetian prison.

And thanks to the spells Asana helped us cast, money wasn't going to be a problem. Maybe we were to blame for my father's death because we fixed the board to make sure we'd be comfortable whilst we played out our Kaetian games.

Ms. Chadwick, my father's assistant, was now sat in front of me in Chris's lounge, laying out files on the coffee table which would reveal the dice we'd rolled.

Father always said she ran the company for him, and without her it'd all fall apart. Now it was her job to make sure I didn't fall apart.

"I went to the house and picked up the items you mentioned, and those your father specified in his will he wished you to have. Are you sure I can't convince you to go and look around yourself?"

I shook my head, letting my hair fall over my face.

"I understand. Are you sure you want your mother's piano delivered here?"

I nodded my head, still not looking up.

She paused. "Kerella?"

It was a command, and she was silent until I obeyed. I slowly lifted my gaze to her stern, pragmatic face, and focused on the tip of her nose. Her dyed blonde hair was pulled back in a tight bun, her rimless glasses were perched on the end of her thin nose, and her makeup was flawless and conventional.

"Your father was happy in his last few days with us. He was aware he wasn't the best father in the world. He never really knew how to handle your 'energy'. That you reached out to him and gave him a second chance to set things right meant the world to him. It was all he talked about. I want you to know that."

I didn't know him. What she described was a conversation I couldn't even imagine him having. I had no idea who the man in the grey suit even was.

I let the tears fall down my face without fighting them.

She gave me a quick sympathetic look, before pushing her glasses up her nose and picking up the first file.

"So, you'll be getting a lump sum up front, then another when the sale of the house goes through. After that, your father set up your finances, so you'll get a monthly payment, with some flexibility should you require any large down payments, for weddings, houses, children, and so forth."

She passed me a sheet of paper.

"No, no." I thrust it back at her. "That's too much. I don't want it. Give it away."

"Now, don't be hasty. You may not think you need it now, but one day, when you have children, you'll be happy about it." She placed the sheet on the coffee table.

"I'm not having children. Can I donate it? Maybe, build a new community centre with a stage and a computer room, and pay for people to train as nurses?"

"Certainly. In fact, your father was involved with several charitable causes. I'll send you through their details in case you want to support the same organisations.

"But what about the community centre and the nurses?"

"Well, as they seem to be causes you care about, I'd be happy to help you set up a bursary. The community centre would be a bit more costly and require finding a suitable plot of land, but I'll put together a project spec and we can take it from there. In fact, I'll take your ideas to the board; I think they may be interested in contributing to these as well."

She put her mother of pearl pen down on the files. "Like father, like daughter." She said, looking me directly in the eye. It was meant as an affectionate gesture, but made me sink deep into myself. "Gerald hated spending money on himself too. I think he'd be proud of the decisions you're making." She started rearranging the files. "Anyway, we don't need to set anything in stone today, but you'll need to think about things like writing your will, and double check all the things on this list before we meet with the solicitors next week." She raised a kindly, efficient smile. "For now, I've left the items we discussed in," She fished a set of keys out of a clear plastic bag and put them in front of me on the table, "your car."

"But I can't drive!"

She stood up, slipping her pen into her suitcase and snapping it shut. "I guess it's time to learn. Until then, make sure you get anyone who drives it fully insured."

I stared at the bunch of keys. "Thank you for all your help."

"I'd do anything for your father; Gerald was a wonderful man." She nodded and headed out.

I picked up the keys and looked at them. I recognised two of them.

I had my flat back; now I could escape to the life I had before all of this madness.

I could go home.

I put the keys back on the coffee table, suddenly not sure if I wanted to go backwards.

"So, Tu-Ker, what did the old man leave you?" Tyler asked, swooping into the room.

"Oh, a car and my flat." I said, trying to gather all the files together quickly.

But Tyler saw the breakdown before I could hide it.

"Just a car and a flat?" He said, picking up the piece of paper and giving me an accusatory look. "Holy fuck! We hit the motherload!"

"Tyler!" Chris snapped from the doorway.

"What?"

"Can you please help Nick close up the café? Lucy's not feeling well, so she's gone home."

Tyler dropped the summary of my 'winnings' on the coffee table and slouched off, muttering something about slave labour.

Chris sat down opposite me.

"Do you need a hand moving? Or do you want to do it in the middle of the night, so we don't find out until after you've gone?"

"How many times can I say I'm sorry?"

He held up his hand. "I'm sorry... Do you need a hand?"

I looked at him. "Any chance I could stay here a bit longer?"

"Of course. Mi casa es tu casa."

"Thank you. This is a bit too much for me at the moment. It's all big decisions, the meaning of life, and babies."

"Babies?" Is there something I should know?"

"What? No! Ty and I are still not really together. But do you know if I could?"

"Okay, in at the deep end." He took a deep breath and looked out of the patio doors. "If you genuinely feel you love Tyler, then it's a choice you need to make."

"Wait! No! I mean, babies! Not sex! What would happen if I had a child whilst I'm down here? Is it even possible?"

"Oh. Phew. That's a little bit easier."

I smiled at him. Things were starting to feel our crazy kind of normal again.

"Okay, so, from what I remember, Kaetians only have one child per family."

"Yes, that's what I remember."

"Biologically, they can have more, but the children are exiled and the parents punished, so extra pregnancies are avoided or covered up."

"Nice place."

"The night you were created, Asana and I performed a ritual. There were chants, relics, a metallic tasting potion, and a lot of ridiculous ceremonial Kaetian nonsense. After that night, my life expectancy was the same as Asana's, and those three thousand years passed on to you."

"Lucky me." I said, my voice dripping with sarcasm.

"It's something a lot of people would kill for. Anyway, I don't know what parts of that night were necessary for conjoining my essence with Asana's, but I'd guess, you would at least need the potion. Without that, your child would live as long as a regular human, and you'd see them die before you could take breath. Also, if you conceive them here, there's no way to know if they'd even travel to Kaetia when they leave this realm."

"Did you and Asana have children whilst you were here?"

"Veronica and I did not have children."

"Asana was called Veronica?"

"And she was so beautiful. During her time on earth, she was very sad we didn't have children. We didn't know that was a blessing at the time."

"What were you? Erm, what was your profession?"

"I worked the land. We were comfortable, but not affluent. It was a time of simple pleasures. There was an olive tree in the garden, which produced the nicest olives I have ever tasted. The road to our cottage had lemon trees growing on either side: the smell was divine. I always knew I was home when that citrus smell was in the air. Once, we saw Leonardo Da Vinci. I think."

"Did working the land make you happy?"

"I think there are only so many lives I can fall into the same profession, before I have to admit that I love nature and the wonder of plants."

"I don't know what I love."

"What about your art?"

"Well, of course I love that, but it's hardly useful, like nursing, or growing food."

"Hoping not to sound too Kaetian, but art is one of the most important aspects of every society. Art comes from the human soul. It captures and records the emotion of a time, or it can help challenge existing perceptions and inspire positive changes. When we talk of past societies, their art is one of the first things we discuss. I would never describe art as not being useful." He took his hat off and put it down on the coffee table. "Is art what you want to do with this life?"

"I think so. But I feel it would be selfish."

He turned around to look at my selkie. "I think if it's what you want to do, it would be selfish of you not to commit to a lifetime of creating your art for this world."

"I sometimes think of, maybe, doing a proper art course. Just to give me some kind of structure and confidence."

"Well, that is what you should do. It's not like you can't afford it."

"Would you be upset if I left town to do that?"

"I'd miss you, and I would be sad, but as long as you told me you were going and let me help you, I wouldn't be upset."

I jumped up and threw myself across the room, crashing down on Chris and pulling him into a tight bear hug. He fought to free his arms, then returned the embrace.

"I'm going to be a proper artist." I whispered into his shoulder.

"You've always been a proper artist." He replied. "You're just going to learn how to do it the lower realm way."

43: A PAIN IN THE COCCYX

The kettle clicked off. I lifted the lid of my mother's blue teapot and poured the water into it. The light from the cool, grey sky caught the flow, turning it into a shimmering silver stream. I slotted the lid back into place and carried the teapot through to the dining room, where Chris and Tyler were sifting through every piece of paper Ms. Chadwick had delivered. It seemed my father had kept almost every scribble I'd done since I was first able to hold a crayon. And from a very early age, I'd been channelling Kaetian images.

I placed the teapot on the green trivet, resting my fingers on the crack by one of the clawed feet. I looked out of the window and saw my mother smiling at me. She lifted her arms in the air and danced in circles.

Was she in Kaetia? Would I ever see her again?

"Earth to Tu-Ker." Tyler snapped his fingers in front of my face.

"What?"

"Why did you rip me in half?"

"What?"

"Here!" He said holding up the paintings of him that had got torn when my father had confiscated my Kaetian research.

"That happened before I met you."

"There's no way I pissed you off before we even met, so why rip these up?"

Chris snorted.

"I got in a fight with my dad, and actually got injured trying to save those paintings. They were ripped because we were fighting over you." I looked at Chris. "That was the night we first met; when I knocked you into that bush."

"Ah, so Tyler was to blame for that pain in my coccyx." He said.

"Some things never change." I winked at him.

"Hey!"

"Oh, come on Ty, we're just teasing you." I poured the tea into the awaiting mugs.

He held the best painting up, piecing it together. "I look nothing like I do in Kaetia."

"Of course you don't. You're a completely new biological entity, with different parents and different genes." Chris answered him.

"Will everyone from this realm look different in Kaetia?" Tyler asked.

"No. Just us. We'll return to our real bodies when we die. Mortals who go to Kaetia take on a form based on their perceptions of who they are, which most of the time is pretty similar to what they looked like down here."

"So, there's no point in getting Tu-Ker's face famous?"

"What on earth are you talking about? I've no interest in being famous!"

"But wouldn't it be useful in the fight against Laescenno if everyone on earth knew we were Gods and were on our side? You've got the money to make it happen."

"That's the last thing we will be doing. We'll either get locked up for being delusional or killed by some religious fanatic."

"Could we set ourselves up as an iconic lifestyle couple, so people at least know us?"

"No!" Chris and I said in unison.

"Can we at least buy a bigger place? It's going to be so cramped with both of us in that flat."

I gave Chris a look, and he nodded.

"I best go take Tris for a walk." Chris said, heading out the door.

"You guys need to work on your undercover skills if we're going to have any chance in Kaetia. What don't I know?" Tyler said.

"We're not going to be moving into my flat."

"You bought that house I sent you the link to?"

"No." I took a deep breath. "I'm moving to Edinburgh. Without you."

"What? No! You can't do that! Have you forgotten: I'll be tortured and executed if people don't think we're together?"

"I'm not going to do anything that'll undermine our 'relationship'." I said making air quotes. "I just need to find myself, see if I can do an art course, and learn a bit more about these human things."

"And fuck half of Scotland whilst you're at it."

"Okay, I'm not going to slap you, but you bloody well deserve it." I felt my chest grow tight. I wanted to bail on this conversation, but I knew I had to get through to Tyler. "Sit down. I'm going to tell you some shit I really don't want to."

He looked at me suspiciously but sat down on the grey couch and I perched next to him, fixing my eyes on the blue teapot.

"When I was younger, my uncle sexually abused me. I've never had a genuine relationship, sexual or otherwise, but tripped blindly from one guy to the next, whilst they took what they wanted, what they expected from me, and what I'd been programmed to believe I was worth. Sex to me is not love; it's a complicated fucked up mess, and for so long it was the only thing I believed people could want from me. People here treat me like something to be passed around and laughed at."

"Okay, so some people make jokes about you, but you kind of ask for it. It's not like they know your sob story every time you open your legs. You have to grow a thicker skin. *You* won't be tortured to death because of *their* misunderstanding."

"Tyler, do you listen to yourself when you speak?"

"Do you? I'm trying to tell you I'll be murdered, and you're making it about you and something that happened years ago. You're always so rude, constantly correcting me or telling me to shut up, and you're all googly eyes at me until the second my life depends on you, and then you turn into Miss Ice Box."

I felt tears stinging my eyes. "I'm not doing anything to put your life in danger, I just want to go to Edinburgh for a few years. I'll not be having sex with anyone; the thought of Asana or Chris poking around in someone's head and getting a full live action replay of that is enough to put me off."

"But why do you have to go to Edinburgh?"

I took a deep breath and tried to remember all the points I'd planned to say. "I want to get away so I can learn to remember that I matter; that I am who I am, and not what other people project on me. I want to get away, so my past actions aren't being thrown in my face as expectations of how I should be treated in the present by people who never understood me, but used me, or ridiculed me, or bitched about me." I'd lost myself in the words. I couldn't remember where I was going, or what I'd already said.

"And what should I do while you're there?" He spat out.

I shrugged. "I dunno. You can have my flat, and I'll set you up a monthly payment. I'm not trying to hurt you."

"Yeah, well you did." He stood up, walked over to the table and leant heavily on it. Then he blew a long stream of air out of his nose, banged the table with his fist, and stormed out, slamming the door behind him.

I sat there in silence for a few minutes, trying to work out how I could've handled things differently.

I really wished telling Tyler to fuck off wouldn't lead to horrible repercussions, because at the moment, I'd be quite happy never to see him again. I picked up my mug of tea and headed towards the café gardens.

I found Nick on his knees digging up carrots around the back of his shed.

"Hi."

"Oh, Kerella, hey." He said, swinging back so he was sat on the ground. He ran his soil covered hands through his dark blond hair.

I sat down next to him and took a sip of tea.

"You didn't bring me one?"

"Sorry, I didn't think."

"It's okay." He bumped shoulders with me. "I was just teasing you."

"I'm sorry I've been avoiding you since my father died."

"Oh, don't worry about that. How are you doing?"

"Better, thanks. Looks like I'll be escaping to Edinburgh soon."

"That's great! Have you told Chris and Ty?"

"Yeah. Sorry about last time. I shouldn't have involved you in my crazy plan."

"Or at least told me what was going on. Don't you think I'd have understood the need to escape?"

"We've talked it over, and with everything that's happened this year, they understand I need a change of scenery and a bit of space. I'm going to try and find an art course and maybe do some volunteering. Ty's going to stay here, and we're going to do the whole long-distance relationship thing. Which should work, as we're one hundred percent perfect together."

Nick looked down and shuffled through the basket of carrots. Shrugging, he said: "Carrot and coriander soup on the menu tomorrow."

"I'll try to get out for lunch; it was nice last week."

He nodded.

"How've you been?" I asked.

"Well, the house has gone on sale, and everything feels like it's the end of an era. I'm looking out for a flat, but nothing on the market feels right. Chris says I could always move in here for a bit."

"He does like to take in waifs and strays."

"That he does. You know, my father worked here from the day it opened, and I played with Stuart in the garden when we were kids. I used to think of this as my home from home, but I don't feel that way anymore. Nowhere is really feeling like home right now."

"Maybe nowhere is meant to feel like home? Like the universe is telling you to move on."

"Are you telling me to go away?"

"No. Well, yes. Maybe." I stared into the soft brown of my tea, my heart thumping. Was this so difficult because I wanted him to say yes so badly? Or because I was doing the wrong thing, and he was about to shout at me for being manipulative?

"Ker, what's up?"

I took a deep breath. "The company have been wrapping up all my father's affairs, and the person who's taking over is setting up a bursary for people wanting to train as nurses. It would mean a lot to me if you'd think about applying. Maybe you could even escape to Edinburgh, and I won't be alone in a strange city. But you know, whatever, it's not a big deal."

He looked at me, his mouth hanging open, a streak of soil across his forehead.

"I'll send you over the details when I hear more." I got to my feet and started to leave.

He jumped up and grabbed me in a bear hug. "Thank you, Ker. I know you did this for me. And it's... just amazing. So thoughtful."

I pulled away and let my hair fall over my face. "I just asked Ms. Chadwick to set it up. I didn't have anything to do with the details."

"You made it happen."

I dared to look at him. He was grinning. "It's not a guaranteed thing; you'd still have to apply."

"Oh, I know. I just can't believe you'd do something like this for me."

"In a heartbeat!" I said, stealing his phrase.

"Well, I look forward to applying."

In the light of his excitement, the frustration I was feeling over Tyler's behaviour slipped away. I smiled back at him. "Anyway, I've my future to start researching. Nothing's going to change unless I make it happen."

He reached forward and tucked my hair behind my ear. "It's lovely seeing you so determined and positive about something. It lights up your entire face."

I dropped my head down and stared at my shoes. "Thanks." I mumbled and ran off.

44: SAMSON AND DELILAH

To begin with, Edinburgh was just a place I picked at random. It wasn't too far from here, but it was in a different country, somewhere I'd never been, a blank slate, a world of possibilities.

I hit the internet. I bought books. I got a set of notebooks with paintings of Edinburgh Castle, Arthur's Seat, and the Scott Monument on them. I immersed myself in the details and felt myself come alive. The world melted away and I was left with underground streets, body snatchers, extinct volcanoes, and new graveyards to explore.

I was being premature. I'd only applied to two art courses and wouldn't hear back for ages. What if I didn't get in? All this research would just make me feel dreadful if they rejected me. But I also needed the distraction, and Edinburgh was such a fascinating place.

Most of all, I was completely obsessed by a rocky outcrop called Samson's Ribs. Something about the columnar basalt shapes intrigued me and made me feel like I could get through this. It was another premonition, but unlike Regrettable Day, it wasn't about burning things down, it was about reaching out and making a connection. It was a seed of trust. So I indulged it.

A rare book on the geology of the area, which Chris had helped me track down, arrived this morning. I'd made myself a little nest on the grey couch in the dining room and planned to read the whole book in one sitting. Tyler had been staying at Ian's since he'd stormed off last week, taking my car with him, and Chris would be working all day, so I was alone with my notebooks, the saltire blanket Chris had bought for me, and an endless supply of tea.

As I turned page after page, I grew a bit disappointed. The book wasn't quite the cornucopia of amazing facts I'd hoped it would be, but it was fun to dredge through each page, picking out the bits of information that appealed to me. Like before the continents drifted, the land I lived on now was in a completely different part of the globe to the land that would later be Scotland, so the rocks were totally different. Considering that in Kaetia, stones were supposed to possess magical properties, I was sure that was significant. I also loved the idea of living on an extinct volcano. Reading about all the lava flows made me think of Chris's mountain. I'd asked him a couple of times to tell me how he'd created that, but like with a lot of things, his memory was fuzzy and he couldn't, or wouldn't, tell me the details.

Someone knocked on the door.

"Hello?"

The door slowly opened and Tyler stuck his head into the room.

I sighed and rolled my eyes. My perfect day was ruined.

He came in, as did the memories of what happened in this room last week. I wrapped my blue protective blanket tight around myself. It wasn't a Kaetian cloak, but it was so soft, it felt much more protective.

"I'm an ass." He got out before I could tell him to fuck off.

"Yeah. Tell me something I don't know."

He placed a brown paper bag on the table.

"No fucking way!" I gasped.

"Chris told me what to get."

I snatched up my baguette and checked he'd got the order right. He'd forgotten 'no tomatoes', but they could be removed.

"What do you want?" I snapped at him. Suspicious, but also stuffing the end of the baguette into my mouth and feeling the hard crust against my gums.

"To apologise, to crawl, to tell you I'm sorry." He said, pulling out a dining chair and collapsing onto it.

I finished chewing and swallowed. "Did Chris tell you what to say as well?"

"Not that bit. Even I can see when I'm out of line."

I stared at him with my rip-you-apart glare.

He squirmed.

"Three more baguettes and we'll be even." I said, putting the baguette on the table to finish later.

He smiled awkwardly. "Let's make it four."

"Without tomatoes."

"Oh shit!" He slapped himself on the forehead. "Yeah, Chris did tell me that."

"Well, try to remember next time."

"I promise."

"So, how's Ian?" I asked.

Tyler shifted in his seat. "He was fine. I totally beat his arse."

"You weren't with Ian the last few days." I didn't know where this was coming from, but I felt it to be real.

He stared at the floor.

I shook my head. "So when you sleep with random women, it's not a death sentence on your head?"

"I was hoping no one would find out."

I sighed. "Well, if anyone does, tell them we have an 'arrangement'."

"An open relationship?" Tyler asked, eyebrows raised sceptically.

"Of course! Fuck half of Scotland whilst you're at it. As long as you're discrete and don't make me into a laughingstock."

"And you're okay with that?"

"Yes!"

"Wow. I wasn't expecting this."

"What were you expecting?"

"I dunno. My balls in a vice. Sanctimonious preaching. You getting Chris to poke my eyeballs out."

"It's almost as if we've been talking different languages. I've said all this to you before; why would you think I meant something else?"

"Because girls don't like their men sleeping around. I didn't think you really meant it."

I stood up, still wrapped in my blue blanket, waddled over to him and bopped him on the head. "Okay, I know Kaetia is dreadful for the condescension, but you're also British. Do not refer to me as a 'girl' and yourself as a 'man' in the same sentence."

"Does this mean we're up to five baguettes?"

"Six. But listen to the words I'm fucking saying!" I untangled myself from the blanket and threw it over his head. "We only need to pretend we're in love. This is not a real relationship. I don't care if you sleep around. But it's probably a good idea to hide it from Chris."

He dug himself out from under the blanket and hurled it onto the couch. "And once again, my 'not-girlfriend' kills my sex life. You say one thing, when you really mean the opposite."

"How've I done that?"

"It's completely impossible to keep something like this from Chris whilst I'm living here. You know that. He's the overprotective type when it comes to you. The second he has the slightest suspicion I'm not treating his little princess how he wants, and I'm just a body hidden in the woods. Or is that your plan?"

"Ty, I've already offered you my flat, and to give you money every month. Stop looking for the negative in everything and just bloody well move in there already. Let a friend help you out. Enjoy this life. Stop fucking moaning."

"Why would you do all that for me?"

"Because you're my friend, and immortal soul mate. And we will get there. I promise."

He stood up and came to stand in front of me. He opened his arms, and

I stepped into the hug, my body stiff, and my arms unable to find a comfortable position.

"This is going to sound lame now, but I came to tell you I'm okay with you moving to Scotland." He kissed the top of my head and stepped back.

"Thank you. But I wasn't waiting for your permission."

"I can see that." He said, turning to the table and rummaging through my books on Scotland and Edinburgh. "Seriously, you need to learn how to search the internet, it'll have a lot more information than these books."

"I know how to do my research, thank you. These are what I turned to after three days on the internet."

He picked up a piece of paper which I'd scrawled some notes on, the crease forming down the centre of his forehead. "Have you been spying on me? Is that how you knew I wasn't with Ian?"

"No, that was just a lucky guess."

"Then how come you're writing about Samson?"

"What's Samson got to do with you?"

"Samson, as in 'The Man of the Sun', betrayed by Delilah who knew his weakness." He shot me a suspicious look.

"Tyler, we're not Samson and Delilah: that story was around way before we were born."

"I know that. I'm not an idiot." He snapped. Then he laughed. "But you know, we are gods; there may be some prophetic references to us dotted about." He winked.

I was completely confused. "Why would that make you think I was spying on you?"

"I've been writing a song exploring different lower realm Sun Gods and heroes. I started with a verse on Samson. So why are you writing about him?"

"I've been researching Arthur's Seat in Edinburgh, which folklore says has a giant called Samson buried underneath it."

"Hmm." Tyler said and put the list back on the table. "Weird coincidence."

I sat down on the couch and pulled the blanket over my knees. I was finding Tyler harder to read than usual, so tried to move to safer ground. "So! New song! Want to play it for me?"

Tyler sat down next to me, turned around so his back was against the armrest, and put his legs over my knees. "It's not really at that stage yet. What about you? Are you working on anything?"

"I've been bouncing around a few ideas, about how I want to say so much, but don't know how to."

"I dunno, you manage to say an awful lot, if you ask me."

I poked his leg. "Oi! You know what I mean! I feel I should have some kind of positive impact whilst I'm down here, but I'm the last person to be a spokesperson for any cause."

"So don't speak."

"You telling me to shut up?"

"No! I mean, you say so much with your music and your art, possibly too much, why do you need to talk as well?"

"I guess."

"I miss our music." Ty said.

"You know what I've been thinking about a lot lately? The Bubble Interlude!"

He laughed, slapping his legs. "Oh yeah! I'd totally forgotten all about that! Kaetia does pop music... badly!"

"Birgitta was such a darling."

"And you were such a clueless idiot."

"Hey, I was raised in a tower! How was I supposed to know Denmark and China weren't the same place?"

"Ask before you assume you know all the answers?"

"Well, when I get back, I'll be different. Asana warned me this would happen, but I didn't realise Kaetians were so lost in their arrogance."

"When you get back, pretend you're still the same. You may know more about this place, but there's still an awful lot about Kaetia you don't know."

"Well, you'll be by my side to teach me." I said, reaching out to squeeze his hand.

"Not like you get a choice in that."

"Ty." I said, looking into his brown, contact lens free eyes. "You're not a bad choice. You're just not a now choice. And you're going to make a wonderful Golden Son of Kaetia."

45: SAMSON'S RIBS

"**O**h my god!" I jabbed at the train window.

"I guess you've never been to Edinburgh by train before? The castle is a bit of a surprise!" Nick said, pulling his green leaf-patterned rucksack down from the overhead storage area.

"I've never been to Edinburgh at all!" I said, letting my eyes drink in the dramatic rocks leading up to the castle, imagining the lava that cooled to form the stone that was passing by the window.

Nick headed towards the doors. I grabbed my bag and followed him.

I bounced from foot to foot as we waited for the train to arrive in the station. I'd spent the last two months researching Edinburgh and I was finally going to set foot in the city! I couldn't remember the last time I'd been so excited.

"You know," I said to Nick, "seventy-eight people matched all the basic criteria for the bursary, and only three people got one. And one of those people was you! And I had nothing to do with that. That is how awesome you are."

He smiled and blushed a bit. "You have mentioned that a few times. You can stop now."

The train arrived in the station, the doors slid open, and I jumped down onto the dark grey platform.

There was a sandwich half trodden into the tarmac and a crowd of people waiting to get on the train. A woman with a pink suitcase roughly pushed past me to be the first into the carriage.

The noise was too much. The people were too much. Everything was happening. This was a mistake. Why would I choose to live here?

I let my gaze rest on a leaf in the pattern of Nick's rucksack as he walked ahead of me, and I focused my mind on the next thing we had to do.

Leave the station.

We ran up some steps away from the platform, then walked down the central overpass, passed advertisement boards, food stalls, and people. Everything was trying to grab my attention with a call to action.

The train had been late, and we had to run to make it to our first appointment. Nick knew where he was going, all I needed to do was be his echo.

We ascended a long, steep staircase, and then we were in a main street. It was raining. A bag piper was playing Scotland the Brave. A bus whipped by spraying water into the air with an explosive hiss. A toddler was screaming.

I slipped my umbrella out of my pocket and opened it. My carefully laid plans for these two days hadn't involved rain, but I had prepared for it. Nick pulled the hood of his red rain coat up and ploughed on through the chaos. I followed.

Before long, the crowd thinned. Nick led us through the quieter backstreets, occasionally checking the map on his phone.

Suddenly, we came to a wide-open green space lined with trees. The air smelled cleaner and there was only one other couple nearby. I looked down the park and was shocked into breathlessness at the sight of the hill I'd become obsessed with. "Look Nick! Look! It's Arthur's Seat!"

"Yes, I know." He gave me an amused smile, ducked into a small shelter, and pulled his hood down. "We've ten minutes before our appointment, and it's just down that road there." He said, pointing at a curved avenue. Did you want to go over the details?" He said, digging in his bag and pulling out his folded-up printouts.

I took a long look at my extinct volcano, thinking about later today, when I'd be walking up those ancient slopes. Then I followed Nick into the wooden shelter. This space was just round the corner from his first choice of flat to rent. Now I could see why he'd picked it, as very little else about it had appealed to me.

Although I'd already read over the details online a couple of times, I took the printout from Nick and looked again at the small two bed flat over the row of shops. Ty had thought I was stupid for limiting myself to Nick's budget. I'd told him he was an arrogant wanker, and that we were here to learn about the lives of human beings, not roll around with golden playthings. If I were honest, I was so scared about all the change, I wanted the security of having Nick around, even if that meant living in a flat which was smaller than I was used to. Many people would think it was a great place to live, and it was a lot bigger than my Kaetian tower, with a door I could go through at any time. But since my inheritance had come through, my head had been filling up with exciting images of what my new home could look like. I was sure, once Nick saw how amazing the flats I'd chosen were, I could convince him to let me cover more of the rent.

The rain drumming on the roof of the wooden shelter beat out a gentle hypnotic tune. The line of trees in front of us was sparkly in the droplet-infused grey light. Nick was providing us the time and space to transition from the race through the city, to venturing into an unknown property, without me needing to explain to him that this was even a thing. Samson's Ribs were so close I could imagine how they'd look. Darker than in the photographs, because of the rain, dripping pristine water onto the bushes clinging to the rocks beneath them.

Two flats to view, then we were hiking out to see them.

"Right! I'm ready!" I declared, handing the dogged bits of paper back to Nick.

He took them from me and tucked them into the side pocket of his rucksack. "Just give me a few more moments." He said, staring out into the middle of the expanse of grass.

I watched the rain falling onto the soft blanket of green with him. After a couple of minutes, he announced: "Okay! We're good to go!"

"Excellent!" I said, and in my excitement, grabbed his hand as we headed off. He held it back, and it felt too awkward to let go.

But it also felt fantastic.

The entrance to the flat was between a sandwich shop and an out of business plumbing supply outlet. Nick pressed the intercom button and the door clicked open without us announcing ourselves. We headed up two flights of stairs, and at the top, a young woman was waiting for us. She sighed and slipped her phone into her pocket before looking at us. "Mr. Fenwick? Hi." She shook Nick's hand but ignored me. "As you can see, this is a two-bed flat in a sought-after location, close to the Meadows and the universities." She launched into her sales pitch, focusing on the location and convenience, dotted with very loose descriptions of the actual interior.

As she led us around the flat, I did my best to imagine living here. I'd survived centuries in a much smaller residence and could hire studio space where I could work on my art during the day. The ceilings were high, and the bay windows in the living area and the larger bedroom were quite nice. But the rest of the flat felt cramped and dirty. Nick quietly inspected each of the rooms, nodding slightly to himself. I spent more time observing him, and thinking about how my feet were sticking to the carpet, than really looking around. I knew I'd hate the flat, but I could live here for a year, if that's what he wanted.

We left the flat, as a young couple arrived, wide eyed and smiling. They immediately asked the letting agent what parking was like on the street.

We traipsed down the stairs and returned to the rain. I popped my umbrella open and raised it over my head.

Nick sighed. "Well, that was a disappointment."

"What were you expecting? For them to have photographed the wrong flat?"

"That was by far the best option in my price range. I know you want somewhere a lot nicer, but I'm not sure it's going to work."

"Let's just see the next flat, and then go for a lovely walk. Once we're all the way up there," I pointed to the top of Arthur's seat, "we'll be looking down on everything, and that will give you a new perspective."

"A walk isn't going to change my feelings about the rental market. But we'll discuss it when we get home." He said, heading off through the park.

I followed him, spinning my umbrella as I walked, watching the droplets fly off like I was in my own little water feature.

We passed through the streets of Edinburgh. I was now able to enjoy looking at the architecture and the landscape. I didn't think about where we were going, until Nick suddenly came to a halt.

"Tadaah!"

I looked at him confused.

He gestured to the shop on his right.

"Edinburguettes." I read the shop sign. "Design your own baguette or try one from our Scoterrific menu."

"I thought we could try out some baguette shops while we're here. See if we can find your new favourite hangout." Nick smiled sheepishly.

"Let me guess: Chris told you to do this?"

"No. I've just seen you come back to the Acres a few times carrying a baguette, and you always looked so happy. I wanted you to have that here too."

We went in and I ordered a brie, black olive, lettuce, and houmous white baguette.

The crust was softer than my usual baguette, the lettuce was mixed leaves rather than iceberg, the brie tasted stronger, and the olives were sliced instead of whole, but it was great to know I'd have something similar to my favourite treat in my new city. And knowing that Nick had cared enough to seek this out for me, made me feel like crying. I'd live in a pokey flat for three years if that's what he wanted to do.

We walked up to the flat I really wanted. It was in a wide residential street. The white stone buildings were neatly outlined with uniform black wrought iron fences. The rent was well over double than that of the first flat, but it was spacious, modernised throughout, had three bedrooms, and an amazing view of King Arthur's Seat.

There was a fresh bouquet of decorative thistles, lavender, and cream roses on the shiny black marble counter in the kitchen, and the man who greeted us appeared to have a genuine smile as he showed us around the flat.

I loved the smooth, wooden floors. The settee looked clean and wouldn't need two throws over it to make me feel like I could sit on it. The view from the living room window had me standing, staring for a good few minutes.

Nick fidgeted and didn't really look at anything as we toured the property, then walked off the second we got back to the front door.

"Thank you." I mouthed at the agent, before running after Nick.

The rain was much harder now, and the wind was picking up, so I didn't even bother with my umbrella as I ran down the street to catch up with Nick.

"Look, I'm sorry Ker. There's just no way I'm going to spend that much on rent. If you want to go ahead and take it with someone else, that's okay. It was just a bit upsetting seeing you so excited about it."

"Okay, I have an idea; please hear me out."

He stopped, turned to face me, and shrugged. "Ker, I don't want to throw all my savings away on rent. That's not why I sold the house."

"Okay, okay, okay. So, if we take the other flat, I'd need to rent some studio space, right? If we take that place, I wouldn't need to, so I could cover two thirds of the rent, and it wouldn't be charity. We could make the studio the smaller bedroom between the other two. And that also means if you brought someone back with you, you wouldn't need to be self-conscious about me hearing you through the wall."

"Ker, it's still too much."

"And, and, and, I was talking to Ty about how he'd be visiting, like all the time, and he said he should pay something towards the rent too, so you could count us in for three quarters."

Nick hmphed. "I'm not sure we can really count on Tyler."

"What do you mean by that?"

He turned and walked away from me.

"Nick, what do you mean by that?" I said, louder, stomping after him. My wet hair sticking to my face.

"Ker, it's not my place to say anything."

"Too late, you started this. Why can't we count on Tyler?"

"Ker, don't make me do this. I like Ty. He's a good guy."

"So, what's the problem? You two have been friends longer than I've known either of you. You know we're good for the money."

Nick stopped. "You know you can do a lot better than Tyler, right?"

"Yeah, but he's the one I choose, so what difference does it make?"

He took a deep breath and sighed. "I don't want to be the one to tell you this… Tyler's been cheating on you."

"No, he's not."

"I'm sorry. Yes, he has. With at least two women, that I know of."

"No, seriously, he's not. I know all about it. I told him it's okay with me."

"You know?" Nick scowled and shook his head. "You don't have to put up with this."

"Of course I don't have to! I made this choice. What are you implying? That I'm too stupid to know my own mind?"

Anger was burning through me. I was furious that I was having to lie about my relationship with Tyler, that Nick thought I wasn't able to understand my own emotions, that I wasn't going to get to live in that flat with Nick, that my perfect day was falling apart.

At least I could still get out to Samson's Ribs.

I decided Nick didn't deserve anything else from me, so I turned around and strode off in the direction of Arthur's Seat, glad the rain would hide the tears streaming down my face.

I missed the curb and fell into the road.

I screamed in shock.

Nick was there in an instant.

He pulled me up and away to safety as a car swooshed by and beeped its horn. He wrapped his arms around me.

I was dirty and wet, and my ankle hurt. But hey! I was so wet a bit of dirt wouldn't make any difference. I screwed my face up in determination, shoved my wet hair out of my face, and stepped in the direction of Samson's Ribs.

My ankle buckled. "Ow! Ow! Ow!"

"Kerella, stop."

The rain was no longer hiding my crying, as I heaved and whined.

"All I want to do is go to Samson's Ribs." I sobbed.

"Okay." Nick swallowed. "How about we check into the hotel, freshen up, see how your ankle's doing, then if you're feeling up to it, we'll get a taxi out to see them?"

"I want to walk out there now." I snapped. "That's how I planned it."

"I really don't think that's a good idea with this weather and your ankle."

I started to limp away. My ankle didn't hurt that much. But I was soaked, cold, and it would be an eight mile walk out to Samson's Ribs and back to the hotel.

"I can't just get a taxi! I have to go there by foot. That was my plan." I whimpered.

"You're going to be living here soon. You can walk out there as much as you want."

I looked into Nick's face, framed by his stupid red anorak hood.

"Hotel." I conceded, quietly.

Nick called a taxi for us and let me use him as a crutch until we'd checked in and climbed up to our rooms.

Having delivered me to the safety of the door to my room, he took his warm arm from around my waist. I was feeling a bit calmer, having had time to adjust to the change in plans. I smoothed my wet hair back from my face, and ran my fingers over my cheeks, in case my makeup had run.

"Ker, I'm sorry. I know it's your choice who you get involved with."

I pulled Nick into a deep hug. The warmth of his protective body sank into mine; I ran my hands through his floppy hair and I felt safe as he wrapped his arms tightly around me. I pulled back slightly and looked him directly in the eyes. I took a deep breath, reaching out and holding onto the doorknob of his room. "Tyler and I have an arrangement." I said.

At that moment, I was conveying everything I meant.

But then I dove towards my own room, swiped the card, let myself in, and closed the door behind me.

I slowly collapsed down the wall, leaving a dirty wet streak down the paint. It was one thing for Tyler to risk his life by getting close to other women, but I couldn't disconnect the act from the potential consequences.

This was a side of my life that could never happen.

I was a god. One day I would judge mortals and choose who would live and who would die. One day I may grow up to create obscenely tall and dramatic mountains.

But I could never stand in front of Nick and tell him how I really felt.

46: THE UNSPOKEN

We signed a lease for a flat a bit smaller than the one I originally wanted, and without the view, but slightly larger than Nick's choice, with the agreement that I would pay two thirds of the rent to use the extra room as studio space. I was more than happy to let my dream flat slip away. I'd realised that any sacrifices to create my perfect home life should be mine, and not forced onto someone else. With all the moulding and coercion I'd been through, you'd think I'd have worked that one out by now.

Chris was driving me and my stuff up in his van next week. Nick would follow the week after. Although our courses didn't start for a few months, we both wanted to find some volunteering to do, so we could find our feet in the city.

Tyler had really made my old flat into his own, and although it was painful to see it in such a state, it was nice to see the old Ty returning. He was getting a bit too enthusiastic about our open pretend relationship, which made me even more grateful that I was leaving town for a few years.

A plot of land had been secured for the new community centre, and several local businesses were involved with pledges of leisure equipment, computers, and musical instruments. 'Chaddy' was outdoing herself, and although I wasn't keen on it being called 'The Tomlinson Centre', after Chris explained that it was highly probable that she'd been in a relationship with my father, and this was more about her than me, I decided not to complain.

This evening, Nick and I were having a little goodbye party at the Acres. Nick was in the café preparing the food, and I was sorting out the drinks in the kitchen.

"Knock knock!" Fus called down the hall as he and Mannie came in.

I squealed, put down the glasses that I'd been arranging, and ran through to meet them.

I threw myself at Mannie. "It's been months! How was America?"

Mannie looked at Fus, a big smile on her face. "Go on, tell her. I know you want to, and you won't be able to keep it a secret."

Fus held up his left hand which bore a white gold wedding band. "We got married! And, and, and," he said, resting his hand on Mannie's stomach, "we're going to have a little baby Mannie!"

I threw my hands to my face as I started to cry. "That's amazing! I'm so happy for you!" I dragged Mannie into another hug, and Fus joined in, wrapping his arms around both of us.

"Did I hear that correctly?" Chris said, coming through the patio doors. Fus nodded, grinning from ear to ear, and went over to shake Chris's hand. They wandered off into the garden.

"But you!" Mannie said, "You look… taller; there's something different. Edinburgh is going to be so lucky! Come on, sit down, and tell me all about it."

We sat down on the settee and Mannie rearranged her bright pink pashmina.

"I decided I wanted to do an art course, to see if I could learn more about how to use my art to have a positive impact on the world. I've also found an Autistic support group. They have a meeting for survivors of sexual abuse, and I've an interview for a volunteer position to help in their art therapy sessions. I was hoping I could use you as a reference?"

"Of course! That all sounds great, but please tell me you aren't giving up on your music?"

"No, I'm not giving it up, but I am setting some boundaries. I see it as something I shared with my mother, so I'm going to enjoy it the way I want to enjoy it, and I don't think I ever want to get back on a stage after last time. It just isn't what works for me."

Mannie nodded and smiled.

I pointed to the piano crammed into the corner of the room. "That's my mum's piano. I've been writing a new song on it. Want to hear it?"

"If it's anything like your last song, definitely!"

"Well, it's very different, but I think you may like it. It's called 'The Unspoken'."

I got up and went over to the piano, taking a quick look around to check none of the other guests had arrived, before I opened my heart up to one of the few lower realm mortals I cared about.

> I am a fragile mess:
>   my life a dark and scary place.
> They made it clear I did not belong
>   so I learned to hide my face.
> They tell lies about me:

    keep changing their version of the truth.
They shift the sands beneath my feet;
    feed their stories and burn my proof.

I may stutter.
I may cry.
I may fall over my words
    and make no sense.
But I stand up for those in pain.
They tear me down; I stand up again.
For those who are told
    what they feel is not valid,
For those hounded
    by prejudice and lies,
for the scarred,
for the broken,
for the freaks and heartbroken
    I hold out my hand,
        and together we say
            the unspoken.

I took their words inside,
    made their fictions a part of me.
Left my self unidentified;
    now I stand in the debris.
The stories that they tell,
    weave a net without a hole.
But I'll rewrite their narrative as
    I grow beyond their control.

Change comes through
    a thousand
        brave
            small
                voices.

These are my choices.

I may stutter.
I may cry.
I may fall over my words
    and make no sense.
But I stand up for those in pain.

> They tear me down; I stand up again.
> For those who are told
>   what they feel is not valid,
> For those hounded
>   by prejudice and lies,
> for the scarred,
> for the broken,
> for the freaks and heartbroken
>   I hold out my hand,
>   and together we say
>   the unspoken.

Mannie was quiet for a few moments and then she said. "Wow. Just Wow. That was so raw and honest and brave. If I ever get a band going again, I'd love to perform that."

I felt that familiar tearing sensation, when things start to go wrong and I had the choice to appease and fawn, or state my personal preferences and upset someone.

I ran my finger along the top of the music stand, trying to think of words which wouldn't offend, whilst charging in without a planned script. "I'm not sure it would feel right for you to perform it. It's all about my personal experiences and insecurities. You're so confident and the opposite of broken."

She didn't say anything in response and looked out of the patio doors at Tris. I wanted to take it back, to let her have the song, to do anything to make her like me again. I tried to think of something to say, but nothing came to mind.

Eventually she turned her attention back to me. "I understand that, and agree, I'm probably not the right choice of performer for your song. Thank you for being honest with me. I get carried away sometimes when I hear good music. But I'd also like to add that not everyone who appears confident is free from damage on the inside."

"Oh, I'm sorry. Are you okay?"

"Oh yes. It's all very much buried in the past. There was a time when I was picked on horribly at school, and your song spoke to that little girl in me."

"Ah! Well, thank you." I slid out from behind the piano. "Phew!" I said, feeling relieved. "I really have to get used to people being reasonable when I tell them how I feel."

Mannie laughed. "If anyone has trouble with that, they have the problem, not you."

"Hey! Tu-Ker! Oh my god, you have to see this!" Tyler said, charging into the lounge. "Oh, hey Mannie! You back?"

He thrust his phone at me. A video started playing of some cheesy eighties pop music. I took his phone from his hands.

"No. This can't be. Oh my god."

"Yep, that's our little Birgitta."

I sat down heavily next to Mannie. Kaetia never felt more real than at that moment.

"She was such a funny character. Look at her pigtails!" I said, transfixed by the tiny video.

"Do you know her?" Mannie said, squinting at the screen.

"No, not really." I said.

"Then why are you crying?"

"Oh!" I wiped my face. "It's just a sad story. She had all these plans but died way before her time."

I handed Ty's phone back to him, and he mouthed "Good save." at me before using the excuse of our audience to lean down and kiss me gently on the lips. He gave me a playful wink and headed out to chat to Chris and Fus, who'd been joined by a couple of people I didn't know.

I saw a disapproving look flit across Mannie's face.

"Let me get you a drink." I said, jumping up. "I got some of that guava juice you like."

"Thanks."

I grabbed a glass of white wine and a guava juice from the kitchen, but when I got back to Mannie, Kat was sitting next to her, hearing the big news. I quietly placed the drinks down in front of them, pretending the wine had been for Kat, grabbed my jacket, and snuck out of the door.

I was just about to go through to the gift shop when Tyler came running up to me. "Hey, Tu-Ker, where are you going?"

"I just wanted to say goodbye to the sea."

"Great, I could do with a breath of fresh air."

"You avoiding Kat too?"

He laughed and put his arm over my shoulder as we walked up through the Acres. I put my arm around his waist. It may have been fake, but this was starting to feel like the best relationship I'd ever had.

We walked quietly through the woods and to the coast.

"As I'm leaving for a few years, I'm going to show you something I've never shown anyone before." I said to Ty, leading him to the rocks that guarded my secret ledge. "You have to promise me, you'll never bring a girl up here, okay?"

"I promise." He said.

I started to climb the rocks.

"Seriously? You expect me to climb up there? I'm wearing a new shirt."

"Come on, it'll be worth it, I promise." I said, leaning down and holding my hand out for him.

He clambered clumsily to the top, and I jumped down on to the ledge. Tyler landed next to me.

"Okay, I have a stain on my shirt, but this is pretty cool."

"Once, I nearly fell off the edge. I'd fallen asleep and was getting so confused between reality and my dreams, I had no idea which world I was in when I woke up."

"I felt like that a couple of times." He sighed. "Imagine trying to explain that to a mortal."

"Oh, they'd just think we're crazy." I sat down, my feet dangling over the edge.

Tyler sat down next to me. "I think we are crazy."

I leant my head on his shoulder and watched the seagulls swoop and dance throughout the ice blue sky. He reached out and gently took my hand.

After a while, he quietly said: "Please don't go, Tu-Ker."

"Ty, we discussed this. You can visit as often as you like, and I'll come back regularly. It's only for a few years, then we can get a house together and maybe get married. Then it'll look completely real."

"But I want it to be really real. You're going to meet someone in Edinburgh and fall in love with them. And then I'll be tortured and executed."

"Look, Ty, I care for you; I'm not going to put you in danger."

"Do you love me?"

I paused before responding. "I'm going to be completely honest with you. Right now, I don't feel that way. But we've hundreds of years to make that happen."

"You'll fall in love with someone else; I know it. No one really cares about me. Everyone thinks I'm dispensable. Just some good time guy they forget after the party."

I stood up. I'd rather be back at the Acres with Kat and feeling awkward than putting up with this. "Tyler, you're not dispensable. You are the only person who can remotely understand what's going on in my life, and that means one hell of a lot to me. Please, just be patient."

He got to his feet. "I'm scared."

I looked at his vulnerable face and pulled him into a hug. "There's nothing to be scared of; I'll look out for you."

He shoved his lips hard against mine.

I pushed him away. "Tyler, stop it."

He tried to pull me back close to him.

I stepped backwards and slipped on a bit of moss.

"Be careful! I nearly fell over, you idiot!" I slapped his arm.

"Tu-Ker." He whispered, grabbing me, and holding me close for a few seconds.

And then he let go.

My feet slipped from under me, and my hip collided with the edge as I went down. Tyler's unnatural pondweed-coloured eyes widened as they grew further away, and the air whistled past my ears.

THE SETTING SUN: PREVIEW

I slammed into the rocks so hard I became stone and my senses reduced to fire. I was unable to move, only to exist within the pain of my broken body and accept the torture of the light and its fickle presence, burning through my eyelids one moment, and forever absent in the next.

Time passed by in waves and tides as my soul floated on the sea far from my body. Slowly, I was pulled back to the pain, to the strict regimen of the cycles of the sun, to the heat that crammed into my throat like a gritty rag.

I became solid, my form lying like lead on an unforgiving surface and the sound of the ocean became a hot wind that roared through windows and sent debris scratching between the walls.

Had I died in the fall?

If so, why was I still in my body?

And if I were still in my body, why could I not move?

I focused on my fingers, urging them to move.

It grew dark.

I drifted to sleep and dreamt of a realm where I was free to run along the cliffs. Where I was feral and the rocks were my kin.

I woke with the dawn and tried to move my fingers again. They felt so far away, neglected, and forgotten; like the hinges of a doll that had not been used for decades, but they once moved, and could move again.

The joints began to flex.

I pulled my fingers in further. They caught on sheets.

My tongue moved, and the tip cracked. I sucked saliva through long neglected glands and brought my mouth slowly and painfully back to life.

Someone came into the room and closed the shutters.

I listened to the familiar creaking and scuttling sounds of the tower walls.

It was growing dark again before I tried to open my eyes.

The torch light flickering under the door illuminated enough of the room to confirm I was back in my bed, in my tower.

In Kaetia.

Tyler had fucking killed me.

The bastard.

I felt all the excitement and plans for my life in the lower realm deflate.

I thought of all the paintings I would never bring to life, how I was never going to leave a message of hope for someone like me, how all that pain and suffering had led to nothing. I thought about how I hoped I could patch myself up enough from my trauma to walk through Edinburgh with my head held high, not scurry around slouching over an imaginary ball of shame I'd been handed when I was still too young to know what was going on. I thought about my dreams of coming home to Nick and talking about real world things, not ridiculous Kaetian bullshit, which was all I was going to have for over a millennium now.

I felt a stab at the thought of Nick. At least now I wouldn't have to see him fall in love with someone else, whilst I was trapped in the claustrophobic pantomime of romance with Tyler.

Tyler.

Mull'aman.

Had he pushed me off the cliff, or was he reaching out to catch me as I slipped?

I shifted my weight in the bed and felt something hard digging into my spine. Rolling slightly to the left, I fished clumsily under myself and retrieved three stones. I couldn't tell if they were Asana's protection stones, or Laescenno's curses, so, to be safe, dropped them one by one out of the bed onto the slate floor.

The door burst open and a Pader strode to the foot of the bed.

Looking twenty-five years older than when I last saw her, Melingad raised her right eyebrow as she looked down at my emaciated body.

"You're back a lot earlier than we expected."

I tried to make a sound, but my throat was too weak. I managed to move my head in a nod, but I wasn't sure if she could see the movement.

She smirked in a manner that would have made me feel like squirming if my body had been up to such actions.

"Welcome back. I think you'll find a lot has changed whilst you've been sleeping. I'll go inform the Council and our new leader that you've returned." She took a couple of steps towards the door, stopped, and turned to me slowly. "Don't go anywhere." She said with a chuckle, before heading out and closing the door, sealing me back into the darkness.

GLOSSARY

ABBIE (ABIGAIL FARLEY):
Abbie was a frequent attendee of the community centre until she became involved with drugs. She committed suicide at age fourteen. She inspired the song 'Porcupine Fairy' co-written by Chris and Mannie.

ASANA:
The only 'ranking' (actively pursuing their divine Kaetian duties) Supreme Kaetian. Mother of Tushenta, married to Kasaman.

BECCA (REBECCA EDWARDS):
Becca is the daughter of Margaret Edwards, who was in a relationship with Gerald Tomlinson (Kerella's father) for a couple of years. During this time, Becca became Kerella's only friend.

BIRGITTA CARLSEN:
On her arrival in Kaetia, Birgitta's talent as a positive, upbeat, feel-good musician was considered a useful skill and she was quickly put to work within the nineteenth tenet, celebrating the wonders of Kaetian society through music.

THE BLACK MOUNTAIN:
Known as 'The Red Mountain' by those who live there because of the red veins within the black igneous rock, 'The Black Mountain' is a dark mirror of the yellow sandstone mountain into which Kaetia is carved. It is home to the Redwaek, Kasaman, and his allies.

BLADE OF SETT:
The blade went missing, or was destroyed, after the murder of Tushenta's grandparents and great grandparents. The Blade of Sett is the only known way to prematurely end a Supreme Kaetian's life. It is said to have a diamond blade.

THE BLAZING COURT:
The Blazing Court is some kind of mystical event shrouded in mystery. Sett was chosen at the first Blazing Court. There are twenty-one Guardians of the Blazing Court, whose statues decorate the Courtyard of the Arcane. There is reference made to them standing judgement over Kaetia's adherence to the twenty-one tenets. Each year, the Celebration of Kaetian Society is held in front of the statues to show how well Kaetia has respected the tenets, in hope that the guardians will lift the curse.

CELEBRATION OF KAETIAN SOCIETY:
Every year, the Supreme Kaetians, Higher Kaetians, Lower Kaetians, and guests, come together to celebrate Kaetian society. Through a series of lectures, dramatic presentations, worship, visual art, and musical events, evidence of Kaetia's adherence to the twenty-one tenets is presented to the twenty-one Guardians of the Blazing Court

MS. CHADWICK (NAOMI CHADWICK/CHADDY):
Personal Assistant to Gerald Tomlinson, occasionally referred to as Chaddy.

CHRIS (CHRISTOPHER HOUGHTON):
Chris grew up a poor boy in Sheffield, the only son of a single mum, who died when he was sixteen. At eighteen, his girlfriend got pregnant. Thankfully, she was from a wealthy family, so it did not interrupt his plans to study history at Oxford University. Unfortunately, a couple of years into his degree, Chris got into a serious car accident, in which he sustained a bad head injury, leading to problems with his memory. He moved into The Acres with his uncle whilst he rehabilitated from the accident. When his uncle died, he inherited The Acres.

COMPOUND (KAETIAN COMPOUND):
The Compound is the living, working, and social areas of the Higher and Lower Kaetians, protected by the Pader Guards. It is carved into a sandstone mountain, although over the years, extra space has been created by building more towers on the outside of the existing accommodations.

CONJOINING OF ESSENCES:
In Kaetia, after a wedding has taken place between two individuals with different lifespans, there is a ritual that takes place for the individual with the shorter lifespan to acquire the same lifespan as their partner. When one of these individuals is a Supreme Kaetian, the other person will also absorb the power to conduct Phronesis (judge newly arrived lower realm mortals and strengthen their spiritual essence so they can survive in the Upper Realm).

THE COUNCIL:
During the Kaetian period covered in The Casa Martyrs, The Council is comprised of sixteen Higher Kaetian men. The Supreme Kaetians have a figurehead role, but no real power.

COURTYARD OF THE ARCANE:
The Courtyard of the Arcane is the large amphitheatre near the top of the sandstone mountain into which Kaetia is carved. It is built around a fountain

which is the only source of water in the whole of the Upper Realm. The three gnarled columns which contain the living areas for the Supreme Kaetians loom over the courtyard, and twenty-one statues surround it, each with one palm held out facing the sky.

THE CRATER OF THE DEAD:
When a person from the lower realm dies, their spirit has about a one in eight chance of traveling to the Crater of the Dead. There, it starts as a ghostly whisper and slowly starts to take on a corporeal form. Once the individual becomes solid, a ranking Supreme Kaetian will hold them in a blue light, witness their life, and judge them. If they are considered worthy, their spiritual essence will be strengthened so they can survive. If not, they will crumble to dust within about ten days.

THE CURSE:
Kaetians believe their land is under a curse. This curse means there is only one source of water in the whole of the Upper Realm, the fountain in The Courtyard of the Arcane.

When the land was cursed, Kaetians were presented with twenty-one tenets, and informed that if everyone in Kaetia obeyed the tenets, the curse would be lifted.

DAXA PRAJAPATI:
Daxa is a young girl who attends the community centre and follows Mannie around. When she was six, she found Abbie after she'd taken her own life in the community centre toilets. Since then, she doesn't talk much, but loves making daisy chains.

DEMETRIUS:
Born near Constantinople in 1432. Demetrius fought and died at the siege of Constantinople in 1453. He died when an arrow hit him in the shoulder and he fell off one of the city's walls.

EDDIE TOMLINSON:
Eddie Tomlinson is Kerella's uncle. He sexually abused her when she was younger.

ELOVETTA:
A Kaetian musical instrument that takes about forty years of practice to be proficient at. It's a bit like a harp-piano, where strings are brushed, plucked, pushed down, and peddles affect the effects.

FUS (RUFUS PENNY):
Fus is the drummer in The Casa Martyrs. He's also a counsellor at the community centre and in a relationship with Mannie.

GALLERY OF SETT:
The venue which displays the official collection of art selected to represent Kaetian values.

GERALD TOMLINSON (SEE MR. TOMLINSON):

GESTRICK:
Gestrick is an elderly Lower Kaetian woman who works in the gardens.

GIOVANNI:
Born near Milan in 1455. Giovanni had a quiet life, worked the land, married Veronica, and around 1487, saw Leonardo Da Vinci. He died in 1525.

THE GUARDIANS:
There are two categories of Guardians.

Each of the twenty-one tenets has a Higher Kaetian family assigned to it. The 'ranking' family member is responsible for leading Kaetia's understanding of, and adherence to, that tenet.

There are twenty-one Guardians of the Blazing Court. These are represented by twenty-one stone statues in the Courtyard of the Arcane. During the Celebration of Kaetian Society, Kaetians try to convince these statues that they are adhering to the tenets.

HESHRIK:
Heshrik was the Guardian of the Nineteenth Tenet until his retirement, when the role was passed onto his son, Mull'aman. Heshrik was responsible for Tushenta's musical education and taught her how to play the Elovetta.

HIGHER KAETIANS:
There are twenty-one Higher Kaetian families. Each family is assigned one of the twenty-one tenets, and the 'ranking' member of the family is responsible for ensuring Kaetia's understanding and adherence to that tenet.

Individuals born to a Higher Kaetian couple when the proper rituals are observed, (The Conjoining of Essences), have a lifespan of three hundred years. Only one child is permitted for each couple. Extra pregnancies are punishable by exile or recruitment into the Pader Guards, so most are covered up.

Higher Kaetians wear a red cloak to denote their status, and their cloaks are fastened with a brooch with the emblem of their tenet.

HIGHER REALM MORTALS:
A higher realm mortal is anyone born into the Upper Realm where no ritual for Conjoining of Essences has taken place with a Lower Kaetian, Higher Kaetian, or Supreme Kaetian. Their average lifespan is about seventy years, not including traumatic death.

HISTORIANS:
The Historians are a clandestine group of Kaetians who like to share old objects and try to work out what happened in the past.

HYRENSUS:
Hyrensus was the Guardian of the Sixth Tenet when Asana first sparked and became available to be paired off. He originally lined himself up to be Asana's partner, but Asana's family all declared the recently deceased Demetrius to be the perfect mate for her.

Hyrensus's son, Laescenno, is the current Guardian of the Sixth Tenet.

JENNY CARLISLE:
Jenny is the guitarist in Angel Waste. She has long, straight, dark red hair, and a tongue piercing.

KAETIA:
Kaetia is comprised of the Kaetian Quarters, the Kaetian Compound, The Crater of the Dead, and the town that is built around the base of the mountain.

KAETIAN COMPOUND (SEE THE COMPOUND):

KAETIAN CONDUIT:
The raised path that leads from the Kaetian Compound to the Crater of the Dead. There's a similar ridge on the other side of the Crater which leads into the Black Mountain.

KAETIAN ELDERS:
Kaetian Elders are mentioned in passing when Tushenta muses that only a select few Kaetian Elders are permitted access to the original text of Sett's tenets.

KAETIAN MOTIF OF THE BLAZING COURT:
A stylised depiction of The Courtyard of the Arcane with twenty-two stars in the sky.

KAETIAN PATHS:
The corridors and pathways which formed part of the original structure of Kaetia. They are many millennia old, and Sett would have walked these routes. They are considered sacred, so those who can set foot on them is limited.

KAETIAN QUARTERS:
The Kaetian Quarters consist of the three Kaetian Towers, and a small area between them, which is referred to as the 'staging area' for the Supreme Kaetians, their guards, and any entourage, to get prepared in before venturing into the Compound. There is one entrance, a large ornate archway, with an iron gate which can close in emergencies.

KAETIAN SPARKS:
A colloquial term for Phronesis.

KAETIAN TOWERS:
There are three Kaetian Towers and they are located at the top of the Kaetian Mountain. Partly carved into the natural peak of the mountain, partly built out of roughhewn sandstone blocks, these towers form the living quarters for the three generations of Supreme Kaetians. During the time of The Casa Martyrs, Tushenta lived in the smaller tower and Asana in the largest tower. The third tower is boarded up, but before his exile, Kasaman resided in that tower.

KASAMAN:
Kasaman is Asana's husband and father of Tushenta. He is suspected of murdering Tushenta's grandparents and great grandparents. He is considered to be some kind of devil figure, who uses sorcery to harm Kaetia and makes redwaek to make even the skies dangerous.

KAT (KATHERINE KOH):
Kat is a computer programmer in an on-and-off relationship with Tyler. She's best friends with Mannie.

KERELLA TOMLINSON:
Kerella is an artist living in the north of England. She likes walks in the countryside, brie salad baguettes, white wine, and playing the piano.

KERELLA'S FATHER (SEE MR. TOMLINSON):

KERELLA'S MOTHER (SEE MRS. TOMLINSON):

LAESCENNO:
Laescenno is the Guardian of the Sixth Tenet, Head of the Kaetian Council, author, and Tushenta's oldest acquaintance. He is two hundred and thirty years old. His daughter, Melisia, has recently given birth to a baby daughter, Khora, and his wife has recently died.

LETHIAN PLAINS:
Beyond Kaetia, are the Lethian Plains. These are completely devoid of water, swarming with redwaek, and crossed by rivers of lava. Despite this, there are still a few settlements out there.

LIBRARIANS:
Librarians are the individuals in Kaetia with the responsibility for preserving Kaetian records and books. Some believe they use their power to rewrite history.

LOWER KAETIANS:
There are fifty-six Lower Kaetian families. Lower Kaetians have a lifespan of one hundred and fifty years. Their living quarters are divided into north, south, east, and west, each with their own focus on the nitty gritty running of Kaetian Society. Within each quarter, there is a hierarchy of fourteen families.

THE LOWER REALM:
The world in which people live and die, gathering experiences before the chosen ones are transported to the Upper Realm.

LOWER REALM MORTALS:
Lower realm mortals are born in the spiritual world beneath Kaetia and have an average lifespan of seventy years. Those who are delivered to Kaetia, and judged worthy by a Supreme Kaetian, live out the rest of their unlived lifespan, only dying early if they meet a sufficiently violent incident.

MANNIE (AMANDA BROOKS):
Mannie's family came to England from Minnesota when she was three. She became good friends with Katherine Koh at the age of ten. The two were inseparable until Kat went to university and Mannie stayed at home. Shortly after, Mannie met Fus.

Mannie secured employment at the local community centre as a counsellor, and helped Fus get a job there too.

She's vegan, loves going to the gym, and wants to save the world.

She is the vocalist in The Casa Martyrs.

MARGARET EDWARDS:
Mother of Rebecca Edwards (Becca) and proprietor of 'Shambles', a seafront souvenir shop, which sells beach supplies, new age stuff, and Kerella Tomlinson's artwork. She was in a relationship for a couple of years with Gerald Tomlinson, which ended on amicable terms.

MARTIN MILES:
Martin is the drummer in Angel Waste. Kerella broke his finger and gave him a black eye a couple of years ago.

MATHEMATICIANS:
A group of people in Kaetia who may live in the walls and eat babies.

MELINGAD:
The Head Pader and a guard in Tushenta's detail. She is loyal to Laescenno and reports every detail of Tushenta's life to the Council.

MELISIA:
Laescenno's daughter and mother to Khora.

MERDIANTS:
Merdiants are individuals who are not Supreme, Higher, or Lower Kaetian, who have been given permission to trade goods and services for Kaetia's greater good. No trades within Kaetia are legal without permission, and Merdiants are given a large medallion, which must be displayed prominently, to show they have permission to conduct such activities.

MIAREANAS:
Miareanas is a Lower Kaetian. She is the daughter of Yuescret and friends with Mull'aman.

MIKE (MICHAEL LEWIS):
Mike is in a relationship with Becca. His legs were amputated after the car crash in which Stuart died and Chris sustained a head injury. As part of his psychological rehabilitation, he started volunteering at the community centre.

MULL'AMAN:
Mull'aman is a Higher Kaetian and Guardian of the Nineteenth Tenet.

NICK (NICHOLAS FENWICK):
Nick is the Deputy Manager of the Acres. He loves growing food to eat, and wants to be a nurse working with cancer patients.

NUIHUE:
Nuihue is a young Pader Guard. Her mother is a friend of Asana.

PADER GUARDS:
Pader Guards are female warriors who defend Kaetia. They wear black cloaks with red streaks down the back. They are armed with long, pale swords which are held in their right hand, and small dark daggers, which they use with their left hand.

When they have qualified as a Pader, they wear a grainy yellow paint on their face. When they have fought in battle and eaten the flesh of their fallen comrades, they wear black around their eyes, and when they have taken a life, they wear a streak of blood down their face.

They are recruited from women who are rejected from a romantic pairing, get pregnant without permission, or volunteer to sign up.

PHRONESIS:
When a lower realm mortal is delivered to the Crater of the Dead in Kaetia, they are judged by a ranking Supreme Kaetian. During that process, they are held in a blue light, allowing the Supreme Kaetian to witness their entire life, all their thoughts, and the depth of their personality. If the individual is judged worthy and a potential asset to Kaetian society, through a process called phronesis, their spiritual essence is strengthened, to enable them to survive in the harsh Kaetian world. After undergoing phronesis, they will only succumb to death through old age or violent means.

RANKING:
'Ranking' means that a Kaetian individual is actively pursuing their divine duties. For each Higher and Lower Kaetian family, there is only one 'ranking' individual at a time. That ranking individual is responsible for leading the specific sector their family is devoted to. For Supreme Kaetians, there may be up to six ranking members, who are actively judging mortals and conducting phronesis in the Crater of the Dead.

RED (FERMENTED RED WEED):
In the Lethian Plains, a red grass grows despite the lack of rainfall. This is fermented to create a drink called 'Red'. It is the only alcoholic drink in Kaetia, and a rampant illicit trade in 'Red' takes place.

REDWAEK:
When a lower realm mortal is held in a Supreme Kaetian's blue light, through a process of phronesis, their spiritual essence is strengthened so they can survive in the Upper Realm. However, the Supreme Kaetian can absorb the spiritual essence into themselves instead, creating a redwaek.

An individual not judged worthy, will just be left with a weak spiritual essence, and they will turn to dust in about ten days. A redwaek will survive, but slowly rot and become deformed along the lines of the individual's psychology. Some grow wings, some grow extra heads, some remain mostly humanoid. But they all lose connection with their humanity and their powers of reasoning.

They remain loyal to, and will obey, their creator in their own way.

RETH'SATAR:
Reth'satar is the Guardian of the Fourteenth Tenet and member of the Kaetian Council.

SETT:
After the curse was cast on Kaetia, a virtuous individual was chosen to be the first Supreme Kaetian. This was Sett. She was presented with the twenty-one tenets and the responsibility for teaching these rules to the other Kaetians. She put these tenets into a book, which is now only available for Kaetian Elders to view, and only after years of spiritual preparation.

SPARKING:
When a Supreme Kaetian reaches a certain age/biological threshold, their palms start to emit a blue light. After this occurs, they are of an age to be married.

SPIRITUAL ESSENCE:
People born in the lower realm have a spiritual essence which connects their physical manifestations to their souls. If the individual is brought to Kaetia on their death, they are faced with four fates.

1. They can run into the Lethian Plains without judgement, and they will turn to dust within ten days when their spiritual essence breaks

and their body becomes an empty vessel.
2. They will be held in the blue light of a Supreme Kaetian, rejected as worthy or useful, and will turn to dust within ten days.
3. They will be held in the blue light of a Supreme Kaetian, judged worthy and their spiritual essence strengthened so they will live out the rest of their lifespan in the upper realm.
4. The Supreme Kaetian sucks the spiritual essence out of them and the lower realm mortal is transformed into a redwaek.

STUART KING:
Stuart is Chris's cousin. He died in a car crash on the day of his mother's funeral.

SUPREME KAETIANS:
Supreme Kaetians are the direct descendants of Sett. They have a life span of three thousand years, and the ability to shoot blue light from their hands, enabling them to see into the souls of lower realm mortals. They are responsible for judging the mortals, and can choose to leave them to fade into dust, strengthen their spiritual essence so they will survive in Kaetia, or suck out their spiritual essence turning the individual into a redwaek.

They are called gods, as they judge mortals arriving in the upper realm, can put on a fancy light show, live for three thousand years, and can't be killed through violent means unless that involves a specific dagger which is widely believed to no longer exist.

SYREME:
Syreme is the Guardian of the Fourth Tenet and member of the Kaetian Council.

THE TENETS:
The tenets are twenty-one rules for Kaetian society originating with Sett and passed down generation to generation. Each tenet has a family from the Higher Kaetians assigned to them, who act as that tenet's Guardian.

MR. TOMLINSON (KERELLA'S FATHER):
Mr. Tomlinson is Kerella's father. He runs Tomlinson and Co. which is a large company which generates a lot of income. He was in a relationship with Becca's mother, Margaret Edwards, for a couple of years.

MRS. TOMLINSON (KERELLA'S MOTHER):
Sarah was an eccentric professional pianist. She married Gerald Tomlinson and gave birth to Kerella. She was consumed by guilt when she found out

Kerella was sexually abused in her own household and began to drink heavily. She fell out of a window and died when her daughter was twelve.

THE TOWN:
The area around the base of the Kaetian Mountain where higher realm mortals, lower realm mortals, Merdiants, and a few other people live. The streets change every few years and, in the centre, there is a market.

TUSHENTA:
Tushenta is the daughter of Asana and Kasaman. She's a Supreme Kaetian and about two hundred and fifty years old. At this age, she's still an adolescent, so has not yet assumed any roles of a ranking Supreme Kaetian, such as visiting the Crater of the Dead, performing phronesis, or taking on any leadership roles.

TYLER ANDREWS:
Tyler is the son of an English teacher and Physics teacher. He fell in love with Katherine Koh at university and dropped out of his Media Studies degree to follow her back to her hometown after she graduated. He's the guitarist and vocalist in The Casa Martyrs.

UNSEASONED MORTAL:
A lower realm mortal that arrives in the upper realm can be sensed by a Supreme Kaetian up until they have been 'seasoned'. 'Seasoning' is an informal term for the process of phronesis. Once a mortal has been judged and accepted into Kaetia, they have been 'seasoned'. Those yet to be judged or rejected, are unseasoned. Should a lower realm mortal be turned into a redwaek, technically they are no longer unseasoned.

THE UPPER REALM:
The upper realm is the entire world accessible from Kaetia. This includes The Black Mountain, The Lethian Plains, and places not explored or discussed in this book.

UPPER REALM MORTALS:
Upper realm mortals are individuals born in the upper realm whose parents did not go through the 'Conjoining of Essences' ceremony to make their offspring Lower, Higher, or Supreme Kaetian. They have the default lifespan of about seventy years.

VERONICA:
Born near Milan in 1455, Veronica was the only daughter of a moderately wealthy family, who went on to marry Giovanni, but never had children. She

died in 1530.

WALK IN THE LOWER REALM:
When a Supreme Kaetian sparks, they are paired off to a suitable mate by the Council, and before the marriage is official/consummated, the Supreme Kaetian and their partner are sent into the lower realm to live and die in a mortal body. The couple then experience the lives of the people they will be judging and fall in love with each other without the confusion of the Supreme Kaetian status.

YUESCRET:
Yuescret is a Lower Kaetian, friend of Asana, and mother of Miareanas.

ABOUT THE AUTHOR

Hello, I'm Moti. I'm an author and an artist. I live in Fife, Scotland with my two cats and my amazing husband.

I am a late self-realised Autistic woman, with a PhD in Politics and a large tarot deck collection.

You can find all my latest news on my blog.

www.motiblack.co.uk

Thank you for reading my book.

Printed in Great Britain
by Amazon